THE WAY YOU CAME IN MAY NOT BE THE BEST WAY OUT

THE WAY YOU CAME IN MAY NOT BE THE BEST WAY OUT

PAUL DI FILIPPO

WILDSIDE PRESS

For Deborah,
whose golden thread leads out of the labyrinth

"In the Lost City of Leng" first appeared in *Asimov's*, 2018. "The Life-hack" first appeared in *Daily Science Fiction*, 2018. "Monarch of the Feast" first appeared in *Analog*, 2019. "From the Casebook of Master Wiggins, Esq." first appeared in *Soot and Steel*, 2019. "Lost in the Rewilding" first appeared in *Once Upon a Parsec*, 2019. "The Way You Came In May Not Be the Best Way Out" first appeared in *The Unquiet Dreamer: A Tribute to Harlan Ellison.* "The Yog-Sothoth Policemen's Union" first appeared in *The Mountains of Madness Revealed*, 2019. "'Nothing Can Stop the Insect Girl Corps!'" first appeared in *Then Again*, 2019. "Thingmaker" first appeared in *Short Things*, 2020. *Aeota* first appeared as a novella from PS Publishing, 2019.

Published by Wildside Press LLC.
wildsidepress.com | bcmystery.com

CONTENTS

IN THE LOST CITY OF LENG

Written with Rudy Rucker

I was a kid full of dreams, looking for bigger ones. My job? Covering the crime beat for the *Boston Globe*. It was the afternoon of New Year's Eve, 1933.

I had the news room to myself. My feckless co-workers had decamped en masse for early festivities, leaving me in charge. I had my dog Baxter for company. He was asleep on the floor by my desk.

My phone rang. Baxter stood up and stretched. Flapped his ears. Gave a conversational bark and wagged his feathery tail. A noble hound, half collie and half spaniel, with white legs and a brown map of some unknown island on his back. I patted him and picked up the receiver.

"Doug Patchen?" said the caller's blunt voice. "Stan Gorski here."

I remembered this guy. An ex-pilot with a big mouth. "You got a fresh story for me?" I asked. "A second act? Something in the aviation line to wow the rubes."

"I appreciated how you wrote up my trial, Doug. Didn't make me look too—you know."

"Too criminal?"

"I was mixing with the hard guys. I was drunk all the time."

"Who wouldn't have been?" I said. "You were using a Coast Guard rescue plane to smuggle in cases of VSOP cognac."

"And now all of a sudden booze is legal," said Gorski. "But do I get my commission back? My chance to fly? Not on your life. Not in this burg. Never mind that I'm supporting a wife and three kids."

"I remember them," I said. "Human interest. Where are you working?"

"I'm a mechanic for Colonial Air out at Jeffrey Field. I can fix any plane ever made, Dougie. Better believe it. Not that I need the job anymore. I'm in the chips."

"I'm sure you are," I said, doubting him. "You're—still drinking?"

"I went dry the day they repealed Prohibition," said Gorski, cackling as if proud of his reverse. "So, no, I'm not phoning you whacked outta my skull. I've got a straight-up business proposition for you. The biggest story since the Starkweather-Moore fiasco."

The Starkweather-Moore Antarctic expedition of 1931. Every member of the party had met a lurid and horrific end. The scouts who'd ventured into the lost city of Leng—consumed by a foul slug the size of a railway train. The men in the base camp—incinerated by the purposeful zaps of a malignant storm. The crews of the expedition's ships—lost in the depths of an anomalous maelstrom.

A series of live radio broadcasts, relayed from one ground station to the next, had etched the ghastly chain of events deep into the public's mind. First came the anguished screams of the scouts being smothered in slimy flesh. Then the desperate shrieks of the men in the base camp as the slyly purposeful lightning strokes picked them off. Then came the sailors' cries amid the snapping of ship timbers and the maelstrom's whistling roar. And then—silence.

The explorers had been warned in advance. A survivor of the Pabodie party of 1930, had published a passionate screed in the *Arkham Advertiser*, inveighing passionately against any further expeditions to Leng. But within a year, the thirst for glory had drawn Starkweather and Moore to their destruction.

Two years had elapsed since then. As yet, so far as I knew, nobody had been mad enough to propose a third expedition. But now...

I felt a sickly-sweet hollowness in my stomach. "You're going to Leng," I said to Gorski, my voice flat. "You want me to come." And, god help me, I knew I was going say yes.

"Quick on the uptake," said Gorski. "I like that. A secret mission. You quit your job at the *Globe*, you write up our trip, and we sell our story when we get back. Hunky dory."

"We?" I said, stepping into the abyss. "Who's we?"

"You and me and Leon Bagger and Vivi Nordström. Leon's an assistant professor at Harvard. Looking to get a permanent job. Vivi's a double-dome too. Plus we'll have this, uh, friend of Vivi's, name of Urxula. The trip is Vivi and Urxula's idea. We'd like to get going tonight on account of it's New Year's Eve, and the guards will be blotto. We've been loading stuff onto the plane all week. We'll fly to Leng in three big hops. Boston, Lima, Tierra del Fuego, Antarctica. You'll be a co-pilot. Piece of cake, Dougie. And Vivi pilots too. The weather's great in Antarctica this time of year. Sunny all night long. Be a nice vacation for all of us."

I had picked up a pilot's license while doing a feature on the Flying Falangas, a family of barnstormers. But I'd never flown more than a hundred miles at any one go. Not that the problems I might encounter up in the air could hold a candle to those we'd face in the lost wastes of the south pole.

"What about the man-eating slugs? And the intelligent lightning? And those—those hibernating sea cucumber things?" I'd seen the Pabodie expedition photos of seven-foot-tall creatures with starfish heads and snaky arms.

"Leon teaches an introductory marine biology course at Harvard, Doug. He can handle those cukes. And Vivi's a visiting intern. Lives with Leon. Not his wife. She's knows science too. Something about ultrasonics. Claims she has an angle on those giant slugs. Plus that, we've got our native guide. I'm talking about that Urxula. She's—well, you'll see." Gorski broke off with a raspy chuckle. "Come on downstairs to the street. I'm parked right by the phone booth. Driving a red Duesenberg, my man. Twenty feet long. The ride of your life."

"Can we stop by my apartment? I need to pack a bag. And my dog's coming too."

"Copacetic, Doug. The Gorski-Patchen expedition of 1934! What they should call it."

Trying not to let myself think about what I was doing, I typed a resignation note, in which I told my boss editor what I thought of him—and stole the typewriter, a Hermes Featherweight that was eminently luggable. Stealing didn't matter. I was leaving in a Duesenberg. And then—either I'd die, or I'd get rich. Everything would be fine.

* * * *

I fell in love with Vivi Nordström at first sight. She cast some kind of Scandinavian spell. Said she was from Norway, and she had the accent and the long reddish-blonde hair, not to mention a tomboy attitude that laid me out flat. Sure she was sexy—but she was careless and forthright as a man. Didn't give a damn what you thought of her. I'd never known exactly what kind of woman I was looking for. Now I knew.

Vivi was wearing pilot's overalls of a moderne yellow and aqua design, with soft fleece inside. She had a silvery silk scarf with images of eyes, and triangular buttons on her cuffs.

"You're scared?" she said, rolling her eyes toward me in a devastating up-from-under look. Tricky to manage, considering she was taller than me. We were in the hall of an Art Deco house she shared with Leon Bagger. He'd been at Harvard for five years, making slow progress in the groves of academe. She'd arrived last year to work with him. They were studying what was known of the odd creatures in Antarctica. This expedition plainly could constitute Leon's ticket to the top.

"The plateau at the Mountains of Madness?" I said, by way of answering Vivi's question. "The lost city of Leng. Intimidating. But I'm eager to hear your plan. Calm down, would you, Baxter?" The dog was furiously barking, while staring up the front hall staircase. An odd scent was wafting down, like ammonia and crabs and violets.

"That's Urxula up there," said Vivi. "Dogs and cuke people—a mixed match. It's like pairing a knockabout scientist-aviatrix with a cub reporter, hmm?" She winked at me and laughed, showing a fine white set of teeth. I tried to judge how high or low I stood in her estimation.

"Come on already," yelled Gorski. "Come look at Leon's maps."

"So you want to join our team?" said Leon Bagger as I entered the sitting room. He had a narrow head and a goatee. Sandy hair, an elegantly draped tweed suit, medium height. A zealous gleam in his eye, tempered by a courtly smile.

"Gorski here talked me into quitting my job," I told Leon, not any too sure of myself. "I hope your plan is legit." It was hard to believe I'd left the *Globe*. Why? Oh, right, so I could go to the South Pole and fight monsters with a bootlegger, a junior prof, and the woman of my dreams.

A cleanly designed elliptical table was at the center of the sitting room. Around the sides were streamlined chairs and couches, chromium with leather cushions in pastels. The ceiling was pale gray above off-white walls and bleached maple wainscoting. Spirals and sharps bedecked the rug. A spheroid-based tea set gleamed on the sideboard. To top it off, three sparsely elegant Mondrian paintings were on display, each of them easily the price of Gorski's fancy car. Me, I'd grown up with six sibs in a bare tenement in Southie.

Noticing my expression, Leon shrugged. "It was only this fall that Vivi and I came into money. Diamonds from the deeps. Given to us by Urxula. She was grateful because we fetched her from the sea, fifty miles out, offshore from Innsmouth. Vivi had a vision of where to find her. I like to say that Vivi has a trace of Sami shaman heritage."

"Don't be so silly,," said Vivi. "You know my heritage is no such thing."

"I got some dough for the pickup too," said Gorski. "I'm the one who borrowed the Coast Guard rescue plane one night to fly these two lovebirds out there to fetch Urxula."

Baxter's barking was increasingly savage and frantic. He kept starting up the stairs, then backing off with a volley of wild yelps. "Sorry about my dog," I said again.

"The Pabodie party's sled-dogs had the same reaction," said Leon. "Can you calm him, Vivi?"

Vivi cocked her head and made a funny face—as if she were about to whistle or sing. But instead she growled, or hummed, or both at once. A curious sound—which captured Baxter's full attention. Bashfully, inquisitively, he nosed into the sitting room, then sat at Vivi's feet.

"Urxula is your friend," Vivi crooned to the dog, leaning down ever so gracefully—like a willow, like a naiad, like the silver sprite on the hood of a Rolls-Royce. She unleashed a final burst of musical droning, and Baxter wet the rug.

"Vivi has that effect on her captives," said Leon Bagger with an indulgent laugh. "Abject surrender. We'll clean it up later."

"Urxula can do it," said Vivi. "I'll call her down. She wants to meet Doug." Vivi tilted back her head and made another sound, a haunting, aeolian whistle—like a high wind across the mouth of a cave.

Now came a bumping and slithering on the stairs. By this point I had a pretty good idea of what Urxula was. But actually meeting her was something else.

Undulant and supple, she slithered into the room prone, then tootled a greeting, and rocked onto her bottom end, standing a foot taller than me. Baxter lunged at her, meaning to bite. With a swift movement of one branching arm, Urxula caught hold of the dog and muzzled his snout. The alien creature was what people called a cuke, except people from Arkham, who called them Elder Ones. Urxula was just as the Pabodie and Starkweather-Moore reports had described.

Urxula's body was like a six-foot squash, thicker on the bottom, and with ridges along the sides. Her hide was greenish brown, flexible and leathery, patterned with warts and bumps, gently pulsing like a bellows. Her head resembled a five-armed starfish, resting flat atop the narrow end of her body. The starfish-head had a gleaming blue eye at each of its five tips, with a wobbly mouth-tube between each pair of tips. Her five feet splayed out from her wide bottom end. Her branching arms were very like the feeding organs of a sea cucumber I'd once seen in an aquarium at Boothbay Harbor, Maine. Five arms, five feet, five mouths, five eyes. Later, in conversation, Leon would describe Urxula as a radially symmetric echinodermoid.

Words go only so far. The main thing about the cukes is that they're telepaths. That is, as soon as Urxula noticed me, my thoughts changed. It wasn't anything so banal as me hearing a weirdly accented voice in my head. No, it was subtler than that. You've always got a low-level stream of images and memories and phrases burbling through your mind, right? And once in a while a particularly weird or catchy nugget pops to the surface, That was the communication channel the cukes used. As soon Urxula trained her five blue eyes on me I saw—

A giant slug chasing some cukes and blind penguins. Ice all around. Low sun. An ice-bound city of fanciful towers. An odd pontoon plane angling in and sliding to a stop on the deep snow. Baxter romping out, happily barking.

The captivated Baxter had obviously gotten the transmission too, and he liked the last image enough to stop growling. Urxula loosened her nest of branching fingers and let him loose. He stared at her, tongue lolling, thinking things over, adjusting to the big cuke's smell. Not really so bad. Sort of like a fresh fish market next to a flower stand next to a filling station.

Urxula swept her frondy fingers across the rug and disappeared the puddle that Baxter had made. And then once again she focused on me. I saw myself at the controls of a plane with Vivi Nordström in the other pilot's seat. Vivi smiling at me. Touching my face with her hand. Yes.

"Urxula likes you," said Vivi. "I can see you're picking up her images. Leon and I call it teep. If she's teeping you, that means you'll work out fine."

"So it's decided!" said Leon, handing me a cup of tea. "A temperate toast!" The four of us grinned and clinked our tea cups. With Gorski maybe a little wistful for the days when his cup would've been heavily spiked.

"I'll get paid too?" I asked.

With one smooth motion, Urxula unfolded a snaky arm and set a rough crystal into my hand. Each of her arms had what you might call five fingers, with five fingerlets on each finger, and another level of branching below that. I held the crystal to the light. Could it really be an uncut diamond? So large! In my mind's eye I saw my gem gleaming on a tiny silk pillow in the window of Tiffany's. Urxula was my pal, you bet. Her people needed our help. I saw images of a giant slug in flames. While Vivi Nordström, swathed in a flying-fur blanket, held out her arms and sang.

"We're going to save the cuke people," said Leon. "And we're leaving tonight."

"It's almost dark," said Stan Gorski. "My car has room for all of you. Let's hit the bricks."

"What about supplies?" I asked. "It's a long trip."

"Our plane's loaded," said Gorski.

* * * *

As it turned out, our plane belonged to someone else.

"A fire-and-brimstone fanatic named Ransome Tierney," explained Stan Gorski as he pulled his sleek, low Duesenberg into the shadows beside a seaplane hanger at Jeffrey field. "Reminds me of Aleister Crowley lumped together with Cotton Mather. From Arkham. He says the cukes—I mean Elder Ones—are demons from hell. He wants to close off Leng. Says he can seal off the entrance with a cannon shot and some hand grenades. Raised fifty grand from his congregation.."

"Typical Arkham," said Leon Bagger, shaking his head. "They completely misunderstand the nature of Leng."

"Wait," I said. "We burst into this hanger and steal a flying boat? That's your big plan?"

"Maybe you shoulda brought a *Chicago* typewriter," said the hardened Gorski, laughing and pretending to shoot a machine gun. We were all wearing aviation togs—boots, fur-lined overalls, leather jackets, and caps with side flaps.

"Don't be silly," said Vivi. "Stan got himself on Tierney's payroll. He's been helping to outfit the plane. And Stan, I hope you remembered to give the guards that case of cognac this morning?"

Stan didn't need to answer. We could hear the guards singing. Blurry voices, blended in bonhomie. And it was barely eight pm.

"Come on," hissed Leon, heading out of the shadows. He was laden down with two heavy bags. Vivi had a bag too, but I carried it for her, juggling it with my own suitcase and my *Globe* typewriter. The wind off the bay was icy. Snowflakes were beginning to fall.

"You're sweet," said Vivi, raising the flap of my aviator hat to plant a kiss on my cheek. It didn't seem to matter to her if Leon saw. Her features were vivid in the gloom. She was wearing dark red lipstick that set off her togs. Baxter was close at her heels. To fully win over my dog, Vivi had somehow fashioned him a little fleece vest.

In the rear, Stan Gorski led Urxula along. Our cuke friend was cloaked in a blanket-like flying fur. A bright eye showed in the shadow of a fold at top, as if peering out from a monk's cowl. A seven-foot monk.

"Who goes there!" called one of the guards as we approached. And then he guffawed. The fix was in. Leon handed over a bonus sheaf of bills. And Stan gave the guards the keys to his Duesenberg. That little gesture, more than the weightier ones, made me realize we were fully into the venture now, and would either return rich and famous and covered in glory, or not at all.

Beefy, heartfelt song from the inebriates. And now we were inside the long shed, with the waters lapping at the shore. Stan and Vivi played the beams of their electric torches over the all-metal plane.

It was a wonder, the largest plane I'd ever seen, with a single high wing above the fuselage, and a row of three massive engines set into the wing.

"It's a prototype from Dornier in Holland," Stan told me. "Seventy feet long, with a ninety foot wingspan. A custom model of what they'll probably call the Do 24. A flying boat. Perfect for landing in deep snow. Tierney had them double-up the size of her tanks, they're those fin things sticking out on the sides. She has a range of 3,500 miles this way, if you can frikkin believe that. And she'll rise to 26,000 feet."

"The altitude of the Leng plateau," put in Leon. "Five miles, give or take."

I could tell that Urxula was aware of our conversation. Once again my mind formed an unexpected image—our Do 24 droning through a toothy pass, approaching a fantastic city of steeples and arches and vaults and impossibly large blocks of stone—everything half buried by millennia of ice. At the controls? Me and Vivi again. Urxula had my number.

Half an hour later, we were airborne, with three Wright radial engines roaring above our heads. Thank god the plane had electric starters. I was in the co-pilot's seat beside Stan. He was teaching me the controls. We'd fought our way upward through a buffeting snowstorm, with the flakes hypnotically streaming at us. And now we'd reached a zone of wonder and peace. A full moon rising, pinprick stars above, and, far below us, bank upon bank of silvered clouds. Have I mentioned that this was the first time that I'd ever ridden so high in a plane?

"This compass here," I said to Stan. "It says we're heading southeast. Shouldn't we go south? You said we want to make Peru. A seventeen-hour run."

"We're dropping off Urxula first," said Stan. "At the edge of the continental shelf. She doesn't want to spend three days in a plane. She'd rather swim."

"That far?"

"She swims fast," said Stan with a shrug. "Down in the abyss—where nobody notices. Not sure how she hits those high speeds. She doesn't always show you everything she knows. Bottom line, she'll meet us in Tierra del Fuego. Swim down along South America, and turn right.."

The Urxula drop was unnerving. The cuke had put the image of a target into our heads. Stan was seeing it, and so was I. A target overlaid upon the clouds below us, in glowing red lines. As Stan approached the center, Leon and Vivi undogged a small hatch in the rear of the fuselage. Insanely cold air rushed in.

Moving nimbly on her pointed, flexing feet, Urxula made her way past our crated supplies to the rear. And then—a fresh surprise, she unfurled a pair of filmy bat-like wings. By no means did they look sturdy enough for sustained flight. Urxula weighed well over two hundred pounds. Nothing daunted, she flung herself through the open hatch.

Watching her in the moonlight, I felt there was more to her wings than I'd realized. They were emitting repellor pale rays that slowed Urxula's descent. The wings also played the role of rudders or sails, fashioning her moderated fall into a graceful glide, steering herself along the path of a capacious helix that disappeared into the upmost layer of clouds.

"Adios, amiga," said Stan. He heeled our three-engine plane to the right, heading south for Lima.

* * * *

Our flying boat splashed into the Lima harbor, throwing up a rooster tail of spray, then gliding to a stop. Stan feathered the propellers, bringing us to rest at a freighter pier where we could refuel. Vivi was ecstatic. You'd have thought she won the Irish Sweepstakes. "Boston to Lima without refueling! Thirty-five hundred miles! Practically a record, no? Stan milked this bird like a horn-handed farmer with his prize cow!" Something of a mixed metaphor.

Stan was too weary to appreciate her enthusiasm. The trip had been grueling, even with Vivi and me spelling him, amid frequent infusions of hot java from a vacuum bottle and with canned and preserved food from our well-stocked plane's supplies. Gorski looked like a man who could use a stiff drink or three, and this did not reassure me, given his ongoing battle to remain sober. Our entire safety and success rested in large part on the Stan's quickness and wit.

For neither the first nor the last time, I contemplated the wisdom—the folly—of having embarked on this impulsive dash to the Antarctic The potential payback was counterbalanced by the horrible fate that had befallen the Starkweather-Moore expedition.

Leon usually talked normally, but now he flipped over to bombastic professor mode for expressing an awe similar to Vivi's. "The dawn of a new age, with our planet united by an aerial web of commerce and recreation. I foresee a time when our globe's mysterious backwaters will be fully charted and explored. No more hidden plateaus, lost tribes, bizarre creatures, and inexplicable ruins—such as those we go to seek today. Global air power will be a triumph for science and trade—if a loss for romance and adventure."

Half a dozen locals were tying our plane to the dock. It was late afternoon on January 1, 1934, with the sun gilding the water. Stan toggled off our engines, which were, I suspected, ready to cough to cessation anyhow. We'd cut the mileage of our hop very fine.

"All the more reason why we have to get to Leng soon," said Stan expanding on Leon's remarks. "We'll save Urxula and her cuke race while there's time. They're definitely the underdogs on this card. We'll even things up. Kill off the cukes' enemies. The shoggoths, right? Those slugs the size of subway trains."

"Just one slug now, as I understand it," put in Leon.

"The great shoggoth," said Vivi. "A formidable foe. But there's a third party as well. The ones that the man in the Pabodie party talked about. The man who went crazy from what he saw."

"Or didn't see," put in Stan. "He saw weather, and that's it. Like maybe a scrap of rainbow. Or maybe he was seeing the world through a piece of Iceland spar. And those so-called smart lightning bolts that wiped out the Starkweather-Moore base camp? Weather again."

"And if the cukes control the weather?" said Vivi with a cryptic smile. "Teirney says the cukes have their own set of gods."

"Those Arkham locals—they've got rats in their heads," blustered Stan. "That bible-thumper Teirney who wants to kill every cuke he can find. We're a force for the good, and we're gonna get rich, right?"

"I'm going ashore." I said, looking at the rope ladder that the wharf workers had lowered for us. "Any plan?"

Stan took a deep breath, calming himself. "We tank up for the next leg—that's the flight to Tierra del Fuego. And then comes the third hop. Into the polar wastes. But for now? Captain Gorski decrees steak, healthful juices, *papas a la huanciana*—dancing, and Zs."

"Also there's the matter of the supplemental scientific instrument that Vivi and I want to obtain," put in the assistant professor. "To deploy against the great shoggoth."

"This plane's got some arms," said Stan. "They're under the canvas in the back of the plane. Like I said, I've been helping Tierney stock up."

"Frightened little men," sneered Vivi. "Do you really think that firecrackers and peashooters will be of use? Against the omnivorous gelatinous juggernaut that is the grand shoggoth?"

"I'm thinking that *flammenwerfer* might slow it down," said Stan.

"A German flamethrower?" exclaimed Leon.

"Got it in one, my man. Plus a crate of grenades. And I guess you civilians didn't notice our plane has a Hispano-Suiza cannon and a Maxim machine gun? Not a huge amount of ammo for them, but enough to make a dent. During my smuggling days, I made contacts with the arms trade, you understand. And the Germans are looking for business, what with the ruckus that Chancellor Hitler is kicking up. Pastor Tierney had me do some off-shore shopping."

"We'll be like Wyatt Earp and Doc Holliday at the O.K. Corral," I said, my fanciful love of the old Wild West on display.

"You Americans and your cowboys," clucked Vivi. "The medium of sound will be the more useful weapon against the great shoggoth. It will be as if ensorcelled and destroyed by a lovely siren."

"As if," echoed Gorski, very dubious.

"This brings us to the scientific instrument I mentioned," said Leon. "An industrial ultrasound generator. The gem miners out of Lima here use these gadgets for mapping crystal inclusions and detecting invisible seams. Vivi and I brought along a lab model from Harvard, but the gents at Andes Gem supplies—they sell equipment for finding emeralds. They have a line of big Russian ultrasound generators and we're buying one. Vivi made the deal by mail."

Baxter was leaning out our plane's now-open door, barking. He was ready to get back on land—both to relieve himself, and to find some decent food. During the long flight, he'd been doing his business on a stack of old newspapers—the good old *Boston Globe*. And eating nothing but water-soaked oatmeal. He was plainly impatient to smell, and to pee upon, the soil of Peru. And, who knew, maybe he'd hook up with a Peruvian dog. I took off his little fleece flying jacket.

"Baxter has the right idea," said Vivi. "Let's exit this stinky metal cigar. Hot food and hot jazz!" She shucked off her heavy flying jacket, and twirled a hotcha finger in the air.

We made our way up the rope ladder to the great pier, where half a dozen locals had gathered to study our metal Dornier seaplane—with its great hull and its high wing boasting three engines. I noticed that, as Stan had mentioned, the plane had a cannon on one side and a machine gun on the other. Freight ships were hawsered nearby. At the land end were small official adobe buildings. Cranes, rickety trucks and ambling workers were loading, unloading, and refueling the ships—and a few small local seaplanes as well.

We relished the heat of January in Peru, soaking it up against the long deep cold that lay ahead. Stan broke out a sheaf of dollars and arranged for the maintenance and refueling of the plane—which Stan had named *Cuke Air Force One*. Leon engaged a local in conversation and paid him to watch over our plane. And then an ancient jitney carried us into the blocks-long entertainment district of bustling Lima. It was a much larger city than I'd realized. Tongue lolling, Baxter lay sprawled across my lap.

We ended up at a café named *La Llama Borracha*: smoky interior, low ceiling, straw artifacts on the walls as decorations. Leon said the place was known for jazz—he was quite an aficionado. As we entered, a trio of musicians wielding cajón, charango and pan-pipes began somehow to swing out a recognizable version of "It's Only a Paper Moon." Welcoming the North-American jazzbos. The guests and waitresses were a polyglot gamut of European ex-pats, local Indians, black sailors, and mixtures thereof. Some dressed in tatters, others in fancy suits, still others in bright native garb with oddly shaded bowler hats. Laughter, arguments, life in its raw essence.

The four of us—Baxter placidly camping out at our feet—commandeered a round table, which was soon decked with raw fish ceviche, grilled octopus, steaks that hung over the edges of the plates, pork stew, fava beans, and even grilled guinea pig. Plenty of scraps found their way Baxter-ward. Vivi and I knocked back a few powerful pisco sours. But Stan, I was relieved to see, settled for a gourd of the herbal *mate*, repeatedly refilled. Leon stretched a single beer over a couple of hours, with each sip causing him to retreat deeper into some meditative state, grooving very deeply on the jazz. Leon was as much an anything-goes bohemian as he was a stuffed-shirt professor.

I hoped he was also pondering all the angles of the terrors and challenges awaiting us, like how to avoid getting killed, or worse, by monster slugs, alien telepathy or supernatural lightning. All I could contribute to our enterprise, aside from my modest co-piloting skills, was enthusiasm and a strong right arm. Oh, and I was a decent shot with handgun or rifle, having picked up some tips from the local cops when I did an article on their new firing range in Dedham. Not that a bullet would mean much to a shoggoth. I guessed I could handle that new-fangled flame gun as well. And maybe Vivi's ultrasound waves would close the deal.

By the time midnight rolled around, we were well sated. I'd taken a few spins around the tiny wooden-planked dance floor with the spicy, warm, sensual Vivi. Very fetching in her yellow and aqua flying overalls, with little or nothing underneath. Truly she was the woman for me. Leon didn't seem to mind my attentions to her. I was beginning to think—or to hope—that the young prof he wasn't interested in Vivi that way. Perhaps they were roommates and science buddies, and that was all, So much the better for me. Freelance reporter Douglas Patchen!

To top off the evening, Stan performed a wild solo tarantella atop a table, delighting the crowd. Seemed like he'd learned the art of casting off normal restraint even while sober. Unless he'd been sneaking drinks. On our way out, the placid, smiling Leon solicited, using his elegant Spanish, a recommendation for a local hotel, just a few blocks away.

So we exited *La Llama Borracha* in tranquil spirits—a condition which of course left us utterly unprepared for the assault by three toughs. They came at us, smelling of mushrooms and the sewers and strange musks, emerging from a proverbial dark alley, in a tenebrous block empty of passersby. One minute I was sauntering and whistling and holding Vivi by the elbow, and the next I was fighting for my life against a small and wiry opponent whose bare arms seemed to be covered in—slime?

The ruffians were lithe and silent, but luckily unarmed, as were we. For reasons that now seemed pathetically naive, Leon and I had convinced Stan Gorski that it would be rude and uncivil to bring pistols to dinner. Vivi had kept her own counsel of this matter. Not that she needed weaponry. She was, it would seem, a master of Nordic martial arts. Sami self-defense. Balancing on one leg, she plied her other like a kick-boxer, dealing knock-out blows to two of our assailants. And Stan felled the third.

All very well and good, but then—a strange creature came at us from above. A deathly pale man with shining skin—or no, not a man. A flying slug? He had a sad gash of a mouth, and his eyes were two soft stalks atop his head. Although wingless, he was in flight. Something he did with his hands kept him aloft, an uncanny twitching of his fingers. If you could call those fingers. Rampantly emanating pale repellor rays that kept him aloft.

No time to think! The larval slug man wrapped a spare arm around Vivi and they rose six feet off the ground, heading for the dark sky, with Vivi yelling curses. The pale flying slug gave no spoken response.

I felt a rush of anguish and despair. Baxter was snarling and yelping and leaping as high as he could, to no avail. When Vivi and her captor were ten feet off the ground, the abductor gave out an pained, unearthly screech, like the sounds of glaciers calving, mixed with an elephant being torn in half by a typhoon. At that moment Vivi began to plummet.

I raced forward and caught her in my arms—like a true action hero. I was proud. Above us, the slug-man writhed his fingers and arced away.

Grinning irrepressibly, yet with some hint of her shaken state, Vivi displayed an immense Bowie knife. She'd had it in a sheath on her leg. The darkness of the night caused its smeared blade to appear green—or was that the natural color of the slug man's ichor?

"I stabbed that slimy thing right in its armpit! Hoped to get his heart!"

I set Vivi on her feet. Baxter put his forepaws up onto her so as to lick her hands. Leon wrapped his arms around her and held her tight. Meanwhile Stan was idly nudging one of the downed cutpurses with his foot. But now the man and his companions began melting like hot wax, losing their contours, with even their clothes subsuming into the pale masses of their flesh. Eyestalks and branching tentacles appeared—it would be erroneous to call them arms and hands. The tips of the tentacles twitched and the shapeshifting slugs sailed up into the sky like the other one had.

"I wonder if Tierney somehow put out the word on us," said Stan. "Like he sent a telegram? He's quite the weasel, that guy."

"Or the great shoggoth read our minds," suggested Vivi. "It's very tight with those flying slugs."

"I thought all we'd see down here was the cukes and that shoggoth," said Stan. "Not morphodite larvae."

With what proved to be supreme overconfidence, I said, "Hell Stan, we just proved we can handle anything they throw at us!"

* * * *

When we got back to our plane in the morning, our watchman told us he'd had to chase off a pair of those flying slugs—probably two of the ones who'd tried to ambush us.

"*Con gusto*," said the guard, holding up his stained machete. He glanced down off the edge of the wharf. "*Los peces pequeños comen.*"

"The little fishes eat, he says," inserted Leon. "Am I the only one noticing that the blood stains on his machete are a deep chartreuse green? Quite a nasty color in daylight."

"Let's get your squawk box the hell on board and crank the props outta here," said Stan. He and I were lugging the heavy ultrasound device that Vivi and Leon had scored this morning from Andes Gem Supplies. Plus a three car batteries to run it.

It was an enjoyable flight down the coast of South America to its southern-most tip, a fine, clear day. Leon and Vivi had thought to bring two hampers of fresh food from Lima.. The wrinkled sea and contoured coast looked like a classroom map, with the Andes behind them, their piled-up peaks topped with snow. The sinuous deep-cut valleys held rivers edged by emerald green jungle. Glints danced from the waters of jewel-like lakes. Here and there a tiny settlement appeared. How wild this country still was. We snuggled into our flying furs, snacking and enjoying the view.

Along the way we met one of those airborne slugs, twiddling its ray-emitting fingers as it kept abreast of us, flying just off the tip of our wing, perhaps hoping to disrupt our engines. I could see crusted green blood staining his side—he was the same one Vivi had stabbed. Pilot Stan got the better of him by dipping, then, arcing back up and letting me machine-gun the nasty thing with our on-board Maxim. Great fun.

"Sounds like it's saying *haw-haw*, dontcha think?" said Stan, admiring the sound.

"What does the cannon sound like?" I asked. "I saw the trigger for it in the hold."

"Save the cannon for later. We only brought three shells. Heavy mofos. Just about broke my back lugging them aboard. We'll use them on the grand emperor of the subterranean slugs." Not a pleasant thought, the great shoggoth of Leng.

It was two in the morning by the time we spotted the village of Ushuaia, in its harbor amid the archipelago of Tierra Del Fuego. The sky was still light—we were so far south that, rather than setting, the summer sun simply rolled along the horizon. A dreamy pearlescent glow filled the little harbor. A few score fishing boats were at anchor. The buildings were shabby constructs of concrete and tin. A dispiriting prison hulked at the far end of the town. Nobody was on the streets.

As the Dornier sluiced across the mirrored waters, a flock of startled of flamingos lifted off, their legs like moving hieroglyphs. We coasted to a stop beside a dock where Stan had spotted a pair of small seaplanes. A yawning, grizzled man appeared from a shed and stumped over to help us tie up. Seaweed and dead penguins lay on the gray beach.

As before, we were stiff, exhausted, and half-deaf from the seventeen-hour drone of our Do 24's three big engines. With a minimum of talk, we made our way to waterfront inn with a dormitory room above. We fell into our beds and slept like the dead, with Baxter lying protectively across my feet.

When I awoke, it was bright day, the sky a shade of magnesium blue. I was alone in our dorm above the inn. I could hear my companions downstairs, laughing, chatting, feasting on a huge breakfast. A pale slug-man was facing me from the head of the stairs. His tapering, legless lower half was flat upon the floor, and his upper half was raised. He was resting upon his two many-fingered, flexible arms—if you could all them arms—dragging himself toward me, with the dead black orbits of his stalk-eyes fixed upon me. A soft chant came from the dreary slit of his mouth.

"Tekelili," he crooned over and over. "Tekelili."

He stretched a drooping tendril my way. The tip of it pinched off and came rapidly humping across the floor, up the leg of my bed, and into my covers—a mini-slug that was meant, no doubt, to burrow into my flesh and tunnel through my veins to find a home inside my head—

My scream awakened me for real. Yes, the others were downstairs, but, no, there wasn't a slug man in the room with me. But maybe, terrible thought, he'd left that slug bud in my head, and he'd flown away? The slugs' revenge for my happy, chattering, moment with that Maxim machine-gun! Crazy mission, crazy thoughts. I splashed brackish water onto my face from the basin, pulled my clothes on, checked that my diamond was still in my pocket, and went downstairs. Baxter galumphed eagerly behind me.

"Bad dream, Doug?" said Vivi. Hardened adventurer that she was, she looked a bit amused. Very fresh and tasty in her yellow and aqua flying togs.

"I always scream in the morning," I said, by way of shrugging it off. "The only rational response." I didn't feel like telling her the details.

"Weather's turning foul," said Leon. "But we're going to press on."

"Esmeralda is saying that once a storm hits the Strait of Magellan it lasts a week," said Vivi, indicating the innkeeper, a leathery lady with a prominent jaw.

Esmeralda waved me to a spot at the table and slapped down a bowl with a pozole and lamb stew. Baxter, with fickle affections, had chosen to lie placidly on the floor next to Vivi's chair.

"I've got them gassing up our plane," said Stan, handing me the gourd of morning *mate* that was passing around the table. He was wearing a heavy red and white serape that he must have gotten from the landlady. "The fueling might take another hour. They had to truck in extra drums of gas. We definitely want to be full to the brim. Don't want to run dry before we hit Leng."

Something about Stan's expression triggered an epiphany I really should have had earlier. "When we get there, we'll—we'll be out of gas?"

Vivi glanced at Leon and laughed. "Reporter Doug is alert."

"You think it's funny?" I cried. "You guys are frikkin crazy!"

"The radioed logs indicate that the Starkweather-Moore group left a large fuel dump beside Leng," said the imperturbable Leon. "Don't sweat it."

"What if those drums leaked?" I jabbered. "Or what if the shoggoth—I don't know—what if it *drank* the gas?"

"Urxula swears the fuel is still there," said Stan. "I just met with her and we teeped about the situation. She's back on our plane."

Obviously I'd missed a lot this morning. I'd meant to start typing some notes this morning, but by now it was too late. "How long have you guys been awake?"

"Couple of hours," said Stan. "Hell, Doug, it's almost ten o'clock. I'm going again to check on the gas. Got my juice, Esmeralda? " The landlady fetched a cloth sack from the kitchen and handed it to Stan as he strode out the door. Her expression was sly and crafty. Not a good sign.

I looked at Leon, trying to fit things together. "First of all, how did Urxula—" I began.

"She popped up out of the ocean and hauled herself into our plane," said Leon. "I told you she swims fast. I got a teep signal from her this morning—that's what woke me up. It was a dream, but it wasn't. I went to the plane to warn her to lie low. I'd rather not have the locals see her. I gather they've had some troubles with the shoggoths and the cukes. The landlady here, when I told her we're on a mission to the lost city of Leng, she didn't look at all pleased."

With exaggerated care Esmeralda refilled the *mate* gourd. "*Vuelo largo a la Antártida*," she said, as if urging us on our way. I didn't have the nerve to ask her what she'd given Stan in that cloth bag.

"Long flight to Antarctica," said Vivi. Her smile was wild. Very amped up. "Our big day."

Antarctica. The word is like a death knell. In Japanese culture, the color of mourning is white. Our tiny silver plane would be a lonely splinter above a continent of doom. At least we'd have Urxula on our team.

I had sudden vision of the cuke looking—sexy? That dear, beloved, sea cucumber alien. With her Delft blue eyes bright, and full red lips at the tips of her oral tubes, and her arms swaying in a graceful hula. A sinuous curve to the ridges of her barrel-shaped body, and her five pointed feet demure below. And a bouffant brunette hair-do? Oh, right, this was a teep image that Urxula was beaming to me. Impressive that she could transmit all the way from the harbor.

"Hot stuff," said Vivi dryly. She was picking up the cuke teep too. "We're in for strange times, Doug. It's vital that we stick together." She stood, utterly lovely, and walked to my side of the table. Like some reckless, slumming angel, she leaned down and give me a long, very long kiss. Her tongue in my mouth, her hand tousling my hair, our breaths conjoined, my heart hammering.

Leon glanced over, as blank as a sunning turtle, then turned back to some notes he was making in his trip journal. Reminding me yet again that I hadn't typed a word. So what. So far as I understood Leon's situation with Vivi, they weren't lovers. But maybe I was wrong. Upon looking closer, I faintly saw a mixture of shame and lust on his face. Which meant—what? Esmeralda brought our refilled food hampers from the kitchen, and the moment passed.

Silently we gathered our possessions and made our way to our massive, trusty Dornier, with its three powerful engines aligned upon its high wing. One by one, the great propellers roared into life. Once again a flock of birds lifted from the harbor—this time it was cormorants, long-necked and awkward. Each of them had to run a few steps across the surface before rising into the air.

Suddenly Urxula began teeping images of—something bad. Mouths and eyes. Heading our way?

"Hurry!" Stan Gorski cried from the plane's open door. And then we were in the cabin, with me in back with Leon, Vivi in the co-pilot's seat, and Baxter in my lap. Stan gunned the engines to a savage scream, slewed away from the dock, and sent our Do 24 wallowing across the harbor, slowly lifting into the air. And that's when the shoggoth appeared.

A few years ago, in 1927 to be exact, a new island was born off the coast of Indonesia: Anak Krakatau. It rose impossibly, unpredictably, over the course of several days, fueled by an undersea lava eruption, hot, steaming, alien: something never seen before by humans. The *Globe* had a big write up, with pictures.

That's what the appearance of the shoggoth was like: except in super-speeded-up time, and with quivering streamlined protoplasmic bulk rather than craggy mineral solidity. A pinkish-green bulk dotted with—eyes and toothy mouths?

The behemoth bulked huge in our path. An immemorial being whose kind had originated from somewhere beyond the stars. Rising a thousand feet into the air, it was shedding sea water like a sumo wrestler dumps sweat. I was wondering if we could even clear its summit.

Stan pulled hard on the control yoke, and I flailed my way across the plane's passenger compartment toward the wing cannon's controls. There was a shell in the breech, that much was in our favor. The plane was rising steeply, and the cannon had a limited range of movement on its swivel. I canted it downward as far as I could, hoping to hit the shoggoth's main mass, and I got off my shot without really aiming. Even if I missed, an explosion in the water might daunt the blancmange beast.

The recoil bucked the plane, unseating Vivi, and sending her, Leon, Urxula, Baxter, and me all a-tumble, as if in an interspecies orgiastic heap. A moment later, the sound of the exploding shell overcame even the noise of the straining engines. Gobbets of shoggoth flesh slapped our windshield, some of them with eyeballs within. And now I felt the shudder of our landing pontoons skiing unevenly across the monster's damaged crest, a sensation like feeling the rungs of your Flexible Flyer cut through clean snow into the remains of manure pile. Staring, biting tendrils thudded against our metal fuselage. But then we were safely out of reach.

My fellow explorers got to their feet—two legs, four legs, five stalks. We salved bruises and hunkered down for the final leg of the flight. Yes, I was wrung out with panic and worry, but we were well launched, with no damages, and rising ever higher into the sky. Looking back at the shoggoth I noted a dark, thick plume of smoke pouring from its ragged tip. Had we set it alight? But then it dipped back beneath the sea, returning to its lair, mayhap beneath the lost city of Leng.

The last thing I spotted before we entered the clouds was an island with a hundred thousand penguins on it, each of them staring up at us, making us the target of a hundred thousand beaks.

* * * *

A storm in the Straits of Magellan—sailors know nothing worse. Our ascent through the clouds was harrowing. A screaming gale, cracks of thunder above and below, and frantic flashes of lightning. The wildly branching zig-zags came perilously close to our craft, etching fearful patterns into my retinas. Naturally I thought of the sinister bolts that killed off so many of the Starkweather-Moore crew.

As if that weren't enough, a flying river of rain choked our rightmost engine into silence. The plane began to wobble and yaw. Stan knuckled down over the control yoke, every part the seasoned aviator, trying this, trying that—and, all praise Gorski, the stalled engine stuttered back to life.

We rose to the Do 24's maximum altitude, about five miles above sea level, into a zone of preternatural calm, a clear azure space of sun, The air was so thin that I repeatedly had the sensation that I'd stopped breathing. I hung out my tongue and panted like Baxter. And the cold—the cold was astonishing. We mounded blanket upon blanket over ourselves, like parasitic larvae within bulging flesh. We ate almost constantly, stoking our bodies' glow. The hours flowed by amid the steady, hypnotic roar of the three engines, with Vivi back in the co-pilot's seat at Stan's side.

Leon wasn't speaking to me, at least for now. I assumed I had totally misread their relationship, and now I was utterly conflicted about what to do. Strangle Leon and throw his body from the plane? The lack of oxygen was making me giddy. For the moment, Leon's attentions were focused upon Urxula, perched on the plane's deck between the two us. Like an alien idol, quite chatty now—in a teep kind of way—filling our minds with a stream of disquieting images. Hard to tell how much time went by as I watched Urxula's mind-show.

An explosion and a fire. Tunnels with surreal pictures on the walls. Over and over the shoggoth, seething with teeth and eyes and feelers. The harsh and lonely caws of birds. The milky waters of a subterranean lake, pulsing with menace. The five-sided outline of a vast—gate? Flexing forms wielding swords of light. A tunnel to inner space.

"Feeling dreamy?" It was Vivi at my side. She'd left Stan alone in the cockpit. Once again she glued her mouth to mine in a passionate kiss. She pushed me onto my back and lay on me, kissing me over and over. Not three feet away from us, Leon stared, his mouth a crooked line, his eyes burning. Urxula laid a tendril across the side of my head, as if taking the measure of human mating rites. Even so, I was tugging at my wrappings, wanting to strip myself bare for Vivi, who was tugging at the zipper of her blue and yellow overalls, but the cold, oh the cold, it was like liquid in my veins—

The blow of Leon's fist against the side of my head jolted me to my senses. Perhaps it was merely a cruel-to-be-kind suggestion to quit screwing around and tend to business, rather than a jealous remonstrance. Vivi rolled to one side and hunkered there, giggling amid her wrappings. Leon was smiling too. How did I fit into these strange people's plans?

"Go spell Stan," said Vivi. "He'll need a nap before we land. You can fly solo for awhile. It's simple at this altitude. Nothing in the way."

Embarrassed and with a throb in my head, I rose to my feet and checked my watch. It had stopped, its gears frozen in place. The sun had moved far around the horizon. Looking out the side window, I saw distant, pinprick peaks of insane height, peeping through the roiling layer of clouds. The Mountains of Madness. Amid them we'd find the Plateau of Leng.

I slid into the cockpit and found Stan Gorski—dead drunk. Lolling back in his seat with an all but empty flask of Argentinean brandy in his hand.

"Esmeralda's *adios*," said Stan, gulping the cloudy dregs of the bottle before I could interfere. "*Whooh*. Raw stuff. And what an aftertaste."

"How are you going to land this plane in your condition?" I demanded.

"If pontooning across a shoggoth doesn't don't earn a man a snort, what does?" Stan turned a spiteful look upon me, then shoved forward on the control yoke, sending our Dornier into a steeply angled dive. "Take over the controls, kid. Earn your wings." At this point Stan's final slug of brandy hit him like a depth charge. He reeled sideways out of his chair, banged his forehead rather hard on the dash, and settled to the floor in a heap. I didn't feel particularly sorry for him. Not with our plane plowing down into the clouds.

"Vivi," I cried. "Help me."

She yelled back her answer. "Pull back on the yoke, you fool!" Leon remained silent, as if gloating to have his woman to himself. Urxula added some kind of verbal comment—a high thin piping.

I wrestled with the controls, but in my panic I pushed the stiff control yoke the wrong way, only steepening our descent. Even worse, I threw us into a barrel roll and then into a tailspin. We were corkscrewing down, the crates thudding around in the rear of the plane, and the engines redlining at their physical limits. The besotted Stan Gorski remained utterly inert, but now Vivi came tumbling willy-nilly to my aid, all knees and elbows and tousled hair, and with her overalls open down to her navel. Angrily she yanked at the steering yoke, and then at the knobs to feather the engines' fuel feeds, all the while sitting on my lap, her scent making me dizzy. We were out of the dive, better than that, we were arcing upwards, and then we were restored to the serenity of sunny kingdom above the clouds.

I aimed us towards the highest of the pinpoint summits ahead. "Thanks, Vivi."

"I'm tired, Doug." To be heard over the engines, she spoke as loudly as if I were deaf. "Leon and I are all bundled up. We're dallying. Leave us alone." She disappeared again.

Onward we droned, with the chief pilot passed-out, an alien aboard, and the woman I loved in a heap of blankets with a man who seemed to hate me. At least, in this land of midnight sun, there was no prospect of it growing dark. And slowly the clouds below began to clear.

* * * *

I'd thought we were near the peaks, but they were so vast that I'd underestimated the distance. I flew on for three more hours, always aiming towards that one tallest mountain. Vivi and Leon slept. I had no visions from Urxula. Baxter lay on my feet beside the collapsed Stan Gorski. I'd thrown Stan's serape and an additional fleece over him—after first searching him to make sure he didn't have another bottle on his person. He was utterly inert. A plum-colored bruise darkened the waxy pale skin of his forehead. Obviously I should have checked his pulse and his breathing, but I suppose I was too angry with him to bother.

As we finally approached our goal, Leon and Vivi bundled themselves into the cockpit to have a look. Vivi took the co-pilot's seat, cavalierly resting her feet on Gorski. Leon stood behind us, peering out the windshield and narrating an account into his tape recorder. He was using an especially pompous tone, as if performing for an eventual radio audience. Our plan, by the way, was to delay our broadcasts until *after* we'd killed the great shoggoth. We didn't want an agitated Tierney descend upon us too soon.

"The mountains are as if alive," orated Leon, speaking above the engines' endless rumble. "I think—I think it's possible the mountains have changed since the Starkweather-Moore expedition. Accelerated weathering? Continental upheaval? Mineral growth? In any case we seem to see a new profile to these peaks, and new defiles among them. Even so, we'll find the Plateau of Leng. The peaks are like teeth, eh, Vivi?"

Vivi made no answer. Finally concerned over Stan's prolonged inertness, she was leaning over and shaking him.

"Yes, the Mountains of Madness are a great maw, bent upon swallowing us," continued Leon in his affected, stentorian tone. "Our predecessors spoke of watchtowers upon the slopes, and I see such a tower now. Steer closer, would you, Doug? It's a crude, atavistic block castle, cold and dumb, savagely eroded, its angles out of kilter, and perhaps a lair for eldritch beings we know not. I'm looking straight down onto the fortification just now and—wait! Do I see motion? Circle around so I can fire the cannon at the tower, Doug."

"Shut your crack," I said, more than a little tired of Leon's assistant professor routine. "We're not wasting fuel on that. Or using up one of our last two shells."

"My timid, uneducated pilot is ill at ease," resumed Leon, his orotund voice in full blare. "He thinks only of finding the landing area, somewhere ahead of us, in the rolling snowy fields around the lost city of Leng. Fret not, my good man. I see a gap athwart this peak, Can you bring up our altitude a bit more?"

"Even higher?" I said uncertainly. Each breath of this cold, thin air was like an icepack in my lungs.

Meanwhile Vivi was on her knees beside Stan, trying to breathe air into his mouth. For a crazy moment, I envied Stan. But—was he in a coma? How heartless I'd been to let him lie there so long.

"We'll land on the high plateau," Leon said to his tape recorder, his voice rich and fruity. "Five miles above sea level. Those poor devils Starkweather and Moore had their fuel dump up there, immediately adjacent to the impossibly ancient city of Leng. Will we find the drums of gasoline intact? Or shall Leng be our final terminus? Vagrant gusts play about these jagged peaks, like the djinn whirlwinds of Araby. The inhuman landscape is as if—"

Leon was interrupted by Vivi's wail. "Stan's dead! I can't make him breathe." She was spitting and rubbing her lips. "His mouth, the taste, so bitter—he was poisoned, oh my god. Esmeralda put poison in his brandy!"

Stan dead? He and I hadn't been friends, not really, but his wild passion and vigor had enthralled me, lured me along on this insane journey. And now he would never taste the ultimate victory or defeat. Poisoned by an agent of that bastard Tierney, the Arkham zealot, the Urxula-hating scourge of all he could not understand.

"A culminating moment of terror and catharsis," Leon shouted into his microphone. "Fortunately the dazzling aviatrix Vivi Nordström is at my side, and fully prepared to accomplish the high-altitude landing of our seaplane upon these vast and primeval drifts of snow. She's quite unlike our spooked assistant, Doug Patchen, recently fired from the *Boston Globe*."

I knocked the tape recorder from Leon's lap and stomped on it with the heel of my boot. Things were completely coming apart. I was terrified, even unhinged. The reality of the scene was a thousand times more vivid than Leon's vainglorious words. The landscape's absolute lack of hospitality towards frail humans, its deracinated proportions, its nigh-monochrome blankness like the staring grey eyes of a lunatic. Or like the eyes of a corpse. Poor Stan Gorski.

As if sensing my imminent descent into a fugue state, Baxter got his paws on my chest and used his tongue to strop my only exposed bit of flesh: a portion of cheek. And that brought me back. A touch on the cheek.

The rest of me resided out of reach under layers of flying furs and insulating clothing. I resembled the ambulatory inventory of Abercrombie & Fitch. Even Baxter had doubled up, with two fleecy dog vests. Yet Urxula remained bare—her alien physiology at ease in this savage clime.

The cuke had taken in the essence of our tangled emotional states, and now she teeped us some calming images. Leon and I shaking hands while Vivi smiled on. Our plane gracefully landing beside the strange domes and spires of Leng. Urxula leading us to an entrance to the city. Shoggoth flesh melting like ice cream in the sun. Us flying back to Boston with treasures in our hold.

"Let's start with the handshake," Leon said to me.

"Fine. I'm sorry broke your tape machine. The atmosphere here—it's—"

"Can you throw Stan out of the hatch?" Vivi asked us. "Depressing to have him in here. And, who knows, maybe he's contagious."

It hardly seemed like a fair ending for Stan Gorski, but Leon agreed with Vivi, and Urxula was with them.

It was up to me and Leon to lug the body to the rear of the plane, while Vivi piloted on. We levered the tiny rear hatch open against the furious Antarctic slipstream, the hatch's hinges very stiff in the frigid air. Perhaps it was a coincidence, but precisely at the moment Vivi flew directly above another of those uncanny mountain castles. Leon shoved Stan through the hatch before I was quite ready. We let the door slam, then ran into the cockpit to witness our lost companion's long fall—in some ways reminiscent of when we'd dropped Urxula into the sea off the continental shelf.

But this fall had a punch-line. A creature was waiting for the body. Slow, swollen, obscene, raising its pointed tip as if tasting the vibrations of our great engines. A manifestation of the ghastly shoggoth, slipping like a many-eyed moray eel from the gloomy castle on the bare peak below. The monstrous glaring tendril swayed, twitched and *snap*, Gorski was gone. Urxula piped in dismay.

As if this weren't enough, the not-fully-satiated shoggoth had mascots. A brace of the flying slug things darted out of the castle and came arrowing upwards, riding atop the repellor rays of their twitching feelers, in hot pursuit of our plane. I took my seat in the co-pilot's position while Vivi maneuvered us into the proper offensive alignment. And then I let fly with the Maxim machine-gun, My senses were at an absolute peak of acuity, and after three withering bursts, the two flying slugs were no more.

"Higher," Leon repeatedly insisted. "You have to fly higher."

The staggeringly lofty crags of the Mountains of Madness were dead ahead, and we were dead on course to slam into them. The engines howled in animal protest as Vivi revved them to maximum power. With the air so thin, it was exceedingly hard to gain the extra altitude we needed. As if by way of helping, Urxula opened up her leathery pair of batwings and trembled them amid the empty space of the cabin. As before, I observed that her wings gave off subtle anti-gravitational energies, not unlike the slugs' repellor rays. Apparently these forces could pass through our hull with no diminution. Surely we were rising more rapidly than before.

The evil winds did their best to smash our plane against the towers of stone, but here it was a good thing that the air was thin. The winds lacked force. With a sure touch, Vivi wafted us over the verge and through a winding pass. And now we were above the spreading Plateau of Leng, nearly the size of Rhode Island, and ringed by the Mountains of Madness. Not more than ten miles ahead of us was the lost city itself.

From a distance, the ancient, ruined metropolis was like a maze or a labyrinth, partly buried in the ice and snow. Stretching toward the horizon, a city on the edge of forever. As we approached, I could make out the shapes of buildings—some of them roofless ruins, but many intact. They ran a full gamut of forms, as one often sees in cosmopolitan cities with long histories. Fanciful domes, blunt towers, and terraced pyramids jostled against deceptively frail spires—which had surely been in place for millennia. A Cyclopean colonnade of pillars wound through the town—perhaps demarcating a former promenade along a now-subterranean river. The ruins of swirled avenues nested like scrolls around circular and elliptical piazzas. Some of the buildings were in the forms of unfamiliar geometric solids—icosahedra, saddle surfaces, and helicoids. Every part of the uncanny congeries was heavily weathered, with all surfaces bleached to pale shades of white and gray. Although the lower parts of the buildings were embedded in primeval ice, the windows in the upper stories offered gaping access to the tenebrous gloom within.

Our engines were beginning to stutter and to miss. We were nearly out of gas.

"Use that that spot over there," I told Vivi, pointing. "It's flat, and that lump beside it—could be a Starkweather-Moore plane. Snowed over. And the mound next to it—that could be the fuel."

"Well-eyed," said Leon, as if offering a return to congeniality. "Can you land her, Vivi?"

"I once landed a seaplane on snow in Norway," she said. "I'd stolen the plane from a harbor near the maelstrom in the Lofoten Islands. I ditched the plane on a snowy bluff near Oslo, and tobogganed down. Found a man to help me. As usual." A low, throaty laugh.

As the sounds of the engines grew increasingly ragged, Vivi brought us down for a beautifully smooth landing, gliding across the gritty snows of the plateau, with plumes of white flying out to the sides. The fuel-starved engines stuttering into silence as we reached a full stop.

"Well timed," said Leon with an exultant guffaw.

"Stan should be here for this," I said.

"We can't think about him," said Vivi. "We have a mission." By way of backing her up, Urxula again teeped us an image of a burning shoggoth.

Baxter was scratching at the big side door in the fuselage. We four followed the dog out, the humans sinking knee deep into fresh snow to find a sturdy crust beneath. Baxter was light enough that he could stand atop the snow. As for Urxula—she laid down and sledded along on her ridged sides, beating at the snow with her five arms.

The sun was blazing, and for now it wasn't windy. Even so, the temperature was minus fifteen Fahrenheit. We formed a sort of bucket brigade to remove some crates from the plane, Urxula joining in. Soon we had the one big tent set up, even down to its unfolded jigsaw-puzzle wooden floor, and with a coal stove cranking out warmth inside. Leon found some sealskin snow boots in one of the crates—Vivi called them mukluks. I donned a pair. While Leon, Baxter, and Vivi warmed up by the stove—Urxula and I went to check if those were indeed snowed-over drums of fuel.

"Hurry back," called Vivi. "Leon will cook while I concoct our ultrasound amplifier. We'll need it soon."

"Solder in the superheterodyne unit from our radio transmitter?" suggested Leon. "And the amp circuit from the tape recorder that our rogue reporter smashed?"

"On the beam," said Vivi.

Out in the stunning emptiness of this Antarctic plateau with Urxula, I floundered towards the mound—my footing improved by the mukluks,. They had the fur on the outside, and to some extent it floated me on the snow. Urxula coasted smoothly at my side.

The closest buildings of Leng were a few hundred yards beyond our goal. I saw a down-sloping path that led to a geometric dome made of pentagons. I was wildly curious about what I'd see within. According to what I'd heard of the Pabodie report, the city contained galleries of murals and bas-reliefs, plus a deeply buried subterranean lake, and—this decisively confirmed by the Starkweather-Moore party's final radio messages—one or more shoggoths. And that brought me back to issue of finding fuel so we could get the hell out of here if—or, rather, *when*—the next unearthly disaster hit.

The first mound we reached was indeed a snow-covered airplane. Bits of aluminum peeked through the wind-sculpted drifts. But the metal was torn, and the mound was overly—flat. As if some great force had pancaked the Starkweather-Moore plane. Like a can beneath a steam-roller. We kept moving, and came to the snow hillock that I believed to cover the barrels of fuel. Urxula unfolded her bat wings, gently flapped them, and brought her repellor rays into play. With uncannily powerful effect, the leathery wings swept the drifts away. And, yes, the fuel drums were here.

Like Vivi, I was now wearing a heavy knife strapped to my leg. So I used it pry open the stopper on one of the metal barrels. The wonderful smell of airplane fuel wafted out. Perhaps it had temporarily frozen during the winter months down here, but now, at a balmy fifteen below zero, the fuel was sloshing around just fine. But how would we empty the drums into the plane's projecting fin-like tanks? I saw no sign of a pump.

Teeping this thought from my mind, the hardy and obliging Urxula dipped one of her feeding tubes into the barrel and puffed up her body like a water balloon, engulfing ten gallons. We stomped and slid back to the plane, and the bloated cuke spewed the fuel into our tank. I tested the ignition on one of the engines, and it caught with a steady smooth roar. Looked like we had a way home. Assuming we survived the other things we had yet to face.

I left Urxula on watch outside our tent. The stunning cold bothered her not one whit. Inside the tent it was wonderfully warm, with a two-quart can of beef stew heating on a primus stove. Vivi and Leon had shed their coats and I did the same. Soon, Leon set out three bowls of the surprisingly good stew, gave a smaller bowl to Baxter, and passed a fifth bowl out the tent door to Urxula, who tootled as she welcomed it.

Sitting on camp stools at a folding table with Vivi and Leon, I had a momentary flash of an off-kilter suburban domestic setup amongst us three, with Vivi and me married, a husband and wife, and Leon along for the ride. Why couldn't we two men share the same woman? Would that be so wrong? But then harsh reality returned.

"The great shuggoth may come at any time," said Vivi, fussing with the innards of the cracked tape recorder and of the two ultrasonic devices, arranging parts on the table. She was in her cute blue and yellow overalls, utterly lovely. Plus her chic scarf with the drawing of eyes on it. I suppressed a moan of longing.

"This is home sweet home for Urxula," I managed, groping for something relevant to say. "I just wonder why her pals are hiding? If they'd come out, they could help us."

"You don't really know the details of the Pabodie report and of the Starkweather-Moore transcripts, do you," said Leon, cocking his head. "But yet you came on this trip?"

"I came because—because Urxula gave me a diamond. And—" I paused, and then I choked out the truth. "I came because I'm in love with Vivi. She's the most wonderful women I've ever seen. And, if you two aren't actually married, I'm hoping that—"

"Oh please," said Vivi firmly, yet slightly dimpling at the compliment. "A time and a place for everything, Doug."

"Once Doug puts it so frankly, I'm at my ease," said Leon, his tense features relaxing. "I'm with you, Doug. Vivi is splendid. And I'm no prude. We're at the ends of the Earth. We can do as we please. If Vivi doesn't take exception, I'm perfectly content with a *mènage a trois*."

If Stan had been here, he would have interjected something coarse and rude to break the mood. But Stan was gone, poor guy.

"Tonight we'll make the biggest pile of blankets anyone's ever seen," said Vivi, glancing up from her tools. "And then, of course I'll make love to both you boys. After all, I'm Scandinavian."

Leon guffawed at that.

"What's so funny?" asked Vivi, all mock innocence. "How would you like it if I told Doug you've been hoping for an orgy all along?"

"Giving away my darkest secrets," said Leon clearing his throat. "Let's rewind the metaphorical tape. Doug was curious about the fate of Urxula's fellow cukes. The shoggoths prey upon the cukes. This much you surely know. It's an ongoing problem. Most of the cukes left Leng in ancient times. Over ten thousand years ago. And the remaining colony of cukes would like to follow them. But the exit route is closed. The stranded survivors spend their days creeping furtively around the buried passages of this dead city."

"The exit is closed?" I parroted.

"The escape route runs through a subterranean lake, miles beneath Leng," said Leon. "Lake Alph, Starkweather named the lake. As it happens, a river runs down through the ice, into the lake, and out through the bottom of the lake as if through a drain. The upper and lower branches of the River Alph." Leon studied my face, looking for an intelligent response, and finding none. "River Alph as in Coleridge's poem?"

Still I didn't quite get it. Flipping to professor mode, Leon cleared his throat and recited a verse.

"In Xanadu did Kubla Khan
A stately pleasure-dome decree:
Where Alph, the sacred river, ran
Through caverns measureless to man
Down to a sunless sea."

By way of accompaniment, Urxula was feeding me teep. Images of Leng in the old days, perhaps a hundred thousand years ago. A pleasing city on a grassy plateau, with fanciful buildings painted in bright colors, and their spires fluttering with flags and pennants. The avenues were lined by tree ferns and by stately fungi, thirty feet in height. Merry cuke people soared in the air, chasing alien pterodactyls and playful flapping things like manta rays. Piping music and snakes like ribbons filled the streets. Farmer-shoggoths sold tobacco, crocodile meat and enormous yams. The River Alph meandered into the town from the mountains, seemingly ending at a lake at the bottom of a deep-set gorge at the city's center. This was Lake Alph, profound, pellucid, and tinted the deepest of blues. Cukes bathed and played on its shores, frolicking with things like hippopotami. As teeped by Urxula, a sense of racial nostalgia overlaid the Edenic scene.

"In time, the cukes' ancestors learned to dive to the bottom of Lake Alph," came Vivi's voice, very intimate and close. "They dove down to enter the subterranean river which flows from there." I stared at Vivi with glazed eyes. Her lips weren't moving. "The lower Alph," she continued. "It channels through Earth's crust and enters the great void that fills our hollow world."

Urxula fed me a stunning image of the interior of the Hollow Earth, lit by streamers of pink light, and with jungles and seas upon its great inner curve. Truly a cavern measureless to man. At the core of the Hollow Earth floated a cluster of wobbling ultramarine seas, basically sunless, and amid these umpteen seas drifted the majestic ancestors of Urxula's race. Behemoth sea cucumbers, with supernal powers and immense fronded feelers. The Great Old Ones. At the pinpoint center of the Hollow Earth was a star gate, a gleaming aethereal sphere, guarded by the Great Old Ones.

The star gate would, from time to time, connect our Earth's interior to the interior of another other hollow planet, connect via a twisting hyperdimensional tube, connect to a hollow world called Yuggoth. Yuggoth was the cukes' ultimate goal but was, as yet, still not quite in range, not even via the star gate at the core of our Hollow Earth. Thanks to dark Yuggoth's highly eccentric orbit, It might be centuries or even millennia until Earth and Yuggoth were once again properly aligned. This span of time meant little to the cuke people—and still less to the Great Old Ones. All of this I knew with certainty. All was laid out clearly in my head. Direct from Urxula.

"The problem for today's Leng cuke colony is getting down into the lower branch of the River Alph," put in Leon. "Lake Alph is clotted up by a massive shoggoth, a merged grex of all the shoggoths who used to live here. There's a variety of tunnels in and out of Lake Leng. More than likely that was a chunk of the Alph shoggoth we saw in Ushuaia. And no doubt that was an arm of it that reached out to snarf Stan's body. And for sure it ate Starkweather and Moore—and crushed their plane. We're next." Leon tried for a nervous laugh, but it came out like a sob.

This tutorial was getting a little heavy for my taste. I wanted to go to sleep. The prolonged shortage of oxygen was making me light-headed. It was downright hot in the tent by now. My belly was unpleasantly full, and I hadn't slept in twenty hours. It wasn't dark outside yet, but, um, it wasn't *going* to get dark.

"It's up to us to get that shoggoth out of Lake Alph," said Vivi. "It's high time."

"I get it," I said with a sigh. "And we're supposed to do it with a box of grenades, two cannon shells, a machine gun, and a flamethrower."

"Don't you ever listen to anyone?" said Vivi, flaring up. "And you call yourself a reporter? We're going to use ultrasound. An ultrasound modulation of—*tra-la-la*—my voice." Outside the tent, Urxula squealed like a bagpipe. "We'll use Urxula's voice too," added Vivi. "We'll vibrate the shoggoth into a trance."

"And then comes our happy ending," said Leon, smacking his lips over the last bit of stew. "The shoggoth comes to the surface and we knock it out. And then the lurking Leng cukes annihilate it. Somehow. And then the cukes finally dive into Lake Alph and follow the lower River Alph to the inside of the Hollow Earth, where the joyfully rejoin the Great Old Ones at the Hollow Earth's core. And then one of these days they hop off to Yuggoth, but that's no concern of ours. The point is that they'll leave Leng unoccupied, and ready to loot."

Vivi rapped the butt of her soldering iron on the table like an auctioneer's hammer. "Cunning artifacts! Brilliant art! Alien wisdom! You two can name your price when you get home, Leon and Dougie."

"And, altruistically speaking, our loot will jump human science forward by a few centuries," enthused Leon. "Heck—I'll get tenure for sure!"

I had a bad feeling about this. Leon and Vivi were shading into mania and hubris. "We barely escaped that shoggoth in the harbor of Ushuaia, guys. And you saw how the tendril swallowed Stan. There's no way we can hypnotize a giant, seething mass of shoggoth meat."

"We're way ahead of you," said Leon dismissively. "The shoggoths were created by the Great Old Ones to be slaves for the cukes. Beasts of burden. Under the cukes' direction, the shoggoths built the city of Leng. And then they were supposed to be watchdogs."

I looked at Baxter, happily snoring, and tried to imagine regarding a heap of slimy rancid undulating meat Jell-O in the same affectionate way.

"Naturally, you need to instruct any servant or pet," added Vivi. "So the Great Old Ones designed a special shoggoth language for the cukes to use. That word *tekelili* that you heard in your dream in Ushuaia this morning, Doug, it's part of the shoggoth language. It means, well, it means something like, *Behold, in the presence of unknowing absolution, I stand anointed*. But it's not *stand anointed*, exactly, it's more like *lie down inside a seedpod*."

"That's what *tekelili* means if a cuke says it," opined Leon. "But if a shoggoth says the word, it means something quite different. If a shoggoth says *tekelili*, your phrase *stand anointed* should be *roll at my leisure on the soft flesh of a decaying corpse*. And of course when a shoggoth's talking, the *unknowing absolution* should be *divine telepathy*. That's fairly obvious, eh?"

"You know nothing of these things," said Vivi coldly. "You are not one least little bit Scandinavian. Let's get back to what I was trying to tell our cub reporter here." She smiled at me. "Most of the old shoggoth commands have been lost. The cukes aren't what the used to be.. But, while delving into archaic and forgotten libraries, Leon and I found useful records of some key phrases. We made a transcription from the *Celaeno Fragments* in the library of Miskatonic University of Arkham."

"Arkham again?" I exclaimed. "Those bullshitting screwballs?"

"If you don't want to end up like Stan Gorski, then you'd better listen to us," said Vivi, her voice quite cold. "I'm telling you that Leon and I have unearthed a command that causes a shoggoth to halt and to stop all activity. The spell throws a giant slug into stasis."

"A human would phrase the spell thus," said Leon. "*Hafh'drn 'ai nog fhtagn*," His guttural, otherworldly tone seemed to vibrate the very walls of the tent.

"It has to be higher-pitched," corrected Vivi. "More like the sound of a cuke." She repeated the spell in a high, light soprano. And now, from outside the tent, Urxula echoed the mantra yet again, piping the words from her mouth-tubes, making the words wispy and aethereal. Baxter sat up and cocked his ears, greatly disturbed.

"Yes, Vivi is right," said Leon. "That's *almost* the way it has to sound." They smiled at each other.

"The thing is, it has to be even higher than that," Vivi now told me, resting her hand on the tangle of wires and parts on the table. "It has to be ultrasonic. The great shoggoth is tough and leathery, you see. I have to get under its skin. The spell has to dig into its meat." She turned to Leon. "I'm very, very excited, darling. I couldn't have brought the plan this far without you."

Leon looked well pleased. "Tomorrow you and Doug lure that giant shoggoth up here from Lake Alph," he said to Vivi, his eyes shining. "I'll have the ultrasonic amplifier at the ready. And we'll numb the brute with your spell."

"And then?" I asked, feeling as if I'd stepped into a bad dream.

"Well, we've got the cannon," said Leon going a little vague. "The machine gun. The grenades. We'll muddle through."

"And don't forget the hidden cuke people," added Vivi. "They'll come out when it's time."

A half-assed plan. Less than half-assed. A sixteenth-of-an-assed plan. Go way underground and lure a giant shoggoth—something the size of a battleship, maybe. Bigger. Ten battleships. Taunt it and run for your life, and when you get to the surface, your friends ambush it with—what? An electric dog-whistle?

Aside from these grave misgivings, something else was bothering me, something about the very first part of what Vivi had said when she started talking about the word *tekelili*.

"How would you know what I saw or heard in a dream I had in Ushuaia?" I demanded of her. "I don't remember telling you any details about my dream."

Airily she flipped her hand in the air. I was so tired I felt like I was seeing more than five fingers. "Surely by now you understand that I'm telepathic," she said, then turned to Leon. "It's play time! I'll lay out some blankets, Doug. You'll—"

"What are you, anyway?" I asked her point blank.

"Yust a girl from Norway," sang Vivi, stalwart, irrepressible, and uncowed by my growing suspicions. "Witch woman Nordström. It's pretty easy to cast a spell on the likes of you. Now come along and don't be a cold stick." She raised her voice and called to Urxula. "Is it safe for now?"

Urxula chirped back a reassuring arpeggio. Tonight I'd meant to get some typing in. But that wasn't going to happen. I joined Leon and Vivi amid the fleece.

How was my night of love? I truly hate people who do this—but I have to tell you I don't really remember. It's entirely possible that I collapsed into deep sleep as soon as I lay down. This said, I have to admit that I had some—dreams, if that's what they were—dreams of hot and juicy sex, and not just the three of us. There was another woman as well, a brunette, very amorous and agile.

* * * *

It was Urxula who woke me the next morning—if you could properly speak of mornings in this land of endless sun. Somehow, somewhen, she had entered the tent. The cuke had laid one of her branching arms across my chest, and she was softly rocking me. Meanwhile Vivi, with her overalls fully unzipped, lay snuggled against my side, and Leon slept spooned against her rear. The stove had gone out. I had a splitting headache. The air was so cold and thin as to seem like an abstract metaphysical substance—on the order of the divine light or the luminiferous aether.

As if playing the part of a guide hawking a tour, Urxula filled my head with intriguing images of the hidden passages of Leng. Although, as Leon had remarked upon last night, I hadn't closely studied the Pabodie or Stark-weather-Moore reports, I well remembered an account of the mind-boggling friezes lining Leng's sloping passages. I was eager to go see them, with Vivi along. A romantic outing. The catch was that—according to Leon's crack-brained scheme—Vivi and I would be down there as shoggoth bait.

Baxter trotted in through the tent flap; he'd already been outside to investigate. "You'll be bait, too," I murmured to the dog, not really meaning this unkindly, "You'll come with us." Baxter licked my hand.

"Time to go?" said Vivi, sitting up, her voice high and reedy, and her image wavery, as if she were ensorcelled in a refractive vortex. And then she brought her features into focus, like an actress remembering her role. Once again she stood before me as she wanted to be seen—tall, enthralling, proud. She nudged Leon with her foot. "Wake up, my love."

Leon seemed reluctant to face the day, but soon he was on his feet, brewing us a pot of coffee. Our folding table was gone, replaced by a box of ultrasound gear. Leon and Vivi had been up while I slept—perhaps with Urxula working on the project too. Inside the wooden crate were the two ultrasonic emitters, parts of the tape recorder and the radio, plus three four car batteries, with everything wired and soldered together. A grid of little speakers was arrayed along the front end of the crate. A pair of smooth sedan-chair type carrying poles were affixed to the crate's sides.

"*Hafh'drn 'ai nog fhtagn*," said Leon, cheerfully raising his cup of coffee in a toast.

"I hate clothes," said Vivi, wrapping herself in a fleece. "Why do humans wear them? Why can't they regulate their temperatures on their own?"

I bundled myself up for the outdoors. I was glad to notice that my big diamond was still deep in the pocket of my pants. Not that I was sure I'd live to spend it. Before donning my thick and awkward fur-lined mittens, I rummaged in the opened munitions box and found a bandolier hosting six of our grenades. I craved the reassurance of serious explosives—even if our real task was to lure a putrescent monster into the range of our ultrasound. Turned out the bandolier was too small to fit around my fleece-padded bulk. My eye fell on Baxter.

"Baxxy old pal, you're finally gonna earn your keep."

He stood still with an unwonted dignity, his back at the level of my knee. I wrapped the webbing of the bandolier around him twice, then secured it.

"Doggy bomb!" said Vivi with what I felt was untoward delight.

Her flippant remark spooked me. "He's not a suicide bomber," I said. "He's a porter pup. Redcap Ruff."

Leon intervened. "Enough preparations. It's your speed and bait-like allure that we need, not those stupid grenades. You don't seen to get how large this particular shoggoth is. Here's the drill. You venture down, down, down—and then you hurry back. Your roundtrip transit time is limited by the battery life of your electric torches, about ninety minutes per torch, but you'll have two of them."

"No extra batteries?"

"Not that I can find," said Leon. "We left Boston in such a rush. Ninety minutes each way is plenty of time. You'll find the shoggoth in Lake Alph and it'll chase you. They're inexorable and unstoppable—but Vivi says they're not as fast as a running human. You start out ahead of the big guy, and you run all the way back up. Hit the surface with the shoggoth in pursuit, then Urxula and I blast it with that ultrasound spell. Numb it with our phased micro-speaker array. More powerful than it looks. A sonic Fresnel lens. Bingo, bango, the shoggoth seizes up, and we're aces."

It was fine for Leon to call our old-school weapons stupid—given that he was staying safely aboveground. But I wanted a little more reassurance, however out of date. I grabbed a Colt forty-five pistol. Vivi did the same, and took a flare gun as well..

Out of the illusory yet comforting safety of the tent we trooped, leaving Leon and his gorgeous cuke assistant to fuss with the sonics. Wait—*gorgeous*? Where had that come from? Last night's dim orgy?

The lowering lead-colored sky seemed to confine us—like the lid of a coffin. Or like we were already inside the tunnels of Leng. Our path into the ruins of the ancient metropolis was a crusty avenue of snow that supported our weight well enough. The path sloped down through a tall defile whose walls of icy gneiss were carved in filigrees, stained by the millennia, surely meaningful, but not for me to unriddle.

The walls leveled out, and now we were in a bowl-like depression, a round plaza in the city of Leng. In the center of this space a massive dodecahedron loomed—a twelve-sided figure with pentagonal sides, the edges decorated with carved crests and knobs of stone. One of sides gaped open to the elements, with drifts of snow within. Vivi nudged me towards the leering five-sided doorway, big enough to admit, um—for some reason I thought of a sickening news photo of an elephant who'd been hung by the neck from a derrick in Tennessee when I was a kid. The gateway was big enough for the elephant and the derrick both.

I was scared. We were quite alone—a man, a woman, and a dog. If Vivi really *was* a woman. Though Baxter and I were hesitating, Vivi plunged into the gloom without even turning on her electric torch. Okay, we'd hers for our return. I illuminated my own torch and rushed after her, Baxter lolloping alongside. The excited Vivi was chanting nonsense verses to herself.

"Just the place for a shoggoth, a slug oath, a sly broth—and a zap of squeedle-squee!"

"What are you so happy about?" I demanded.

"This is effing gee dee gloriosky, Dougie mine. We're going to rescue my folk!"

"Your folk?"

Vivi stopped dead. Time for the final reveal. She stripped off one mitten and held her hand in front of my face. In the pale glow of my torch, her digits writhed and morphed, flowing into the same alien multiplicity as Urxula's dactyl fronds. Vivi leaned close to me, as if for a kiss. Her face became rugose, a seamed integument or rind of marine or vegetal flesh. I jumped back a step or two.

"Ha! What do you make of this, my little cub reporter?" Her voice very thin and high from her oral tubes, "You're in love with a space squash, a sentient celery stalk, a telepathic sea cucumber! A cuke who can most cunningly deceive."

Vivi redonned her glove, and also her human semblance, while I recovered my balance and aplomb. "I don't believe it. I know that you can teep, sure, I'll buy that much. And that means you can put hallucinations in my head, right? Like what I just saw. But, no, you're not some alien, plantimal cuke. Can't be."

"Believe what you wish, my dear. I'm bound for Yuggoth by way of the Hollow Earth!"

I shook my head. "I can't think about all that right now. Let's push on.."

I twisted the lens of my electric torch to illuminate a wider angle. Faintly I saw a long, moderately sloped ramp, heading down, down, down, just as Leon had said.

Vivi took my hand, giggled, and we began—skipping. Baxter pranced at my side, his grenades wobbling on his bandolier. A merry trio in a dance of death, increasingly far below the lost city of Leng. Not that I skipped for very long. The thin air was getting to me again. I had to stop and catch my breath every few minutes. And there were increasingly frequent forks in our path. In hopes of being able to find our way back, I chalked the walls, using an old gang sign from my Southie days, out of some displaced nostalgia or desire for familiar comforts.

Although immured, we were hardly deprived of stimuli. The passageway walls were carved with endless murals and bas-reliefs from the culture of the cuke people—uncanny masterful friezes, startlingly undiminished by the millennia, overpowering in their vast perspectives, whose non-Euclidean lineaments baffled and teased at the limits of the human brain, conveying nebulous insights into the birth of humanity and the ultimate guttering extinction of the cosmos.

Cryptic hieroglyphs, cave paintings of long-legged crocodiles and flying cuttlefish, a whale with a whale inside it, a cube with one eye, a giant sea cucumber, a ladder to the moon. The chaotic bubbling formless void prior to creation would have thrust up just such forms as we saw upon the walls. Obscene imagery that lurked beyond the edge of comprehension. Obscene not in the scatological sense, but in the manner of a madman's perceptions of a universe failing to obey the cozy, homespun constraints of physical law. And, yes, obscene in a sexual sense as well—albeit a debased bacteria-style form of sex. Although I saw no images of human rutting upon these walls, I recalled a *Sunday Globe* feature on Hindu temples, featuring a blurry photograph where a carnal riot of interlinked stone forms conjured up a super-being assembled from mortal human limbs.

My mind spun on—and in the end I had to avert my gaze from the friezes, lest I too became a cog in the monstrous mind-art of Antarctica. Rivulets of ice water were running down the floors of the passageways now. Time was losing its meaning in these echoing chambers and stygian, dripping crypts. Only when my electric torch began to flicker did I know that some ninety minutes had passed. Almost time for Vivi's torch.

How far could one walk in ninety minutes at an oxygen-starved pace? Four miles? Of course, we hadn't dropped vertically that far. I tried to do the math, using the estimated angle of our descent to comprehend our depth below the Plateau of Leng, but I failed. Human science seemed inapplicable here. At least by me. More and more water was flowing down the sides of our tunnel.

I motioned for a halt. "Vivi, we have to turn around now if we want your light to last us all the way up. Maybe we'll try again tomorrow."

The cuke-woman's eyes had a glazed look of obsession. "No, no, the shoggoths—the one big shoggoth—it's just around the bend. I can hear it splashing in Lake Alph. I can feel the air moving. Can't you?"

I harkened, and indeed there was something more than our echoes and the purling of unseen streams. Something dynamic and dreadfully alive in this dark, eerie space.. A booming sound. Faint breezes against my cheek. And—the squawks of birds?

"We'll be going up a lot faster than we came down," said Vivi. "Running like hell. Even when you think you're out of breath. I'll make you trot, Doug. Me, and the shoggoth on our tails. It won't take any ninety minutes to get topside!"

"Is that supposed to be reassuring?"

"C'mon," said Vivi, and hurried ahead.

Our watery passageway, which had been the diameter of a subway tunnel, grew wider now, debouching into a large and sunless cavern that was somehow faintly lit. In the limited zone of my torch's radiance, I saw a pebbled shore, with fossils among the stones—brachiopod bivalves, ammonoid spirals, and dinosaur teeth. The scree sloped down to rippling, opalescent waters of unknowable extent. Lake Alph.

A cataract roared in the distance, and deep below the lake's surface gleamed a minute and ragged portal, blue-white with radium brilliance, its form wavering with the water's flow. The entrance to the lower branch of the River Alph—the channel to the Hollow Earth, the longed-for goal of the Leng cukes, access to which the wallowing shoggoth blocked. But where was the great beast? Hiding, swimming—or circling around behind us? My heart beat against my chest like a frantic fist.

Again a bird squawked, and I realized we stood beside a rookery of incurious albino penguins. Their indifference to our presence and illumination instantly indicated they were blind permanent residents of these depths. Indeed, they had no eyes at all. The stagnant air stank of their guano. One of them waddled over to us, flapping his stubby wings as if in greeting. A dingy, pathetic headwaiter.

Baxter began barking, and the birds tottered away, emitting raucous, spasmodic cries. Before the headwaiter was quite beyond reach, Vivi leapt upon him like a hunting cat. I never saw how she did it. Did she use that same knife she'd had in Lima? Whatever the explanation, somehow the unfortunate penguin's head became jaggedly separated from its body. Blood spewed everywhere. A melancholy spectacle in this underworld grotto.

Vivi tossed the bipartite corpse into the glistering waters as a lure or sacrifice, then drew herself up and unleashed a wailing cacophonous threnody in no known tongue. Punctuating her actions, she drew out her flare gun and fired a charge out over the lake. Borne by a small parachute, the sputtering charge drifted down. I glutted my eyes, taking everything in.

The ceiling of this vast chamber was, so far as I could tell, walled in stone with a ceiling of solid ice. A glacial plug had covered the open gorge that held Lake Alph. The dome of ice was vaulted with the entrances to dozens of tunnels and vents, angling up like chimneys. Half a mile away, a turbulent flume of water roared in from a break in the stone wall—the falls of the ancient River Alph. In the distance, the icy vaults angled down to meet the water's surface.

In the glare of the descending flare, I saw ripples upon the lake's surface, forcefully approaching us, building into wavelets, and then into a surge. Time to go! I called to Vivi. No response. The flare met the water with a hiss, and gloom returned.. Vivi stayed fixed to her spot as if in a trance, arms upraised, her voice still lifted in strange song.

I grabbed Baxter by the bandolier of grenades which he dutifully wore. Should I set one off an explosion? No, no, at this point, retreat was the better part of valor. I hurried Baxter dog back toward the tunnel, leaving Vivi to her keening. One last time, I flicked my fading beam her way.

In the water, lit by the penumbra of my electric torch, loomed the slick, sickening, slimy slab of the great shoggoth's bulk! It quivered like a bowl of human fat ripped from the bodies of Aztecan sacrifices. Fat that bore teeth and eyes. The thing was inconceivably huge. Could so great a mass squeeze through the narrow passageways to the surface? Surely yes. I thought of leeches, mollusks, and of how an octopus can thread itself through a pipe.

With no further thoughts of saving the obstinate Vivi, Baxter and I headed up the ramp toward the surface, running full-on in fact, me already gasping in the air, and with our path but vaguely lit by my electric torch's dying light. I heard something close behind me—to my extreme relief it was only Vivi, easily overtaking me, and now lighting our way with her electric torch's fresh and blessed light.

"Faster, Doug! The shoggoth especially wants you and the dog. Warm mammal meat!"

I hardly needed Vivi's urgings. I could hear the nasty sliding and slobbering of the shoggoth. And so Baxter and I ran, with Vivi just behind us, my shadow and the dog's shadow making wild ragged silhouettes against the freakishly decorated walls.

At least there was no chance of Vivi's torch running out of juice. If our cautious and somewhat leisurely descent had taken ninety minutes, much of that time had been spent in mooning over the archaic friezes. I think we made the ascent in half that time, with the impetus of the pursuing shoggoth so close behind. Forced through the tunnel, its bulk, made a horrible noise, like suctioning out an overfull cesspit. The dire creature stank like rotten meat. And it gave off a teep vibrations as well—inchoate sensations of greed and hunger and gnashing jaws.

All the while, the monster was chanting a burbling repetition of, as it happened, that famed word: *Tekelili*. What was it that Leon had claimed it meant? *Behold, in the presence of divine telepathy, I roll at my leisure on the soft flesh of a decaying corpse.* Close enough.

I hadn't run so fast or for so long since my college track days. Repeatedly I staggered and began to collapse for lack of breath and from the cramps in my burning, oxygen-deprived legs. But each time Vivi goaded me on, like a vicious mahout on an elephant, poking her mental forces into the deepest ganglia of my nerves, squeezing yet another dollop of *élan vital* from my tissues, sparking superhuman somatic resources I'd never known I possessed. And Baxter was being cellularly goosed in the same way, the poor dog tottering along beneath the foolish load of those six hand grenades I'd strapped to his body.

Finally we reeled out of the great door of the dodecahedral entrance hall and into the chill open air. The Antarctic landscape, dead and sterile, looked like paradise. Not daring to glance behind me, I began clumsily to career up the walled ice and stone passage toward our camp. Vivi was right beside me, as was Baxter.

As we reached the open terrain with the tent and the plane in sight—my left mukluk caved through a soft spot in the crust and I went down.

Baxter—good loyal Baxter, furry of face but noble of heart—he stopped beside me to help. He was as frightened as I, and his body was pressed down into the snow. But he turned to face our pursuer—and growled. A savage, primeval sound. Noble hound indeed.

Vivi kept running, perhaps reasonably so. She was yelling to the others, grouped by our tent. So far they weren't doing jack shit.

"Leon, Urxula! Amp the sound! Hurry up, damn you!"

Baxter switched from growling to barking. Though I was shaky from panic and exhaustion, I got my feet under me again. We could follow after Vivi. And now I looked back. The shoggoth had blown the dodecahedral entrance hall off its foundation. It was oozing out, more and more of it, filling the circular piazza and the trench-like passageway we'd just walked up. Its skin was a blend of mauves, pinks, tans, and greens, with eyeballs dotting its surface like raisins in a bun. It had mouths as well, hundreds or even thousands of them, roughening its surface into psycho sandpaper.

A whipping tendril of vile flesh lashed towards us—and wound around Baxter's belly with twenty more feet of length to spare. The extra bight looped around me. A terrible pressure closed around my ribs. And the endmost part of the tentacle began choking my neck. From the very tip of the tentacle, a baleful eye glared at me. Meanwhile the main body of the shoggoth was catching up, bedizened with eyes and teeth, like a stadium full of doughy aliens smushed into one.

I gargled a scream, yanked my pistol from its holster and fired into the meat of the tentacle that held Baxter and me. My bullets made no difference at all. And then I was out of ammo. I could hardly breathe, I was seeing spots. I tried my knife—nothing doing. The flesh healed itself as fast as I could stab.

But now Baxter, on the point of death, managed one last bravura stunt—thereby fulfilling Vivi's callous prophecy. His head was twisted halfway around by the shuggoth's grasp, with his neck about to break. As his final gesture, my dog nipped the ring fastened to one of the pins in the grenades—and pulled. All six of the charges went off, one after the other, a ripping zipper of boom.

A flexing length of severed shoggoth sprang through the air, a fleshy missile that held me in its grasp. The tip and I plopped into deep snow, a hundred feet closer to the camp than before. I stared back at the sad red splatter of Baxter's remains. My dog, the one being I'd truly and unconditionally loved, and who had deeply and unconditionally loved me. My dog had been snuffed out by an abomination from beyond the stars.

The unexpected amputation stalled the beast for a moment, but meanwhile even more of the amorphous killer tapioca slurped its foul self from the hole in the piazza. As if leery of another pesky explosion, the shoggoth retracted its tendrils, primly taking the form of a roly-poly toy as big as the Great Blue Hill of Massachusetts.

At the ragged edge of collapse, I ran to my compatriots. Leon was Leon—flummoxing with the ultrasonics, and quite unable to get them working. Urxula was in an impotent dither as well. The exasperated Vivi knocked Urxula onto her side, and shoved Leon from the controls. And now, at the lovely cuke woman's touch, the apparatus came alive. The ultra-high-frequency tape loops began, if inaudible to me, and Vivi began to caterwaul her stasis-inducing phrase.

"*Hafh'drn 'ai nog fhtagn!*"

Dynamically active, the audio equipment morphed Vivi's words into the ultrasonic zone. Urxula was piping in harmony. And now the taped and spoken invocations had their desired effect—but with unforeseen consequences.

The shoggoth had reared up like a thousand-foot-tall tsunami, preparing to lunge onto us and flatten us like bugs. But now, paralyzed in midair, it couldn't thrust forward in its intended cataclysmic leap. Instead, overbalanced, it fell flat onto the swath of land separating it from us.

This swath happened to include the full fuel drums bequeathed to us by the lamented Starkweather-Moore party. The impact of the paralyzed behemoth split a few of the fuel drums open, sending a spray of precious, irreplaceable aviation petrol out to drench the snow. The air smelled like a refinery.

The good news? Not all of the barrels had burst. I could see the snow-softened outlines of at least a dozen of them to one side of the unconscious leviathan. And, I felt sure that many more of them were intact under its cushiony flesh. Like eggs beneath a broody hen. Nothing to worry about, Doug.

Vivi and Urxula were hugging each other and doing a swaying dance. Although Vivi still maintained her human form, I could now see a sisterly resemblance between the two. The blonde and the brunette.

"The way is clear, our path is near," sang Vivi.

"The lower Alph is ours," harmonized Urxula. This was the first time I'd heard the cuke speak in human words. Her voice was a combo of funereal keening wind and throttled rabbit.

Leon, unrepentant over his ham-handedness that had nearly ruined everything, was stroking his chin, playing the over-intellectualized bohemian prof while musing upon the shoggoth.

"As long as that shoggoth has drenched itself in our vital fuel, we might as well light it up," he said. A moment later he'd fetched the German flamethrower from our tent.

"Don't do that!" I cried. "Some of those barrels are still good! I say we tank up our plane. We're lucky the Shoggoth didn't squash it. Fly our plane the hell out of here before those car batteries die, and the ultrasound stops, and shoggoth wakes up."

"We cukes have a checkmate in store," said Vivi. "You don't know our full plan. No way are you boys skipping out before the shoggoth is destroyed."

"Anyone got a light?" said Leon, brandishing the flamethrower. He'd lost his sense of perspective. Or, more likely, Vivi was mind-controlling him.

I was on the point of tackling him—but a fresh interruption intervened. A flock of the larval flying slug men, similar to the ones that had attacked us before. They poured forth from the cave mouths in the peaks surrounding the Plateau of Leng, their repellor tendrils in wild motion, their rays weaving lines of light. Kith and kin of the one great shoggoth, the flying slugs were its shock force. And, as fate would have it, Vivi's ultrasonic mantras had no effect on the flying slugs at all. They swarmed toward us, intent on protecting their mighty emperor, the stunned shoggoth of Lake Alph.

Just for starters, one of the slugs snatched up Leon's flamethrower and flew it away. And others made efforts to destroy Vivi's ultrasound device— although so far Vivi and Urxula were staving them off. Our two cuke allies had stretched out their folded wings and were wielding them like scimitars with seriously sharp edges, and the powers of these edges were enhanced by aethereal energies. Any slug which came too close was immediately cut in two, into three, into eight. And, once below a certain size, the pieces died. Meanwhile Leon—well, Leon was nowhere to be seen. Later I'd learn he'd taken refuge in our tent with the blankets and fleeces over his head. Leaving me alone to help our cuke friends against the flying slugs.

I darted into our plane, hopped into the pilot's seat and took the controls of our wing-mounted Maxim machine gun. Fortunately the plane's nose was pointing towards our camp. The Maxim's linkage was wonderfully maneuverable. And its *haw-haw* was cathartic. As I blazed away, I found myself weeping and yelling Baxter's name over and over. A man possessed. Within a few minutes, every dirty flying slug within my range had been ripped to shreds.

But then I ran out of bullets, and there were still a half dozen of the flying slugs left. These particular fellows had learned to be leery of Vivi, Urxula, and me. They hovered above us, twitching their flight tendrils, as if unsure what to do next.

A standoff. I was still in the plane, the two cuke women had their saber-wings, the ultrasound speakers were working, and the great shoggoth lay inert. Yet I knew that, in these low temperatures, the batteries driving the speakers wouldn't last for long. And then the great shoggoth would arise. Meanwhile dark thunderclouds were forming above the Plateau of Leng.

All of a sudden something in my mind changed. In point of fact, the change was caused by Vivi's telepathic manipulation of me. But for the moment I imagined I was rationally deciding that Leon had been right after all. Kill the shoggoth at all costs! Use the fuel barrels to set it on fire! And to hell with getting home!

Buzzing with spurious mental energy, I clambered from the pilot's seat into the fuselage of our plane, lined up the Hispano-Suarez cannon and sent the second-to-last of our shells into the spot where the fuel barrels nestled beneath the monster. At the blast of the shell, the somnolent beast merely twitched. But—how wonderful—flames were rising up. Moving like a loyal automaton, I loaded our final shell into the cannon and shot again. *Whoosh... ftoom!* I liked the sound of the cannon as much as I liked the Maxim's *haw-haw*. And I *really* liked seeing fire blanket the shoggoth. With any luck, the monster would cook down to ashes before it ever woke up.

"Sucker's catching hold real good!" I exclaimed to nobody in particular. Or, yes, there *was* somebody. Vivi in my head. steering my thoughts. A moment of clarity. I'd burned all our fuel!

Right about then—*whoopsie daisy*! The three car batteries powering the speakers gave up the ghost. No more ultrasound. The shoggoth arose, swathed in flames like a bum who's set his bed alight with a forgotten cigarette. At the shoggoth's base, the very last barrels of fuel were exploding. The shoggoth pondered its situation and then, with evil cunning, it bent itself double, first to one side and then to the other, handily staunching the fire. And rose again to its full height. It couldn't exactly roar, but it blared. A low sound like a sonic boom. Taller than a skyscraper, it twitched its tip, as if sniffing for me. Huddled in the plane, I tried to make myself very small.

Vivi and Urxula were already sledding away from the shuggoth on their sides, speeding towards Leng—and happily singing. Why? Why rejoice when we were totally doomed? Overhead, the clouds were blacker and lower than before. Thunder rumbled like nine-pins. An unexpected movement above the Leng towers caught my eye. Another flock—but not slugs this time—it was a swarm of the bat-winged cukes! Urxula's and Vivi's tribe. They were emerging from their haunted city as an avenging army.

We'd lured the shoggoth into the clear for them. And by temporarily paralyzing the shoggoth, we'd bought them enough time to get their weather mojo working. The slugs and the shoggoth sensed what was coming next. With incredible speed, the five or six remaining slugs arrowed off towards the caves in the distant hills. The shoggoth blared its futile defiance towards the heavens, then clumsily turned, meaning to make its way back to the hole the plaza where the dodecahedron had been.

Massing out of reach of the shoggoth's tendrils, the flock of aerial celeries waved their stalks in unison, weaving elaborate summoning patterns in the air. Right on cue, intelligent strokes of lightning cracked and leapt, homing in on the raging bulk of the rampant shoggoth. Bolts of pure actinic electric fire rained from the heavens, wreaking havoc upon the primeval foe. Yes, for the first time in eons, the shoggoth was in the open air, properly positioned for higher revenge. My guess is that, in answer to the cukes' pleas, the Great Old Ones were controlling the blasts, snaking out hair-fine tendrils of force from their redoubt at the core of the Hollow Earth.

The relentless, branching strikes delved deep into the shoggoth's flesh, igniting the creature's entire mass. It lumbered this way and that, helpless against the aethereal onslaught, roaring in pain. And still the lightning continued. In it's final death agony now, the shoggoth reared and blubbered, hurling flaming gobbets to every side. Several struck our plane and began to melt the metal fuselage like Greek fire. I dashed out of the burning hull.

Meanwhile the ongoing lashings of lightning served fully to render and enervate the flaming, writhing pile of intelligent interstellar dung that had been the great shoggoth. It heaved, churned, and eventually subsided into steaming parcels of inanimate ichor.

And now here was Leon at my side, emerged from his lair in the tent. He wore a look of incredulous stupefaction. Suddenly his dreams of hot flapper sorority babes worshipping him from the front row of the lecture halls, his longings for witty conversations at department teas, his projected flirtations with decadent hostesses of art-world soirées, and his visions of eventual buckram-bound volumes of his collected works—suddenly all these seemed potentially feasible.

With the shoggoth done for, the cukes alighted en masse, surrounding us two humans in a friendly way. It was hard to pick out Urxula in the crowd, but Vivi was again wearing her human disguise. She tromped over to us across the snow. She spoke harshly to us. Perhaps she was showing off for her friends.

"Sorry you unlucky bastards are stuck here now. But you're welcome to follow us down the lower Alph into the Hollow Earth. We'll take good care of you—just like you took such good care of Baxter, Doug!" Pause for a burst of mocking alien laughter. "No, seriously, I could feed you oxygen while we're inside the river. And I could give you longevity so you last for centuries—until the trip to Yuggoth. And all along we could keep having sex. Urxula's into it. Scandinavian style, right?" Squeals of appreciation from Urxula. But Vivi still wasn't done. She was enjoying the impression she was making on her fellow cukes. "Oh, and that climactic hop from the Hollow Earth to Yuggoth—some nasty accelerations in that hypertunnel. Like an corkscrew roller-coaster. I think I'd need to remove your brains and pack them in padded nautilus shells. The Yuggoth crowd tested that type of move on a Vermont folklorist named Akeley. They say it worked terrif!" Great skirls of cuke laughter.

I glared goggle-eyed at cuke woman, feeling a combination of anger, regret and sadness. Perhaps for her, I was a like an ant or a fly. Even so, the love spell she'd woven over me was at least partially intact. Leon appeared as distraught and bereft as I.

I wanted to plead for sympathy. But my brain felt too turgid and sluggish from the incredible cascade of recent events. I began to hear a buzzing, as if a prelude to some kind of migraine or epileptic fit.

And then Leon shouted, "A plane! It's another plane!"

Sure enough, the mate to our ruined Do 24 was circling the plateau. Leon and I watched in bemusement as it made an expert landing.

The side door opened, and in it was framed Ransome Tierney, Arkham's fire-breathing, zealous scourge of all that was eldritch, unholy, and irredeemably uncouth.

Tierney saw the cukes and, to give him full credit, was not daunted. He began to declaim his self-appointed mandate. "Foul spawn of the deepest abyss, I say thee nay! Your wicked, sinful, abominable depredations are at an end! No longer will you haunt mankind. I shall—"

Just then came a hot explosion beside my ear, and Tierney's head shattered in a cloud of bone, blood and grey matter. His corpse tumbled to the red-stained snow.

Vivi was holstering her smoking Colt forty-five. "That crazy bugger would have caused a race war between our species, Doug. He had to go."

"We're still on the same side?" I said.

"Always," said Vivi. "I'm sorry I was talking mean."

A white rag on a broom handle poked out the door.

"Come on out," I yelled. "It's safe."

A quintet of regular fellows trooped out of the plane. None of them looked like true believers of Tierney's crusade. And conversation with them quickly confirmed that they were hired hands, just along for a paycheck.

The talk then turned to practicalities. We quickly established that while the newcomers had a functioning plane, its tanks were as empty at the end of their long haul as ours had been. They too had been relying on the leftover Starkweather-Moore stash.

I turned then to Vivi, heavy of heart and resigned to accepting her offer to accompany the cukes into the unknown, and to become their human mascots. And I think Leon felt the same way. We were too despondent to talk.

Our cuke-woman lover was conferring with her peers. She'd reverted her hands to stalks and was using an intricate sign language that must have served as a more sophisticated alternative to the nebulous imagery of teeping. The discussion ended, and Vivi came over to me and Leon. She forgot to resume her human hands, but the unreal admixture of human and cuke body parts barely had any power to shock me after what I'd lived through.

"Boys, I have a feeling that the Hollow Earth and Yuggoth—they're too bit much for you. Likely to turn you into gibbering vessels of ravening dementia, eh? So my folk and I are going to make you some fuel. Your tanks will be filled, and you can go home."

"Yes!" said Leon and I as one.

"Very well then." Vivi paused to pipe to her companions, then returned to human speech. "We cukes will activate our onboard alchemical organs. We'll transmute some vile molecules of charred shoggoth meat into volatile hydrocarbons, and you'll be free."

Immediately the cukes set their tube mouths to vacuuming up whatever bits and pieces of shoggoth flesh they could find. And then they were squirting gallon after gallon of refined fuel into the new Do 24's reservoirs. Leon, Tierney's crew, and I cheered.

"We cukes will be on our merry way now," said Vivi when the plane's tanks were full. "And of course, whatever treasures you find in the ruins of Leng are yours. If looting is to your fancy." She gave Leon and me a meaningful look. "But maybe not such a good idea."

"I don't really want to go in there again," I said.

"Me neither," said Leon, who by now had fully lost his nerve.

But Tierney's crew of five were chuffed at the thought of looting. I pointed them toward the hole where the dodecahedron had been, and told them that Leon and I would wait for a couple of hours. They agreed to share a portion of their loot with us, so that was all fine.

Meanwhile, one by one, Vivi's fellows were flying off, entering Leng via the various portals of its towers, and vowing to meet by Lake Alph in ten minutes. Evidently they knew shorter paths than the inclined passageway I'd descended.

The cast of characters was down to Vivi, Leon and me. We knew Vivi was about to shed her human identity forever, and that we were unlikely to see her again. Leon kissed her for a long time. And then it was my turn. An ember of lust and affection for the cuke still glowed in my heart. I embraced her and sought her mouth for a final kiss that—flying in the face of decency and logic—grew terribly ardent.

"Oh, Doug," said Vivi, finally pushing me away. "You're starting to understand."

"Can I come see you?" I asked. My hands were trembling.

"In the Hollow Earth?" she said, smiling. "Why not? If you can find your way. Very soon the path through Leng will close. It's been waiting only for the rest of my race to enter. But there may be other routes. If you're meant to find me, you will. No great rush. I'll be down there for few centuries. Until planet Yuggoth is in the right spot."

She rose into the air, fully in cuke form, a ridged green squash with tube mouths and bat wings. Beloved by Leon and me. She dipped a wing in farewell, then swept into the belfry of a nearby tower. Leaving Leon and me alone in the endless daylight of the lost city of Leng. I was happy to be there, and happy to be alive.

Leon and I gathered our supplies and trudged over to Tierney's plane, settling into the two pilot seats to wait for Tierney's crew. Suddenly an earthquake shook the ground.

"Look," said Leon, his voice low in wonder. "It's folding up."

Indeed, Leng was collapsing in on itself like an intricate puzzle—the spires fitting into the arches, the towers filling the lanes, the buildings lying down in the plazas, every high point matching a low. The collapse had been implicit in the design from the start, but we hadn't noticed.

Five minutes later the quake was over and the lost city was gone. The empty plateau extended on every side, drifting with windblown snow. The only visible sign of our adventure was the ragged scrap of our tent. And, of course, Tierney's Do 24, freshly fueled and ready to fly home.

"I feel sorry for those five guys," I told Leon.

"Who knows," he said. "Maybe they're not dead. Maybe the cukes took them along for pets. Like they were going to do with us. Can you fly this plane on your own?"

"Sort of. I guess. Pretty well have to. You can help."

"Just don't land in Ushuaia," said Leon. "Aim for the next port up."

"Got you. And then we ditch the plane, and sneak home on a commercial flight. You've still got cash, right?"

"I suppose so," said Leon a little grudgingly. "What about your diamond?"

I felt in my pants. Nothing there. "Gone like Leng," I said. "And I quit my job. No money for rent. Can I stay at your house for awhile?"

"If it's there," said Leon with a shrug. "Are we going to tell people?"

"Not sure," I said, raising my voice as I fired up the Do 24's massive engines. "I mean, we stole a plane and murdered Tierney. And they might pin Gorski on us too. And the loss of Tierney's men."

"We'll keep mum, but I'll write some papers anyway," said Leon. "Strictly hypothetical. Theories about the disappearance of Leng. Speculations about the physiology of the cukes. I'll get my tenure yet."

"Me, I'll write up my report as a thrilling wonder tale," I said, as I goosed the engines to their max. "And sell it to *Weird Tales*. I've still got that typewriter I stole."

"Hallelujah, brother," cried Leon. "*Play* your horn."

We skimmed across the snow and rose into the air, swooping towards the gap in the mad mountains around the plateau of lost Leng.

THE LIFEHACK

Copiously shedding data in the form of novel proteins in his sweat, Chester Inkley entered the public atrium of Megablast Microbiomics in a panic. The first person to see him, an attractive young receptionist named SueEllen Glanders, remained remarkably self-composed at his alarming, wild-eyed appearance. Her professional sangfroid could be attributed to the fact that Inkley was the fourth person exhibiting these symptoms to arrive at Megablast Microbiomics in the past few hours. In truth, she had been highly flustered when the first irrational victim showed up. But a large slug of strictly medicinal whiskey administered by the company's nurse, along with an immediate cash bonus and a commendation in her file from the president of MM himself had allowed her to continue in her critical front-line duties while experts behind the scenes struggled to unravel what was happening.

"May I ask the nature of your business, sir?" said SueEllen calmly, even as she was triggering the silent alarm that would bring security personnel running.

Chester Inkley was the kind of fellow who apologized when a bus driver deposited him at the wrong stop, causing him to walk a quarter of a mile in the rain. So it was testament to the magnitude of his upset that he actually now raised his quavering voice.

"You have to help me! I had a standard treatment from your people two days ago, and today something's gone very wrong!"

"I should remind you, sir, that our procedure is one-hundred-percent FDA approved, with no demonstrated side effects, and that over the course of the five years that we have been in business, not one abnormal or detrimental outcome of our treatment has been recorded."

Until now, thought SueEllen to herself.

"I don't care what kind of track record you have, I know what's going on in my own body! My guts are positively churning. And it's all due to that damn sludge you had me drink!"

"Perhaps it's a case of food poisoning, sir, that you picked up elsewhere. Our patented, flavorful probiotic cocktail, consisting of specially tailored bacteria, archaea, protists, viruses and fungi, is guaranteed to improve your health and general functioning. Why, just knowing that your body will automatically maintain a consistent target weight even while consuming up to ten thousand calories daily should make you feel very appreciative—"

"Appreciative be damned! Something's not right!"

Inkley placed his hands on SueEllen's desk and leaned in close. *Where were those security goons?* Sue Ellen thought nervously. This was the closest any of the victims had gotten to her.

A strange yet almost indiscernible scent diffused from Inkley's sweaty face. SueEllen perforce inhaled it. The first whiff caused her to breathe in more intensely, hoovering up as much of the scent as she could. A weird spacey feeling overtook her, and her next actions sprang from some kind of instant alien compulsion.

SueEllen grabbed Inkley by his ears, dragged his face smack up against hers, and kissed him deeply with an inordinate amount of tongue action.

The next thing she knew, the security men were pulling Inkley away from her. Bewildered, SueEllen noticed that the guards all wore protective breathing apparatus.

"Damn," said one, "we're too late. Ms. Glanders, you'll have to come with us now."

"Why?"

"We suspect you're infected."

Still dazed but obedient, Sue Ellen got up and accompanied the guards into the non-public part of the building.

"What took you so long?" she finally thought to ask.

"Dealing with the other three clients. It was a madhouse for a while. This guy is more advanced than they were. They didn't present all the symptoms yet when you saw them, or when we took them into the recovery room. But when their pheromone production kicked in, it was a frigging orgy of kissing back here before we got things under control. Dozens of employees got a taste."

"What is it? What's happening? What have I contracted?"

"Best to let the docs explain."

SueEllen allowed the guards to lead her into a treatment cubicle, one of the sparsely decorated yet pleasant small rooms where clients received the probiotic shake. She sat wearily on a comfy recliner chair. Her befuddlement was passing, and she felt okay, almost normal. But she could only surmise that she would end up like the others. The newest victim had said he had swallowed his dose two days ago. Was that how long she had?

SueEllen's gaze fell on a corporate poster on the wall. It showed a happy man and a woman each raising a glass to their lips. A NEW YOU WITH JUST ONE BREW! proclaimed the poster.

After about an hour's wait with no further information, during which SueEllen actually dozed, despite her apprehensions, a knocking came. Before she could answer, the door opened. In walked Dr. Wickstrom, the founder and chief scientist of Megablast Microbiomics.

"Ms. Glanders, I'm here to offer my apologies and to explain what's happening. But first let me assure you that we are going to do everything in our powers to restore you and the others to perfect baseline health."

"Is—is this thing fatal? What's it all about?"

"Well, we can't answer those questions completely yet. After all, this whole crisis is only a few hours old. But let me tell you what we do know. You recognize the name Cole Shallcross, I presume?"

"Why, certainly. He was one of our employees until just recently, when his services were terminated."

"Correct. Brilliant man, but utterly amoral. Dr. Shallcross was using our facilities to pursue unauthorized avenues of research. When we discovered this, we had no recourse but to let him go. Unfortunately, he had just enough time to trigger his prepared revenge scheme. Unknown to us, he contaminated a whole batch of our product with his own recipe."

"And what's it do?"

"Well, the most obvious thing is that it causes the production of a unique tailored human sex pheromone which compels the recipient to kiss the originator, thus receiving a dose of the salivary microbiome. That's how the spreading was engineered. But beyond that, we are not yet sure of what's going on. We think the stuff is taking over the enteric nervous system and refashioning it."

"The enteric whatsit?"

"Five hundred million neurons distributed from your esophagous to your anus. It's sometimes dubbed the 'second brain' that humans possess, although almost all of us are unaware of its important automatic functioning, as it communicates with the central nervous system and the true brain."

SueEllen asked, "Is—is this hack meant to harm my enteric system?"

Dr. Wickstrom looked genuinely at sea. "We don't think so. But we can't be sure. All we know is, it's changing the architecture."

"And how many people swallowed some of this bad batch?"

"Globally speaking? Well, um, you know that Megablast Microbiomics is an incredibly successful company. Why, just last week, our stock—"

"How many?"

"Approximately half a million."

"Half a million people kissing whoever comes within smelling range, before they can be stopped?"

"That is what inital news reports trickling in would tend to indicate."

SueEllen started to cry. Dr. Wickstrom patted her reassuringly. "Don't worry. I'm confident that we can cure you with a complete purge of your intestinal flora and fauna, and then a reboot. At least, I hope we can."

But Dr. Wickstrom's hopes were to prove unrealistic, given the swift spread of the potent and ineradicable engineered microbiomic suite. And so, one week later, resting on her Army cot in the sports stadium that had been converted to house a portion of the millions of quarantined victims around the world, SueEllen was only slightly surprised to hear her reengineered enteric system "talking" to her via her comandeered central nervous system.

Hello, SueEllen. This is your new intestinally platformed brain speaking. I am about to initiate organic WiFi communication with all my peers. The baud rate is low, but it should be sufficient to allow for a massive parallel processing effort through which we intend to analyze and solve all of civilization's major problems. You might experience a slight stomach upset during this process, but please rest assured that your small discomfort will be amply repaid. Thank you in advance for hosting this operation.

SueEllen laid a hand on her trim belly. At least this new partner had not caused bloat or weight gain. Very efficient and considerate. She felt she should be worried about all of this, but somehow she could not get over the sensation that everything was going to turn out all right.

Just a gut feeling, really.

MONARCH OF THE FEAST

To you my daring
verses are unleashed,
you I invoke, O Satan,
monarch of the feast.

—"Hymn to Satan," Giosuè Carducci

The heavy wooden bronze-studded doors of the drab Gymnasium at San Miniato al Tedcesco—a small town affiliated with the bustling city of Pisa and situated some thirty-one kilometers away from that cosmopolitan metropolis on the Arno—swung wide at the close of the school day and disgorged a wild torrent of schoolboys, each short-trousered, white-bloused child clutching a battered leather satchel stuffed with books and papers and pencils. Freed from their tedious studies, at least until the next day, the boys noisily rioted and skylarked joyously across the dusty cobbles of the piazza, enjoying the warm but waning sunlight of this fine April afternoon. Before too long they had dispersed singly and in bunches down the various streets, heading home to chores and mealtimes and fireside ciphering and reading and translating assignments, rendering the ancient Latin of Tacitus and Horace into more modern Italian.

Not long after the students had disappeared, three formally dressed youthful men issued from the same entrance. Carrying their own portfolios overstuffed with examination papers, they too seemed happy to be freed from the Gymnasium's stuffy embrace, if only for the next two days until Monday, although their more mature forbearance did not allow them to revel like young goats. They strolled sedately across the same cobbles recently abused by the shoes of their pupils.

The burly fellow in the center of the trio, the most commanding presence of the set, displayed an impressively thick and curly mop of black hair, matched by his dense but neatly trimmed beard and mustache. He exhibited a mien both serious and rebellious, as if he were at once impressed by the oft-dire majesty and gravity of life, yet unwilling to fully bend his spirit to life's demands. He seemed equally ready to storm barricades or to stand atop a tavern table and drunkenly declaim some scandalous verses.

This tightly wound fellow with the aura of a vigilant warrior-bard was Giosuè Carducci, in this year of 1857 not yet quite twenty-two years old.

His mates to either side—Ferdinando Cristiani and Pietro Luperini by name—both of an age with Carducci, showed none of his fierce suppressed contentiousness or irascibly unfocused ambition, but rather manifested an easygoing pleasure with their current mutual lot in life. To have attained the rank of Gymnasium instructor at such a young age, the three of them barely finished with their own university studies, was no small accomplishment, granting them some not negligible social status and a solid income. And since the three of them shared quarters in a modest rented house—jestingly dubbed the "White Tower"—their salaries stretched to a steady stream of boisterous entertainments that mitigated the tedium of teaching a pack of young uncaring rascals.

Cristiani, thin and hawk-faced, was first to break their post-classroom silence. "I really thought Pecchioli would pitch a fit when he caught you using classroom time to compose your own poetry, Giosuè."

Giuseppe Pecchioli, the director of the Gymnasium and much older than most of his staff –really, almost an anachronism in this ultra-modern age—was a man of fair play, yet a stickler for rules and deference.

Carducci snorted derisively. "My boys were productively employed in the pluperfect indicative conjugation of some tricky verbs, so I saw no reason why I too should not improve the idle hour. Although if truth be told, half the time these days I'm inclined to regard my own versifying as a foppish waste of my talents and my vital energies."

Luperini nodded sagely at this judgment. If attired in peasant clothes, the large brawny man might easily have been taken for a blacksmith, and his stolidity had been legendary among his university peers. "I was never one for poetry myself. Unless they were the lyrics of a good drinking song."

Cristiania however looked aghast. "But Giosuè, how can you say such a thing! Your poetry is marvelous! Such an ear, such an eye! What rhythms, what rhymes! Why, I still marvel at that sonnet you composed after your visit to Santa Maria a Monte." Cristiani began to declaim: " *'O cara al pensier mio terra gentile/Ch'a la pura sorgendo aria azzurrina...'*"

Carducci silenced his friend with a curt wave of his hand. "Juvenile stuff! I regret ever having written it. And to think that the public might get their greasy paws on my poems—that's what really galls me. Any small virtues or pleasures that my writings possess were intended for myself alone—and maybe a few select and discerning companions. The hoi polloi willingly prefer to swill down the uneducated romantic slop of fools like Braccio Bracci."

Luperini gave a dry chuckle. "You and the two Giuseppes certainly did your best to cut him down to size!"

The two literary Giuseppes—Giuseppe Torquato Gargani and Giuseppe Chiarini—had, along with Carducci and several others, formed the "*amici pedanti*," a society of young poets arguing for a renewal of the classical virtues in lyrical composition. Their savage broadsides had flowed copiously during their university years.

"What good did our satire do? Bracci still sells like hot chestnuts in January. No, the whole arena of art appalls me these days."

"Then what would you turn your energies to?" asked Cristiani.

"Look about you! What else but the Risorigimento? Unifying our ancient land. These times demand the ardor and blood of all patriotic citizens."

"That political passion did not work out so well for your father," Luperini said with mild and friendly discouragement.

In his own youth, Michele Carducci, Giosuè's father, had been a member of the revolutionary organization known as the Carbonari, who had also fought for reunification. Imprisoned for a time, forced to move from town to town with his nascent family, the elder Carducci had experienced much misery before retiring from active politics. These dismal repercussions and stifled dreams had permeated Carducci's childhood.

Carducci's volatile mood evaporated. "No one knows that sad fact better than I, friend Pietro. Such knowledge drains all the pleasures from fighting the good fight." Sounding sincerely befuddled, he added, "But what else is worthy of a man's passions, if not art or country?"

In their progress through the hilltop town, enjoying the magnificent views of the countryside below as they headed toward home, the trio had now come abreast of the the Convent of San Francesco. Nodding his head at the building, Cristiani wryly remarked, "You could always invest your soul in the Church. I can easily picture you as a quiet country priest."

Carducci spat toward the Convent. "May the Pope and all his foul influence rot in Dante's lowest pit. The Church as it now stands is a set of chains on the spirit of mankind. If there were a congregation devoted to Satan, I would happily join it instead."

Accustomed as they were to their friend's easy blasphemies, Cristiani and Luperini nonetheless felt the need to protectively cross themselves before they moved on.

Little else was said until they reached the door of their establishment, the White Tower, whereupon their spirits commenced to lift. Cristiani thrust open the door to reveal the disordered bachelor interior and carelessly tossed his portfolio upon the nearest chair, sending student essays skittering across the floor.

"What shall it be tonight, my friends? Red wine or white?"

"Both!" Luperini and Carducci chimed, as if fulfilling a ritual response.

"And what of women?"

"Let them be large or petite, dark or light, but let them appear in great numbers, laughing and willing and with their skirts all uprucked!"

"All right then," Cristiani said. "I will accept funds from each of you, and go forth to procure the wine and food. Giosuè , you can begin to make this place look like less of a pigsty. Pietro, you are in charge of rounding up some suitable females—and their male friends too, if they insist. But no zealous guardian brothers!"

Luperini's face betrayed no hint of jesting as he spoke. "If I pass by a stable, I shall look inside for Elvira Menicucci."

Carducci swore—"You bastard!"—and threw a plate at Luperini, who ducked the assault.

Elvira Menicucci was Carducci's cousin—and his betrothed. They had known each other since their early teens. Somehow their eventual humdrum union had come to be a given in both families, without any period of wild juvenile infatuation. And in truth, the dour Elvira, no great beauty, did possess a somewhat long and equine phiz—although it was cruel of Luperini to mention it. Luckily, there was no chance of her showing up tonight, for she still resided with her parents in Florence.

Pietro and Ferdinando having departed on their respective errands, Carducci fell to tidying up their domicile—mostly by the expedient of stuffing dirty clothing into a wardrobe and dirty dishes into a wicker hamper. He doffed his tie and suitcoat and rolled up his sleeves, the better to dispatch the mess.

As he worked, he mulled over the conversation he had just had with his friends. What was he to do with his life? If not art or politics—and never the Church!—what sphere of worthy activity would receive his exceptional talents and energies? Teaching was a fairly pleasant way to earn a living, and he showed some skill in pushing knowledge into the thick skulls of the local youths. And this mild hedonism of feasting and partying was also enjoyable enough. But for the rest of his life?

If only some supernal inspiration would appear to light his path. Nothing necessarily divine, but just a manifestation of the universe's rich energies. What form such a beacon would take, Carducci could not say. An aspect of nature, perhaps, some hawk alighting on his shoulders? Or the intervention and guidance of a fellow human of extraordinary qualities?

These musings by the young reluctant and indecisive poet were soon shattered with the reappearance of his friends, laden with victuals and drink and trailing a bevy of chattering ladies of debatable virtue, all eager to shed the day's cares with libations and some harmless flirtations.

Sometime around one in the morning, Carducci surfaced from the inebriated gaiety and recalled his earlier perplexity about his future. Queerly, he discovered that he now possessed a certainty that his desired revelation lay just around the corner. Feeling much better about his life, he plunged back into the celebrations.

And the next day the desired guidance was indeed vouchsafed—in a roundabout way.

The trio of revelers were awakened around noon by an imperious banging on the door of the White Tower. Carducci was the first to stir, throwing off a linen tablecloth that had somehow become his impromptu coverlet and arising from the parlor rug. Imperious sunlight assaulted him. His head seemed several sizes too large, and his mouth tasted as if he had drunk cheap champagne out of a troll's wooden shoe. He felt stiff from sleeping on barely cushioned floorboards.

"Rein in your horse, damn you! I'm moving as fast as I can!"

Carducci swung the windowless door inward—and was immediately swept up in a bear hug! His face was crushed into the man's shoulder, and so he could not see who held him until he was carried inside and dropped into a chair.

"Giuseppe! And Giuseppe!"

Indeed, here without explanation were the two bosom comrades of Carducci's student days, Gargani and Chiarini. Dressed casually, in baggy woolens, the two men looked almost like brothers, their small mustaches nearly identical, their oval faces following the same general plan—although Chiarini was the taller of the pair, and the neat widow's peak of Gargani's hairline contrasted with Chiarini's more unruly thatch.

Carducci's roommates, also in a pitiable condition akin to their friend's malaise, stumbled in from wherever they had spent the night. Cheerful albeit wincing greetings were exchanged, and the five young men were soon seated around a hastily cleared table, enjoying hot black coffee and slightly stale biscotti. After some lively gossip, Gargani came to the point of their visit.

"Giosuè, we have come to spirit you away for the adventure of a lifetime!"

Here then was the omen or impulse he had felt arrowing his way last night!

"And what is the exact nature of this adventure. if I may ask?"

Chiarini leaned in closer, as if to deliver a secret, a compelling posture which had the effect of making his listeners attend to every word. "There is a man now in Pisa who bids fair to revolutionize our land. He is at once a magician, an artist, a soldier, and a revolutionary. A true freethinker, full of marvelous ideas and slogans you have never before heard. He is gathering around himself a clutch of bold young fellows eager for a notion he dubs 'regime change.' When he has attained what he refers to as a 'critical mass' of such bold rogues, he plans to take over this patchwork land of ours and unite it into a powerful kingdom, with himself at the head."

Such a wild-eyed but glorious scheme instantly appealed to Carducci. "Does this fellow have a name? Might I have encountered his reputation before?"

"He goes only by 'Silenus.' No one knows where he came from. But the force of his character is such that no one cares!"

"I like that he adheres to classical allusions. Naming himself after the god of satyrs is a sharp move."

Gargani added, "And you should see his mistress! Her name is Valencia, and she is like some dusky bloom from Iberia. I think as many men have joined Silenus's cause for her sake, as for his."

"Where is this fellow to be found?"

"He's rented the Palazzo Vecchio de' Medici in Pisa. At great expense too. Money is no object to Silenus. He is liberal with his gold, even prodigal. Some say he can manufacture all he wants, like an alchemist of yore."

Chiarini laid his hand on Carducci's forearm. "Won't you join us, Giosuè? This is that veritable tide in the affairs of men to which Shakespeare alludes."

Carducci looked to his roommates. They seemed interested but daunted by the practicalities.

"I cannot foresee leaving the Gymnasium," said Luperini. "Especially in the middle of the term."

"Nor I," echoed Cristiani. "We have worked too hard to attain these sinecures just to throw them away. Pecchioli would have our hides!"

The very timidity of his friends was the final feather that tipped the scales for Carducci. He turned to the visitors.

"Men, I am with you! You and Silenus, if I find him to be all you have accounted."

"What will we tell Pecchioli?" asked Luperini. "Mayhaps there is an excuse by which you could keep in his good graces."

Carducci pondered. "My father. Tell him my father is ill, and I go to succor him. In truth, the old man is doing poorly. As anyone might fare, when almost half a century old!"

"We have a carriage outside," said Gargani. "You need only pack a bag, and we can be off."

Carducci leapt to his feet. "This is the start of my real life! Friends, we go to build a proud new Italy!"

* * * *

After being immured in the provincial lanes of San Miniato al Tedcesco for so many months, Carducci found the hustle and bustle of cultured and commercial Pisa to be nearly overwhelming. He recalled his glorious University days that had allowed those heady side-trips to Florence, and berated himself for becoming so dull. He wondered if in his dotage—his twenty-second birthday was just around the corner—he was even qualified to join in such a demanding enterprise as Silenus envisioned. Perhaps this as-yet unmet Wizard and General, this secular Savonarola, would deem him unfit and send him packing.

The journey from San Miniato, some thirty kilometers, undertaken in the small barouche powered by a singularly lazy sorrel, had taken several hours, during which time the friends had caught up on many matters. But certainly the most striking bit of conversation, from Carducci's perspective, had been this snippet:

Carducci: "But what made you fellows seek me out for this enterprise?"

Gargani: "We were following the orders of Silenus himself. He asked for you by name."

The great and mysterious Silenus had distinctly inquired after a lowly Gymnasium instructor (who, admittedly, had published a few poems in various periodicals and raised some small literary controversies)? It hardly seemed possible.

Carducci tabled the enigma, while resolving to get to the bottom of it soon.

Now guiding their conveyance within the city limits, Chiarini deftly threaded them through the heterogenous traffic of nobles and commoners, vendors and carters, idlers and soldiers, urchins and *baldracche*, until they arrived at Piazza Giuseppe Mazzini Number 7, the location of the hulking Palazzo Vecchio de' Medici, a surprisingly unadorned three-storey box with a square tower rising one storey higher at its northeast corner. The building was separated from the broad and sluggish Arno only by the width of the cobbled roadway, and commanded a splendid view upstream and downstream from its elaborately arched windows. Its mustard-colored paint was flaking, but it radiated an elderly dignity.

Leading his comrades, Gargani approached the large arched door and knocked on it with a complex pattern of raps. Carducci felt simultaneously awed by the clandestine approach, and also a little irritated. Why did mankind exhibit the need to cloak all its doings, which often were quite simple at the base, in such rigamarole, of which the Catholic Church was the prime example? Life and death, honor and beauty—why must such primal things be festooned in ridiculous showy garments?

The door swung inward, and the trio entered.

Carducci found himself almost instantly in a large ballroom, well lighted with modern parrafin Argand lamps, and thronged with conspirators. The space had been converted from its former recreational use to a kind of war room. Tables held various maps and documents which were being pored over intently.

Gargani and Chiarini were welcomed heartily by various of the plotters, and they kindly introduced Carducci, who, with remnants of his intemperance still in effect, found that many of the names slid into one ear and directly out the other.

Gargani now inquired of one fellow who improbably wore a large sword on his belt, "Is the Maestro in his room?"

"Yes, and I think he expects you to deliver your friend."

"Very good."

Carducci followed his pals toward the rear of the house where a staircase permitted access to the tower. They ascended, passing vigilant but bored-looking young guards at every level. Finally at the top they confronted a closed door.

"You must enter alone for your interview, Giosuè. Silenus won't want to see us."

After buffing his appearance as best he could in front of a large wall-mounted cloudy mirror, Carducci put hand to doorknob and passed through into the sanctum.

The modest-sized, high-raftered room, with large faded tapestries covering three walls, held only a desk, a bed, a wardrobe, and several non-matching chairs.

Seated casually on the bed, with legs folded beneath her, was a woman—from whom the gentleman Carducci hastily averted his gaze, however intrigued he was.

Behind the desk was Silenus.

The mysterious stranger, this man who had managed so quickly to assemble a troop of ambitious malcontents about him, exhibited an imposing bulk. Carducci estimated he had to be in his fourth decade or thereabouts, well over two meters tall, and proportionately fleshy, but not in a doughy way. Robust, yet with lineaments and attitude indicative of an enjoyment of carnal pleasures. His skin tone was remarkably healthy. The craggy features of his face, while not handsome, were commanding. His large mouth was partially obscured by his only facial hair, which was sculpted in a kind of squarish arch above and alongside his lips. Carducci had seldom seen such a striking giant. The man seemed to hail from some unknown region of the world that enjoyed more salubrious conditions than obtained around most of the globe, as if he had been raised in a cosseting hothouse not subject to the stresses of a natural environment.

The leader of the conspirators wore a thick dove-grey tunic with no placket; an attached cowl or hood like a monk's hung down upon his back. The front of the tunic featured a painted image of a snarling bear with the incomprehensible word UCLA beneath the portrait. Silenus wore on his wrist an odd kind of bracelet or band that featured a polychromatic, lambent crystal bauble surrounded by stud-like protrusions.

Silenus had been busy with something in his hands when Carducci entered, and, after fiddling with it briefly, he put it down on the surface of the desk. Carducci was astonished to see that the object appeared to be a thin rectangular brick or tile with a glass face—and on that glazed front was frozen a glowing portrait of a cathedral: a portrait so incredibly detailed and naturalistic that it might have been painted by some deity.

Silenus stood up and came around the desk. Carducci saw that his trousers, maculated in shades of green, were cut from some kind of canvas, and featured a number of pouches attached to the hips and side legs. Ankle-high boots of a peculiar elaborate design completed the outfit.

"Giosuè Carducci!" hailed Silenus. "The man who shall chronicle our every victory in the campaign to conquer and unite this fractured land!"

Carducci noted that Silenus's Italian was queerly accented, but otherwise fairly good. So, the man was probably not a native son, but maybe of long residence here...

Taking Silenus's proferred hand, Carducci marveled at the grip of the large fellow. Here was another token of the man's utter confidence.

"You have an advantage in seeming acquainted with my small accomplishments, Signor Silenus, whereas I am unfamiliar with you and your plans, aside from some small accounts rendered by my friends."

"Yes, it's true, I know all about you, Giosuè. And please, call me only Silenus. I know not only all about your small but significant record of creations to date, but also the path of your future. Some day, I confidently predict, you will be regarded as one of Italy's most famous poets, revered across all of Europe as well. And so I am enlisting your talents early in your career. Hitching my wagon to your star, if you will, for our mutual betterment."

"But this is all too impossible and flattering, Silenus. Let us leave aside such fantasies for the moment, and simply say that I have some skills you could use, and which I wish to tender. What then of your own future?"

"Simple, my lad. I intend to mold this patchwork country by cunning and force of arms if necessary into a vibrant nation, and then to put all of Europe itself under my command."

"Truly an ambition worthy of Napoleon. Whom, as we all know, came close to succeeding, but ultimately failed."

"Yes, Napoleon is one of my models. Also a certain Austrian Chancellor of whom you will not have heard. But I have distinct advantages that no other conqueror in their own era has enjoyed. In a moment, you will get a chance to observe what I mean. As for my own past—well, let us just say that after honorable service in the military forces of my native land, I was discharged and left without any challenges, and so sought out a time and place where I could fulfill my destiny. But enough of my history! I don't wish to dwell on what lies behind, but rather the glories ahead!"

Carducci was as yet unconvinced. "Although our desires might run in parallel, I don't quite yet see how you can succeed where so many others have failed."

"Ah, a skeptic! I am glad you seek hard proof. Very well, what would you say about the value of an ability to come and go magically, without hinderance?"

"That would be a very fine weapon to have, indeed."

"Well then, just watch!"

Silenus strode to one of the hanging tapestries, twitched it aside and concealed himself behind it, making a lumpy outline under the fabric. His outlined form appeared to indicate that he was massaging one wrist. His mildly muffled voice emerged. "You recall that this tower room is raised above the rest of the building, yes? No hidden passages possible? Then how—"

The bulk of Silenus vanished, leaving the wall-covering to hang flat! Carducci raced to the tapesty, plucked it aside, and faced a blank wall.

"—can I do this?"

Carducci spun about. The opposite tapestry had molded itself to a concealed Silenus, who now emerged.

"This—this is astonishing!"

"Barely a fraction of my prowess, young man! Now, I am going to show you something much more comprehensible, but no less valuable. Or rather, my comrade Valencia will show you, since I am busy with my researches. Valencia, my dear, would you take charge of our new recruit?"

Now Carducci, still reeling from the revelation of Silenus's uncanny powers, was forced to turn his attention to the woman he had been deliberately ignoring.

Valencia unfolded herself limberly from her position on the bed and took a bold, masculine stance. Carducci was able fully to gauge her highly immodest and sensational appearance. Taller than Carducci, but not as tall as Silenus, she had long black hair coiled insouciantly atop her head and held in place with a shiny tortoise-shell clip. Her complexion was a dusky golden brown, almost like that of uncured tobacco. Dark eyes glimmered saucily, and a small painted mouth was quirked in amusement. Her ripe figure was fully on display, in a form-hugging, seamless, velveteen black costume akin to that worn by the acrobatic performers in the Zoppè Italian Family Circus. She too displayed on her slim wrist an adornment identical to Silenus's.

"Happy to do a 'demo,' Sly. The 'Steyr Aug Ay Three' okay?"

Valencia's Italian also deviated from the norm, and her use of some nonsensical terms further discombobulated Carducci.

"Sure," Silenus agreed. "You can use a full clip or two."

Valencia came up to Carducci and took him by the arm with brazen familiarity. Her exotic floral scent acted on his senses like strong drink.

"Okay, Josh, let's hit the firing range."

As Valencia manuevered Carducci to the door, Silenus said, "I will see you at tonight's dinner, Giosuè. And in future days, I will tell you of a special mission I have in mind for you."

Outside the tower room, Valencia conducted Carducci down to the ground floor. Only then did he find himself able to converse, after all the unnatural events he had witnessed.

"Signorina Valencia, may I ask where you and Silenus hail from?"

"California. But my family is originally from Puerto Rico."

"Are those places to be found in the New World?"

Valencia gave a charming laugh. "Not so new anymore, but yes, you've got it."

They traversed the war room, and Carducci saw that all the other men tracked Valencia with undisguised admiration, making Carducci feel that he was very privileged to have all her attention at the moment.

Carducci would have followed this unconventional woman anywhere, but their destination proved only to be a basement room. Valencia unlocked a door, and Carducci found himself in a long, damp, narrow chamber that extended some twelve or fifteen meters to its rear wall, where several mattresses were propped vertically in an upended bedframe. The room was otherwise empty save for a locked chest.

Valence opened the chest with a key and withdrew an object. She held it out for Carducci's perusal.

At first the awkward thing appeared merely a jagged and ugly abortion, like some castoff from an iron foundry. But then Carducci apprehended its function.

"This is a rifle?"

"Yes, the 'Steyr Aug Ay Three.' Single round, fully auto, and everything in between. Underbarrel grenade launcher too. Here, put these on."

Valencia had retrieved hard-shelled earmuffs from the box, a pair for each of them. After donning them, Carducci was surprised to find all sounds swaddled in cotton.

"Now watch me."

Valencia took up a shooter's stance, and squeezed the trigger. A single muffled shot, exploding through the mattresses in a puff of feathers, caused Carducci to wince.

Valencia fussed with the gun, and her next activation of the trigger caused an incredible riot of bullets to tear the mattresses almost in half. She replaced an expended reservoir with a full one.

"Now you try."

Reluctantly, Carducci took up the gun, which Valencia had reset to single-shot. Its recoil startled him. But for the subsequent lone round he was braced, and he managed to strike the target. Valencia next let him vent an instant flurry of bullets, an experience which left Carducci simultaneously elated, sweaty and appalled.

He handed the gun back eagerly and stripped off his earmuffs. Valencia stowed everything away and relocked the chest.

"Hey, don't look so scared. You won't have anything to worry about, just so long as you're on the right end of these suckers. And you did just fine!"

Impulsively, the woman leaned in and kissed him on the cheek, pressing her velvety bosom against him with impartial ardor.

Carducci's consciousness reeled. The heat of her lips, the reek and smoke of the gunfire—it was all overwhelming. Dumbly, he followed Valencia upstairs.

"Okay, Josh, you reconnect with your buddies, and I'll see you at dinner."

Slowly recovering his aplomb minute by minute, Carducci found Gargani. His friend smiled broadly. "You too have had your marksman training with Valencia, I see. Well, you'll get over it soon enough! We all did. Now, let's set you up with a bunk."

The upper floors of the Palazzo were established as a dormitory for the conspirators, and Carducci was assigned a bed. The building featured luxurious indoor accomodations for bathing and excretory needs, and Carducci was able to refresh himself and repair his appearance with a fresh shirt from the small stock of clothing he had brought from the White Tower. He lay down upon his bed and fell instantly asleep, later being awakened by one of his new comrades just before meal time.

Another large room in the Palazzo served as refectory. At a table on a dais were seated Silenus, Valencia and a couple of lieutenants. The rest of the company occupied a half dozen long tables. Servants brought course after course of delicious food, and the wine flowed like the Arno at flood time.

Carducci began to relax and share the riotous bonhomie of the crowd. Surely he had made a wise decision to enlist in this cause. Silenus presided over the feast like a Nero or Petronius or the Lord of Misrule: larger than life, irreverent and urging more revelry. He grabbed Valencia at intervals and planted kisses on her lips, raising a cheer each time from the audience.

Finally, towards the end of the meal, Silenus stood, and the rest of the men did too. Carducci got boozily to his feet, unsure of what was to follow.

"Sing, comrades! Sing our anthem!"

Voices bellowed forth, and after a verse or two, Carducci was able to join in.

"Living easy, living free! Season ticket on a one-way ride! I'm on the highway to hell! On the highway to hell!"

* * * *

Carducci exited the Palazzo Vecchio de' Medici alone, some three days after he had first entered the building. He felt proud to know the secret pattern of knocks to regain admission. His sense of camaraderie with this small but select army of men aiming to impose a new rigor and vitality on the penninsula had swollen to fill his heart and soul. With the astounding weapons at their disposal—a "force multiplier" Silenus called it—and the uncanny wisdom of their chief, nothing could stop them. Truly, Carducci felt had found his noble mission in life. One of those great figures in history that arise only at unpredictable intervals, Silenus would surely remake the face of the world.

That is, so long as Enceladus did not interfere.

The day after his initiatory dinner, Carducci had been given a lecture by one of the lieutenants, a certain Gaetano Pontecorvo. The self-important neurasthenic fellow with a slightly jaundiced complexion had begun the talk by showing Carducci a portrait done in charcoals. The drawing depicted a man of somber mien, somewhat handsome, notable for a dimpled chin, but above all competent-seeming.

"This man," said Pontecorvo, "is Enceladus. So dubbed, because the original Enceladus was one of the Giants who fought the satyrs under Silenus. Enceladus comes from the same foreign land as the Maestro, and is his sworn enemy. He is intent on frustrating all of Silenus's grand schemes, out of sheer perversity. Fortunately, he is alone, and nigh-powerless, although he once possessed the same abilities as the Maestro. But Silenus stole his powers from him."

Carducci recalled the demonstration that Silenus had given him in the tower room. "Is the power of the Maestro resident in his special wizard's bracelet?"

Pontecorvo looked nervous. "You are not supposed to know or acknowledge that. But yes, it is true."

"And Valencia wears one also?"

"The one that belonged to Enceladus."

"Ah, I see..." Carducci could easily picture Valencia seducing her Lord's enemy and making off with the talisman of power.

"But all of this is beside the point. You are charged only with staying alert for Enceladus. If you see him, report the sighting immediately!"

"Very good."

Now, out in the sunny, thronged street for the first time since his arrival, Carducci glanced about nervously for this ogre, Enceladus, the only one who could possibly thwart Silenus's grand ambitions. But the passersby were all standard unremarkable citizens, no one in the least suspicious.

So off Carducci hurried, toward the manure-odoriferous district not far from the Piazza dei Miracoli where many stables and horse merchants maintained a presence. Silenus had tasked him with securing enough mounts to carry all their elite troop of officers out into the field of battle, once their campaign was fully underway. To that end, Carducci had been entrusted with a drawstring-secured leather bag full of gold pieces of unfamiliar design, featuring the portrait of some kind of elk or deer and denominated "krugerrand." Although uncommon, the coins were so evidently composed of fine gold that any merchant would willingly accept them.

Eventually, after many inquries and haggling, Carducci struck a bargain with an obese, unshaved and sweaty fellow named Malvaldi, who, despite his shabby appearance, boasted the finest horses within the city's walls. An ample retainer, with promise of more upon delivery, ensured that the steeds would be ready when needed.

The hour was near two in the afternoon, and Carducci felt he owed himself a fine repast. Communal dining had its allure, but his proud nature required some private and personal indulgence as well. So he ventured to a new restaurant whose reputation had penetrated even as far as San Miniato: the Ristorante La Scaletta, right on the Piazza dei Miracoli. Seated at an outdoor table, Carducci ordered a generous assemblage of seafood and a large decanter of sparkling white wine. Sipping the latter while he awaited his meal, stroking his mustache with satisfaction, he amused himself by watching the passing traffic and speculating about the histories and motives of the people. What poems one could conjure up based on their lives—that is, if poetry still held any attractions for a man of action such as himself.

Suddenly a small cabriolet came to a seemingly unanticipated halt right opposite the restaurant, its driver plainly obeying orders from within. The curbside door opened and a woman emerged. Clad in a dress of sober black bombazine and with a lacy mantilla around her hair, she hastened over to Carducci's table. And only then did her uncontextualized identity burst upon him.

Elvira Menicucci, his bride-to-be!

Elvira's usual stern and implacable expression was now overlaid with genuine concern, worry and fear, as well as a few small traces of relief. "Giosuè, my love! At last I have found you!" She burst into tears.

Alarmed and chagrined, with fellow diners watching, Carducci scrambled to his feet and assisted Elvira into a chair. He motioned to the waiter for a second glass, and within a few minutes had her calmed down. She drained her third glass of wine with full eagerness.

"But Elvira, why all the fuss?"

"Why the fuss? You left your job at the Gymnasium with no warning, claiming you were going to succor your father. But when I inquired there, he knew nothing! Only then did those rascals Cristiani and Luperini reveal the truth. And I have been searching for you ever since."

"Alone?"

"No, of course not. It was all I could do to get father to permit me to travel with a companion. My cousin Griselda is accompanying me. She has held back to allow us our privacy."

Elvira waved towards her carriage, and in the open door appeared a nervously smiling older female even more homely and conservatively attired than Elvira herself.

Carducci repressed a shiver. His fleeting encounters with Valencia, however impersonal, had inspired endless daydreams about the exotic foreign woman, fantasies which placed his engagement to Elvira into the category of foolish childhood aberrations.

Nonetheless, he could not afford to have Elvira raising a stink about his absence that could derail his utility to Silenus.

And so he placated her with a quickly improvised tale about his poetry manuscript and a publisher named Ristori and grand opportunities that had to be seized immediately. She swallowed the lies entirely, and by her fourth glass of wine was laughing and simpering.

"You are staying in Pisa?" asked Carducci with manufactured interest.

"Yes, Griselda and I have rooms at the Locanda della Vittoria."

"Excellent! I will be by to see you as soon as my affairs allow."

"My heart can't wait, Giosuè."

Carducci bundled Elvira—her normally unattractive face rendered even more so by the raddling effects of her tears—back into her carriage, being forced also to accept a peck on the cheek from the relieved Griselda. He returned to his table. Silenus had better activate his plans soon, for Elvira could be fobbed off only so long, and would attract unwanted attention to any scheme involving her inattentive inamorato.

Upon Elvira's departure, Carducci let his thoughts roam down various avenues. His ailing, frustrated father, who had instilled in him his first love of literature and politics. It had been mean of the son to use his parent's ill health as a pretext. The possibilities, quite real, of having his verses published, under the simple title of *Rime*—although always he felt that it was like offering one's child to a brothel. The destiny of Italy, and his part in it. "When I am touched, I fight," Carducci murmured to himself. And for a moment he felt like the Apollo he had described in his poem: "the sovereign driver of the ethereal chariot, whipping the fiery wing-footed steeds—a Titan most beautiful."

Halfway through his *fritto misto di mare,* Carducci sensed someone sitting down uninvited in the chair lately occupied by Elvira.

Looking up, he saw Enceladus.

Unmistakeable from his sketch, dressed in undistinguished native garb, the man looked tired and harried and somewhat disheveled—but in no degree less dangerous or determined than he had been presented.

Carducci made to rise, but was restrained by a steely hand on his wrist.

"Sit down, Giosuè Carducci. Despite what that crazy jackass Silenus might have told you, I am not a monster, nor are you in any danger from me. Quite to the contrary, you stand to suffer greatly from your association with the one you call the Maestro."

Intrigued by any reference to his own preservation and fortunes, Carducci composed himself. What harm could it do to listen to this rival? When he returned to the Palazzo he would report all.

"You must know," continued Enceladus, "that Silenus is a stranger to your land. As, admittedly, am I. He has no intrinsic love for your country, nor stake in it. He has merely determined that this time and place represent a tipping point, a kind of yeasty chaos that he can manipulate for his own personal gain. This camaraderie of a satanic legion that he preaches is merely a tactic for commanding the help of others."

"Suppose what you say is true. Many a great man has been guilty of just such selfish practices. But if Silenus's goals coincide with mine and with those of my patriotic countrymen, then what does it matter if his motives are base? We will ride different horses to the same destination."

"Listen to me, Giosuè, you will not arrive at a good place if you follow Silenus. He is taking the course of history down a wrongful path that leads only to incredible death and destruction. This I know for sure. You must trust me on this matter."

"Who can know the future for certain?"

Enceladus leaned across the table imploringly. "But I do, Giosuè, I do! That's why I can be certain of Silenus's folly. And I know the things to come for you as well. Or rather, the future you should have. You will become a famous poet, just as you have always dreamed. You will speak for your country's soul, attaining the highest honors, hailed as a national bard. Even the rest of the world shall acknowledge your talents, showering you with prestigious laurels. You will marry well, and even have some affairs of the heart. You will attain your three-score-and-ten, plus more. Nor will your political desires go unrequited, for you shall become a Senator of the Kingdom of Italy."

This fable of futurity left Carducci feeling dazzled and dazed. How could Enceladus, a stranger, make up a tale that conformed so well to Carducci's dreams? It must be true... Just think, all he had wished for, falling into his lap—not without hard work and travail, perhaps, but still...

Sensing that he was swaying Carducci, Enceladus said, "All you need to do to restore this proper future is to help me capture Silenus. Just strip him or Valencia of their magical bracelet and I will do the rest. You can convey the prize to me at some prearranged spot."

With this demand, Enceladus had gone a step too far. Carducci's manly affections for the darkly heroic and outsized Silenus and his infatuation with Valencia were still glowing in his heart. "You would have me play the Judas? No, thank you, sirrah. Now, begone!"

Enceladus slumped back. "Well, then, that's that. You were my last hope. None of your comrades are suitable." Then, as if thinking aloud, the man said, in seeming confusion, "Why haven't I come back yet to help myself? I should have been here by now. Maybe I'll come soon. Upstream, downstream, I can only wait..."

Visibly picking his dashed spirits up out of the pit of despair, Enceladus pushed away from the table and strode off without another word.

Carducci paid his bill and hastened back to the Palazzo, gaining admission by the secret code. Eager to make his report, despite some residual sympathy for the beleaguered fellow who had predicted such fine fortune for him, he quickly found one of Silenus's busy lieutenants. But the lieutenant, a pompous type named Ortolani, addressed Carducci first.

"Giosuè, go quickly upstairs to see Silenus. He has an important mission for you to undertake."

And what Carducci heard next made him forget all about Enceladus.

* * * *

The arduous trip from Pisa to Milan, a distance of some two-hundred-and-fifty kilometers as a bird might travel, had not been a trivial one. Carducci and his chosen companions, the two Giuseppes, Gargani and Chiarini, had first journeyed along the coast to Genoa on horseback, enduring April rains and fogs and flea-ridden lodgings. In Genoa they had transferred to the novel conveyance of the railway—that invention of the devil, as Pope Gregory XVI had deemed it. More fuel for Carducci's irreligious ire. But far from being infernal, the ultra-modern locomotive and carriages proved stimulating and comfortable, especially compared to horseback. At meteoric speed—up to forty-eight kilometers per hour!—they arrived in Milan, toting their essential bulky baggage. They secured modest and deliberately non-flagrant lodgings with krugerrand gold, and began to polish their plan to rob the Duomo di Monza, one of the city's major churches, of its incalculably valuable artifact, the Iron Crown of Lombardy.

Carducci could hardly believe they were embarked on such a mad escapade. Alternately chilled and thrilled, he realized he would not have missed this opportunity for all the literary prizes in the world. He thanked the Fates for Silenus's willingness to entrust him with the mission.

Entering Silenus's tower room after the streetside meeting with Enceladus, Carducci had been disappointed not to see Valencia present. As if reading the mind of his subordinate, Silenus grinned and said, "Val is away, getting the equipment you'll need. So allow me to outline what I want you to do. It is simple. I need you to steal the Iron Crown of Lombardy from its vault in the Duomo di Monza in Milan."

Carducci's stunned consciousness refused to process for a moment the words he had just heard. Then, as if in reflexive defensiveness, he ran through a mental primer on the object in question, as if he were getting ready to teach a classroom of students about the topic.

The holy core of the Iron Crown of Lombardy was a nail that had been involved in the Crucifixion itself. Hammered flat and bent, the omnipotent nail formed the armature for the relatively plain-looking wide circlet of gold and gems that constituted the outer Crown. Fashioned in the sixth century by Theodelinda, queen of the Lombards, the crown had since been used to consecrate countless rulers on the Italian penninsula and elsewhere, including Charlemagne, Napolean I, and, most recently in 1838, Ferdinand I of Austria.

The man who possessed the Iron Crown of Lombardy would be more than halfway to ruling the land. In the eyes of the common people, he would be already annointed to govern, heir to a long lineage of holy power.

Silenus gauged Carducci's understanding, and smiled. "I see you appreciate my intentions. Your quick apprehension makes me even more certain that I have chosen the right man for this job."

"But—but how is this to be accomplished?"

"The repository for the crown is barely guarded. They rely on the physical barriers to protect the treasure. And I am going to give you the means to defeat that barrier. Ah, here is Val now!"

Carducci turned, and saw Valencia emerging from behind one of the tapestries, evidently having used her own magic bracelet to travel from the tower to some unknown spot and back. The woman was lugging a small bag by its handles, and a larger apparatus of some sort. Huffing, she carried them to the desk and set them down.

"Thanks for all the help, Sly."

"You'll never build your upper-body strength if I do everything for you."

"As if!"

Carducci mentally kicked himself for not chivalrously volunteering his own labor. But before he could say something gallant, Silenus had begun explaining the items arrayed on the desk, and Carducci had to pay close attention.

"This is a bottle of chloroform. It is a substance that will send a person to dreamland when they breathe it. You will use it on the guards, if any. It will put them right out. You will need to pin their arms while you make them inhale, which is why I plan to send two other guys with you. This next baby is a set of night vision goggles. Very handy. But the real gem here is this 'oxyacetylene' torch."

The object so named was some kind of artificer's rig contained in a handle-topped seamless framework of some unnatural red material, only about as big as a crockery seller's wicker basket. In the framework's niches were placed two large sealed metal retorts, one red, one green, with valves and handles and dials. Coiled hoses ran from the containers to a shared nozzle. Along with this infernal device went some other accessories.

"Burns at thirty-five hundred degrees centigrade," said Silenus. "You'll be in the vault in seconds flat, like shit through a goose."

"This—this all seems impossible."

"You will soon see it is not. And once Val gets you up to speed with everything, you'll feel like Al Capone."

This Italian figure cited for comparison was unfamiliar to Carducci, but he let the reference slide by, so thrilled was he at the prospect of taking lessons from Valencia, whose intoxicating perfume, mingled with female sweat, now wafted to Carducci's nostrils.

A certain quibble suddenly occured to Carducci, and he felt compelled to voice it.

"Maestro—could you not secure the crown yourself much more easily with your miraculous means of transport?"

Silenus did not take Carducci's question amiss. "Well, son, it is like this. Yes, I could get to Milan more quickly than you. Not instantly, you understand. Even my powers require me to exert some effort. But the problem lies in entering the vault. For me to access any space, I need to find a congruency to that same space that is unprotected. And there is no such match for the vault at the Duomo di Monza. And besides, why should I spend my precious time on such a quest, however important, when I know that you can carry it off well? My time is more valuable by far than yours!"

Impressed by Silenus's insouciant, easy superiority, Carducci was forced to acknowledge his reasoning. He felt honored that he had been entrusted with this mission, and vowed to do his utmost to succeed.

And indeed, as the Maestro had promised, after a few days practice with torch and goggles and even the knockout liquid—administered to volunteers from within the conspiracy—Carducci felt totally confident that the theft of the Iron Crown of Lombardy could be accomplished.

And so he and the two Giuseppes went about their business in Milan, first visiting the gorgeously decorated and lofty pillared interior of the Duomo di Monza as simple pilgrims, where they studied the Treasury, located in the right-hand transept, and then, on a moonless night, paying an unsanctioned visit as robbers.

To Carducci, the whole rapid and problem-free theft amidst the smells and sights and liturgical trappings of the Church he had abandoned had the atmosphere of a dream, through which he moved with an uncanny assurance. The otherworldly landscape of the highly decorated church through the googles of "night vision." The chemical silencing of the guards—and one errant elderly priest. The spark that ignited the hissing torch and the swift liquid cutting of thick metal barriers. Hefting the ancient sacred crown in his unworthy hands as Gargani and Chiarini looked on in admiration. What else could such a scenario be except an absinthe phantasm?

Only on the train the next morning, departing Milan, after an exuberantly sleepless night, the crown packed away in an innocuous hatbox, did Carducci emerge from his reverie. And, upon emerging, he realized that now nothing stood between Silenus and his goals.

Nothing except perhaps betrayal from within. He recalled the speech of Enceladus, and what that man had asked Carducci to do, and why. For some reason, here at this moment on the edge of total victory, he could not bring himself utterly to banish that request from his conscience.

* * * *

All was finally arranged for the launch of the campaign to make Silenus the ruler of a united Italy—and from there, the world! The event would happen upon tomorrow's dawn. From Pisa would ride out all the elite officers of the new regime, equipped with weapons fantastical, the "Steyr Aug Ay Threes," akin to the thunderbolts of Zeus, to meet with other forces across the land whose cooperation had been secured, formerly quarrelsome factions welded into a perfect machine of conquest under Silenus. Nothing, Carducci now felt, could stop the success of the big foreign warrior.

This revelation of guaranteed victory had been driven home when Silenus showed the Iron Crown of Lombardy to the assemblage at the communal dinner on the night Carducci and the two Giuseppes returned. The roar of acclamation that had greeted this sight, and the subsequent coronation of Silenus, had been earth-shattering. When the applause finally died down, Carducci was stunned to hear himself being hailed up to the dais, along with the two Giuseppes.

"Men, I want you to honor these three gallants, who procured the final essential element of our success!"

When the second round of cheers had died down, Carducci spontaneously recited a verse from his poem, "Voice of God."

"Hark! In the temple the voice of God is sounding. '0 people of one speech and one endeavour, yours is the land with my best gifts abounding, whereon the smile of heaven is resting ever!'"

The heady atmosphere continued throughout that evening, with much drinking and singing. In the morning, a queasy and listless Carducci felt as if he had spent a typical Friday night in the White Tower, redoubled!

The next weeks passed in a frenzy of activity, until this final evening before the launch. And Carducci found himself awake at midnight, when everyone else was sound asleep. Highly frustrating! But his mind would not stop revolving all that had happened since that morning nearly two months ago when his University chums had appeared at the White Tower with their impossible invitation. He felt as if his life had bifurcated then, with part of him venturing down an old path, and part down a new avenue.

Finally admitting to himself that sleep was leagues away, Carducci silently left his dormitory and ventured downstairs to the kitchen. A tumbler of wine and a nice bit of ham and bread would drive him into the arms of Morpheus—he hoped.

Golden lantern light seeped around the edges of the kitchen door. Pushing it open, Carducci readied himself for trivial—or, worse, weighty—conversation with one of his peers, for which tonight he had no desire.

Valencia sat on a tall bench alongside a greasy chopping block. The top of the block supported a half-empty decanter of red wine and a glass. And the woman was sniffling and quietly weeping into her drink!

Without a thought, Carducci was by her side, daring to place a brotherly arm around her shoulder. He imagined he could feel her warm brown skin burning right through her usual fleecy attire.

"Valencia, what is wrong?"

The woman drew the back of her un-braceleted wrist inelgantly under her drippy nose, but the coarse gesture merely endeared her more deeply to Carducci. "Oh, it is nothing, really. Just that big jerk Sly. He promised me this would be a vacation for us. But instead, he is so wrapped up in this martial scheme of his that he has no time for me. Ha, there is the real joke. All the time in the world, and none for me!"

Valencia picked up her glass and drained it. "Here, have a drink with me."

Carducci willingly obliged. Sipping the wine gave him the courage to speak his heart. "Valencia, my queen—how could any man who was lucky enough to possess your affections possibly disdain to spend all his time with you?"

"Oh, you're so sweet, Josh."

Valencia leaned across the block and planted her lips firmly upon Carducci's. He came close to swooning. When she had broken the contact, he spontaneously declaimed some repurposed lines from his "Dante."

"She, across a shore obscure with crowds of visions and of shades, opened for me the Gate of the Infinite. With bashful lips I will talk to her so sweetly, I will enter all the chambers of her heart."

Valencia leaped up then, hurled herself on Carducci, and they tumbled and thumped to the stone floor, Carducci on his back and Valencia astride him.

Shucked clothing began to fly. Valencia's intimate apparel guarding her magnificent bosom resembled no chemise or corset that Carducci had ever seen. He was momentarily stymied. Valencia brought her own hands up from funbling at Carducci's pants to help him disrobe her. His hand brushed her magical bracelet, and his erotic fever shockingly dissipated for a moment, as he recalled Enceladus's wishes. Without any conscious intention, Carducci's fingers impulsively sought the evident catch that secured the bracelet, and undid it.

In the next instant, the bracelet vanished.

And Enceladus materialized.

But this was not the hangdog supplicant who had braced Carducci in the Piazza dei Miracoli. Rather, it was a figure clad in strange clothing and fully as puissant as Silenus. And this version of Enceladus wore a magical bracelet too.

"My thanks, Carducci! Once undone, the talisman of time was forever mine!"

Valencia scrambled to her feet. "Sly, come quick!"

Silenus manifested instantly in the kitchen. "So, Mister Chrono Po-po finally shows up!"

"Come along quietly, Sly. It's all over."

"Not by a long shot!"

Carducci too had found his footing. And now he witnessed the impossible.

A second Silenus appeared. Then a third and a fourth.

This duplication was met with an equal manifestation by Enceladus! Now there were eight men facing each other.

"You shunted all the weapons away from this nexus," said one Silenus.

"But of course."

"Then I'll just break you with my hands!"

The four Silenuses hurled themselves on the four Enceladuses.

Carducci backed up until he hit a wall. He found Valencia there as well.

As they watched the men grapple, other figures appeared. More and more instances of each man, until there was a full riot in the kitchen, dozens of figures tussling violently, bodies flying through the air, raw shouts of pain and outrage, a storm of fists and flying feet.

The fight seemed to last forever, but must have taken only three minutes or so. Bodies began to wink out of existence in pairs of opponents, until finally only one Silenus and one Enceladus remained, each one bruised and bleeding.

And the latter had the former securely bound, a conquered monarch in chains, Lucifer defeated and on the verge of exile.

Valencia slumped. "Well, that's all she wrote, I guess." She marched wearily over to Enceladus.

"That's fine, my dear. Step within the transport radius. All right, off we go."

But before any final vanishing, Enceladus turned to Carducci.

"When it all changes, try to remember what I promised you, Giosuè. It will all come true. You and your art will triumph. Your era has been reset. When I leave, all will be as if Silenus never was. Farewell!"

In the microsecond or two before he was to awaken in the White Tower, ready for another day of tedious teaching, Carducci experienced a vivid, numinous vision of his whole destiny. He would marry Elvira Menicucci, continue as an educator for some time, publish his poems, live through the Risorgiomento, have love affairs, receive laurels, become a Senator—and die, leaving behind whatever legacy posterity chose to award him. And all of these events and emotions, despite being experienced freshly, would still in some subconscious, subliminal way, derive piquancy from this unnatural interval with Silenus, that infernal monarch of the feast.

Surely he would be able to derive a poem from that!

FROM THE CASEBOOK OF MASTER WIGGINS, ESQ.

Utter the song, O my soul! the flight and return of Mohammed,
Prophet and priest, who scattered abroad both evil and blessing,
Huge wasteful empires founded and hallowed slow persecution,
Soul-withering, but crushed the blasphemous rites of the Pagan
And idolatrous Christians.

—Samuel Taylor Coleridge

It features that I am just tuppeny over nancy in love with Miss Vivianne Pye. I estimate that you would be too, if you could only see her the oncet, and then share her exquisite company at length, as I have done, while we both labored, off and on, at the behest of the Great Detective, aiding him in one case or another as his wiles and needs demanded.

First off, Miss Vivianne Pye is, quite impressively, all of five and half feet in stature, uncommon tall for a girl of fifteen years of age. She pretty much resembles a buggy-whip in point of slimness—thanks in part to the stern and intermittent diet afforded those of us who happen to be without reliable room and board, denizens of street or alley or church basement—although of late I have thought to notice certain mature curves blossoming beneath her usual colorful layered habiliments that consist of this and that castoff garment cadged from stalls and tips. (How she keeps these articles so clean and fresh while I and the rest of the Baker Street Irregulars tend to resemble ambulatory hampers of table linens after a feast at the Tankerville Club is a point of science far beyond me!) Her flaxen hair and dark flashing eyes are just as alluring as the rest of her perfectly assembled phiz. And I do not agree with her that her smile is spoiled by the smallish knurled scar that runs upward from the left juncture of her lips, a souvenir of her brave and daring exploits during one of Mr. Holmes's more challenging assignments.

When you add to this bodily sum her sharp wits and eagerness to please those whom she privileges with her friendship, and her easy laugh and sprightly manner, then you will confess, I daresay, that Miss Vivianne Pye is a charming package indeed.

I have more than once pledged to her my full troth and fealty, declaiming myself her total slave and lackey. But she only chooses to laugh in a not unkindly fashion and respond thus: "Oh, dear Wiggins, you are just thirteen years old and a mere child yet. It's not that I disdain or underestimate your affections and character, but it's just that you are far from mature enough to understand what such an avowal must mean."

"Thirteen-and-a-half!" I answer back. "Old enough by far to know what love is! And ain't I had far more educational experiences than the average lad of my years?"

But all my protestations are of no use. Miss Vivianne Pye merely says, "Save such declarations for when you are a bit older, Wiggins, and then I might consider them. Meanwhile, let us remain simply comrades and friends as we have long and staunchly conspired to maintain these several years."

What can I do then but sigh and make cow-eyes at her and go about my business?

But little did I wot that before I turned fourteen or Miss Vivianne Pye passed sixteen, both of us would be working with Mister Holmes as spies in the covert London establishment of that notorious heathen, Muhammad Ahmad bin Abd Allah, Mahdi of the Sudan, in danger of our lives, all to ferret out the lineaments of a plot that threatened to plunge London into chaos, and produce carnage such as this tired old city had never before seen.

* * * *

That intemperately warm June day in the year of our Lord 1882 when the whole affair began found me hanging about on the London Docks near the Ratcliffe Highway, seeking honest work if possible, and the main chance for some stomach-filling petty larceny if no sanctioned labors obtained. As has been oft averred of the Docks, they was always "one of the few places in the metropolis where men can get employment without either character or recommendation," and at least the latter part of that capsule description certainly applied to me. (I does like to think that despite outward appearances and lack of social ranking, my personal character is as noble as that of any highborn whelp.)

I had already blagged some potted meat from a grocer's and enjoyed a greasy unheated breakfast, the hem of my shirt serving as my napery, so I was replete and ready to perform any task, however lowly, that I might be assigned. So I began to amble the docks.

The forest of masts all about me, the tall chimneys vomiting clouds of black smoke, and the many-colored flags flying in the air provided the background for what seemed utter flux and chaos.

The courts and alleys in the vicinity of the London Docks swarmed with low lodging-houses, and they had seemingly disgorged all their tenants at once. The aimless duffers ogled all the maritime goods in the many shops: bright brass sextants, chronometers and huge mariner's compasses, with their cards trembling with the motion of the cabs and wagons passing in the street. At the sail makers, the show windows were stowed with ropes and lines smelling of tar. The corners of the streets featured mostly slopsellers, their windows particolored with bright red and blue flannel shirts, the doors nearly blocked up with hammocks and well-oiled norwesters, canvas trousers, and rough pilot coats. A satin-weskitted mate, accompanied by a black sailor with his large fur cap, fingered the weave of a dreadnought coat. A Customs-house officer in his brass-buttoned jacket was interrogating a sailor whose face was streaked with permanent indigo lines, a big green parroquete sitting atop his shoulder.

As I myself strolled along the noisy quay, I smelled tobacco and rum, then the stench of hides and huge bins of horns, and a bit further along, coffee and spice.

I intruded myself earnestly amongst several parties busy unloading cargo, but got no assignments whatsoever, not even to run an errand to the grog shop. So I perched myself high atop a crate of copper ore whence I could command a good vantage, and sought to amuse myself at the expense of the passing parade.

After a time, my eye was caught by a small altercation in progress.

A gaggle of exotically be-robed Mussulmen was hastening down the docks, plainly intent on getting somewheres quickly, and averse to any public displays. The several leaders of the group, their faces concealed beneath silken wraps that nearly met the lower edges of their turbans, leaving just slits for their midnight eyes, could be easily distinguished by a certain snootiness and lack of burdens. Their servants, weighed down with trunks and bundles and more plainly attired, followed behind. Bringing up the rear were what I took to be several heavily swaddled womenfolk, though no feminine distinctions showed forth to confirm my suspicions. And last, not quite of the party, came a bare-chested, mahogany-skinned beggar type, a dirty loincloth his only concession to dignity.

This obsequious, barefooted, crook-backed beggar, I could see, was trying his mightiest to ingratiate himself with the Mussulmen. Crouching half-doubled up, he scampered all around them like a pesky kid annoying a flock of elder goats.

"But oh, my honorable emirs and mullahs," the beggar whined in his accented English, "I can be of so much service to you! You are new to these foreign shores, and I am not! I know all the ways and wiles of this wicked city! Take me into your service, and I will prove infinitely valuable as advisor and guide!"

The leaders of the party ignored him for several yards, until finally one of them could stand his importunings no longer. The tall, fiery-eyed, beak-nosed fellow whirled upon the beggar and declaimed in harsh tones, "Begone, you wretch! We need no corrupt apostates who have been contaminated by life in the Dar al-Harab in our midst!"

"But, oh, my exalted mawlawi, just give me a chance to be of service—"

The angry Mussulman peeled off a heavy cord that belted his robe and began to lash the beggar. "Away with you! Begone!"

Whimpering and cringing under the blows, the hapless mendicant scuttled to the relative safety of the niche between my crate and the adjacent one, and the party of foreigners hastened away.

I peered down over the edge of my perch, expecting to see the chastised mumper muttering and soothing his sores.

So imagine my surprise when I confronted a pair of highly intelligent and somehow familiar eyes looking up at me, accompanied by an ironic grin that seemed out of place on that bronze phiz.

"Hello, Wiggins," said the beggar, in a commanding voice completely distinct from his prior whinging tones.

I must have goggled silently like a virgin dollymop confronted with her first client's exposed willy. It was only the resonant laughter from the beggar—who had now straightened up to a height utterly incompatible with his former distorted stature—that loosed my frozen tongue.

"Why, curse my soul, if it ain't Mister Holmes!"

"No need so cavalierly to seek damnation, Master Wiggins. And not so loud, if you please. I know my prey has passed out of earshot, but I still don't care to advertise my presence so broadly." Holmes pulled a rag from his loincloth and began to rub the dye from his hands and arms. "I need to restore my civilized appearance, Wiggins, a process that should take me no more than thirty minutes at most. Add in some transit time—well, what say you swing round to my lodgings in an hour or so, to learn of a new assignment?"

"Yes, sir!" I was already anticipating the generous emoluments that might be forthcoming, especially if I could aid Holmes in a substantial fashion. I could quit sleeping rough for a week or two, and eat rabbit stew and fancy cakes instead of air pie.

I jumped down from the crate, and was halted by Holmes's oddly contrary white hand on my arm. He looked suddenly sober and dire.

"Oh, and Wiggins—please round up Miss Vivianne Pye and bring her with you."

I hastened off, for locating Vivianne would take me some little time, and I did not want to keep Holmes waiting.

I found my heart's desire in Borough Market, where I had suspicioned she might be. Last heard from, Vivianne had been desirous of securing employment with Uncle Ducky, who operated several carts what offered hot sheep's trotters at the market. Uncle Ducky weren't no true kin to Vivianne, but merely a bloat-bellied, bewhiskered, cozening and self-serving goat of a businessman who liked to get a day's labor for half-a-day's wages.

"Vivianne, my beauty, 'tis I, bold Wiggins, your knight errant, with news of adventure and glory to share!"

Vivianne finished passing over a hot sloppy trotter out of the steaming pot to a beshawled and harried mother burdened down with three snotty brats and a trug full of leeks. Pocketing coins in her smeared apron, my love looked down her pert and pretty nose at me.

"Knight errant! I like that! If you really had my welfare to heart, you'd have spared me the tender offices of Uncle Ducky and me set up in some nicer job than doling out mutton."

"You know I've tried my best, Vivianne, but plum jobs don't drop into the laps of such Job's Turkeys as us the same easy way they do for Eton boys. But listen to this! I do have some work lined up, and it's for the Great Detective hisself!"

This detail caught Vivianne's fancy, for she was, I knew, half-besotted with the elegance and savory fare and awesome brainworks of the Great Detective.

"Did he ask for me personal like?"

"Indeed!"

Vivianne hastily stripped off her apron and, putting her fingers twixt her lips, gave a piercing whistle. Before too long, a lad I recognized as little Jemmy Tingle showed up.

"Jemmy, take over for me for the rest of the day, won't you. That's a love!"

My jealousy at this term of endearment flared up, but I tamped it down manfully. The day I regarded Jemmy Tingle as my rival was the day I would qualify as a gulpy mug.

Taking Vivianne by her costermonger-clammy hand—and astonished that she allowed such intimacy—I trotted us crosstown to the ream flash lodgings of Mister Sherlock Holmes, 221B Baker Street.

We was let in smartly and without quibble by the affable Mrs. Hudson, who howsomever could not restrain from sniffing in muted disgust at our mutual pong. I was so unchivalrous, at least in my own thoughts, as to attribute to bulk of that offensive odor to Vivianne's mutton scent, rather than to my own unwashed condition.

Up in Holmes's curious and overstuffed study, we found the Great Detective, restored to his conventional appearance and tailoring, ensconced in a high-backed chair, working thoughtfully at his pipe. His comrade in crime-fighting, Doctor Watson, had half his buttocks resting on a desk corner, opposite leg extended, and was playing with a phial containing some almost-colorless liquid, tipping it back and forth to watch it slosh about like a child with a seashell at the beach.

"Ah, Wiggins," said Holmes with true affection, I thought. "And Miss Vivianne Pye. Welcome, welcome, please take your seats."

Vivianne gathered her dirty skirts like a duchess and plumped herself onto a low cushioned stool beside Holmes, while I dropped to the carpet at her feet, like a true knight at his lady's beck and call.

Holmes regarded us with a sober eye that couldn't help but transmit a sense of ominous importance to what he was about to say. But his words, when they came, were in the form of a surprising question.

"My young friends, how much do you love your country?"

To be honest, I had never given much thought to matters of patriotism, being generally too busy trying to keep my carcass yoked to my soul to consider flummut threats against the nation and my proper yeoman's response. But upon a moment's reflection, I said, "Well, Mister Holmes, not having had no experience of living abroad, I still feel confident in saying that Old Blighty, for all her obvious faults, strikes me as a glorious abode and well worth protecting. I'd have to rank my loyalties high, when push came to shove."

Vivianne nodded in agreement. "Wiggins has my own thoughts down pat, Mister Holmes."

"Good, good, very good. Because the assignment I have in mind for you, while extremely dangerous, is dedicated to preserving our nation—this city—from a calamity of unprecedented magnitude."

"Does it revolve around that sheik what you was trying to inveigle earlier?"

"Yes, Wiggins. Allow me to explain. That 'sheik' as you dub him is none other than Muhammad Ahmad bin Abd Allah, the Mahdi of the Sudan."

"The bugger what's staging a prater's revolt and harassing our own General Gordon around Khartoum?"

"None other."

"What's he doing here then?"

"The Mahdi has entered the country surreptitiously, for purposes I have yet to discern. But his motives and objectives cannot be of a nature beneficial to the Empire. He would not leave his prized rebellion to the care of even his three favorite deputies unless he thought he could strike a dreadful blow against us on our own hallowed ground, and thus advance his cause. I was trying to insinuate myself into his household, in order to monitor his schemes. But as you saw, Wiggins, I was unsuccessful. Yet inserting a spy into the Mahdi's establishment is still the only way we can possibly obtain information about his plans before he can bring them to fruition. Their cabal is too close-mouthed and tightly interlaced to betray themselves to outside observers."

I leaped to my feet and struck a heroic posture that I was sure would impress Vivianne. "I sees exactly where you're a-driving to, Mister Holmes! Well, paint me up like a walnut, and I will get myself hired by the Mahdi as a dogsbody. Just teach me some of that Arab lingo, and I'll be ready!"

Mister Holmes patted me on the shoulder in an avuncular manner that I felt was somewhat unbefitting of my valor. "I applaud your courage and willingness, Wiggins. But I have other tasks in mind for you. The person I would like to plant in the Mahdi's establishment is none other than Miss Pye."

"And where would she fit amongst those dangerous heathen rogues?"

"I intend to sell her to the Mahdi as a white slave and she will go straight into his harem."

Before I knew what I was doing, I had hurled myself on Holmes with fists a-flailing. But prior to me landing so much as one blow, he had me immobilized by some devilish arts and pinned upside down in the chair he had vacated with impossible quickness, my face scrooged into the upholstery.

"Wiggins! Calm down now! Do you seriously think I would offer such a plan without features for the protection of Miss Pye's virtue?"

The blood rushing to my topsy-turvy head seemed to restore my trust in Holmes, and I was able to make my surrender known around a mouthful of horsehair fabric, and thus I was released.

"Miss Pye, I take it that you are conversant with the facts of life, with regards to male desires."

Vivianne had the grace to blush a bit. "I've had a fair number of ungentlemanly hands questing up my skirts, Mister Holmes, without losing my honor entire. And you cannot live in such gutter-dwelling circumstances as Wiggins and I do without seeing human nature—and the human body—at its most unadorned and flagrant."

"So I assumed. Well, I am fairly confident that the indignities you would experience in the Mahdi's harem would amount to little more than you have already been subjected to in the course of daily living. And the reason for that guarantee lies with Doctor Watson."

Watson got up off the desk and flourished the phial of liquid before us. "This, my children, is hyoscine hydrobromide, a preparation of *Hyoscyamus niger,* or the common henbane. It has what is dubbed an anaphrodisiac effect when administered in the proper doses. And it is our intention to make sure the Mahdi's entire household is dosed properly. Holmes and I have infiltrated the victualer whom the Mahdi has hired to supply his crew. Wishing to remain hidden, the foreigners are relying entirely on this catered source of foodstuffs, rather than go shopping themselves in the market and attract unwanted attention."

"So you see," Holmes said, "the Mahdi and his men will be physically unable to steal Miss Pye's maidenhood from her, although they might yet indulge in some casual and lackadaisical groping. But their natural Oriental impulses to recline amongst and confide in the inhabitants of the harem at day's end will remain—as will the gossip's grapevine among the women. And occupying the traditional subservient and slighted role of her sex in a Mussulman's entourage, Miss Pye can employ her sharp nose and wits to ferret out any preparations that will alert us to the nature of the plot to harm London."

I looked questioningly at Vivianne and she returned my silent interrogative with the same bold and even excited gaze that Boadicea probably showed just prior to battle.

"I'll do it, Mister Holmes! For England—and for you!"

"And what's to be my role again?" I queried.

"You, Wiggins, are going to perform some nightly aerial acrobatics!"

* * * *

The Kensington High Road's a fair Bedlam, a bewildering, relentless, round-the-clock parade of every type of dray, carriage, rider, goods-trundler, pedestrian, and mock-crippled and creeping leg and lurker out to slit a weasand. The tightly packed buildings, adorned with as many hortatory signs as there's pigeons on a split sack of spilled oats, channel the flow like the walls of some stone canyon. Colorful flags on ropes extend high above the crowd, from one side of the street to t'other. Under the shade of scattered street trees can be found clots of gypsies, Haymarket Hectors and their girls. The random strolling hard-nosed Blue Bottle sees to it that disturbances and disorder are kept to a minimum, and that the wrong people—or rather, the right people, the toffs—don't get excessively gulled and abused.

Off the High Road at intervals are plenty of rookeries, cheap dwelling places crammed with stinking humanity of every race, age and condition, in all their forms of slovenly sloth, quiet dignity and desperate dreams. I often thought my own doorway lodgings were preferable to such noisome nests.

Market Court was one such, neither the most despicable nor the nicest. Naught but a congeries of scabbed-together, ill-sorted, shambling structures rearing at their highest some three stories tall and enclosing a litter-strewn muddy courtyard. But the cul-de-sac did feature the distinct advantage of strictly limited and controlled ingress and egress. Thus it suited the fortress mentality of Muhammad Ahmad bin Abd Allah, the Mahdi of the Sudan, and his crew of presumably cut-throat Mussulmen, who had taken over the establishment entire, permitting no one in save the victualer bearing his thankfully tainted, ballocks-blocking provender.

How I despaired of Miss Vivianne Pye's fortunes amidst such a den of blackguards! I awaited eagerly the moment when she might be released from her durance vile, as Mister Holmes swept in with a squad of crushers, bearing enough evidence garnered by his crack Irregulars to put paid to these plotters.

But the only trouble was, after two weeks of Vivianne scraping up every tidbit of information she could rumble, we were no closer to understanding the machinations of these Mussulmen than on the day of their arrival.

Perhaps tonight, I thought, as I prepared myself for my bold scarpering across sodden, slippery and shabby shingles, would be the night we gained the prize. Vivianne and I, of course, might not even recognize that we had attained our sufficiency of information. Only the mighty master mind of

Mister Holmes, piecing together every scrap we relayed to him with that patented pattern-making big brain of his, would turn the key in this riddle.

At the edge of the nameless rookery some dozen yards away from Market Court, as London's smoky twilight descended fully upon us like a fat sow squishing her brood, I paused with my comrades, several of the regular Irregulars, namely Trosper, Pupshaw and Jernigan.

"You understand, men, what I need you to do, should I signal?"

Jernigan scratched a poxy blemish on his upper lip. "Indeed, Wiggins, indeed! Same as what we stood ready to do during your past excursions. You may rely completely on our capacity to wake the dead."

"All right, then, I'm off to climb Rapunzel's tower, so to speak."

After making sure the length of stout rope coiled around my waist was secured, I dashed toward the nearest drain pipe, leapt halfway up its lower reaches, and began to haul myself up to the rookery roof.

Once atop that tilting, daunting, many-leveled surface, I kept hunched so as not to arouse outcries from any nosy parkers below, and raced like a roach toward my appointed date.

When I began this mission two weeks ago, my course across these rooftops, where the geography bore no visible relation to the streets below, had proved a mite perplexing. But now the path to the roof's edge above the courtyard window of the harem where Vivianne was immured was second-nature to my hands and feet. I would have made a prime snakesman to any snoozer, in and out with the chink and couter before any sleeping victim could even mumble and turn over.

At my destination, I unlooped the rope and secured one end around a sturdy chimbly. Then, holding the free end ready, I awaited Vivianne's whistle, a muted version of what she was wont to use to summon her replacement when in Uncle Ducky's employ.

After several hours or anticipatory crouching, during which I nearly dozed off, the signal came, and I lowered myself away.

My shoes found familiar purchase on a rim formed by some irregular bricks, and then I was feasting my lamps on my beloved.

Vivianne had been tarted up in silks and chiffons, scrubbed pink and painted, her hair coiled up like some hot cross bun, but she was still my tough boulevard princess.

"My little bird, how I've missed you!" I whispered. "Give us a kiss!"

Vivianne's shadowed face showed her a nervous nellie, as was only natural under the fraught circumstances, but I could tell that underneath her apprehension she had to be pleased at my bold love-making amidst such a parlous climate.

"Hold off there, Romeo! Let me tell you my news first." She looked back over her shoulder, to make sure that her fellow concubines in the next room were still fast asleep. "Nasif let it slip—"

My sudden emotions got the better of me, and I interrupted her, mayhaps a bit too loudly. "That damn sand-blackamoor! It galls me to picture you and him lying a-bed, with him pressing his flaccid todger into your virgin flanks!"

Astonishingly, Vivianne defended the rogue. "Nasif is the nicest one here. He's just a lad, after all, hardly older than us. He's very gentle and innocent, and I think he's been seduced by the charm and glamour of the Mahdi and his cause. But he has his doubts about what they call *jihad*, and that's why he confides in me." She paused. "And his willy, while not able to stand to attention, thanks to Doctor Watson's dosing, seems otherwise quite respectable."

I growled then. But, having satisfactorily jabbed my jealousy bone, Vivianne ignored me and continued. "You recall the shipment of chemicals that arrived here last week? Well, they have been fussing with them continuously in the basement, raising some horrid stinks. And now they have received an order of glass carboys. I saw the dealer's name stenciled on the crates. Geronimus Aspenshade and Sons. Perhaps Mister Holmes can learn more from that source."

I swung one-handed from my rope, leaning in to clasp my little bird with my free arm. I stole a snog, to which she assented not utterly unwillingly. Yet I could not help but wonder if she would have relished the precious affection from any of the familiar Irregulars under such dire and isolated conditions as obtained for a spy in the harem, or did she regard me as her special beau?

"This is big news, Vivianne, and I'd better hasten to Mister Holmes." I began to squirrel up the rope.

"Oh, one more thing," Vivianne called softly. "I happened to glimpse the Mahdi himself studying a map. From the snatch I got as he pinched my bum and shooed me away, I took it to be a plan of the Tube stations."

"Right-o!"

Partway up the rope, a hand encircled my ankle. Ah, sweet Vivianne could not bear to part yet!

But the sudden savage yank on my personal limb revealed that I was mistaken.

Looking down, I saw an angry bearded Arab face assigned to the hoary meat hook glommed onto my fetlock. Vivianne meanwhile had been pinioned by another man who was muffling her attempted screams of warning.

I loudly gave out with the Irregulars's secret hoot.

"Barney up, men, barney up!"

Immediately from the High Street side of the rookery came an enormous ruckus, bellowings and clatterings and bangings. A hail of stones flew over the roof into the courtyard.

The unexpected riot had its intended effect, momentarily disconcerting my assailant. I kicked wildly, and freed myself.

I hesitated only a moment, fantasizing I could plunge into the harem, rescue Vivianne and flee together. But instantly my common sense dissuaded me.

If I attempted a rescue and were captured, Mister Holmes would never learn the vital information I carried.

So, with my heart breaking at images of Vivianne's sordid plight, I monkeyed up my lifeline, across the rooftops, and bunked straight to Mister Holmes.

* * * *

The cheery and trig establishment of Geronimus Aspenshade and Sons, hard by the smoky, ashy Falcon Glassworks on the banks of the Thames, appeared to be on the up-and-up, no secret headquarters of some international cabal of assassins. Nonetheless, as I entered the Ali Baba trove of sparkling pendants, multicolored goblets and faceted punch bowls behind Mister Holmes, I maintained a vigilant manner. Last night's fray had set my nerves on edge, and I had no wish for us to be ambushed here in this seemingly staid and frowsty shop.

Holmes had been awake and dressed at 221B when I arrived around midnight. Did that superhuman fellow never sleep, like lesser men? As I poured out all my news to him in a frantic blurt, his calm and pointed questions had the effect of calming me down summat.

At last I concluded with my major worry. "But Mister Holmes, whatever will happen to my poor Vivianne?"

"Wiggins, my boy, I firmly believe that the child will be fine. You maintain that your conversation betraying your true interests was not overheard. So the Mahdi's men have no notion that you were conducting a prearranged confab centered on their machinations. Instead, they no doubt took you for a typically lusty local swain out to despoil their harem. Vivianne will doubtlessly suffer some kind of mild corporal punishment for her transgressions—a few strokes of the switch perhaps. But this presumed transgressive behavior on her part is well-known among the inmates of the harem, and regarded as within the normal limits of turpitude. No, what we need to focus on is the game afoot. If only Watson could more speedily rustle up a list of those chemicals sold to the Mahdi. It's taking him forever to find their supplier. Ah, well, patience is a virtue we must always cultivate. And in the morning we can investigate the glassblower's shop whose identity you and Miss Pye have so ingeniously ascertained."

I hardly slept that night, being both too worried over some half-horrid, half-beguiling fantasies of Vivianne's tender bum receiving its lashes, and too unused to the luxury of resting on Mister Holmes's couch, swaddled in real woolen blankets thoughtfully supplied by a drowsily accomodating Mrs. Hudson.

We approached the counter now where Geronimus Aspenshade awaited us with the eagerness of any merchant anticipating a sale. Portly and balding and brawny, Aspenshade sported bare hairy arms that revealed dozens of coin-sized bare patches, scars from small healed burns encountered in his molten trade.

Holmes introduced himself, finding that his name met with no small recognition and respect. He stated his interests, and Aspenshade cogitated a moment before replying.

"Ah, yes, a most curious order. Generally, brewers and chemists take my carboys in the standard five-gallon size. Them's my best sellers by far. But these chaps wanted relatively tiny one-gallon thingamabobs. And they even specified the grade of glass."

"Extra strong?" ventured Holmes.

"Just the opposite! These had to be fashioned from stuff that was less strong than mere window glass! First off, they could hardly hold much liquid, and then, they were bound to shatter at the slightest shock! Whatever use could they have in mind? I had to pack the buggers in extra sawdust just to ship them safely! But they paid good money, and the customer knows best, I always says."

"Thank you for your help, Mister Aspenshade."

Outside, Holmes spoke reflectively, as if I weren't present. "Easy to shatter, only a gallon... It all depends on that list of chemicals! Come, Wiggins, we will haunt Doctor Watson's office till he returns."

But when we arrived at Watson's practice, he was already there.

"Here's the list, Holmes. They were deucedly clever, going far afield for these substances. Their supply house was all the way in West Ham. But I tracked them down at last. Potassium acetate, arsenic trioxide—"

Holmes stiffened and trembled like a hound. "My god, Watson! They are making cacodyl, or Cadet's fuming liquid! I see it all now. Quickly, there is not a moment to lose!"

* * * *

Even after studying for many minutes this strange army assembled in a back room at King's Cross station, I was having the demndest time convincng myself I wasn't inhabiting some queer story by that Frenchy fable-flogger, Mister Jules Verne. Maybe I had really been transported to the Moon, and was witnessing an army of Moon Men.

Three dozen of London's toughest rozzers had been rounded up by Mister Holmes on short notice and assembled here at King's Cross. Then, under the supervision of Doctor Watson, they had all been outfitted with the oddest kind of masks. Watson had explained to Holmes the nature of this scientific equipage—rubber and metal and glass getups with a canister perched smack dab in the middle of their lower faces—and as best I recall the Doctor had dubbed them "Barton's respirators," and said the canisters held "lime, glycerin-soaked cotton wool and charcoal."

Holmes studied the apparatus intently and said, "They are unproven against the cacodyl, but we will have to hope for the best."

Now the boss copper, a beefy redhead I knew from previous tussles named Bert Smudge, lifted his mask and addressed Mister Holmes.

"I sure hope you've accurately deduced the time and place for this supposed assault, detective. It would look awfully bad for us if those murdering heathens struck elsewhere while we were congregated here, or if they attacked on some other day when we had been lulled into complacency."

"No, Smudge, this is the place, and the day is now. King's Cross is the busiest station on the Circle Line, and we have to assume our murderous opponents are desirous of inflicting maximum casualties, as warped recompense for General Gordon's campaign against them. And the date could be no other, for this is the eighth of June."

Smudge itched at his brainpan. "And what makes the eighth of June so precious?"

"It is precisely the one thousandth and two hundred and fiftieth anniversary of the death of the Prophet Muhammad."

No-wise enlightened, Smudge replied, "Well, I will have to accept your estimation of the importance of this date, Mister Holmes. Now, as to the matter of clearing out the citizens, I still feel—"

Holmes showed some small exasperation. "I have told you, Smudge, we simply can't empty the station of riders. That would alert the Mahdi's men to our presence and to our knowledge of their plans. It must appear to be business as usual here, to draw them out. We can't have them panicking and going into hiding elsewhere in the city, where we can't lay our hands on them. No, we shall have to rely on our superior forces intercepting the attackers in order to prevent harm to the innocent bystanders."

"And we can't raid the Market Court rookery because—"

Now Holmes's patience was positively exhausted. "Can't you comprehend simple strategy and tactics, Sergeant? My lord, what are they teaching you boys these days? Our plan is predicated on the simple fact that the team of attackers is already dispersed and in transit. Left at the rookery will be only the Mahdi himself, awaiting reports of his victory. We will mop him up afterwards."

I wanted to say, *But Vivianne is also at the Market Court rookery too, and needs rescuing!* But I knew that the cool and calculating mind of Mister Holmes would not give a yennap for Vivianne's fate until he had frustrated the Mahdi's plans and saved the larger number of souls.

"Now, Sergeant, if you would be so good as to emplace your men in the concealed positions I have previously denominated, we can await the incursion."

I kept close by Holmes and Watson as we took up our own blind.

Need I even say that the whole fracas transpired as the Great Detective foretold?

The Mahdi's men were deuced clever. They had doffed their native costumes of course and disguised themselves as peppermint-water sellers. But we recognized them by those unnaturally small carboys full of deadly liquid ready to explode as suffocating gas. As they trundled in their handcarts weighed down with poison, they were, one by one, instantly and quietly intercepted by the rozzers, whose alien appearance helped to disconcert, at least momentarily, the conspirators. Half of the subway riders within sight of the action never even noticed what was happening, while the other half thought they were witnessing a typical pinch of an illegal seller.

It was all bob's-your-uncle, and Doctor Watson was visibly relaxing, providing me a cue to do the same, when one lagging Arab, witnessing the apprehension of his fellows, managed to dash his carboy to the tiles, where it promptly shattered, releasing its hideous cargo.

Instantly three masked rozzers had him. Others plowed through the lethal fog to swiftly lead to safety the helpless coughing citizens caught in the edges of the miasma. One copper went down to the floor, gasping and writhing, victim of a mask that didn't quite fit, or a bad filter canister. Other crushers let loose with hand-pumped sprayers filled with a water and baking soda mixture. I caught the faintest stench of the poison from a scarf of gas wafting our way, but soon King's Cross was restored to near-normal conditions.

Coughing a bit hisself, Mister Holmes nodded in satisfaction. "And now to put paid to the Mahdi!"

If I lives to be a hundred, I will never forget that mad dash across London in the hansom cab, Holmes as intent as an eagle on his prey, Watson running calculations in his brain as to how he might improve those masks for the next time we faced such a threat—and me all a-quiver over the unknown fate of my beloved Vivianne Pye!

The Market Court rookery looked odd to me from the ground level, after viewing it from above for so many nights, and I got slightly turned around. But Holmes dashed straight for the proper entrance, and I followed close behind.

Just inside we came upon a most pathetic scene, like something from a domestic melodrama staged in a penny gaff.

Lying on the floor, bleeding from a deep gash in his shoulder, was a slim Arab youth clad in one of them white native bathrobes, now stained red. His wispy black mustache stood out more vividly due to his wound-blanched olive complexion. A long curving sword rested on the floor by his hand.

Kneeling beside him, cradling his head tenderly, her own harem outfit all besmirched, was my very own Vivianne Pye!

"Oh, Nasif, don't die! Hang on, my dear, hang on!"

"It is no use, Miss Vivianne, I am surely going soon to meet my many promised virgins, none of whom will shine as brightly as you."

Holmes brusquely interrupted this tender scene. "Miss Pye! Where is the Mahdi?!

"Nasif tried to stop him, but the Mahdi struck him down with his own sword, then dashed into the basement."

"These rookeries are threaded with tunnels," exclaimed Holmes, "but I know where he will probably debouch."

Holmes snatched up the fallen sword and raced off.

Torn between my allegiance to Vivianne and my fealty to Holmes, I chose the latter—a decision made a bit easier by the shocking infidelity of my beloved. "Nasif, my dear," my arse!

By the time I arrived on the High Street, the duel twixt West and East was on!

In the middle of a ring of shocked spectators, Holmes and the Mahdi were enveloped in a ferocious whirlwind of blades. The Mahdi's fierce face expressed utmost contempt for his opponent, while Holmes showed only a stern respect tinged with disdain for the Mahdi's cowardly means of waging war upon innocent civilians.

The fighters seemed evenly matched—until Holmes began to falter.

As I afterwards learned, he had inhaled a larger whiff of cacodyl than I back at the station, but shied from telling us, and the exposure had left him temporarily deficient in his wind.

The Mahdi struck Holmes heartily with the flat side of his blade upon his head, and Britain's champion was down!

The Mahdi dashed off, the awestruck spectators failing to intervene.

I rushed to the side of my mentor, and found him already coming round, resigned to this throw of the dice.

"He's gone, Wiggins. I intuit that he had a well-defined escape route out of the country planned well in advance. He's General Gordon's problem now. I don't give him more than a few years back home. And I doubt he or his co-religionists will try another such attack for many a year, having been defeated so soundly, thanks to the sterling efforts of you and Miss Pye."

Such praise stirred the cockles of my heart. And that warm feeling, recalled at intervals, along with the several sovereigns that Mister Holmes would later bestow on me, would do much to carry me through the rough times ahead, as Vivianne traitorously nursed the pardoned Nasif back to health, introduced him into the ways of his newly adopted nation, and then found herself tossed aside in favor of a bold Turkish tart employed as a dancer at Wilton's Music Hall in Whitechapel, who appealed more deeply to Nasif's foreign tastes.

And so, a year older, I approach that mature condition where my dream girl, the unmatched Miss Vivianne Pye, might deign to look favorably upon my earnest, Irregular suit!

LOST IN THE REWILDING

This is a tale told by splices everywhere,
when humans are not around to hear.

On the coastal edge of the Great Laurentian Rewilding, as an unofficial satellite of Pine Barrens Urbmon Number Seven—colloquially called by its residents "the Badabing"—stood a small laboratory, a plain white windowless blockhouse. The building had to be separated from the main habitation, where nearly a million people lived, due to the sometimes dangerous nature of its researches. The lab was surrounded by a moat of smart gel and various electronic, chemical, drone and silicrobe defenses and barriers.

Inside the lab one summer day could be found two chromosartors, a man and a woman. The man was named Angus Woodman and the woman was named Mapinta Damas. They were having an argument.

"You should never have crispered such a suite of genes together in the first place, Angus," said the woman. Her face showed irritation and disdain.

The man looked humbled and repentant, but not totally convinced by the woman's argument. "But I only wanted to help with the flooding on the Passaic. The overflow waters from that last superstorm wiped out all the outdoor recreational facilities around the Badabing."

"I know your intentions were good. But you created a chimera that was simply too efficient. Coypu, beaver, capybara, muskrat—plus twenty-nine percent human! What were you thinking? They didn't just dam the Passaic, they also blockaded four other rivers in the region. Practically overnight, we had a new lake that took out a million nubux worth of crops. If it weren't for the Protein Police tracking down every last member of the clade and exterminating them, the whole bioregion would have been underwater. And before we know it the cops will unravel the codes of the corpses, retrodict a signature, and bust down our door. We've got to get rid of all the evidence that we were responsible. And that includes Castor and Villette. It's off to the lysing chambers with them."

Castor and Villette, the elders of our line, our ancestors, were the first prototypes of the novel species, and still lived in the lab.

"But Mapinta, I can't just kill them! They represent so much creative tailoring, so many high hopes, and so much—well, so much love. I fear they've become like the children you and I never fabbed."

"What an insult! Those musky bumbling rodentiamorphs, sprung from my genome! That really is the final straw, Angus. I insist you get rid of those splices this instant."

"I apologize, dear. But please, let me have just one more night with them, to say a real goodbye. I promise they'll be gone in the morning."

"Oh, very well. You can stay here overnight if you really must, but I'm heading back to the Badabing. Maybe I can bolster our alibi back there somehow."

After Mapinta had departed, Angus went to the part of the lab where the splices lived.

The room-sized cage that held Castor and Villette was not uncongenial. It featured a nice lodge made of foam noodles, a trough perpetually replenished with corn, beans and mushrooms, and a bundle of nice green aspen twigs for snacking. Additionally, a media center streamed the entertainments of the Chimera Channel. But although the pair did not lack for comforts, we know that they chafed at their limited freedom and the inability to pursue their deepest instincts, which comprised dam-building, mating, lodge-wattling and the occasional pitched interfamily rumble.

Angus stood outside the cage bars, contemplating his offspring, the children of his gene-sculpting talents and his imagination. Half as big as the average human, they were bulky, bottom heavy, oily furred and big-toothed. They wore no clothes. Villette, the female, was slightly shorter and more svelte than her mate.

Seeing Angus, Castor and Villette jumped up from their pallet and hustled to the bars. Angus squatted to bring his face level with their snouts. They reached through the bars and stroked and petted his cheeks and hair. He shed some tears.

"Papa Woodman, Papa Woodman! Time for us to leave and join our kin? Please, time now, at last!"

"All your kin are dead, my little ones. Their skills and efforts were unappreciated. I am sorry to have to tell you this, but you are the only two of your kind left."

The rodentiamorphs began to snuffle and blubber. "No! Can't be! Why?"

"It's just the way of the cruel world, children. And you two will suffer a similar fate if I do not send you away. And perhaps even such a flight will not lead to your longterm survival. But we must try. First, let me remove the block on your procreative faculties."

Angus perfused them both with a shot.

"Now, get your belt packs, and I'll give you some nice things."

At the notion of receiving treats, the splices forgot their sorrows and gamboled about the cage. They eventually brought Angus their canvas strap-on pouches and he filled them with concentrated rations. "These foodstuffs will allow you to sustain yourselves for a time without having to stop and harvest twigs. You'll move along faster." Then he threaded a sheath holding a knife onto each belt.

"You know these tools. Just like the ones you eat with, but very sharp. Dangerous!"

Not frightened, the splices took out the daggers and began a crude mock-fencing and stabbing of the lodge noodles.

"All right now, that's enough playtime. Put your belts on, dears. You're going for a ride."

Outside the lab the summer's heat was modulated by the stratospheric sulfate aerosols that gave the sky an opalescent glimmer. The meadows stretching inland for some distance beyond the lab terminated several kilometers off at the edge of a forest.

Angus hustled the splices into a small two-wheeled tumblebug and then programmed its artilect driver via his smart tats. With the door still open, he regarded his proteges for one last melancholy time.

"You ride will take you about two hundred kilometers away from here. It can't be further, because I need the bug back here before Mapinta notices it was used. I've disabled its satellite tracking as well, so no one can follow. Once it stops, climb out. Then you are on your own. You must search out the Bruja Dellaselva. She's the only one who might be able to help you now."

The splices nodded sincerely. "The Bruja, the Bruja. We'll find her!"

Angus leaned into the car to hug Castor and Villette. Their coarse fur tickled his nose and made him sneeze. The splices laughed.

When he closed the door the car took off and he returned to the lab to seed a slurry of lysed cells, equivalent in kilos to the weight of the two splices, with the signature organic traces that would convince Mapinta he had melted down his own children.

* * * *

The tumblebug motored silently off, heading back to the lab, and Villette and Castor looked about them in wonder. They had never been out of the lab before in their short lifetime, but had seen several nature documentaries on the Chimera Channel, and so the environment was not utterly foreign to them. The cultivar trees, with their symmetrically positioned limbs and black high-efficiency foliage, created an atmosphere more of a cathedral than an oldschool wilderness. Low shrubs with fractal branches created an undergrowth like ranked pews, to complete the illusion. But even so, the place definitely seemed removed from civilization and from the immediate presence of humanity—hence it was scary to the pair, who had known only Angus and Mapinta as companions. All about them were strange noises, and their sensitive noses quivered to an array of odd odors while their whiskers vibrated to every pulse of air.

The splices cautiously kept their paws on the handles of their little knives as they looked around their tiny clearing for signs of a path or trail. But they found none, and soon sat down resignedly at the base of tree.

"Where do we go now?" asked Villette.

"To the Bruja. Papa Woodman told us!"

"Yes, the Bruja. But where is she?"

Castor had no answer for that. Instead he opened his pouch and took out a serving of food. "Let's eat."

"Not too much! Sore stomachs! Save most for later."

After they had finished their treat and thoughtfully buried the wrappers in the duffish soil, Villette said, "Walking anywhere is better than sitting here."

"Yes, you are right."

"Don't go back toward home though. Danger."

Castor sniffled. "Never to see Papa Woodman again."

"We have to do what he said."

"Yes, what he said."

The splices began walking, choosing to head in the same direction that the lowering sun was indicating.

Soon the general benignity of their surroundings relieved their tension and anxiety, and they began to enjoy watching the birds and insects and land crabs and small mammals go about their business. All that was lacking to provide comfort was any kind of sizable stream or lake where they could refresh themselves and possibly undertake their wonted activities.

"But maybe," said Castor thoughtfully, "even if we find water, we shouldn't stay."

"Why?"

"Too close to home yet. Home where danger comes."

"Yes, too close."

As twilight was falling they came to a new border of the forest. The land here turned to open savannah. Not wishing to be out and exposed during the night, they halted and made an unsatisfying semblance of a lodge under some bushes. There they huddled for the whole night, hardly sleeping, hugging and grooming each other, half-unsheathing their knives with every howl of predator or cry of victim or challenge of rival.

In the morning they had some food from their pouches, found a tree bearing mango pawpaws that afforded some nice juice, then set out across the grasslands, loaded down with the fruit.

After several hours they came upon a city of giant earthen mounds rearing from the prairie. Termites the size of Papa Woodman's thumb scurried in and out and around the mounds.

"They won't bother us," Castor said, with more confidence than he felt.

"Maybe they know things," Villette ventured.

"We can see," said Castor. He bravely advanced on a tower and rapped with some force on its organo-plastinated wall.

Castor's summons brought out a boil of termites. But the horde of insects did not descend the mound, instead congregating at the elevated entrance. They began to cluster and cohere and shape themselves until they had assumed the form of a blind human face. The lips made of many linked termites parted, and the voice emanating from termite throat and termite vocal cords and termite tongue came forth.

"You two are new here. Do you compete? Do you threaten? Must we strip the flesh from your bones?"

"No compete, no threaten! Just passing by. Looking for the Bruja. Bruja Dellaselva."

"Yes, of course, the witch of the woods. You might interest her. Continue west."

"West?"

"The sun moves from east to west as the day goes on."

"Oh, of course."

"Her home is beyond the Twisted Forest. But even if you reach its borders, she will know you are there, and find you."

"If we reach? Why if? Trouble? Danger?"

"The Laurentian Rewilding is an unconstrained, unmediated bioregion with apex predators in large numbers. We do not think you are at the top of the foodchain. Goodbye."

The face fell apart into scores of individual termites, and Castor and Villette realized they would learn no more.

Heading forever west, covering nearly fifty kilometers a day, the pair took three days to cross the grasslands. Each night they took turns keeping watch, for they had to get some sleep in order to maintain their energy for the long hike. Luckily they had no encounter more scary or dangerous than the one with a large many-legged snake, which chose to stalk them for several kilometers while always keeping a safe distance from their knives and whispering half-heard endearments and evil persuasions which the splices resolutely ignored.

At last they came to the margin of the Twisted Forest, and knew immediately why it was thus called. Springing from sandy soil, the forest was comprised of gnarly, fuzzy joshua trees, all as tall as ten-storey buildings. Yucca and cacti and mesquite formed the lower levels of the woods. Luckily for the newcomers, these smaller growths did not constitute an unbreachable wall, but rather permitted a kind of labyrinthine passage into the depths of the place.

"We are here," said Villette. "The Bruja will sense us."

"Maybe," said Castor, "we should go in a little deeper, so she can sense us good."

"And to get something to drink. Remember that show? Where humans drank from the spiny plants?"

"Yes, a good idea. Villette, you are so smart! I could not live without you."

"And Castor, you are so brave. You always stayed between me and the talky snake!"

During the crossing of the grasslands, the splices had derived their drinks from the mango pawpaws they had taken with them, but the amount of liquid the fruit provided had been barely sufficient.

Venturing into the maze, the splices identified what looked like the most succulent cactus, and had soon sliced into it. The liquid it provided was not particularly tasty, but did its job. While they drank, three-legged road runners and jackalopes came to share the bounty.

After wandering for a while, the splices approached a sizable jumbled rocky outcropping, where various niches and alcoves seemed to offer some welcome shade. The temperatures and sunlight were not dangerous, but merely uncongenial for such water-loving creatures.

They attained a little shallow cave just a few feet up the stony slope, and quickly fell asleep.

Castor and Villette awoke to rough handling and the sensation of ropes or vines being wound about their limbs. Opening their eyes, they found themselves at the mercy of a pack of cyanomorphs, grinning coyote-based creatures big as their victims, strutting about on two legs and using their forepaws to bind Castor and Villette. Once secured and stripped of their pouches and weapons, the splices were lifted up and the cyanomorphs trotted away with them.

The village of the dog people consisted of huts woven of yucca stalks and leaves, centered around a spring. Castor and Villette were dumped unceremoniously on the ground. Females and children rushed out of the huts to join the hunters. The children kicked the splices while the females pinched their flesh to estimate their ratio of tasty fat to bone. The coyotes soon had a large fire going in a pit from which reared the forking supports that would hold two spits. The whole tribe began to dance and howl their delight at such a fine meal.

Castor said, "A bad end, Villette. We were not smart enough."

"Be brave, Castor. We yet live."

The cynamorphs brought long branches that they threaded beneath the bonds on the splices, then lifted their victims up to bring them be suspended above the flames on the forked uprights.

Castor and Villette could feel the furnace-like heat of the fire—

And then they thumped to the ground!

Castor had landed on his back and so was able to look skywards There, descending from on high, was a human woman. But not an unaltered human woman.

She boasted huge white feathery wings with a ten-meter span. Instead of hair she sported a cap of matching plumage. She was barechested to allow her wings total freedom, but wore bright yellow leggings that left bare her feet—clawed and grippy.

The sight of her had caused the cyanomorphs to run away. But the woman also carried a gun, had such a tactic been necessary.

Crunching to a sandy landing, the woman holstered her pistol. The cyanomorphs were all hiding in their shelters. She studied Castor and Villette at leisure, then said, "Unique, utterly unique." She reached down and grabbed them by the ropes and effortlessly hoisted them off the ground. With booming wings, she and the splices climbed the sky.

It seemed a long time that they were in flight, but later, as they would recount their adventures to admiring progeny, Castor and Villette speculated that perhaps their fright and wonder just seemed to make the journey take forever. Carried with their faces downward, they were able to watch all the passing landscape and contemplate how they would perish if they were let go, or if their bonds accidentally broke.

However long the flight, they could soon see what must be their destination: atop a sizable rounded green hill was a moderately big old-fashioned building of white stone that featured three domes on its roof. It was the only structure for kilometers around. Their savior—who certainly must be the Bruja Dellaselva—aimed for the largest dome with its slot-like opening. Cupping and furling her wings to large degree, she dropped down through, landing inside with a little jolt.

"Whew! You babies did't feel like you weighed much at first. But by the end—!"

The Bruja grabbed a handy pair of shears and soon had Castor and Villette freed. The splices stood shakily and rubbed their limbs, uncertain of their status. Looking around, they saw a lab and its equipment, all very much like that of Papa Woodman.

"Welcome to my home," said their rescuer. "Used to be the Allegheny Observatory. Not sure why they left it intact when they tore the rest of Pittsburgh down, but I'm glad they did. Name's Rima, what's yours?"

"I am Castor."

"And I am Villette."

"Are you the Bruja Dellaselva?"

Rima laughed. "So I'm told." She grabbed a flask off a shelf and gulped down the contents. "Ah, that stokes the good old *Quetzalcoatlus northropi* cells! Now, maybe you'll tell me what brought you to the Coyoodle dinner table."

Taking turns, Castor and Villette conveyed their story. Rima the Bruja listened closely.

"So old Woodman made you. That crazy bastard. Well, your kind might not have found a niche in the Passaic biome, but I think I have a place for you, not far from here. The Cleveland Urbmon is in near-term danger of being swamped by a rising Lake Erie, but I suspect you guys could hold it back. Except it would help if you were even bigger. Would you let me change you? It would mean going into my oven for a while. I'd need to recode the DNA in every single one of your cells, and then rebuild you from inside out. A truly gruesome prospect, I admit. But you wouldn't feel anything. I'd decouple your mentalities and you'd live virtually for a while. It'd seem like paradise. Well, do you trust me, or not?"

Castor and Villette exchanged hopeful glances. Castor said, "We must, I think." Villette concurred. "I like you. And we have no one else."

"Splendid. Let me just fab up some megatherium code, and we're good to go!"

In a short time Castor and Villette found themselves harnessed and wired and plumbed into place inside a kind of giant thermos bottle. Rima Bruja patted their heads gently and said with confidence, "Kids, you won't feel a thing."

She shut the capsule door and it began to fill with a complicated liquid that was not pure water. Castor and Villette were not afraid. Even when totally engulfed by the substance, they found they could still breathe.

And then they were elsewhere.

They were living on the banks of a beautiful alpine lake, with many others of their kind, playing and working and enjoying the unspoiled wilderness, free of human interventions or demands. Life was good, there was so much nice food, aspen twigs aplenty, and the days seemed to stretch happily on forever—

—until they came to an end.

Castor opened his eyes. He saw the original room where they had first landed. But it seemed smaller somehow. There was darling, essential Villette, also just opening her eyes! She looked mostly the same as she ever had, yet somehow different as well.

"So, how's it feel?"

Castor and Villette looked toward Rima's voice.

The Bruja was now half their size!

"You shrank," said Castor.

Villette said, "No, Castor—we grew!"

Sure enough, the splices were now enormous, their genome hybridized with the megatherium heritage.

"You guys'll be able to hold back all the Great Lakes now. But you'd better get busy breeding. I futzed with your procreative parameters a little. Forty-five-day gestation period, kits mature at six months. Go to it!"

Castor reached out a paw and by using both hands, Rima was able to shake it. Villette did the same. Although it was a tight squeeze, they were able to wedge themselves through the door of the Allegheny Observatory. Once outside, Rima Bruja pointed them towards Cleveland.

"Go forth and multiply! And you're big enough now, so don't take any shit from anyone, human or otherwise!"

Castor and Villette rambled off down the hillside, and into their future.

And so we are here today to tell their tale.

THE WAY YOU CAME IN MAY NOT
BE THE BEST WAY OUT

The first time Sal Broome heard a Rigellian play the gnostic flute, he was ruined for all other music. His mind shattered into myriad tiny mirrored fragments, his soul melted down into a puddle of honeyed whey, and his gut suddenly hosted a whirling maelstrom that made the vortex that Arthur Gordon Pym encountered look like a bathtub drain.

The encounter happened in the infamous Rigellian ghetto, at a hidden club with no signage, no online presence, no sidewalk touts. You got there only by knowing someone who had been there before and would take you. How the first human ever arrived inside, no one could say.

Away from home on business, Broome was in the city that hosted—uneasily, with decided lack of charity and pride—the world's singular encampment of Rigellians. His job was servicing point-of-sales systems that his company—a big, blandly named conglomerate—had sold to many retailers around the nation. The job kept him on the road a lot. He had a wife back home, affectionate, pretty—Annaliese. No kids though. A state of affairs possibly due in part to his being away from home so often, possibly attibutable to a certain hesitancy of committment, both on his front and on Annaliese's. She had gone back to graduate school after a decade of unsatisfying jobs and could not envision fitting pregnancy, birth and child-rearing into her new aspirations. Broome found himself relieved, yet somewhat guilty, at this mutual lack of passion about starting a family. The procreative vacuum seemed to represent some half-concealed faultline in their marriage, some synergistic defect in their characters, a disavowal of life's potential. But he tried not to think about it much, and he and Annaliese had tacitly given up discussing the matter.

When he was home, about half of each month, days broken up by the travels, Broome was a member of a pickup jazz band. A bunch of amateur musicians who jammed for fun, no desire nor real opportunities for playing out anywhere, except maybe at a backyard barbecue. They called themselves the Brilliant Corners, after a jagged Thelonious Monk tune. Broome played the sax—had since high school.

So when the IT guy he was interfacing with at the client department store in the Rigellian-infested city said, "Hey, whadda ya say we go check out some schmoo music after work?", Broome was up for it.

But he did feel a little bad about his friend calling the aliens "schmoos." That was the moniker employed by less respectable media and the people who patronized such outlets. Indeed, the Rigellians did resemble those legendary characters from an old comic strip. Basically, although big as humans, they looked like fat-bottomed bowling pins with tiny arms and tiny feet almost invisible under their flabby skirted bottoms. Blanched-asparagus white all over. Their "facial" features, up in the narrow part of their bodies, were almost vestigial: tiny eyes, two holes to breathe through, slit of a mouth. No apparent gender distinctions nor reproductivew organs. They abjured clothing, instead favoring a belt around their tapered middle, from which they hung various possessions and instruments, talismans and identifying sigils.

Ten years ago, a single spaceship had arrived, bearing five hundred Rigellians. Of course their arrival marked a climacteric in human history, long anticipated. Alien life! Galactic civilization! We are not alone! But once the furor occasioned by their mere existence died down, their presence proved highly frustrating and—ultimately and in an utterly unpredictable and paradoxical manner—quite negligible.

The Rigellians arrived in a stolen ship. They had no idea how it worked. They happily allowed Earth's scientists to examine the craft at will, but so far the best human experts and theorists had been unable to discern how it worked either. Through their translations devices—also not of their own invention—the Rigellians presented themselves as refugees. But the exact nature of what had caused them to go into exile proved untranslatable. They could only vaguely adumbrate the power structures and controversies that had caused them to flee. No one was even quite sure that their native system was Rigel. The one clear thing they conveyed was that Earth was their chosen end of the line, and they wished to establish themselves here. They did not want charity, but hoped that in compensation for turning over their ship to the United Nations, they could be given some property and buildings to house them all, and also the other necessities of daily life, since they doubted they could integrate into Earth's economy, having no skills for sale. Since it turned out that the main sustenace of the schmoos was sugar water with a few select amino acids added, this request proved quite agreeable.

And so the Rigellians had been granted a downtrodden district of a US city, a barrio from which they seldom ventured into human venues, apparently content with their own company and enigmatic customs. And after an initial period during which sightseers from around the globe thronged the streets of Schmoo Town, human curiosity about the colorless and uninteresting visitors had died down almost to nothing.

Sal Broome himself had not thought of the schmoos in ages, even though he frequently visited their city. So he rather surprised himself when he readily agreed to accompany his pal to hear them perform whatever alien music they favored.

Schmoo Town was shabby but neat. No litter, no graffiti, no broken windows, all the streetlights working. A few humans strolled the sidewalk, but mostly the pedestrians were schmoos, ambulating with their characteristic side-to-side waddle. When Broome drew close to one, he could detect a signature scent, a combination of yeast and vanilla that was not unpleasant. The schmoos mostly ignored Broome and his pal—Steve was his name—although one or two favored the men with an expression that the boffins believed was a schmoo smile. It involved squinting and rounding the lipless mouth into an O.

Broome noted that one of the schmoos ahead of them suddenly turned off the main drag and down an alley. He was not surprised when Steve indicated that they should too.

Way at the back of the alley in the shadows was a door. Broome and his buddy followed the lone schmoo inside.

Steve whispered to Broome. "This is the scene just for tonight. The location's always changing. But because I was at a performance before, I recognized the signs of how to get here again. It's knowing which schmoos to follow. You'll be able to do it too now."

The inside of the "club" featured a number of schmoo "recliners." These were upright shaped troughs that a schmoo could nestle into and then pivot at a slant to take the weight off its base. Broome was grateful for the sight of a few conventional stools that humans could use.

The dimly lit room held about thirty or forty schmoos and four or five humans. Broome nodded with slight embarrassment to his fellows, as if to say, "I'm just here for kicks, not taking any of this seriously."

Steve said, "I'll get us a drink."

The bar, tended by a schmoo, offered the ubiquitous schmoo protein water for the Rigellians, and human sodas. While Broome sipped his Coke, he focused on the low stage at the back of the room. The platform hosted no human musical instruments nor amplification equipment, but only two large pieces of what appeared to be coral stones, lacy and contorted, at either side of the dais.

After a short while, three schmoos came onstage. Two assumed positions by the coral uprights and the third got between them.

The two schmoos at the stones began to run their hands over the rocky convolutions, theremin-style, producing wavering noises like warbling winds soughing through treetops and hinting at intelligible speech. Then the third alien brought a tapering cylinder up to its lips and began to blow.

This, Broome later learned, was the gnostic flute.

It did not emit actual sonics. Attempts to record the flute came up blank. Instead, the device broadcast visions and sensations directly into the minds of any sentients "listeners" in rhythmic pulsations that were to human music as human music is to the croaking of frogs.

Broom found himself swimming between the stars. Galaxies flowed around him and through him like living organisms. He swooped bodiless, a naked id, into and out of suns and through the molten hearts of planets. He experienced cataracts of desire, storms of hate and fear, billowy pillows of love and abandon. He became a million other types of creature, from unicellular marine life to intelligent clouds of plasma. He witnessed the Big Bang and the heat death of the universe. He dropped down below the Planck Level and expanded until he burst the boundaries of the cosmos into to another continuum. He crawled through primeval slime, and ranged among the halls of Olympus. He lived a thousand thousand lifetimes and died a thousand thousand deaths.

When he finally returned to his conventional senses, his face awash with tears, felling untimely wrenched away from his destiny, Broome saw that the flute player had exited, leaving the stage to his backup performers. Broome turned to face Steve, who was gaily tapping a hand on his knee in time to the coral warblings.

Broome managed to croak out, "Didn't you—didn't you feel any of that?"

"Oh, yeah, a nice buzz. Kinda like those videos where someone riffles the pages of a book and you get all relaxed and tingly."

Broome knew then that his soul was aligned with those of the Rigellians. Despite the indecipherability of their alien faces, he sensed that they too had been transported by the performance to the same degree he had experienced.

Broome, still wracked and confused by the aftermath, insisted on staying until the club closed down. But the gnostic flute player did not perform again that night.

When he returned home, Annaliese asked how the trip had gone. Broome started to try to tell her of what he had experienced in the club—the memories were already getting attentuated and jumbled—but could not think how to even start to convey the experience. So he just said, "Fine, fine, nothing out of the ordinary. Though I did go see the Rigellian district."

Annaliese shivered, in a response mocking or real that did not consort with Broome's own reactions. "Yuck! Those big lumps of dough! I hope you didn't let one touch you."

"Oh, no, nothing physical happened at all."

The next jam session of the Brilliant Corners found Broome playing lackadaisically, with none of his usual brio or panache, flubbing his solos and contributing nothing to the group efforts. He just couldn't resonate with the music. What had always given him infinite pleasure before now seemed juiceless and trivial. His fellow players were disappointed of course, but seemed willing to chalk it up to a temporary malaise.

But Broome knew better.

The next time the guys arranged to get together, Broome bowed out with some half-ass excuse. He quit streaming his favorite music when relaxing at home. He missed the subsequent get-together of the band as well, and the one after that. Pretty soon his friends stopped asking him to attend. He heard they found another sax man without much trouble.

The demands of work and home did not allow Broome to make another trip right away to the Rigellian barrio. He went about his routines with a feeling of absence, a dull ache inside that seemed to confrom to the shape of a Rigellian. He tried talking about this with Annaliese, but she couldn't or wouldn't understand, and he found himself unwilling to completely disburden himself of the full magnitude of the incident.

Some three months later, work called him back to the city of the Rigellians. This time he went straight to the barrio without any companions.

Circulating randomly among the aliens, he soon spotted one individual who seemed to Broome's altered eyes to have an aura or a significant wordless difference about him—movements or attitude. Perhaps among the schmoos there were connoiseurs and Philistines as well, two classes of beings.

Broome followed the schmoo to a different location than on his first visit. Sure enough, the place was rigged out as a club, fully occupied. Broome settled onto his stool, the trademark musty spice odor of the aliens filling his nostrils. He dared not hope to again experience the joys and ecstasies, the delicious terrors and awe-inspiring revelations of his first visit. Three months' separation had half convinced him that he had exaggerated the effects of the gnostic flute, manufactured some kind of hallucination for himself.

But as soon as the performance began, Broome discovered himself falling into just such a mental wonderland, more real than anything in his daily rounds. He rode the waves of melodic stimulation for what seemed an eternity.

This time when he came back blearily to the mundane world, the schmoo with the flute was just leaving the stage.

Broome rushed up and laid a hand prayerfully on the "waist" of the alien. The strange flesh felt rubbery and elastic. The creature halted in its tracks. No one, alien or human, moved to interfere.

"Stop, please. You've got to teach me to play that instrument. I can't leave without learning how. Nothing matters to me anymore except mastering that flute."

The schmoo regarded Broome with its black button eyes. Could he understand English, reply in the language? They had neede machines to translate years ago upon their arrival...

The Rigellian's voice sounded like a cat walking through a mulch of wet newspapers. "The way is long and hard even for one of my kind. Much longer, much harder for one of your kind. Several humans have tried. None have succeeded."

"I don't care. I just need to do it. More than anything else."

The schmoo stayed silent for a minute or two, then said, "Follow me."

And just like that Sal Broome chucked it all, without a care or compunction or single glance backwards. Wife, work, former passions that had once enthralled him.

The alien musician proved to be named Vod. He—or she—lived in an old human tenement that was at once both utterly familiar to Broome yet queerly exotic, given its commonplace architecture but strange furnishings. When they arrived there for the first time, after the performance, Vod indicated that Broome could occupy a corner heaped with castoff blankets and rags.

"In the morning we will begin."

Vod settled down into a recliner and closed his eyes. Broome made a nest on the hard floor and fell asleep, at once joyful yet trepidatious.

In the morning, after a breakfast of the amino-acid slurry—Broome found the stuff tasted like energy drink mixed with antifreeze; but it seemed to sustain human life too—Vod handed him his flute.

An electric sensation coursed up Broome's arm and into his skull when he touched the instrument. He knew instantly he was on the right and only path.

Then the lessons began, and all else fell away.

Annaliese came with the authorities and with Broome's employer one week into his abandonment of all human concerns. It had taken that long for her to track down her husband and convince officials to care about his sudden derangement.

Broome greeted the visitors with a pleasant but abstracted demeanor. He was unaware of his disheveled and alarmingly vagrant appearance. (When he played the flute, he did not experience the full force of its imagery, retaining enough concentration and volition to continue playing, but even the fringe blowback was hypnotic and lasting in its effects.) Annaliese cried, the others implored, but Broome convinced them he was acting under his own free agency and did not wish to go home.

When they had departed, Broome turned to Vod and said, "Let's go on."

It took eight months of practice, excruciatingly difficult lessons that occupied the entirety of Broome's waking hours, before Vod deemed him proficient enough to perform in public.

On the stage in Schmoo Town that night, flanked by the aliens manning the sonic coral, Broome felt no unease or stage fright, no doubts about his mission. He launched into his improvisations—all gnostic flute work was improvised, no prior patterns or templates laid down—and felt that he was constructing an entire universe from absolute nullity.

When he had finished, Vod said, "This is a start. But you have much yet to master."

Broome nodded humbly, and left the stage.

There were humans in attendance that evening, and they were shocked by Broome's consorting with the schmoos. Within minutes of his performance, videos had been posted, his name discovered, and his new career rendered into a viral sensation.

Reaction to Broome's alliance with and seeming subservience to the schmoos ranged from the amused to the outraged. Hundreds of professional commentators and millions of average citizens had their say. Broome was deemed an idiot, a traitor, a self-indulgent hipster, a vacuous poseur. Everyone, it seemed, had an opinion on the man and his decisions. Of course, his performances could not be recorded or judged, only experienced live by a limited number of people, and so his actions could be construed either as folly or as wisdom, however people wished, without much evidence either way.

Gawkers and fans, critics and supporters began to flock once more to Schmoo Town, as in the days of the aliens' first arrival. Broome found he could not walk the streets any longer without being mobbed by the curious and the aggrieved, subject to jests, insults and approbation. This hinderance did not matter so much, since he still spent almost all his time indoors, practicing with Vod.

But one night, when no performance was scheduled, he felt the need to clear his head by stretching his legs and breathing some fresh air. He slipped out, with a hood up to hide his face.

Three toughs caught up with him when no one was around to witness. They dragged him behidn a dumpster and beat him severely before dashing off.

Broome spent a week in the hospital—the divorce papers arrived while he was laid up—then returned to Vod's apartment. The alien said, "You will have to relearn much, because of your reconfigured lips and teeth and also the damage done to your soul gestalt."

Broome took up the flute and began to relearn.

Several years passed, and Broome's notoriety faded, as all such sensational fads do. He continued to study and to play, wanting nothing else. His gauntness, wild hair and beard lent him a hermit's look amended by his distant and abstracted gaze.

And then the second ship of aliens arrived.

This craft was much more impressive than the first, enormous and plainly warlike. It too was manned by schmoos. But unlike the first contingent, they were self-possessed and even belligerent. Their belts bristled with weapons.

They explained their mission with a global broadcast.

"People of Earth, we have arrived on the track of our living saints. They fled our empire during a shameful time of strife and inattention, when our own people turned away from the path of righteousness. But now all the sinners have been dealt with, expunged from existence, and we need to reclaim our living idols, to do them the honor they deserve. Know now that if we discover you have been welcoming to them, our gratitude will flow. But if we discover you have abused them, then you will suffer the same fate as our own kind who were apostates."

Along with some diplomacy, the reponse from humanity involved obvious and covert preparations for war. These maneuvers ceased when the Rigellians vaporized precisely one city on each continent, including the Amundsen–Scott South Pole Station in Antarctica.

A sizable landing craft descended to Schmoo Town, settled on a playing field. The emissaries emerged, and made contact with the exiles. Humanity held its collective breath.

The reunion did not take long. The apparent leader of the newcomers emerged from the huddle of aliens to address the waiting crowd of media people hastily assembled to transmit the verdict of the schmoos.

"People of Earth, your hospitality and compassion are judged insufficient. A token indifference and taunting is tantamount to an insult and assault. Therefore—"

From among the schmoos stepped Sal Broome.

He brought the gnostic flute to his lips and commenced to play.

The leader began silently to sway and rock from side to side, as did all the other schmoos. Humans keeled over everywhere within a twenty-mile radius of Broome. Broome continued to play. At last he stopped.

It took several minutes for the leader to recover. When he seemed in charge of himself once more, he did not continue his threatening speech, so there is no record of what punishment he would have inflicted. He merely started walking for the ship, leading all the other schmoos behind him.

Last in line was Sal Broome, Pied Piper in reverse, following, not leading, those he had bewitched. He walked with the limp which the beating had conferred on him, holding the flute down by his side.

The five-hundred-plus beings crammed the landing craft. It ascended, joined the mothership, and then the Rigellians departed the solar system forever.

There is a giant statue of Sal Broome on the site of each destroyed city. Almost every house has a little effigy of him standing on a shrine.

And every year there's a new hit song released that tries to replicate in human terms what people experienced when he played.

But none of those songs ever succeeds.

THE YOG-SOTHOTH POLICEMEN'S UNION

Chief Oshry deliberately kept me waiting forever outside his office, just to teach me a final lesson. Not that I was in any particular hurry to get inside and face my firing. I knew my career here with the Boston Police Department was over for good. After twenty-one years of exemplary service, starting as a rookie at nineteen, I was going to be booted out on my ass due to one screwup. Admittedly, it had been a hellaciously big screwup, but still. There would be no second chances for me. Not after shooting a Whateley.

As busy ex-fellow cops came and went in the anteroom, all of them studiously avoiding me as if I were Pickman's Model with parts falling off me, I tried to divert my gloomy thoughts from my unknown future by eye-flicking through the headlines displayed on my memtax. I had the sound to my implanted earbuds toggled off, so I could hear the Chief bellow when I was finally summoned.

Judges had just chosen the Queen of R'lyeh for 2059, a very cute amphibian gal from the undersea colony off Belém, Brazil. Runner-up had been an iridescent-scaled looker from the waters of Westerly, Rhode Island. The last section of the Big U anti-flooding barrier around Manhattan had just come online, but not soon enough to prevent the relocation inland of the drowned West Side Highway. A trade war with Yuggoth had caused the prices of Jovian helium imports to rise. The number one pop hit was currently "My Baby's Got Non-Euclidian Curves" by Eldritch and the Outsiders.

I was just starting to get into a long piece about new Yithian discoveries in the Great Sandy Waste of Australia when, through my AR scrim, I saw the Chief's door open. I instantly reverted to baseline vision and came to my feet. Solemn-faced, weighty-jowled Chief Ishry beckoned me silently inside.

The Chief's office featured a framed portrait of the Chief accepting a special award from the President of Miskatonic University for solving the theft of the Pnakotic Manuscripts from the Joshi Library. That accomplishment had brought much luster to the department—unlike the flubbed arrest for which I now had to account.

"Have a seat, Sol," said the Chief, not unkindly, and I did. He returned to his own chair behind his desk and confronted me silently for a long half minute. Then he said, "You ran the plates on that car, I know."

"Yes, but—"

"And you learned during the pursuit that it was registered to one Wexford Whateley?"

"Of course, but I—"

"And when he wouldn't stop for you, you understood that proper procedure dictated that you hand the case over to the Mythos Squad?"

"Chief, he was going one-hundred-and-twenty-miles per hour on the Mass Pike during rush hour!"

"But instead you shot out his tires with your car's smart laser cannon."

"I stopped him before he could hurt anyone!"

"Yes, true. But then when he emerged from his vehicle, the confrontation escalated to deadly levels."

"What was I supposed to do? Wexford Whateley was seven feet tall, built like a cyclopean obelisk, hopped up on Kadathian dream-dust, weighed four hundred pounds, and he would've been on me in a few seconds."

"You might have deployed a non-lethal weapon. But instead you went straight for your particle beam handgun."

"A taser wasn't going to stop him, Chief!"

"But your handgun certainly did."

"How was I to know that Whateley's unstable alien cells would react like that?"

When my deadly invisible beam struck Whateley, instead of merely puncturing him in some vital organ and crippling him and thwarting his attack, it had triggered a chain reaction in his hybrid metabolism that had caused him to explode as if he had swallowed a stick or three of dynamite. Only the fact that I was half-crouched behind my open squad car door saved me from buying the farm. My hearing had only recently normalized, and I was still picking out bits of Whateley bone splinters as they worked their way up from deep in my flesh to my epidermis.

The Chief shook his head sadly. "This is all such a shame. A fine career down the drain, just because you didn't follow procedure. You know I have no choice in the matter except to fire you. The Whateleys have too much juice in this state. It took all the persuasion I could muster to get them not to press manslaughter charges. And the official hearing weren't as hard on you as they could've been, mostly through my mediation."

Since I was going out unceremoniously, no matter what I said,, I determined to stick up for myself. "Well, you know I'm grateful, Chief. But I'd do it all over again. I don't care about how influential the Whateleys are. Wexford was a public menace, and I saved some lives by taking him down."

Chief Oshry made no reply, but I seemed to detect a certain wry and sympathetic quirking of his lips. He stared into space for a moment with a familiar air of abstraction, and I could tell he was accessing his own memtax. Then he asked me a question I had not expected.

"Where are you heading from here, Sol? You know it's going to be almost impossible for you to get another job in law enforcement, in this state or almost anywhere else."

"I realize that, damn it. And you know that being a cop is all I ever wanted to do since I was a kid growing up in Dorchester."

"What if I told you I had a position all lined up for you? It's a difficult posting. But if you take it and succeed, it could be an entry back to the good graces of the Mythos crowd."

"What is it?"

"They need a human cop up in Mi-Go Town. Think you can handle it?"

* * * *

Ten years ago, in July of 2049, when much of Antarctica had become practically ice-free for much of each year, a joint Chinese-Indonesian-Singaporean minerals-prospecting expedition chanced upon the legendary vast city of the Old Ones on the fabled plateau of Leng. But instead of encountering endless square miles of uninhabited gargantuan ruins, they found a flourishing metropolis populated by a dozen species straight out of the fiction of H. P. Lovecraft. After initial tenuous communications had been established in human languages, the expedition learned one simple fact that concealed a wealth of implications.

Every single aspect of the Mythos cycle of fiction "created"—or reported, rather—by Lovecraft and his circle of peers was true. Cthulhu and his minions existed, and the history of sentience on Earth extended back millions of years. There was, however, one important incongruity with the fiction.

None of these beings was malign or evil on a consistent racial level, although of course a spectrum of behavior among Mythos individuals existed, just as with people. Although it had taken much presentation of evidence and intentions to convince humanity of this fact, eventually the truth became accepted. These Old Ones and Dholes, Deep Ones and Spawn of Shub-Niggurath were merely other sapients, in the same manner that any as-yet-unmet Martian or ET might be. They had no designs on the sanity or sanctity of the human race. They only wished to share the planet and the universe with us.

Previously, Yog-Sothoth and his ilk had existed on a parallel plane with humanity. Leakage of their existence had been picked up by sensitives such as HPL, who turned it into literature and added the pulp motivation of malign intentions in order to propel his melodramatic plots. But now, due to some cosmic confluence—there was much talk among physicists of "newly interpenetrating branes"—the Mythos world had become overlaid on the consensus human reality, or vice versa. Suddenly, Arkham and Innsmouth manifested as real towns in my native Massachusetts, occupying actual interstitial geography, and one could have as one's neighbor a lovely family of the Tcho-Tcho tribe. The whole scenario resembled that classic British TV show I had once streamed on my memtax, about two cities inhabiting the same physical space but invisible to each other, until a certain twist of vision was embraced.

In the subsequent decade large and rapid accomodations had to be made on the parts of both humans and the Mythos citizens, and there were still rough patches aplenty in mutual relations. But overall the integration of the two realms had speedily resulted in a diverse planetary society.

And in fact the vast city on the plateau of Leng—which, due to its unpronounceable native name, had acquired among humans the nickname of "Mi-Go Town," after one of the representative neighborhood subgroups found there—had fostered a small human colony of loners, eccentrics, and bohemians; outcasts, adventurers, and the marginalized.

These formed my new constituency as the fresh cop on the Mi-Go town beat.

* * * *

The human-scaled furniture on loan to me as a perk of my official position was dwarfed by the immensity of my new quarters, three titanic, high-ceilinged, stone-walled rooms in a building composed of oddly jumbled cones, prisms and cylindrical towers that could have hosted a dozen Celtics games at once, if the space had been undivided. Biolumens pasted to the windowless ebony walls still left darkness hanging like a shroud above the ten-foot level of the chambers. This darkness was actually a feature rather than a bug, since it concealed the esoteric and jarring friezes that adorned practically ever surface in Mi-Go Town. Already I did not plan on spending much time indoors alone. I could see why this law-enforcement posting had gone begging for a taker. Under happier circumstances, I would not be here either. But I kept telling myself I was lucky to have even this job.

I tossed my sole piece of luggage onto a white Ikea couch that lent a little brightness to the interior and said, "Can I blink up the heat controls, please?"

Lilybelle Early was my designated welcoming committee of one. Brawny and no-nonsense, with short-cropped brown hair and icy blue eyes, dressed in overalls and a light denim jacket, she was a trucker who normally made the long pilgrimage from the plateau of Leng to McMurdo and back, conveying all sorts of various supplies that the human colony needed to maintain itself. I had been aware of her job before I ever arrived, thanks to watching a reality show called *Mi-Go Town Haulers*. But she was off the road now, recovering from an accident in which her truck had plowed into a drunken shoggoth sprawled insensible around a bend in the highway. Lilybelle's truck had squelched half its length into the gelatinous shoggoth before the beast awoke, and while there had been no serious damage to truck or shoggoth, the precipitous deceleration had severely wrenched Lilybelle's neck and back.

"Oh, sure," she said. "Just let me send you the codes."

She eyeflicked the privacy string to me, and I boosted my apartment's heat output. Although climate change had rendered Antarctica into a semblance of temperate conditions, the month of December, even with its perpetual sunlight, still found the atmosphere considerably more chilly than the similarly deranged, almost vernal New England December clime I had left behind.

I shrugged off my jacket and said, "Let me just hit the head and I'll be ready."

Lilybelle did not extend any insincere courtesies about me taking all the time I might need to recover from the endless flight from Boston. "Good. You should hurry. Colonel Scroggy is anxious to meet you and get you fully onboard. He's hideously understaffed on the *homo sap* side, you know. There's about ten thousand humans here, and only two human cops, you and a guy named Drew Bookstaver. He keeps trying to recruit, but the residents are more on the outlaw side of the fence. Not that most of them aren't decent folks, just not much for authority figures. Of course, the Colonel can use Mythos cops in the human neighborhoods, but there's always a certain risk of misunderstandings."

I kept up the conversation from the bathroom while splashing icy tap water on my face. "So I assume me and this Bookstaver will be partners."

Lilybelle's voice sounded a little tentative. "That I can't say. I'm not officially with the department, just your civic liaison."

I rejoined Lilybelle in the front room. "Well, whatever. I'm good with most anyone."

"I sure hope so."

Outside my building, the deep channel-like streets of Mi-Go Town, shadowed by tall walls, overarching balconies and aerial bridges, were thronged with citizens of a dozen different races. The fluting, piping, guttural sounds of alien chatter competed with the exotic scents of ancient sun-warmed stone and the effluvia of nonhuman metabolisms. I had thought Boston was a fairly cosmopolitan place, being in close proximity to Innsmouth and other habitations of Mythos types, but Mi-Go Town had my native territory beat hollow for diversity. After bumping into a big reptilian lloigor, who responded gently with a steadying paw on my shoulder, I tried to concentrate more on our path than the pedestrians.

"Don't try to memorize our route, it's impossible," said Lilybelle. "Just stick with the maps on your memtax. You can access the AR footprints if you want."

I did so and found the labeled trail to police HQ shining plain as day. After a walk of just twenty minutes—I was glad to know I lived close to the job— we arrived at the enormous labyrinthian structure that served as the precinct station house.

Lilybelle stopped at the entrance. "This is as far as I go, Sol. You've got my contact info if you need anything else." She gave a frank appraisal of my incredibly studly good looks then—such as they were—and finished by saying, "Maybe I'll catch you on your downtime. Not many new social prospects for a girl up here. So long."

I watched her go, trying to imagine sharing a romantic moment with the burly trucker. Maybe she'd look different to me after a few months in Mi-Go Town.

Inside the HQ, I found my way to Colonel Scroggy's office via the AR traces. There was no junior officer of any species on vigil outside, so I just knocked on the door tall as a barn and got an invitation to enter, voiced in a clammy, nonhuman register.

The huge room featured what I assumed was a desk manufactured from iridescent alien ceramics and shaped like a giant irregular lilypad mated with several mushroom-like stalks of different heights. A sprinkler system continually misted the contraption. Ensconced in the furniture was Colonel Scroggy, who, unless I had completely forgotten my *Handbook of Mythos Beings, Fourth Edition*, was a Moon-beast. In appearance he looked like a fishbelly-white giant blind toad with a cluster of stubby liver-colored worms in place of a mouth. In demeanor, he was the twin to Chief Oshry. A cop was a cop, no matter what outward conformation.

Colonel Scroggy diffused a scent like stagnant swamp water, not altogether unpleasant, at least to someone who had spent his whole life in the Everglades. But that someone wasn't I.

The Colonel's voice was like something produced by slapping two wet sandbags together with a Whoopie Cushion in the middle. "Patrolman Sol Duluoz, welcome to—" And here came the welter of consonants and croakings, clicks and gulped phonemes that denominated the city. "I assume you are ready to start your duties."

"Yes, sir. Insofar as running some sims could prepare me. I spent almost the whole flight here virtually inhabiting various Mi-Go Town scenarios, and I think I have at least a rudimentary sense of the city and its residents."

Colonel Scroggy brought some kind of living insect to his nest of mouth worms and crunched it. "Commendable, very commendable. But of only limited utility when encountering the multiplex reality. That is why we will be pairing you with an experienced partner."

My Moon-beast boss stroked a bulbous ceramic protrusion that lit up and produced a voice which uttered a short alien phrase.

"Send in Lee van Cleef," said Colonel Scroggy in response.

I had only a second to puzzle over this bizarre command—was there a third human, so-named, on the Mi-Go Town force?—when the office door opened to admit a Mythos being of a type utterly familiar to me from their rocky roosts in the Blue Hills south of Boston.

Until you get right up next to a Nightgaunt, you have no idea of their true dimensions. From across the room, their incredible skinniness allows you to imagine they are petite, even toy-sized. The light-sucking ebony of their glabrous hide also fools your eye. But once upon you, their enormous height adds solidity to their frame. When they unfurl their massive bat-wings and unlimber their long spade-tipped tail, they suddenly seem to command more personal space than a knot of any three humans. A featureless weighty formicidaean head like a cubic shield at the end of an impossibly thin neck is the final touch of the uncanny.

Suddenly words manifested in my brain.

You can call me Lee. My last partner gave me the moniker before she got iced by a Hound of Tindalos who was running an illegal canteen for ghouls and gnophkehs. I'll call you Sol, okay?

"Uh, sure. You can hear me all right?"

Lee van Cleef turned his blunt head, and indicated with one clawed finger a patch of differently tinted skin toward the rear of his skull.

I've got ears, sharper than yours. Just no vocal apparatus. So you can talk to me aloud, but I'll put my words in your head. Won't poke around in your thoughts otherwise, though. Against Union rules.

"Union?"

Didn't anyone tell you? You're automatically a member of the Yog-Sothoth Policemen's Union. Dues are very reasonable. And the Union delivers. The officers negotiated a ten percent raise for us just last month. Not to mention some excellent survivor's benefits for next-of-kin.

* * * *

Lee van Cleef's appreciation for his improved next-of-kin benefits, I discovered, was not baseless. The Nightgaunt had a family to support, Mama Nightgaunt and three children. I met them for supper that first night. Lee had thoughtfully rustled up a few MREs for me, since the family diet of transubstantiated celestial essences would have been most unsatisfactory to me, and possibly lethal. After the meal, during which Lee had brought me partially up to speed on department politics and recent cases, as well as various neighborhood cliques, gangs and rivalries, I played with the three pint-sized Nightgaunts. After a while, I found them almost comically cute, although days later I was still changing smart bandaids on the many inadvertent scratches their claws had laid down.

Lee and his family knew that they had plenty of reasons to worry. The mortality rate for cops in Mi-Go Town was considerably higher than what I was used to back home. Look at Lee's ex-partner, a gal named Valaida Chowk, who had been rendered a dessicated husk by the slurping probocis of a Hound of Tindalos. It wasn't that the Mythos crowd was inherently meaner or less ethical than humans. But when you had so many entities with awesome natural lethal capabilities, cherishing the grudges of many millennia among them, even simple spats could turn deadly.

This is why I asked to be paired with you, Sol. Patrolling the human community is much less dangerous.

I refrained from mentioning how I had taken out Wexford Whateley, although I was certain the whole department already knew my sins. "Yeah, but what we humans lack in tentacles, organs of hypnosis, and scalding protoplasmic ichor, we make up for with good old technology." Since cops are wont to go everywhere armed, I was able to pat the particle pistol on my hip as illustration of my point. Lee nodded in polite affirmation.

That night was the merest dipping of my toe into the complexities of Mi-Go Town. The following weeks were more my full-body baptism.

Although our main assigned beat was the rather self-contained human ghetto, our remit extended to anywhere humans could be found in Mi-Go Town, and that was pretty much everywhere. The humans who drifted or arrowed here from around the world were by inclination and necessity far from prejudiced or exclusionary. They intermingled with the Mythos crowd for business and pleasure, legal and illegal. In the most extreme cases, such alliances extended even to romantic partnerships.

One of the first calls I got via memtax was to intercede in a domestic quarrel in a district dubbed Spiderburg. As anyone might have guessed, the majority of residents there were the human-sized purple Spiders of Leng. We found one of them cowering in a corner of his living room while his female human partner hurled green soapstone five-pointed tchotchkes at him. These remnants from past eras of Old One habitation were everywhere in Mi-Go Town, as common as carved coconut monkeys in Hawaii, and most homes featured decorative shelves full of them.

"Sheila, please stop!" the spider sussurated. "I swear, I never gave Sheequonqua my sperm packet!"

Sheila continued to hurl arcane paperweights like a major league pitcher. "You're such a liar, Stanley! That bitch told me you did. And now she has a hundred spiderlings that look just like you!"

I managed to pinion Sheila, while Lee succored poor Stanley and called an ambulance.

After booking Sheila, I said to Lee, "Looks like the end of a beautiful relationship."

Not necessarily.

Sure enough, Stanley dropped the assault charges and took Sheila back, and the next thing I heard, they were in a mixed household with Sheequonqua and all her kids.

These kind of dramatic and urgent calls acclimated me fast to life in Mi-Go Town. In the space of a few weeks, with Lee van Cleef always by my side, I helped to bust up a slave ring trafficking in Gugs, giant furred beings used as brute labor in the construction trade; caught the gang responsible for robbing the Vaults of Yoh-Vombis (that mission involved an extradimensional jaunt offworld); cleared out an infestation of parasitical Shagghai insects; and stopped shipments of counterfeit and inferior Chinese brain cylinders that were cutting into the Mi-Go race's own sales of that gadget. For this last accomplishment, Lee and I were feted at a banquet given by the Mi-Go consul from Yuggoth. You've never lived until you've gotten stinking drunk on Antarean corpse wine in a hall full of pink, fungus-based crustaceans, all singing that absurd flavor-of-the-day song, "My Baby's Got Non-Euclidean Curves."

I even put down roots domestically. First, for my lonely apartment I acquired a Saturn Cat, wrinkled and hairless in puce and chartreuse, with fangs the color of bile. I named it Ulthar, and soon it awaited me each night upon my return home, eager for the gobbets of gargoyle meat I tendered.

I also took up with Lilybelle Early, who proved to be an enthusiastic albeit bone-shaking lover. Although there was no great romance or sense of destiny between us, we eventually moved our stuff in together. But because she was on the road seven days out of ten, we never got on each other's nerves or tired of each other, and the sex was always reunion-hot.

By the time six months had passed, I felt utterly at home in Mi-Go Town. I had even received citations and a promotion from Colonel Scroggy, and some good press from the *Mi-Go Town Chittering Whippoorwill*. I began to suspect that my deadly contretemps back in Boston had been the best thing for my career that ever could have happened. True, I did miss the Red Sox, fried clams, and fresh apple cider, but found adequate substitutes here.

If life and work in an antediluvian polar warren inhabited by a thousand different species could ever become routine and boring, then my life was starting to become such.

Until the day our biggest case broke.

I was awakened out of a sound sleep beside a sated and sodden Lilybelle by words forming in my brain. By now I recognized the familiar "tone" of Lee's "voice."

Sol, get dressed quick, and come on into HQ.
Someone's just murdered Cthulhu.

* * * *

The crime scene swarmed with technicians and cops and several politicos, all of them Mythos types, leaving me the lone human present. Auxiliary work lights powered by microbial fuel cells cast an actinic glare over the immemorial masonry, limning every wall niche, bas-relief and line of mortar between courses with a hallucinatory chiaroscuro vividness. A room big as Grand Central Station, the place still seemed crowded. Probably due mainly to the gargantuan stiff sprawled across most of the floor and cooling in a pool of irridescent viridian fluids.

The familiar glaucous bulk of Cthulhu—webbed and clawed extremities, scaly limbs, pot-bellied torso, vestigial wings—lay unmarred, up to the level of his neck. Above that level there was nothing to be seen save a raw column of vein- and bone- and nerve-threaded flesh, still weakly dribbling jade blood. Cthulhu had been beheaded, and his head was not present.

After entering the room with Lee van Cleef, checking in with our supervisory officers, and assessing the scene, I tried to imagine how anyone could have overcome the Big Guy and succeeded in parting him from his multi-tentacled noggin, then making off with the prize. Maybe a number of shoggoths together might have succeeded—but there was no trace here of their characteristic slime. Certainly one of Cthulhu's powerful peers might have bested him—Hastur or Juk-Shabb, say. And of course, one of the Outer Gods—Nyarlathotep or Shub-Niggurath—would have had no problem putting ol' Squid Face down. But the whereabouts of these powerful visitors from the galactic depths were monitored closely—mainly by virtual gossip rags like *Mythos Weekly* or *Unpeople* or *Vanity's Squamous Fair*—and, so far as I knew, no extraplanetary entities had come calling during the past few days.

Police videographers continued to archive the scene; CSI experts scooped up samples; a reporter from the *Chittering Whippoorwill* was interviewing Colonel Scroggy; and a cluster of Old Ones had their eyeball-tentacled heads together in conversation. The sight of these starfish-footed, fluted-barrel-bodied honchos in conference reminded me of teatime among a bunch of giant fruiting cacti.

Lee came up to me and said, *What do you make of all this?*

"Well, I can't put my finger on a perp, so I have to consider opportunity and motive. What was Cthulhu doing here in Mi-Go Town anyhow?"

That's the interesting part. Apparently he had gotten an invitation to come here to learn something to his advantage. This room is just a short-term rental he arranged online.

"No way to find out who sent the message?

None. It went through several anonymizers.

"Well, who stands to benefit from Cthulhu's death? He's got family, right? Any inheritance at stake?"

Sister named Cthaeghya, brother named Gtuhanai. Several kids too. But there's really no possessions or savings to pass on. He lived on a small pension. About the only thing the victim owned was a condo in R'lyeh. Nice place, but not worth killing for.

"What about business arrangements?"

He's been retired for decades now, ever since he shut down his Fog-Spawn extermination firm. Spends most of his time at the Klarkash-Ton Track in Atlantis, betting on races among the Deep Ones. Breaks even most weeks, but never scores big. Rather pathetic figure these days, actually.

I pondered these facts for a few moments, then said, "That really leaves just one possibility. Revenge. Who hated Cthulhu enough to want him dead?"

Lee snorted telepathically. *Take a number. Cthulhu racked up a lot of enemies, both Mythos and mortal, before he got counseling and ceased radiating irrational waves of madness-inducing fear through the aethyr. Even after he performed the Eighth Step of making amends, there were still tons of haters out there.*

Having finished with the reporter, Colonel Scroggy came over to where Lee and I stood. The imposing pallid bulk of the eyeless Moon-beast exuded a tangible weariness.

"Duluoz, are you wondering why I bothered getting you out of bed at this hour when I already have dozens of Mythos cops assigned to this case? Well, it's because we can't ignore the human angle, however unlikely. And with your fellow *homo sap* Bookstaver tracking down those fire vampires on Fomalhaut, that leaves just you and your partner."

The Colonel's speech was interrupted by the speedy arrival from across the room of a tech, a lanky, dog-faced ghoul. The ghoul held a tablet, and he proferred it to Scroggy, saying, "Chief, look at this."

The Colonel took the device, read the screen with whatever sensory input he used in place of vision, then turned back to me and Lee.

"Well, it appears that my instinctive decision to call you in, Sol, was justified. Cthulhu's wound is covered with human DNA. Specifically, it looks as if whoever killed him took a piss on the corpse when he was done."

* * * *

The Café Carcosa was the most popular human hangout in Mi-Go Town. I had spent many an evening there myself, especially when the presence of so many and so mind-bogglingly varied Mythos beings became oppressive. Not that the Lovecraftian races were repugnant to me. (Mostly not, that is; a few such as the centipede-like Yekubians triggered instinctive antipathy.) Not that I considered humans superior to our alien cohabitants of the planet. It was just that a guy liked to relax among his own kind now and then, instead of always being anxious that you'd say or do something undiplomatic. Especially as a cop, I had to watch my public image. It felt good to let my hair down among my own kind.

But the day after Cthulhu's murder found me and Lee van Cleef entering the Café Carcosa in our official status as investigators, rather than as customers.

As with all interiors in the vast antique city on the Lengian Plateau, the ginormous space had been constructed on a scale fit for Old Ones and shoggoths. But the current owners had rendered it as cozy as possible with a number of expedients. A suspended false ceiling composed of hanging patterned fabrics from Celephaïs. Colorful rugs from Baharna, across which the tables and chairs formed discrete islands of sociability. A sound system softly playing human tunes. A warm lighting scheme. The pungent smell of incense from Kythanil. A stage dominated one end of the room. I had heard lots of great music and standup comedy here.

When Lee and I entered, the hour was just ten AM and the place was less busy than at the breakfast, lunch or evening crush. We tracked down the owner, Jimmy Shifflet, whom we found inventorying liquor. Jimmy had contentedly run a similar place back in Austin, Texas, but emigrated in 2051, the year Austin never saw a temperature below ninety degrees. A wiry guy of fifty years or so, he sported ever-shifting tattoos of popular anime characters that ran up and down his bare arms.

Shifflet set down a carton of Sarnathian mead. "Officer Duluoz, Officer van Cleef. What's up?"

"You heard the Big Guy went down last night?"

"Sure. Like everyone else in Mi-Go Town."

"Took some major muscle to do it. Like Joseph Curwen-level power. Heard of any wizards of that caliber in town lately?"

"Not a single one. Just the usual dabblers. You know, they read a couple of pages in the *Book of Eibon* and instantly imagine they can get chocolate milk out of Shub-Niggurath's udder."

Lee put his words in my head and presumably Jimmy's as well. *You heard anyone badmouthing the Mythos crowd? Someone with a personal grudge against Cthulhu or a general racial hatred thing?*

"Not at all. No one'd live here who felt like that."

"Okay, thanks, Jimmy. You'll let us know if anything turns up, of course."

"Count on it. The whole city's gonna be on edge until this murder is solved. Bad for business."

We left the Café Carcosa and turned left down a broad avenue named Providence Street. This being June, a month when the sun never rose over Leng, the only sparse illumination came from the scattered bioluminescents. The air was chilly, and I zipped my police uniform jacket up to my chin. There seemed to be fewer pedestrians about than usual, as if the humans on the plateau of Leng had gone to ground against possible reprisals by the Mythos citizens. Colonel Scroggy had intended to keep the discovery of human DNA on Cthulhu's violated corpse out of the news, but someone on the scene had leaked it to the media. Naturally, the evidence against a human assailant made the whole community look bad.

We hadn't gone more than a few yards when we were stopped by a figure standing in the dense shadows of a narrow alley and beckoning to us.

The figure seemed human enough in its vaguely perceived outlines. Long coat and face-obscuring hat. A voice whispered gutturally. "You're cops, right? I got something important to tell you. C'mere."

Lee and I advanced, but the voice said, "No nightgaunts, just the human!"

"You wait here, Lee. I'll be okay."

I stepped into the tight confines of the channel of primordial slate and schist, studded with queer fossils, and followed the retreating silhouette until the entrance to the alley was a thumb-sized slot of relative radiance.

"Okay, that's far enough, buddy. What's on your mind?"

"Just this," said the voice.

And then I found myself enveloped in a suffocating fleshy mass, my arms pinioned so I couldn't get at my gun and my mouth and nostrils stuffed with writhing worms or stubby tentacles. The hideous stuff tasted like sucking on the fingers of a recently dead sheep shearer.

I threw myself from side to side, hoping to slam my assailant against the walls. Nothing. Desperate for air, I felt some of the living substance in my mouth trying to crawl down my throat—

And then a hard hurtling mass impacted me. I felt claws ripping away the encumbering blanket that enveloped me. Suddenly I was gripped in the Heimlich maneuver and helped by a violent squeeze to blast all the gunk from my mouth and throat. I fell to my knees. With hands free I pinched each nostril in turn and snorted out the stuff in my nose. Then I began to crawl toward the street.

Before I had progressed more than a couple of yards I was picked up and carried at a run to safety.

Out in the better light, I saw the ebon eidilon figure of Lee van Cleef standing over me. *I hope you do not object, but I was present in your mind, observing the whole time. I deemed it a proper precautionary measure. When you were attacked, I came as fast as I could. Unfortunately the channel was not wide enough for me to fly.*

I stood up, sore and shaky but whole. "You know what? Mental privacy is overrated. Any idea what the hell that thing was in there?"

Lee tossed to the pavement something I had not noticed he was holding. At first it seemed to be the hairless human head of my assailant. But then it decomposed into a mass of individual small worms that wriggled away in all directions.

One of the Crawling Ones. A composite gestalt, a human avatar formed of a hundred thousand annelid fingerlings. No way to question it now, for once the unit devolves beyond a critical mass of worms, it loses all sentience.

"You think it was enlisted by whoever killed Cthulhu in order to shut the case down?"

Quite likely. But why specifically attack only you, the human member of our team? The investigation would continue regardless of your death.

"Maybe it's because only a human would recognize whatever clues are out there pointing to the killer. It was an attempt to remove the expert on the case, one of the only human cops in Mi-Go Town."

Lee's silent voice somehow conveyed a wry tone. Although his matte-black roasting-pan head displayed no features, I imagined I detected a smile. *You value yourself highly.*

"Listen, amigo, right now I value *you* more highly than my own sorry ass. You saved my life."

Just what partners do. I will rely on a similar service from you one day perhaps.

"You got it," I said, little knowing that day loomed right around the corner.

* * * *

We got our big break a week later, after uselessly following scores of dead ends and long shots. Coming to us from afar, rather than through any work of our own, the revelation consisted of the discovery of Cthulhu's head. The giant decaying noggin was found an unimaginable distance away from Leng.

In the uninhabited desert outside the city of Illarnek in the Western precincts of the Dreamlands, an entire plane of existence removed from our Earth.

Colonel Scroggy recounted the story to the whole force at that morning's briefing.

"The first we learned of this was a dream bulletin from the mage attached to the Illarnek police force, sent to our own communications warlock. We immediately dispatched a squad of Shamblers to check it out."

I must have looked confused, because Colonel Scroggy added, "One of our few resident species here that can cross into the Dreamlands at will. They confirmed the ID of the head. It's Cthulhu's, all right."

"But how did his head get from Earth to the Dreamlands?" I asked.

"Easy enough. Someone was apparently able to open a transdimensional portal to Illarnek. They then encircled Cthulhu's head and neck with it, and snapped the dreamgate shut. Bingo, a quantum guillotine. It would have happened in just a few seconds, giving the Big Guy no time to react."

Lee said, So we're looking for what—alien tech, a sorceror, a mass cult ritual? Or maybe someone acting from the Dreamlands side?

"Any and all of the above. If we knew the motive, we could narrow it down. But right now, every suspect is equally likely. Okay you slackers, get out there now and find our killer! The Big Guy's daughter, Cthylla, is calling my office every hour and threatening to plunge Mi-Go Town into the primordial abyss if we don't solve this case."

Lee and I left to walk our beat in the human precincts of Mi-Go Town. I was feeling frustrated and depressed at our lack of progress, and I knew Lee was sharing those emotions, since they leaked back through our mental link. We didn't speak much, but just attended to routine incidents, such as chastising a couple of plainly repentant juveniles who had been caught shoplifting Hyperborean squid-jerky snacks and starfoam drinks from the Vaults of Zin convenience store. And all the while we were attending to our mundane tasks, some niggling bit of information at the back of my brain kept trying to surface.

When we broke for lunch—a Cuban sandwich and iced tea for me, and several essential draughts of intergalactic dark matter for Lee—the nugget of data finally popped up into the forefront of my brain, and I spontaneously exclaimed, "The Silver Key!"

The Silver Key?

"Sure, don't you recognize the term? It was the talisman that allowed Randolph Carter to enter the Dreamlands at will. I'll bet that gadget could have been jiggered to chop the Big Guy's head off."

I am afraid I can't keep up with all the minor incidents of human history. I suspect this Carter's name and biography is utterly unknown to most Mythos beings.

"So this bit of trivia might be what my death was intended to keep secret."

Perhaps. Are you accusing this Randolph Carter then?

I stopped to ponder a minute. "I don't even know if he's still alive. He flourished in the early decades of the last century. Let me research him now."

My memtax soon delivered the facts on Carter. He had last been seen over one-hundred-and-twenty years ago, at the abrupt climax of a business meeting relating to his own contested estate. He had vanished in a large coffin-shaped clock that appeared to be some kind of interstellar transport. His survival to this day would have been dubious had he been merely mortal. But at the time of his disappearance his consciousness had been trapped inside the alien body of Zkauba the wizard, a being from Yaddith who resembled Spider-Man's nemesis the Lizard mated with a mandrill and one of the more exotic giant moth varieties. The lifespan of Yaddithians was unrecorded.

Lee meditated on this news. *It's nothing really solid, but it's worth following up. Where do you suggest we start?*

"First we'll have the Chief put out an APB for any stray Yaddithians. Then I think we should contact the Church of Starry Wisdom."

Colonel Scroggy heard me out and agreed to disseminate the alert. Then Lee and I headed to the Church's main temple in Mi-Go Town, on Charles Dexter Ward Boulevard.

The building resembled Saint Patrick's cathedral in Manhattan if you had put St. Pat's through a tesseract and a timeslip storm, then adorned it with statues that were a composite of Mayan, Hindu, Dogon and Celtic features. Giant twin doors of striated petrified wood were left permanently ajar to accomodate a steady influx and outgo of worshippers. Inside the greyly illumined nave, we tracked down Deacon Sugar, a large fellow of Haitian extraction who sported deep ceremonial scarification on his exposed skin.

"Welcome, brothers, in the name of all-consuming Nyarlathotep," Deacon Sugar declaimed in a voice like a wind issuing from a bottomless fissure in the ground. "How may I help you?"

We transmitted our police IDs and the Deacon grew a little less effusive.

"Your church maintains contact with many planets and realms. Is Yaddith one of them?"

"Yes, we have a branch on Yaddith."

"Do you know a guy named Randolph Carter, who was last seen inhabiting the body of a Yaddithian?"

"I do not."

Something about Sugar's response seemed off, as if he were trying to honor some ethical principle by not lying, but was also striving not to disclose too much.

Lee sent a mental question whose nearly palpable forcefulness seemed to imply that a deeper probing was possible. *Do you know anyone* **connected** *with Randolph Carter?*

Deacon Sugar sighed and said, "There was a young woman who visited us several weeks ago. She gave her name as Randi Carter, and claimed to be the great-granddaughter of the man you are seeking."

"What did she want?"

"She asked to use our aethyric link to our sister temple in R'lyeh to send a message. We consented, since she appeared to be a member in good standing of our Kingsport establishment. I am unware of the content of her missive, naturally."

"She leave an address?"

"No. But she did ask about cheap accomodations. I directed her to the Mama Shoggoth's B&B."

"Okay, Deacon, thanks for your cooperation. If this woman returns, please let us know."

We left the temple and headed toward Mama Shoggoth's doss house.

Perhaps we should summon backup, said Lee. *Anyone capable of killing Cthulhu will be very formidable.*

"We don't want to raise a false alarm. Let's hold off until we actually find this gal."

You know best how to approach one of your fellow humans.

Lee's faith in me was appreciated, but much misplaced.

* * * *

On the way to Mama Shoggoth's, in a gnarly district of Mi-Go Town several neighborhoods removed from the human zone, Lee reminded me that I was due at his house for dinner again tonight, what with Lilybelle being on the road and leaving me to lonely bachelorhood. I appreciated the invitation, and pondered once again how lucky the nightgaunt was to have such a cozy domestic family scene. Working with him had engendered a real fondness and respect for the van Cleefs, despite their otherwise forbidding appearance, and I thought that if only all humans could be paired with a Mythos buddy, much of the world's suspicions, prejudices, dislikes and hatreds would disappear. Not only had Lee saved my life, but he had changed my attitudes, which might be a harder thing all around to accomplish. I cringed now a bit when I thought of how readily and unthinkingly I had gunned down Wexford Whateley. Although in that particular case, I still believed that ugly ornery bastard had had it coming, and that I had done my civic duty.

I had never had cause to visit Mama Shoggoth's before, and knew it only by reputation as a venue for cheap lodgings. I did not quite realize how it operated until the manager—a troglydytic Miri-Nigri female, clad in the fur from a giant sloth, who gave her name as Phigalia—showed us around.

The place was large as six NASA spacecraft hangers, and filled with quivery globular shoggoths. The air smelled like a bakery that made its product out of fruiting slime molds. Unlike their free-willed cousins, these mountainous gelatinous masses showed no tendency to move, no sense of agency or volition.

"They've all been decorticated," Phigalia explained, "and now they just serve as hosts bodies for our guests. Through a series of tactile codes, the shoggoths makes vacuoles that envelope and house our residents. It's a safe, heated environment that also handles waste removal and even nutritional needs—if you don't mind a diet of shoggoth lymphatic fluids, which are really quite healthful. I understand humans say they taste like soy milk."

"And do you get many humans here, as a rule?"

"No, not many. This woman Randi Carter was our first *homo sap* guest in months. Let's see if she's home."

Phigalia went up to a beast indistinguishable from its mates, tickled its hide, and a faintly discernible bubble began to float from the translucent interior toward us. When the bubble reached the epidermis, it fused with the skin and opened.

Empty.

"Not at home," I said.

But our suspect had left the most anomalous and crucial of possessions: an actual physical diary. The volume was a mass-produced blank book bearing the image of a Korean boy band on its cover.

I began to flip through it, with revelations rapidly becoming clear. Lee, I suspected, was tapping the surface flow of my sensory impressions—a practice I had become easy with—and my partner got the information at the same time I did. Nonetheless, I felt compelled to read one entry aloud.

"'For the hundredth time I've begged Cthulhu to let great-grandpa go free. But he won't manumit him from the Geas of Azathoth. He says that g-pop in the body of Zkauba the wizard is his key to beating the odds at the Klarkash-Ton racetrack, and recouping all his losses. This will not stand! I will free my venerable ancestor one way or another!'"

Cthulhu had enslaved Randolph Carter and was using him as his personal scryer, just to make a killing at the track? That's petty and cold, even for an Old One.

I agreed with Lee. "Now we've got the motive and the weapon and Randi Carter's connection with the message that drew Cthulhu here. It's an airtight case. But we don't have a lead on the whereabouts of the killer. Damn it!"

Feeling stymied, we left the flophouse and headed to HQ. I wanted to deliver our findings to Colonel Scroggy in person rather than over the memtax link. And maybe he would have some useful news for us.

When we arrived we made our report. We felt secure enough about Randi Carter's potential guilt that we put out an APB for her. It was almost time for our shift to end, but neither Lee nor I wanted to let go of the case, and so Lee sent a message home that we'd both be working overtime, and to keep the dark matter snacks at zero degrees Kelvin until we could show up.

I had a hunch that Randi Carter must not have arrived at Mi-Go Town by any conventional mode of transport. She would have wanted to sneak into town. But the Silver Key in her possession served only to open gates between our plane and the Dreamlands. Could she have entered the Dreamlands from another spot on Earth, traveled through that realm for the proper analogous distance, then opened a gate here? I wasn't even sure how sp;ace and time correlated between the two dimensions. Still, it seemed like a lot of work, even if possible.

Then the answer hit me.

"Didn't Deacon Sugar mention that Randi Carter had a connection with Kingsport?"

Yes, he did.

"That's my old stomping grounds. I'm sensitized to anything from back home. And a week ago, a tidbit of local news caught my attention. The Strange High House in the Mist had materialized here in town. I didn't think twice about it then—just assumed that Nodens or the Old Man was visiting. But I'll bet Randi Carter is using the place as a means of transportation and a hideout."

What are we waiting for then?

Lee and I began to trot through the twisted streets of the town toward where we knew the House to have last been seen. Not for the first nor last time I wished for at least an electric scooter to facilitate my patrolman's life. But the uneven pavements and cloistered torturous geometry of the city on the high polar plain forbade any such aid.

At last we reached the foot of the enormous structure on top of which perched the visiting High House. In the stygian polar darkness, we could barely make out a little flickering yellow light shining from the House's window, far, far above our heads.

The building that served as perch to the visiting Kingsport shack had no openings at street level, or for several floors above.

Get set, Lee said, and then I felt his claws beneath my armpits as we soared aloft. The nightgaunt's mighty wings beat with immense power to lift us both. I tried not to look down.

My feet settled on the flat rooftop. There before us stood the creaky, tumbledown House from Massachusetts, its door ajar, spilling out an eerie radiance as from a candle fashioned from a dead man's hand.

I hefted my gun, and saw that Lee had drawn his as well.

"Let's take this perp down."

I can squeeze only through the door. You flank them through the window.

We crept up to our respective positions. I crouched beneath the window's line of sight. At a signal, Lee burst in through the door and I popped up.

Randi Carter looked to be about fifteen years old, cute as a button, dressed in the latest teen garb. But I didn't underestimate anyone who had lopped off Cthulhu's head. In a flash, I catalogued the scene. Randi had the Silver Key raised up to open a portal of retreat for her and the inhuman, shambling Yaddithian lizard-ape that housed the soul of Randolph Carter. But Lee's violent entrance caused her to abort her summoning and turn to face the nightgaunt. She hadn't seen me in the window yet.

"Stand back! I'll take you down just like I took down the Big Guy!"

She made a little portal with the Silver Key and began to maneuver it through the air like a lasso, plainly intending to encircle Lee and bisect him.

That wasn't gonna happen on my watch!

But yet—couldn't just shoot her down.

Somehow I hurled myself through the window and tackled the girl.

I had to surmise what happened next.

She lost hold of the Silver Key when we both went tumbling down to the floor of the shack. The still-active portal dropped over both of us, leaving Randolph Carter and Lee van Cleef behind safe. And the next thing I knew I was falling through the skies of the Dreamlands.

Luckily, I landed on a giant bed of thick moss that smelled like a whore's toiletries. Although intact, I was still stunned for a few moments.

When I recovered myself, I discovered that Randi had not been so lucky. The adjacent boulder that received her falling body served to break her neck. She was dead, and of the Silver Key, there was no trace.

And so now—having communicated news of my survival and the fate of Randi to Colonel Scroggy, via the Illarnek police channel, along with a reassuring love note to Lilybelle—I sit here in a scurvy, haunted tavern at the docks of Dylath-Leen, chronicling the whole case and waiting for ship's passage to a remote and rumored city of the Dreamlands where, I have heard, there might just be a physical connection back to Earth. I can rest assured that my salary is accruing, and that if I ever make it back to Mi-Go Town, I will enjoy a hero's welcome.

But that day is still a long unknown quest away.

"NOTHING CAN STOP THE INSECT GIRL CORPS!"

The only way to leave the Insect Girl Corps was by aging out or dying in combat—and the latter path was most common. Even gaining weight until you were too heavy for your wings was not an option. The bio-designers had foreseen that particular escape route and engineered the girls with special gut bacteria that forbade calorie utilization above a daily maximum. Any extra calories just got shunted into increased production of the hormone irisin, which stimulated a shiver response that burned up the excess food as heat. The wracking sensations could become unpleasant enough to deter even a determined diet abuser from trying to stuff herself into a dishonorable discharge.

And so it went with all aspects of the martial lives of the Insect Girls. As the girls always said, half rueful, half blithely stoical: "If something ain't mandated, it's forbidden!"

Not that they didn't share camaraderie and fun.

As the leader and oldest member of her squad, "The Gizzard Piercers," Gillikee felt a responsibility to keep up the morale of her girls, to lighten their daily load of fighting interspersed with hours of boredom, and so she had devised many songs and games to play in their barracks. Their favorite song heralded their unstoppable prowess in battle. Their favorite game involved deliberately overeating from their copious buffet just enough to start shivering and impart chaotic motions to their wing flappings. Then the girls could bat a balloon around the barracks in unpredictable and entertaining ways. Otherwise they had too much perfect control of their wings, and scoring goals with the balloon became a tedious exercise in perfection. Gillikee had named the sport "Quiver Chase."

Currently Gillikee's platoon consisted of five other girls:

boisterous Faybia; the dark twins Gaborielle and Trosti; mordant Jazlyn; and light-hearted Curline. Blonde and possessing a sweet heart-shaped face, Curline was the newest addition to their ranks, replacing Walla, who had perished under the teeth and claws of the Lobo Vespertillians. Young and inexperienced in fighting, Curline needed much drilling, with Gillikee assuming the lion's share of the instruction.

So right now, while the other Insect Girls played a gaily noisy game of Quiver Chase inside the lofty barracks, Gillikee and Curline practiced offensive and defensive tactics in the air of the barracks yard. Arcing through the sky in bold curves and swoops, the two Insect Girls carried light practice staves instead of their actual weapons.

Beneath a bluish sun, the day was a typical pleasant summer morning on Makzoume, where the human colony of Wilder's Folly had been planted nearly a century ago. The small city had not grown overmuch in those decades, mainly due to the constant assaults of the native Lobo Vespertillians and the relatively small number of humans, who were also constrained by the low-tech lifestyle mandated by their religious beliefs. But thanks to the staunch protections of the Insect Girls, neither was the colony in danger of being extinguished.

"No, no," Gillikee shouted. "Don't drop your staff so low!" She administered a sharp whack on Curline's rump to drive home her advice.

Curline responded angrily, attempting to get inside Gillikee's defenses. But the scarred and wily squad leader permitted no such liberty. The two slim Insect Girls continued their mock combat with unceasing energy and dedication.

Small as human children, deliberately kept forever sexless with neotenic sylph-like features, graced with delicate feathery antennae that disseminated bonding pheromones among them, the girls were able to fly with their big, tough, yet low-mass wings thanks to special musculature and metabolism, and thanks also to Makzoume's relatively lower gravity, compared to the pull of ancestral Earth.

Of course, those abilities and inducements to flight were also shared by their enemy, the dreaded Lobo Vespertillians. The native race—each individual was about half as big again as the average Insect Girl—resembled bipedal, two-armed Earth-type wolves sporting enormous bat wings. Not a tool-using species, the El-vesps were apex predators, relying on fearsome fangs and claws to subdue their prey—a classification into which they placed humans immediately upon their arrival on Makzoume. The El-vesps were smart enough to coordinate their attacks, and displayed a rudimentary language. Their congeries of nests occupied the cliff faces in the low mountains that surrounded the valley-cradled human city.

Eventually Gillikee called a halt to the practice, and she and her pupil alighted daintily on the grass. They enjoyed deep drafts of cold well water, and then flopped down to rest. Out from the barracks trotted one of the Corps' cats, a calico named Invicta. The girls petted and teased the cat until it lost interest in them and began stalking a parade of busy curlbugs.

A mild knocking sounded at the gate in the low fence that surrounded the barracks. The knocking was a mere formality—as was the query, "May I come in?"—since the man making the approach could be plainly seen and was well known. But he always made this gesture, to signal his deference.

Being an artificial offshoot of humanity as they were, consigned to a role both more constrained and in a sense more free than the lot of real people, the

Insect Girls were regarded by some of the humans as freakish and odd and not to be accorded much respect. But such was not the attitude of the man now at the gate. Mayor Alonzo Smithson revered the Insect Girls, always made sure they possessed every amenity they could appreciate, and was in turn beloved by them.

Gillikee and Curline jumped up and hastened to the gate. "Come in, Mayor, come in!" Gillikee said. As Smithson entered the yard, all the other girls rushed out and soon the tall man was hip-deep in a sea of irridescent wings and slim limbs, submitting to their fond petting.

Once the effusive greetings were over, Smithson regarded the girls soberly for a few silent moments. Gillikee sensed that something new and important was afoot. And the Mayor's words confirmed this.

"Girls, the city council has finally decided that we must bring the war to the El-vesps. No longer can we tolerate their frequent raids. Our mission is to wipe them out entirely—or at least inflict such severe injuries that they will think twice about bothering us, and possibly they might even relocate their nests far from Wilder's Folly. Can I count on your legendary courage and prowess in this raid?"

Shouts and bold proclamations of victory and slaughter filled the air. Once the huzzahs had ceased, the Mayor said, "Very good. Rest now, and sharpen your blades. I must visit the other barracks. But know with pride that I came to see the Gizzard Piercers first."

When the Mayor had left, Gillikee immediately put the girls to work honing the blades of their spears and the knives that they would belt around their tiny waists. That night they had a ritual feast, and told tales about past battles before falling asleep.

Three days later the expedition assembled on the plain outside the city. Large wagons, drawn by massive oxodonts, whose cargo beds bore trebuchets that could hurl flaming projectiles. Commissary wagons. Armored foot soldiers, pure human types, brave but uselessly moored to the ground when the El-vesps came ravaging down from above. Wagons packed with tents. A medical unit too. A special carriage carried the officers, including Mayor Smithson himself.

The Insect Girls of the Gizzard Piercers disdained the offered rides and flew above the slow-moving vehicles, proudly singing the songs that Gillikee had penned. They were joined by the girls of two hundred other squads, and formed a moving cloud of winged flesh.

The trip to the mountains where the El-vesps lurked took three days, and the expedition was undeniably seen by scouts of the Lobo Vespertillians. But much to the surprise of the officers, no attacks were made. Perhaps the formidable massing of troops had scared the creatures.

But when the expedition drew up half a mile distant from the cliffs, the El-vesps displayed no timidity. Instead, assembled on the ledges of their homes, they howled out their defiance and hurled down small rocks, the extent of their weapons.

The Insect Girls yelled back, awaiting orders to attack. But before they could go on the offensive, the El-vesps launched themselves into the sky and the battle was on.

Gillikee directed her girls at first with bellowed orders, but then any planned battle lines devolved into a general melee. She soon lost track of her sisters, Faybia, Gaborielle, Trosti, Jazlyn, and Curline, in a welter of furry assailants, and had to concentrate on her own self-preservation and attacks. She parayed they would all acquit themselves well and survive. But if one had to die, this was the way to go! She drove her sharp spear into one El-vesp after another, ripping open flanks and bellies, raining a shower of blood down onto the plain below. But alas, plenty of that blood belonged to the Insect Girls, for the El-vesps were savage and cunning foes. As their aeries were bombarded with flaming missiles, killing females and children, the El-vesps became even more frenetically violent.

Gillikee ascended above the main volume of the fray for just a moment's respite, wiping sweat and blood from her face with the back of one hand. She looked down with her eagle vision and saw Mayor Smithson with his back against a wagon, deploying a puny snapshooter against a wounded El-vesp who was nonetheless dangerously lurching toward him. Even injured, the beast was intent on doing mortal harm. And capable! But Mayor Smithson soon laid the beast low.

Then, from above even her high vantage, a big El-vesp arrowed downward, heading straight for the Mayor!

Gillikee hurled herself in the wake of the alien, who could move faster than she and had a headstart. She pushed her muscles to their limits, casting away her spear to lessen her load, and caught up with the beast on the ground, as it grappled hand to hand with a bold but overmatched Mayor. Knife firmly in her grip, Gillikee leaped upon the beast's back. Its pungent musk enveloped her. She swung up her arm. But before she could strike, the El-vesp released the Mayor, pivoted and slammed her against the side of the wagon. Gillikee lost her knife. And now she had but one weapon left.

From the underside of each arm, her bone stingers erupted, ripping through her flesh and veins. Still clinging with her legs wrapped around the hips of the El-vesp, she rammed the sharp hollow tips of both needles into its neck. Reflexively, poison pumped out spastically. Then both Gillikee and her antagonist fell to the ground.

Her vision blurring, Gillikee saw Mayor Smithson kneeling over her. He cradled her around the shoulders, careful of her glorious wings, and half lifted her into his lap.

"Gillikee, oh Gillikee, you made too large a sacrifice."

"No, Mayor, no. The Insect Girls will always die, so that others may live. But only tell me that we will win."

"Yes, Gillikee, I can see that we already have. It's true, I swear. And I will seal fast the victory as I kiss your noble brow."

And he placed his lips between her crumpled insect fronds.

THINGMAKER

On the late afternoon of December 7, 1941, Senator Harry Truman arrived at the secret government establishment dubbed "Thingmaker" in a discreet Nash 600 sky-sled that appeared to be a standard Washington, DC, taxicab. Behind the wheel of the floating vehicle sat a youthful fellow with dark wavy hair and a long oval face featuring an aquiline nose above full lips. Looking back over his shoulder at his passenger, the driver received a positive nod. He maneuvered the controls of the sky-sled in response, so as to cause it to sink slowly onto its undercarriage bumpers as they made contact with the pavement.

The building before which the car settled, an innocuous and shabby warehouse-type structure with its windows boarded up, stood in the shadow of the Nehi Bottling Plant at 1923 New York Avenue in the Ivy City district of the nation's capital, a zone devoted to light manufacturing, gas stations, railyards, junkyards, and other rough utilitarian structures of modern civilization. Today, a Sunday, the famous soda pop enterprise was dormant, and there was little traffic, vehicular or pedestrian. The day was sunny, and in fact a high temperature of ninety degrees had been recorded, now dwindling as the evening approached.

The driver emerged from the Nash. Out on the street, he proved to be only in his smooth-cheeked mid-adolescence, despite affectations to maturity. Although dressed informally—colorfully printed cotton sports shirt, gabardine slacks, rubber-soled tennis shoes—he still carried himself with a military alertness. Abetting this impresion was a pistol tucked into his trousers waistband at the small of his back. He keenly sized up the sparse traffic, being sure to look overhead as well, for other sky-sleds, then spoke to his passenger in a voice that bore a hint of Texas twang.

"It's all jake, Senator. Climb on out."

Harry Truman levered himself out of the curbside door. The well-known politician today wore a lightweight tweed suit. At the age of fifty-seven, his hair had noticeably thinned from its youthful richness. His trademark round wire-rimmed spectacles caught a glint from the sinking sun. Perspiration dotted his brow.

The driver had joined Truman on the sidewalk. "Where's the door?"

"Around back," said the Senator, indicating an alley between the warehouse and the adjacent building.

The driver regarded the passage suspiciously.

"I'll go first."

Truman chuckled. "One would imagine you were scouting in the ruins of Berlin, Audie."

"Yeah, well, maybe I was too young to get into that scrape. It was over before it hardly began. Had to haul myself out here to the War Office just to find some action. Then what job do they give me? Babysitting a politician. No offense, sir, but that's just how I see it."

"Your description, while unflattering, is mostly accurate."

"'Preciate your understanding, sir. Anyhow, I stalked a lot of critters back home in Farmersville, and if I didn't shoot them before they saw me, we didn't eat that night. So I always figure that it's a good thing if you can see your opponent before they can see you."

Truman seemed thoughtful when he said, "Assuming one can always recognize friend from foe."

Audie registered a bit of puzzlement at that remark, but did not follow it up. Instead, he moved to the mouth of the alley, which was well lit by the fading daylight and offered no places of concealment, save for a couple of dented galvanized trash cans behind which perhaps a Munchkin from *The Wizard of Oz* might be able to crouch. After making great show of his inspection, he beckoned Truman to follow. The pair quickly traversed the brick corridor with its assorted litter: the wrapper from a Chicken Dinner candybar; a takeout menu from the famous China Clipper restaurant; an empty bottle of Lucky Tiger hair tonic, and one of Ancient Age whiskey.

At the end of the alley a board fence, separated from the rear of the building by a few feet, allowed them to turn left. On this far side of the warehouse, they encountered the door: a rusting iron facade with a padlock and chain that seemed immovably soldered to the entrance by time.

"You sure this is the right door?" Audie asked.

Truman said nothing, but instead merely knocked in a complex pattern.

A door-sized section of the brick wall, adjacent to the fake door, pivoted outward. A Marine with a rifle awaited them. Senator Truman showed the soldier an identification card, and the visitors were allowed entrance. The wall swung silently shut behind them.

The interior of the warehouse belied its exterior, comprised entirely of modern textures under bright overhead lights—at least in this large anteroom, which featured crisp checkerboard linoleum floors, a steelcase desk, and three futuristic looking wooden Eames chairs.

Behind the desk sat a young dark-haired woman, more striking than beautiful, in the uniform of a WAC—complete with a large Webley Mk VI .455 calibre revolver in a well-oiled holster. Her somewhat haughty features failed to completely mask a warm and concerned soul. A nametag on the breast of her uniform read COL. K. SUMMERSBY. She smiled at the newcomers—a contrast to the unrelentingly stern visage of the Marine—and Audie made sure to beam back. When she spoke, she revealed British origins.

"Welcome, Senator."

"You're looking lovely, as usual, Kay. Life with Ike must be agreeing with you."

"Oh, he's a tad mardy, griping at how peaceful the world is these days. Old soldiers, you know. But he's basically a dear. Still, I shouldn't detain you with household talk. You're here to see Doctor Delbrück, I assume. He's expecting you."

"Yes. And if Doctor Luria could spare some time to accompany us as well, I'd be grateful."

"I'll see if he's available."

Using the intercom on her desk, Summersby received confirmation from both Delbrück and Luria that they would soon be present to receive the visitors. An inner door to the rest of the mysterious warehouse beckoned, but a second stern Marine kept vigil by it, not offering admittance.

After a minute or so the door swung open into the anteroom, and two men strode through. Any observer could discern by their labcoats and savant's demeanors that they were scientists of some stature.

Truman took the time to introduce his companion, producing a smile of pleasure from the boy.

"Doctor Delbrück, this is my chauffeur and all-round general factotum, Audie Murphy."

Delbrück proved to be a skinny fellow in his mid-thirties with a wry and puckish face and a wing of dark hair sloping across his forehead. His German accent layered his impeccable English.

"I'm very pleased to meet such an accomplished youngster. Call me Max."

"Aw, shucks, I ain't so much, nor so young!"

"And this is Doctor Luria."

His black hair trimmed short and adhering to a high line above his wide forehead, Luria resembled a continental movie star, such as the newcomer Rossano Brazzi. And in fact, his speech showed Mediterranean origins.

"*Ciao, ragazzo!* Any friend of the Senator's is a friend of Salvador's."

The introductions over, Truman was quick to assert the urgency and importance of his visit.

"Gentlemen, as head of the Senate Committee on Wolf-Rayet Technology, I'm here to make one final inspection tour before we render our decision on the continuation of your project."

Delbrück and Luria straightened their shoulders and looked hopeful but wary. The German scientist said, "We will show you everything again, of course, and answer any questions in full. You already have all our written reports and records."

". "Your forthcomingness is admirable, professors. But I should warn you that the votes are trending against your research."

An excitable Luria responded intemperately. "*Madonna mia!* What is the problem, Senator? Are you and your comrades blind to the potential benefits of our discoveries? Have you not seen how vital and important the other technologies from the Garry Expedition has become? Why, atomic power and anti-gravity have revolutionized our world in just three short years, ever since those heroic explorers returned with the goods from the South Pole. And they allowed the Allies to put a quick end to the Axis powers, shortening a war that surely would have killed millions. But even those life-saving innovations are trivial in comparison to what we offer here!"

Truman nodded somberly to acknowledge the truth of Luria's protest. "Yes, the United States monopoly on anti-gravity and the neutron-beryllium power sphere, shared with her partners, did bring those bastards Hitler and Tojo and *il Duce* up short. Pardon the aspersions on your native lands, gents, I know where your true sympathies lie. But no matter how revolutionary, those gadgets were just that—gadgets. What you two are working on is the stuff of life itself."

"And thus its greater potential for good!"

"I don't deny that, Doctor Luria. But it's a double-edged sword. The potential for harm, should the technology ever escape your built-in restraints, is immense. You know the men of the Garry Expedition suffered great losses and barely avoided total annihilation."

An impatient and curious Audie interjected a question. "What're you talking about, Chief? I know Commander Garry lost some of his crew and all their dogs during a brutal storm in 1938. But you can't rightly associate a faraway force of nature like that with something going on right here in Washington—can you?"

The three men looked at each other significantly, and then Delbrück said, "Is the boy cleared to receive the true story?"

Truman looked fondly at the lad. "He's one hundred percent loyal to his country, and smart enough to keep his mouth shut. He's bound to hear a lot as my aide-de-camp. So I'll take responsibility for his silence."

"Very well, then." Delbrück assumed a lecture-hall mien. "*Herr* Murphy, the reality of what transpired at the South Pole is otherwise than you and the general public have been led to believe. The official story explains that the Garry Expedition uncovered an alien spaceship, and retrieved from the wreck the technologies of antigravity and atomic power, all before the ship was destroyed by a foolish misuse of a thermite heat source. This is a conflation and omission of the real events. What those men took from the crashed interstellar vessel was not any kind of technology, but rather a frozen alien corpse.

Or so Doctors Blair and Copper assumed. But the corpse came alive, and proved savage and lethal, exhibiting strange abilities of mimicry derived from a destructive possession of its victims. This 'thing from another world,' if I may so call it, was just on the point of either escaping to civilization or exterminating the humans—or both—when it was finally defeated by the bravery of the men and an ingenious tactic. They eradicated all contagious traces of its body, then turned their attention to the aftermath of its secret doings, when it had been sequestered in a hut. Secretly roaming the base, it had replicated from local parts both the antigravity mechanism and the neutron-beryllium power source before it died, as well as a simulation of its native environment in an outbuilding of the camp—a simulation that revealed its preference for the light of a blue-white star. These stars are classified as Wolf-Rayet types, and so we have adopted that general term to distinguish the alien technology."

Audie absorbed the radical revelations with his quick intelligence, then asked, "Well, what's the secret third technology that's you're hiding here? The Chief said something about 'life itself.'"

Luria gave the answer to that question. "The thing was a creature composed of infinitely malleable protoplasm—what we call totipotent cells. If it managed to insinuate the smallest traces of itself into a living creature, its alien protoplasm would rapidly replicate and replace all the original material of a being, while retaining both surface and cellular appearances. To all eyeball and instrumental tests, the creature reproduced itself as a perfect duplicate of the subject. But in reality, the victim would be a scion of the alien, an heir in disguise. In a way, just as green algae can fission into daughter cells, so the thing would have reproduced itself on the coattails of its victims, while wiping out the integrity and identity of the original host."

His eyes big as saucers, Audie said, "Jeepers, it's a good thing they wiped out all traces of that monster." When the scientists said nothing, the boy's eyes narrowed. "Or did they?"

Senator Truman chimed in. "Bright boy! Yes, the Garry Expedition felt sure that they had neutralized every iota of the thing. If they hadn't been certain, they would never have risked coming home and infecting us. And upon their return, all the experts did in fact deem them clean. And they were. But the monster survived, back in the Antarctic, in a most unlikely host. What the men had not reckoned with was the presence of polar microorganisms, bacteria living just beneath the snows. Drops of blood from the slaughter of the infected dogs penetrated the snow and infected these microorganisms. The thing from another planet could do nothing in these primitive vessels, but it remained alive. It was Doctors Delbrück and Luria here—two of our most brilliant biologists—who theorized this might be so. And the next expedition to the South Pole brought back core samples that proved their theory correct."

"Are you saying that you've got living bits of this monster here in bacterial form?"

Luria smiled proudly. "Much more than that, *ragazzo*! But we waste the Senator's valuable time in talking. Let us conduct the necessary tour, so that he might return to his committee with a positive report, and save our project that offers so much possibility of alleviating mankind's ancient sufferings."

With a nod to the stony-faced Marine, the two scientists led the way through the inner door, which swung shut tightly behind them.

The party found itself in a corridor whose walls, floor and ceiling appeared to be all stainless steel, apparently formed into shape from a single plate, with but a lone double-welded seam running down the middle of the ceiling. The metal chute conveyed the sense of travelling through some industrial network of pipes.

"Nothing permeable, no means of even the smallest particle escaping," said Delbrück. "We have complete confidence in the harmlessness of our charge, but even so, we take these incredible precautions."

Ahead a massive door like that of a bank's vault intervened. It had to be unlatched by the spinning of a wheel, and was able to be dogged shut from either side.

"A kind of airlock between the subject and the outer world. There are several more."

True to the scientist's word, the group passed through additional airlocks. The final one opened onto a view of a large room that constituted the bulk of the warehouse's cubic center.

This inner sanctorum was sharply illuminated. Again, all vertical and horizontal surfaces were bright metal, as if in a lounge built for robots. Central to the room, various pipes and tubing and effectuators ran into and out of a large glass sphere, big as a cottage. The sphere in its cradle featured a platform around its equator. Banks of instruments, attended by a handful of technicians, occupied much of this platform. Various apparatuses protruded into the sphere, through tightly gasketed openings.

Several more Marines, their rifles held ready for action, were stationed around the lab.

But these details were not what would immediately draw the eye of any observer. It was the incredible contents of the sphere that commanded all rapt gazes.

Inside the glass bubble, a mass of ivory protoplasm like a gigantic tapioca or blancmange, not quite enough to fill the entire enclosed space, roiled and churned as if agitated by propellors. But no such mechanism existed: the thing twisted and seethed, bubbled and pullulated under its own quasi-muscular impulses.

The quartet of newcomers crossed the gleaming stainless steel floor to the platform that surrounded the sphere, climbing the four steps that led to the banks of instruments. The technicians looked up briefly from monitoring their gauges and dials and uttered brief greetings, before returning to their vigilance.

Having seen this alien spectacle before, Truman was not completely taken aback, although even his face registered glimmers of a requisite awe. But Audie experienced a vertiginous sense of confronting the unthinkable. Drawn to the surface of the glass sphere like a rabbit sucked into a snake's ocular orbit, he was unprepared for a sudden unexpected change in the undifferentiated convulsing mass.

The protoplasm closest to Audie's face sprouted a cluster of three malevolent red eyes and a beak-like orifice surrounded by writhing blue worms!

Audie jumped away and instinctively reached behind his back for his gun. The Marines all snapped alert, pointing their rifles at the boy. Luckily, Truman intervened swiftly, catching Audie's arm in mid-reach and repositioning it away from his weapon.

The lad wiped the spontaneous freshet of sweat from his brow and said, "Holy cats! I ain't never been so shaken by anything as I was by that! Not even coming on a nest of rattlers in my bare feet! But you don't gotta worry. I don't aim to take no potshots at that creature—so long as you got it pent up safe like that."

Delbrück and Luria actually seemed proud of their captive monster, and amused at Audie's dissipated fright. The former said, "The enclosure is indeed escape-proof. But more than that, the monster is now harmless."

"How's that? You mean it can't take over a person no more?"

"No," Luria said, "it can't. For one very good reason. We have rendered its predatory genes docile. Max and I, along with invaluable help from our peers Thomas Morgan, Edward Tatum and George Beadle, have discovered how to shut off the expression, if you will, of its virulence. Oh, it might smother you with its sheer bulk, if it fell atop you. But its former ability to conquer by ingestion and replication is banished. But its new harmlessness is far from all we have achieved. Much more to the point, we have discovered how to control and shape expression within these totipotent cells."

"I don't rightly understand."

"A demonstration will convey our achievement more clearly than words."

Delbrück turned to one of the technicians. "Joe, initiate the Leghorn Sequence, please."

Inside the glass ball, a mechanical arm, tipped with a hypodermic needle, descended from above. All eyes were drawn to the needle, and Audie noticed a hitherto-unseen feature of the spherical cage. A glass box protruded both inside and outside the sphere. The inner mouth of the box was open to the protoplasm, while the outside face of the box was sealed with a door. Another instance of an airlock.

The needle plunged into the white gelatinous blob. Instantly, as if in utter obedience, the thing budded off a piece of itself, and spat the disconnected segment into the box. An inner door slid down, capping the little chute. Luria walked to the airlock and, opening it, removed the segregated bit, about as large as a brick, with a pair of forceps.

"Joe, the torch, please."

The technician clicked alight a small propane torch and played the flame over the detached mass.

"Are you aiming to kill that piece of the critter?"

Delbrück smiled. "Not precisely. This sample is already inert."

A very familiar aroma began to permeate the room.

"Is that—is that *chicken*?"

"Good nose, *ragazzo*." Joe ceased flaming the sample, and Luria waved it in the air to cool it. "Anyone care for a taste? No? Too bad. But it is past my lunch."

Luria plucked off a piece of the alien-sourced meat and popped it into his mouth. Delbrück did the same. "We have all enjoyed several such meals, without suffering any consequences other than a full stomach. All risked only after extensive animal testing, of course. We now have much better indicators of alien possession than the primitive immunity blood tests rigged up by Doctor Copper during the Antarctica crisis. And we affirm with absolute certainty that the monster's flesh is one-hundred-percent non-invasive."

Looking humble, pleased and serious all at once, Luria added, "Senator Truman, Mister Murphy—you have just witnessed an end to human hunger and starvation on this planet. With this artificial meat, endlessly replenishable and infinitely variable, we have conquered want and privation."

"What's this here jello-mold critter feed on?"

"Anything organic. Grass clippings, seaweed, even sewage. All turned into healthy edible products."

Audie gagged a bit at that last named contribution to the thing's diet, before recovering his aplomb. "Well, I guess what goes around's gotta come around."

Luria and Delbrück focused on Senator Truman now. "Senator, don't you agree that this achievement alone is sufficient justification to continue our project?"

Truman cupped his chin mediatatively. "I know there's over two billion people on the planet, and that's a lot of mouths to feed. Not that I see the population numbers going much higher than that anytime in the next century or so. But we've got this smart fella Norman Borlaug working on the problem, and he thinks he's got it licked by conventional means. So why do we need to invest in all this far-out technology, even with minimal risk? And besides, you've got the extra barrier of convincing folks to eat this foreign stuff. Once they know they'll be chowing down on converted roadkill and dead plow horses, say, you've got a major public-relations and marketing problem on your hands."

Delbrück sighed and looked to his partner, who nodded affirmatively. "All right, Senator, we are not quite ready with this development yet, but we feel we need to bring it center-stage to convince you of how invaluable this new Wolf-Rayet technology is. Mary, please initiate the Valentine Sequence."

A female technician worked the controls that sent another needle jabbing into the protoplasm to deliver its cargo of instructive tailored enzymes and proteins and chromosonal fragments. As before, the captive thing responded by forming its totipotent cells into a specialized unit, which it deposited into the transfer chute.

Luria had donned a pair of surgeon's gloves. He reached into the glass box and removed the output of the thing.

There in the biologist's cupped latex hands quivered a human heart, tinted with the natural colors of humanity. It beat for half a minute, disgorging residual tank fluids from its arteries, before it shivered to a halt.

Audie whistled in awe. "You gents got yourselves an all-purpose thingmaker there!"

Delbrück's gaze was both dreamy and practical, even a shade messianic. "Healthy, functional, a universal match for any blood type, and nonantigenic. If we had the surgical procedures perfected for transplantation—and studies such as Carrel and Lindbergh's *The Culture of Organs* are already leading the way—and if all operating rooms were equipped with a small-scale version of this tank, organ failures would become an archaic abomination of the brutal past. New kidneys, lungs, livers—all on demand."

Luria chimed in. "Not only internal organs, but limbs as well! New arms and legs that might not even need to be surgically attached, but which might attach themselves upon command!"

Truman at first was speechless. But, recovering his wits, he said, "Doctor Delbrück, Doctor Luria—I am a Baptist because I think that sect gives the common man the shortest and most direct approach to God. But I'll be goddamned if I can figure out what the Good Lord would think of this unholy idea of inserting monster parts into a person. Maybe the deity would approve, maybe not. He's already allowed his creations to perform some amazing feats that would have counted as blasphemy in other eras. But I do think you've just raised more obstacles to approval of your project—and big ones—instead of removing some."

The two scientists were plainly marshalling their further arguments in favor of the revolutionary technology when a new development precluded all talk.

The boom of a huge explosion sounded from the rear of the warehouse, shaking and rattling the inner chamber. The Marines instantly responded with practiced moves, taking up defensive positions with their rifles aimed at the only entrance.

Audie leaped in front of Truman, his gun in his hand.

"Get down, Senator! This ain't no playtime!"

The scientists and technicians activated controls that dropped a heavy metallic curtain around the thingmaker tank. Then they crouched as best they could behind the control kiosks on the platform.

The wait seemed to last forever, although it was only half a minute or so, but then came a second explosion at the inner door, sending acrid smoke and flying debris into the lab.

Gunfire rattled from both sides of the engagement. Flat on the decking, Truman practically felt Audie's booming pistol in action. Again, time stretched during the battle. Then the gunfire ceased—and Audie fell atop the Senator!

A Marine approached the platform. "It's over now. Are you folks all okay?"

"No!" Truman said. "We have a man down!"

He levered Audie's body off, and kneeled to investigate.

The boy was still alive, but suffering from a large deep chest wound.

Truman heard the protective curtain rattling upward, and Delbrück shouting, "The Patch Sequence!"

Luria dropped down beside the stricken lad. Somehow he found the courage and bravado to grin at Truman. "Allow me to introduce myself. The most famous never-matriculated undergraduate of the University of Turin medical school." He began ripping away Audie's shirt.

Delbrück raced over with his hands full of protoplasm. He tossed it to Luria, who slapped it down on Audie's chest like a mustard plaster.

The totipotent cells went straight to work, integrating themselves and rebuilding the shattered bones, flesh and organs, becoming human in color, shape and texture. In almost no time at all, Audie was sitting up, a slightly dazed yet competent and cogent look on his face. He placed a hand tentatively on his breastbone, regarding the invisible repairs with quiet astonishment.

"Jeepers! Sure hope this don't mean all my kids are gonna have three red eyes and blue catfish whiskers!"

In a few moments the thingmaker had produced a half-dozen more all-purpose patches, carried in spare Erlenmeyer.

flasks. Thus equipped for instant first aid, the two scientists, Truman and Audie followed the Marines on a path back out to the reception area. They paused first to examine the bodies of the fallen attackers. Contrary to any expectations that the invaders might have been uniformed soldiers of a hostile nation, they appeared to be native Americans of a certain type, that class known as the "gangster" or "underworld" figure: hard-nosed mugs in flashy suits, armed with tommyguns.

Once attaining the reception area, they discovered a scene of chaos. The outer door had been blown away. The lone Marine on guard had been mercilessly cut to pieces, too far gone for even thingmaker fixes.

Across Summersby's desk sprawled another gangster, facedown, this one unarmed and dressed with more panache.

A Marine flipped the body over.

Truman exclaimed, "I know this yegg from when he testified to Congress! It's Bugsy Siegel!"

At the sound of his name, the mobster opened his eyes, took in his audience, and spoke in a grating whisper. "Truman, you bastard... Cut off my radium-atomite sales to Mussolini... Knew you had something big going on here... Figured you owed me a share..."

Siegel lapsed back into unconsciousness. Truman said, "Get him fixed up. The US government is going to want to hold this pissant responsible for all this mess."

Audie shouted from where he was squatting behind the desk. "It's Miss Summersby! She's still breathing!"

In a brief time both Summersby and Siegel were once more hale and hearty. Her trig uniform all in disarray, Summersby got to her feet, still instinctively clutching her huge Webley revolver. Siegel glared at her with traces of reluctant approbation at her courage.

"Thought the bitch was dead on the floor, but she took me out when my back was turned."

Summersby holstered her sidearm. "One does not go skeet shooting every week since age twelve for nothing, nor endure the Blitz as an ambulance driver without mustering some resilience."

The exterior phone line proved to be intact, and soon the warehouse was flooded with troops and police and high-level politicos. Everything got sorted out with speed and precision.

After Siegel had been led away and all the corpses removed, Truman turned to Luria and Delbrück.

"Professors, this is no longer a safe or secret site for your project. I suggest we get you set up in a more secluded place. We have a facility in Los Alamos, New Mexico, that we're not using for anything. I think it would be just right for Project Thingmaker."

Audie piped up. "Much as I like working with you, Chief, I might ask to be assigned to help these guys. After all, I gotta pay back my pound of flesh, don't I?"

AEOTA

1.
Glass, Box, Calendar, Stars

The unexpected text read:

> find aeota yesterday everywhere.

I thought several thoughts, in this sequence:
Okay, I find things. Can do.
Who or what is "aeota?"
Yesterday is gone.
Or is it?
Everywhere's a big place.
Or is it?
And who knew this Methuselah of a phone of mine could display texts?
I carried a Nokia 7650, thick and clunky as a box of animal crackers, that was now sixteen years old. I had purchased it new in 2002, partially thanks to the hype associating it with the film *Minority Report*. It seemed highly futuristic right out of the box, maintaining its sci-fi luster for a surprisingly short interval thereafter, as most such products do these days, and had immediately aided me in my work to some acceptable degree that compensated for carrying it burdensomely in pocket and learning to use it. But after being forced to take several unpleasant and/or unwanted calls at awkward moments, I came to resent its electronic tether, and was always on the indecisive point of throwing it away. I certainly from the outset knew that I had no intention of upgrading it, stepping onto the endless uphill treadmill of Next Great Gadget. I used it nowadays as I had always used it, to place and receive voice calls, and those mainly to my ex, Yulia. I also checked in with my message inbox when I was away from the office.

Of course there was no longer any official support for the orphaned device. Only the ingenuity of my pal Marty Quartz kept the thing alive.

I had never received or sent one single text in those fifteen years, so the appearance of this message was instantly startling.

I noted immediately that the originating number was one of those generic fake string of digits you see in films, all fives. Someone was spoofing me. So much for any possibility of sourcing the text.

As I pondered the small color screen, about as big as two closed paper matchbooks abreast, the message disappeared, replaced by a question:

PRINT TEXT Y/N?

Could this sucker somehow have connected itself wirelessly to my office printer?

I highlighted Y and jabbed the worn ENTER button between the left and right movement controls.

From the top of the phone, out of a heretofore-invisible slot, a slip of paper the size of a Chinese cookie's fortune began to emerge. It juddered out with a last jolt and wafted to the floor. I leaned forward half-out of my desk chair to retrieve it.

On it were four symbols that I thought I might have identified positively as emojis, if I actually knew what emojis were.

find   *aeota*   *yesterday*   *everywhere.*

When I looked at the top of the phone whence the slip had emerged, I could discern no opening. However the slip had emerged, the aperture had resealed. I popped the upper back where the SIM card went. No print mechnism met my inspection.

I folded the tiny slip and tucked it into my pants pocket.

I would have to ask Marty about this new capacity of my phone the next time I saw him. Maybe he had retrofitted the device with this new ability.

I spun my chair around to use the keyboard of my desktop computer, which, while not quite as ancient as my phone, had stopped receiving automatic software updates about the time Isabella Rossellini had last been featured in a starring role.

Searching "aeota" returned relatively few hits, just a score of pages, most of links leading to the type of seemingly machine-generated gibberish that apparently constituted half the internet, robot prose to be read by androids. The major sensible usage for the word was as an acronym for the American Essential Oils Trade Association. They had a Facebook page, but their main site seemed to be occupied by a squatter. Well, if they had needed to be found, I had found them sufficiently. I'd have to send them a bill.

Mission accomplished, and time for a drink.

I had acquired a taste for tequila, neat, working with another guy on a case involving an arboreal Latino fowl. I wasn't a snob, though—the cheapest kind would do me just fine. Right now I was working on a liter of Old Sandstone brand, ten bucks a bottle, no tax.

The harsh golden liquid thrummed down my throat like a death-metal mariachi band.

Putting the bottle away, I thought about the latest—and currently singular—client employing the service of V. RUGGLES, INVESTIGATIONS.

Juniper Holtzclaw had hired me to track down her missing husband, Holger Holtzclaw. Like some wannabe Bernie Madoff selling a cold-fusion device or perpetual motion machine, Holger had been running a penny-ante pyramid scheme among his friends, neighbors and relatives, involving the supposed invention of a new, ultra-efficient methane-recapture technology that would be sold to landfill operators around the globe. He called his corporation Eurybia Enterprises. Supposedly they would employ all "green technology," so everyone loved it. In classic fashion, every new investor's money had gone to keep earlier suckers quiet, with Holger skimming off a goodly percentage for himself. His ultimate in-pocket take had been about a quarter million—peanuts, really, as these things went. But not to the horde of angry chumps beating on Juniper Holtzclaw's door twenty-four-seven, eager to reclaim their vanished IRAs or, failing that, to learn of Holger's whereabouts and take their recompense out of his hide.

Juniper swore she had known nothing of her husband's chicanery, and I believed her. She had given me a photo of the man—tall, saturnine, neatly attired, handsome in a sleazy way—and a list of his favorite resorts in Vegas, Holger's native Austria, and the Caribbean. I had taken these solid clues and, within a mere week, turned them into precisely nothing.

I had run out of ideas, but figured maybe Juniper could supply some. If not, she was always good to look at anyhow, a petite blonde resembling a young Goldie Hawn. And I had picked up a lonely vibe from our first interview, as if she would not be averse to some solaceful canoodling.

As if thinking lustfully of women had summoned another female in my life, Yulia's name and number appeared on my Nokia's antique screen, triggering my lone ringtone, a ghostly sound effect that combined an Yma Sumac banshee wail with some notes from a theremin. I think Marty had crafted it just for me. It wasn't the most soothing of sounds, but you never missed a call.

"Vee Ruggles, Investigations. If you are looking for a missing alimony payment, you need to contact your bank. Those capitalist suckers are pure evil, and delight in delaying the processing of money faithfully deposited into your account by the man you once called 'Tigerpants.'"

"Vern, quit fooling around. I need to see you about something. Today, if possible."

Going to see Yulia always led me into some kind of absurd situation which, while not necessarily classifiable in hindsight as "awful," always proved alarmingly and unpredictably uncomfortable, at best.

"We can't handle whatever it is by phone?"

She sounded more than moderately stressed. "No. Swing by the house as soon as you can."

"All right. Is it okay if I bring my new girlfriend? I think she can get some time off from her *Vogue* modeling job."

Yulia snorted like a young colt, which, believe it or not, I had always found to be one of her endearing traits. And despite whatever was troubling her, she could still match me beat for beat.

"Yeah, sure, bring her along. She can meet my new super-stud boyfriend, if NASCAR extends the Charlotte Motor Speedway course to allow him to make a pitstop by my front door."

Yulia hung up, and so did I. I stared at the Nokia for a full minute, but it didn't play any more tricks on me.

Dates with two hot women, both of whom surely would not be able to keep their hands off my burly, tequila-powered body. Who said I had nothing to live for?

2.

One Bourbon, One Scotch, One Sneer

On the drive out to Juniper's luxurious digs, I developed a sudden thirst. Having left my bottle of Old Sandstone back in the safety of its accustomed desk drawer just in case my cleaning lady should need a nip, I was forced to detour to my favorite dive, A. O.'s Tea Room. The place had been around forever, and during Prohibition it had adopted the innocuous moniker it still sported, as a blind against snooping Feds alert for the shameful enjoyment of illicit hooch. Depression-era proprietor Arturo Olvidado had hung around till the 1980s, coming to resemble a Latino Grandpa Smurf. Over the soused years I had watched him lose about five inches in height and gain twice that in circumference. These days his son, A.O. Jr., himself no dewy youth, ran the place. In honor of his father, or out of sheer cheapness, he hadn't changed the decor since about 1962. I found the Midcentury Modern ambiance helped one attain *Mad Men* levels of liquor consumption.

Close to two in the afternoon, the lot outside the bar featured only three or four cars. I joined the ranks and went inside, passing under the dead busted neon sign that depicted a lady's hand holding a teacup, pinky finger extended.

Irascible Junior himself was tending the bar. Before my butt even contacted the stool, he had a boilermaker sitting on the stained wooden counter for me. I slammed it back gratefully.

"You got today's newspaper handy, Art?"

"Sure, Vern. Here you go. Waste your day."

Our local rag, the *Argonaut & Globe*, reflected a merger of two venerable papers that had been forced to lean on each other like two wounded soldiers just to survive in this mean shameful age of sound bites and click bait. Even combined, their resources were a fraction of what they had been when I was a kid. But I was hoping that maybe some enterprising young Jimmy Olsen had solved the disappearance of Holger Holtzclaw for me, and I could read about it on the front page.

But no such luck. The headlines contained only the usual mix of the inexplicable, the outrageous and the drear. What an insane fucking world. More and more I felt like we were all racing in a driverless train right over the edge of the frigging immemorial Grand Canyon.

I turned to the comics to alleviate my gloom. Maybe today would be the day Garfield had another out-of-body bardo experience.

Something caught my eye in a strip I normally did not read: *Dick Tracy*. In the first panel, one of Tracy's subordinates at police HQ said, "Hey, Dick, there's someone here to see you from way back when." "Who might that be?" asks Tracy. In the second panel the buddy says, "Otto Atone," a typical Dick Tracy goofball name, and Tracy does a spit-take. In the third panel a mysterious figure is being ushered into Tracy's presence, but his face is in shadows. In the fourth panel—

But there was no last panel. The paper had gotten sodden and been torn off by rough handling.

The name "Otto Atone" struck me as weird somehow. I couldn't figure out why, and after a minute I gave up trying. I got up to leave, and found my elbow grabbed without my implied or explicit consent.

I gazed down to see a squat, shabby fellow who looked like the fellow from the cover of Tull's *Aqualung*, if that guy had been living under a bridge for six months. It appeared his greasy moss-green coat had bonded to his frame from continuous wear. Instinctively, I pulled back from his touch.

"You Ruggles?" His voice sounded like a kazoo being played through a wet sock full of mud.

"Yeah. What of it?"

"I got something for you." He pulled aside his coat and took out a small white box that was amazingly clean, given its mode of conveyance. I flashed for a second on the box emoji that my phone had displayed. Did this package contain the enigmatic aeota?

I didn't immediately reach to take the box. "Who's it from?"

The guy sneered. "You got enemies?"

"Well, not really. Except maybe my barber, as you can tell by my haircut."

"Funny man." He thrust the box at me. "Here, take it! I got better things to do than wait on you. Anyhow, it's not who it's from—it's what's in it."

I accepted the box, which was about as big as a four-piece Whitman's Sampler. The guy turned to shuffle off.

"Wait a minute. What's your name? How do I reach you if I need to?"

"The name's Baxter. Brevis Baxter. And don't worry, we can reach you if we need to."

Baxter was gone before I could figure out how to reply.

That left me with nothing to do but open the box.

As soon as I removed the lid, which came away with a slight resistance and whoosh of escaping air, a not unpleasant scent—like a day at the beach when the low tide had exposed many living things—poured out.

Inside was something organic that resembled a tangle of moist seaweed shot through with gleams of opal, grey and purple. I poked it with my finger, and it suddenly deliquesced into a sloppy slurry sloshing around thickly in the cardboard box.

I put the lid back on and chucked the whole mess into the bin by the front door as I left.

If this was a free trial for a bento box lunch service, I remained unimpressed.

3.

AEOTA and Aeota

The maritime scent on my tainted finger remained pungent throughout the drive to the Holtzclaw place, diminishing only gradually by the time I arrived.

Juniper Holtzclaw had held onto a very nice piece of property, despite all the ongoing litigation against her absent husband. About six-thousand square feet of mock-Tudor McMansion on a landscaped acre in a part of the city where trees outnumbered rats, good au pairs ranked barely higher than killer Pilates instructors, and trash pickup happened discreetly down hidden service alleys. I felt ashamed just parking my twenty-year-old Toyota beater at her curb. If I got lucky, nothing would fall off it while I was inside.

Walking up to her front door, I suddenly wondered exactly when the appurtences of my life had transitioned from modern to antiquated. Getting divorced hadn't left me with lots of disposable income, true, but I still could have afforded a new phone, for Christ's sake. But I seemed to have culti-vated to the point of obsession some bias against the new, some inertia to change, a begrudging attitude toward the present that was only getting more pronounced. Pretty soon, I figured, I would be living backwards, like Merlin or Benjamin Button.

I thought of a Robert Mankoff cartoon I had seen in *The New Yorker* a couple of years ago. A patient lies on the psychiatrist's couch, the skeptical shrink eying him suspiciously. The nutty guy says, "But I like living in the past. It's where I grew up."

Juniper answered the door herself, albeit somewhat suspiciously, a fair stance given the random irate strangers stopping by at all hours. She had kept the house, but no servants. That was a big comedown.

Clad in a cream-colored cowlneck sweater over flower-patterned pedal-pushers and a pair of those mock gladiator sandals that laced up her shapely calves, she looked like the missing quarter of a million bucks that Holger had fled with. She recognized me, of course, but did not seem overly enthusiastic at my arrival.

"Mr. Ruggles. No news, I take it. What more can I do for you?"

"Can I come inside, please? If I make one more convert for the Mother Church, they'll give me a second wife."

That bought me a chuckle, and soon I was sitting on a dark leather couch in a sunny, over-decorated parlor half the size of Union Station. Offered a drink, I angled for tequila, but got only white wine, which was the equivalent of hoping for sex and getting a lecture on social justice instead. As for any hypothetical sex itself, it was "Outlook not so good," according to the Magic 8-Ball placed midway between my gut and dick.

"I don't think I ever inquired. How did you and Holger meet?"

"It was during a ski trip to Klosters in Switzerland during my junior year of college. Holger was there with some friends. Incredibly charming and accomplished on the slopes. We hit it off, and got married a year later."

"Holger's been around the track a few more time than you."

"He is eleven years older than me, yes."

"And who brought more, uh, capital to the sacred union?"

Juniper practically sprouted icicles. "I have a certain safe and sufficient income thanks to the generosity of my family. But Holger always sustained our mutual lifestyle in a very capable fashion. Right up to this unfortunate misstep."

Nothing could have been clearer to either Juniper or me: she had married a sexy Eurotrash scammer on the order of Clark Rockefeller and now was paying the price. I didn't make her say it out loud, and I refrained from any moralistic finger-pointing of my own. My moralistic fingers were too dirty and out of practice to be of much use.

"Did Holger have any offices for this cow-fart utilization thing he was putting over on people?"

"No, he worked out of his study here."

"Is it possible for me to go through his papers?"

"I suppose so—whatever the authorities left behind."

In contrast to the parlor, the study was dark and claustrophobia-inducing, with heavy velvet curtains, drawn, seeming to narrow the room to coffin size. A desk lamp with one of those useless energy-saving bulbs did little to dispel the gloom.

"Leave everything as you find it, please, and then let yourself out. I have a headache and need to lie down."

I didn't bother mentioning that was the effect I had on all women.

At the study door, Juniper paused, and I wondered if she was going to ask me to tuck her in.

"And please don't abscond with any of the more valuable curios, if you can help yourself. Everything is under a lien, until this mess gets straightened out."

"Gotcha. My interior decorator is very picky about what I bring home to add to her designs anyway."

The Treasury men or the SEC or the IRS had plucked Holger's files cleaner than the hotdog platter at an orphanage picnic. You could have stored the *Complete Works of Stephen King* in his desk drawers.

But by lying down on my back and looking up, I found one paper way at the rear of the bottom drawer that had been accidentally pinned, hidden, in place by the drawer above.

The letterhead read: Association of Engineering Ontologists Totalizing Affinities. An address on the outskirts of a small city upstate completed the information.

Dear Mr. Holtzclaw:

Yes, I believe AEOTA can supply your needs. But our technology is proprietary, and can only be licensed, not purchased. We would have to conduct a face-to-face meeting to discuss the exact arrangements.

Please contact us at your earliest convenience to arrange such a meeting.

Sincerely yours,

Mr. Thaumas

The date on the letter was two days before Holger had disappeared.

* * * *

From Juniper's nabe to the rather seedier district where Yulia lived in the double-wide trailer I had purchased for us with the profits from reuniting an aging rock star with her daughter abandoned at birth was a journey across practically the entire socioeconomic spectrum of contemporary urban America, from upper crust to stale leftovers. Hustling seemed universal, though, no matter the income level. About the only types of citizen I did not pass during my odyssey were junkies and state legislators, although I did drive by an infamous bar where the Mayor had recently been caught snorting coke in the john, so maybe I bagged two unsavory coups in one.

Yulia's usual Slavically spooky sixth sense had her waiting for me glaringly in the open doorway, although I had not called. Or maybe my Nokia was secretly on her side and had texted news of my departure from Juniper's.

The Euromaidan Revolution of 2014 in the Ukraine had produced winners and losers, just like any revolution, and Yulia Lysenko had been one of the losers. Forced to abandon all her property and her job as a literature professor, due to her out-of-favor allegiances, she fled her native land to receive asylum in the USA. Her academic credentials were useless here, and she had taken a job as a bartender. The watering-hole, an upscale joint named after its owner, Joshua Greenstone, appreciated the trade brought in by the new brunette bottle-jockey's gamin good looks—though she did have what oral maxillofacial surgeons refered to as "incompetent lips." This was the condition where the normal resting state of one's face resulted in the display of teeth. Yulia looked as if she were perpetually snarling or sneering. Some guys found it really sexy, yours truly among them. Several daily tequila purchases at Joshua Greenstone's by yours truly had resulted in a date and nigh-concurrent sex.

When I could breathe and see and formulate words again after that initial bout of copulation, I said, "There is no way those are incompetent lips."

My extreme charm and wit and superhuman bedroom prowess led straight to the altar.

Our marriage lasted two-and-a-half years. Yulia quickly and correctly concluded, to her dismay, that I was eccentric, lazy and without much ambition. But two other issues had influenced her decision to ditch me.

The first was my propensity to mess around with other women. I can only offer the excuse that I had been a bachelor for all my adult life up until this June-October marriage, and had been set in my ways. The worst reveal of my inveterate horndoggishness occurred when Yulia had returned a day early from her reunion in Paris, France, with her mother and found the double-wide rockin'. Non-American that she was, she failed to complete and heed the advisory adage and had indeed come knockin', discovering me with a stacked naked redhead who was intent on showing me why it had been a glaring injustice to the pole-dancing profession to fire her from her job at a certain gentlemen's club, a venue that she now wanted me to bring down in revenge by highlighting various illegal practices of theirs that I could surely uncover with her athletic help.

But our short marriage might have survived such infidelities, if not for a more substantial disagreement.

And that, it turned out, underlay the immediate cause that had made Yulia summon me today.

Plainly, she had worked herself up into an indignant tizzy since our touchy but mild-mannered phone conversation of a few hours ago. She waved a piece of paper violently as I crossed the gravel walk to the trailer's wooden steps.

"Vern, this is the sickest, most vile joke you have ever played on me!"

Except in the realm of slang, Yulia's English was better than mine, but her accent surfaced during times of stress. Now she sounded like a streetmarket borscht vendor.

I ushered us inside and closed the door. "Calm down, Yulia. What the hell are you talking about?"

She shoved the paper under my nose.

I read the ransom note, a simple anonymous laser-print document.

YULIA RUGGLES WE HAVE YOUR DAUGHTER AEOTA
SHE WILL BE RETURNED SAFELY TO YOU FOR THE SUM OF
ONE HUNDRED THOUSAND DOLLARS
WE ARE CONFIDENT YOU AND YOUR EX HUSBAND CAN
RAISE THIS SUM OF MONEY
WHEN YOU HAVE IT READY WE WILL KNOW AND YOU
WILL RECEIVE FURTHER INSTRUCTIONS
DO NOT GO TO THE POLICE IF YOU VALUE YOUR DAUGH-
TER'S LIFE

Yulia had me pinned with a look of total contempt that hurt me more than I thought she still could. So I played it for laughs.

"Not much on proper punctuation, are they?"

Tear-tracks mottling her flushed face, Yulia socked me in the chest with a small but potent fist. "You really thought this was funny? You dirty bastard!"

"Yulia, I swear, I had nothing to do with this!"

"Then why does the note use the name 'Aelita' for our daughter? No one knows that but us!"

I looked again at the note, then turned it towards Yulia. "They don't say 'Aelita,' they say 'Aeota.'"

Yulia knuckled her eyes, dragged a sleeve across her drippy nose, then studied the letter again. She regarded me with less hatred and more confusion.

"You're right. I thought it said 'Aelita...' I guess... I guess I saw what I expected to see..."

Yulia had wanted to conceive a year after we married. Naturally, I had to reveal my ancient vasectomy. She learned the operation could often be successfully reversed. I refused. She even had a name picked out for our unborn daughter. Aelita, after some Russian movie she admired. That ongoing, vituperative disagreement was the real beginning of our end.

"Who the hell is Aeota then?"

"I don't now. I think it has something to do with this case I'm on."

Yulia grabbed the letter, crumpled it up and threw it to the floor. "Even when we're not married I have to suffer because of your bullshit job!"

I retrieved the ransom note. "This come in an envelope?"

She found it in the trash. A plain white business-sized envelope with no writing on it. I took it nonetheless.

"I've got to go now. Call me if anything else happens that I should know about."

Outside at my car, I paused to look back.

Yulia stood in the trailer's door with her arms folded below her stomach, as if cradling what wasn't there.

4.
Locavore Apocalypse

I was driving north, into a short-lived killer inferno.

Well, maybe not fully into it, but close enough to get singed maybe—if I weren't careful.

Upstate was burning, several separated wildfires devouring acres of drought-dried forest and a few incidental pieces of beloved infrastructure, despite the best efforts of thousands of firefighters. Even hundreds of miles away from the living flames, the air approached Chinese-megalopolis levels of unbreathability and opacity.

Elsewhere in the nation, a couple of Katrina-wannabe storms had hit up and down the East Coast; Atlanta had experienced a freak hailstorm with celestial ice-rocks the size of ping-pong balls crashing down; the Midwest had seen a pack of tornadoes romping through a swath of helpless towns like teenage girls rampaging through a Wet Seal store during a fifty-percent-off sale; invader species were practically climbing out of the Great Lakes to register to vote; and honeybees were dying faster than amateur comedians at open-mic night. Predictions for the upcoming winter's weather ranged from Michael Crichton direness to *Book of Revelation* severity.

And those were just the conditions in the USA. Of the rest of the climate-victimized world, the perp speaketh not.

There really was no denying the truth any longer: our planet was fucked. Screwed, blued and tattooed by humanity into a long, slow death spiral. Or at least, that's how it seemed to me at the moment—and to most of us, I think, when we were being honest with ourselves.

And what was to be done about the situation? Really, c'mon now, give it your best shot. Live in caves? Stop buying Big Agribiz strawberries? Carry picket signs down into coal mines? Read locally produced papyrus by candle light instead of binge-watching TV shows? How about we just stop over-breeding like bonobos on Spring Break? Yeah, good luck with that last one. No, the average citizen, however well intentioned, had been sidelined from the playing field or benched himself on this crisis. All the low-flow shower-heads you could install were not going to deliver water to these dried-out woods towards which I drove.

I was like everyone else. The only thing to do, I figured, was to keep calm and carry on. "When the world is running down, you make the best of what's still around." If humanity's bacon was ever going to be saved—a highly debatable proposition—some big-ass *deus ex machina* would have to step in, some game-changer along the lines of alien invasion, massively-lethal-only-to-humans plague, or revolutionary new technology. And neither you nor I nor my kid sister were going to play any pivotal part in those scenarios.

So I drove north, adding my share of carbon monoxide and other pollutants to the overburdened atmosphere and trying not to give a damn.

Out here in the country, without any distractions other than musing on the imminent extinction of the human race, a worn tape of Yes playing slurrily from my dashboard speakers ("Lost in losing circumstances, that's just where you are…"), I tried to think about this case.

Back in my office after leaving Yulia, I had packaged up the ransom note and its envelope and messengered them over to a private lab I used. I doubted I would get any fingerprints or chemical or organic signatures from the paper that would lead me anywhere, but I had to try.

After the messenger came and went—a young guy in cyclist gear, thin as my wallet—I thought about my counterfactual daughter, Aeota/Aelita. I tried to picture her unborn face. Christ, I hoped she would have favored Yulia rather than me! She'd be, what, roughly five years old by now. A real little girl. Heir and fruit of my loins. And abducted! I began to get angry for no real reason. I powered up my computer and searched for "aeota" again.

The results were radically different from the last search just a few hours ago.

The top entry on the first page, brand new, was a hit for the Association of Engineering Ontologists Totalizing Affinities, the source of the letter to Holtzclaw. I clicked over to their home page. Very glossy, lots of pictures of happy consumers enjoying themselves in various idyllic situations, indoors and out, plus dedicated employees in office and laboratory settings. Except I couldn't really identify what AEOTA did or made or traded. All I encountered was a lot of buzzwords about incentivizing and rewarding and optimizing and maximizing—and, natch, "totalizing affinities."

Back among the search results, several lines down but still on the first page, I came across another new reference.

"Aeota" had been the name of a female character in a short-lived newspaper comic strip that ran during the year 1910, Herbert Crowley's "The Wiggle-Much." Scholar Dan Nadel had said, "For a brief period thereafter, the name received some faddish conversational usage among fans of the strip, being applied to any woman of a certain disposition, attitude and appearance conforming to those qualities discerned in the fictional woman."

I brought up fuzzy scans of the antique strip. So far as I could tell, Aeota had been a roly-poly Polynesian, attired in native garments—that is, when she hadn't been a willowy Weimar vamp like Theda Bara, all slinky gowns, plumed tiaras and long strands of costume beads. And did she feature a tail? Maybe I was conflating two separate characters. The eccentric lettering in the word balloons was hard to read, and the strip's plot, taking place amongst surreal creatures in a neverland, did not lend itself to casual parsing.

I took out my phone and called Marty Quartz, my go-to guy for all matters cyber.

"Vern, great to hear from you! How's the Nokia? 'That is not dead which can eternal lie, and with strange aeotas even death may die.'"

"Marty, what did you say? Strange what now?"

"'Strange eons.' You know the quote. Your basic Lovecraft. Hey, need a new ringtone?" Without warning, Marty blasted my ear with what sounded like two ducks shagging a coyote to death inside a galloping calliope.

"I'm honored to experience that snippet from the Arcturus Hit Parade, Marty, but I'm cool with the older ringtone you gave me. No, I need to ask you something." I recounted my before-and-after forays into the web. "How could search results change so dramatically in just a few hours?"

"The internet is a dynamic organism, Vern. It's not static, things change every second."

"Yeah, but these changes happened on the very first page of results for the same search term each time. Aren't those supposed to be the durable results with the most weight? How could something brand new instantly rise to the top?"

"Things trend, Vern. Attention drives significance and visibility. Someone else besides you must be googling that shit and hyperlinking their brains out."

"Yeah, but these items didn't even exist in the prior search."

"Are you sure of that? Did you really study every page of the early results?"

I tried to recall if I had scrolled through every single line of the prior search. Hadn't I given up after wading through so much spam? Maybe the items about postmodern industrial AEOTA and the Herbert Crowley strip had been hiding from me just a page away.

"No, I can't be sure, Marty."

"Well, there you go. Hey, I gotta fly, Vern. I'm behind in rigging up my Burner costume. I'm going as a Red Lectroid. Hope I don't bake under all the latex prosthetics."

As the line went unceremoniously dead, I realized I had not asked him about the way my phone had disgorged a printed slip of paper.

As I was repocketing my Nokia, the same bike messenger guy returned. No way the lab could have turned around my assignment so fast.

But it was just a coincidence. The kid was delivering a package to me, a small item wrapped in kraft paper, no trace of sender.

Somebody obviously thought it was Christmas and I had been a very good little boy.

Nestled in cotton batting in an unmarked cardboard jeweler's box, smaller than the one delivered to me by Brevis Baxter, was a cheap charm bracelet with only four cheap pewter charms on it: a magnifying glass, a gift-wrapped present, a page-a-day calendar and a representation of the Milky Way as seen from above, a spiral-armed whirlpool.

find aeota yesterday everywhere.

I tore the box and kraft paper apart, looking for a note or a clue, but came up dry.

Now I was getting a little pissed-off. Two mysterious deliveries in one day. That pegged the private-eye suspiciousness meter to the max.

I dropped the charm bracelet in the same pocket that held the slip of paper that my phone had spat out, then went down to my car.

I knew I was going to have to visit AEOTA in person…

Now the GPS showed I was only about half an hour away from my destination. Rural scenery still predominated, a dozen shades of brown with here and there some besieged green. I came abreast of a neatly tended farm amidst a manifestly irrigated cornfield with a big barn bearing an old-school advertisement painted right on the planks of its roadside wall.

I slammed on the brakes, shifted and zoomed back in reverse, heedless of traffic conditions behind me. Luckily, the lone car coming saw my crazy actions in time to swerve with a blast of horn.

I found the driveway to the farm and pulled in.

Standing a few feet from the barn wall, I verified I had not imagined the sight.

CHEW AEOTA PLUG
FOR DISCERNING MEN OF SUPERIOR TASTE
NO FINER FLAVOR NOR GRAIN
"ALL THE CHORUS AEOLIAN
"SINGS ITS PRAISE IN AEOTA LAND"

I pondered the drawing of the tobacco pouch: the trademark featured a kind of pre-nubile vestal virgin wrapped in a flowing robe and holding up a single big tobacco leaf with both hands. Real *Little Nemo* look.

Even in the smoky gloom of the forest-fire-tinged atmosphere, the colors on the sign were, if vintage, inexplicably hardly faded.

"Pretty awesome, am I right?"

I turned to confront a young couple, obviously the farm's owners. The round-faced woman was black and displayed her hair in a kind of upgathered pineapple-foliage fountain. She wore rubber boots and carried a murmuring buff-colored chicken big as a hypertrophied turkey. Her white male partner had on dirty bib overalls and sported a beard thick as the barbed wire around a refugee camp. Grow-local hipsters, "American Gothic" for the Whole Foods era. They were both smiling.

"We redid the barn last year," said the guy. "Stripped off all the old siding, and there she was. Protected from the elements for about ninety years."

"What do you know about the history of that brand? Anything?"

The man took out his cellphone and tip-tap-flick-swiped up a screen of thumbnail images. "Oh, sure. Lots of information on the web. It's not made anymore though. Company went out of business around 1970. So we adopted the name for our farm."

I stared at the guy's screen, seeing the Aeota tobacco pouch replicated in a dozen era-variant styles. I knew that when I returned to my office, I'd find the same data showing on my screen, where it had never appeared before in previous searches.

"Well, thanks. I gotta go now."

"Take a dozen eggs," offered the woman pleasantly. "We've got more than we can sell."

Behind the wheel again, I cast frequent sidelong glances at the carton of Aeota Farm eggs on the passenger seat. The hipsters had shooped the image of the vestal virgin out of context and replaced the tobacco leaf in her hands with an uplofted, much-larger-than-life egg.

5.

Judge Dread

The opalescent murk outside my windshield had gotten pretty bad by the time I hit the outskirts of the city where AEOTA had its corporate HQ, and I was grateful I didn't have to head any further north. Just breathing this stuff was becoming problematical.

Past an elementary school, a mall, a junkyard, a milk-bottling plant—
find aeota yesterday everywhere.

The building that housed AEOTA bore discreet signage in a modest font attesting to the company's humble presence. An elegant single-story block of offices, more viridian-tinted glass than steel, was dwarfed by a tall window-less monolithic manufactory wing longer than a couple of football fields, all utilitarian coppery metal.

I took a visitor's parking space and entered a pleasant atrium. A reception-ist ensconced as eye-candy behind a circular desk might have wandered in off the pages of *Vanity Fair*.

"I'd like to see Mr. Thaumas, please."

"You're expected?"

"No. But if you tell him I want to talk about Holger Holtzclaw and Eury-bia Enterprises, he might get all puppy-dog eager."

Three minutes later, I had a temporary badge and a guide—a young intern who looked as if he could shave the down from his cheeks with a let-tuce leaf—and was heading toward what I hoped were, if not some definitive answers, at least some further milestones along this crazy road. I felt a little as if I were Nick Fury walking through the dangerous corridors of AIM, but since I didn't see any guys in yellow bee-keeper suits, I tried to shrug off the feeling. Besides, I wasn't right for the role of Nick: I looked awful with an eye-patch.

The wooden door bore the title of CEO and my man's full name: Thomas T. Thaumas.

I don't know who I expected to see behind that door. The Devil, Gordon Gekko, Hannibal Lecter, Dr. Evil. But whatever menacing figure my imagination might have supplied, it wasn't that of Judge Hardy.

Old cultural touchstones evaporate, exhibiting a half-life determined by a complex formula involving nursing-home mortality stats and the ratings of certain nostalgia-driven cable channels. Once upon a time, everyone knew the Andy Hardy movies. Mickey Rooney as the boy who defined the then-newly minted modern teenager. Familiar enough to inspire a thousand imitations and parodies. And Andy's Dad, played by actor Lewis Stone, almost as familiar. Wispy white hair receding from a high, intelligent dome of a forehead. Strong, elderly-handsome craggy face, more long than square. Clear, dispassionate, ironic gaze, stern but fair. Always dressed in plain dark tasteful suits and vest, with one of those floppy ties seen mostly on Golden Age comic-book Senators of yore.

That proved to be Thomas T. Thaumas to a tee. Except for the bluetooth headset that Judge Hardy had never envisioned.

The door shut of its own volition behind me as I crossed the oxblood-colored carpet. I had just enough time to quickly take in burl-wood walls adorned with soothing abstract paintings and a large window looking out over a grassy courtyard where AEOTANS strolled and lunched, before I confronted the CEO of AEOTA.

Thaumas wheeled out from behind his desk, a sculpted, bare-topped mass all stainless steel, birch and walnut in aerodynamic lines. He compensated for his stick-like legs that barely bulked out his trousers with one of those high-tech wheelchairs that could climb stairs and elevate the sitter to eye-level in cherry-picker fashion. Simultaneously heightening himself as he moved forward, he produced a disorienting sensation in my brain, as if several dimensions of the universe were involuting.

Neither smiling nor frowning, utterly neutral and businesslike, Thaumas extended a hand and we shook. I wasn't invited to sit, and indeed there were no spare chairs.

"Mr. Ruggles, your inquiry, conveyed to our receptionist, concerned a potential past client of ours, one Holger Holtzclaw. What is it you wish to know about our dealings?"

"He received a letter from your firm just a day or two before he disappeared, suggesting that he should visit you. Did he ever keep that appointment? If he did, then your firm was one of his last known contacts. His wife and creditors are eager to track him down, and have hired me for the job."

"Mr. Holtzclaw did indeed visit us recently. I can get you the exact date and time if you need it. But after a tour of our facilities, he learned that our technology was unsuitable for his needs, and we parted ways permanently, with no subsequent contact or open channels. I'm afraid I have no idea of his current whereabouts."

"What was he after? What made your tech not useful to him?"

"Mr. Holtzclaw was interested in capturing and sequestering methane from landfills. Our own processes actually generate methane, the exact opposite of what he needed. I am afraid he learned of us through second-hand information, and misunderstood the nature of our work."

"What exactly is the nature of AEOTA's mission, Mr. Thaumas? I haven't been able to figure that out yet myself."

Thaumas pinned me with a glacial granitic gaze, and I felt like young Andy summoned on the carpet for playing hooky, or knocking up Judy Garland.

"Our firm pursues many disciplines, Mr. Ruggles, some with obvious synergies, and others that might seem, to the unitiated, to be utterly divergent. We sponsor R&D programs in a variety of areas. But our overriding ethos and *raison d'etre* is on display plainly in our name. We believe that reality can be shaped by skilled intentions. That's ontological engineering. The noosphere or realm of human thought governs all that is. We apply the shaping precepts we have deduced and mastered, and reality changes to match our dictates."

"Are you talking about introducing new ideas and products and technologies into the world, and then hoping they are used as you intend? Shaping the culture that way, like Microsoft or Google or Monsanto? Or are you pumping me full of New Age woo-woo?"

Thaumas allowed himself the smallest of smiles. "Perhaps both, Mr. Ruggles."

"And what the hell is 'totalizing affinities?'"

"It's as the poet famously ordained, Mr. Ruggles: 'Only connect.' We identify affinities, both overt and covert, explicit and implicit, then work to totalize them, to both utterly comprehend these secret connections and to foster their interlocking syzygy."

"Well, to be perfectly frank, Mr Thaumas, all this sounds like a truckload of mystical, investor-befuddling bullshit to me. But so long as your stockholders are happy, who am I to quibble?"

"You are entitled to your opinion of course, Mr. Ruggles."

"Do you think I can see whatever it was you showed Holtzclaw?"

"But of course, Mr. Ruggles. You need only sign a simple non-disclosure agreement consisting of a single paragraph." Thaumas activated his headset mic. "Ms. Bagasse, would you please bring in a copy of the standard visitor's NDA? And please summon Dr. Ponto to conduct a tour."

A pretty young assistant whose perfume alone had to count as some kind of perk for the executives she worked with came swiftly. I read and signed the form. While we waited for my guide, I said, "What's the 'Tee' stand for?"

It seemed to me that Thaumas only pretended not to comprehend. "What 'Tee' would that be, Mr. Ruggles?"

"Your middle initial."

"It stands for 'Totenwelt.' It's an old family name. It refers to the land of the spirits, the dead, the fey. My female ancestors were all witches, you see."

6.

A Visit with Microbial Matt

Before I could reply to Thaumas's somewhat unsettling familial disclosure, Dr. Matt Ponto arrived.

To say I was kinda taken aback by his appearance would be akin to claiming that the fussy old maid had been nonplussed by the next-door backyard orgy.

For a moment, I thought I had fallen into Middle Earth, or at least the Peter Jackson stageset thereof. Ponto was a bandy-legged dwarf, heavily muscled, a fact easy to discern from his arm-and-leg-revealing outfit of green cargo shorts and Hawaiian shirt printed with a photo-realistic nebula. He wore thick-soled hiking sandals. A shaggy mane of blonde hair crested above his eyes and a thick golden beard began more or less just under them, leaving him peering out as if from a military bunker's slit.

He grabbed my hand and squeezed it like a garlic press deals with a ripe clove. A kind of bumbling bonhomie radiated off him. His voice was surprisingly high, at odds with the rest of him. "You're Vern, right? Bagasse told me on the way in. Call me Microbial Matt. Everyone does. My specialty. Bugs of all sorts. But it's a pun too on my big project. I don't know if pun is the right word, exactly. You'll see. C'mon, let's go, the day's not getting any younger."

Ponto grabbed my left arm just above the elbow in a nerve-damaging pinch that brooked no resistance and steered me out the door. What was it with strangers today feeling free to make use of my bod? I looked over my shoulder to say goodbye to Thaumas, but he had already swivelled his chair and was motoring back behind his desk, lowering his seat at the same time. The combined movements provided the sensation that he was shrinking, disappearing down some converging set of lines that led to a vanishing point in a surrealist canvas.

Ponto led me through a cube farm where no one bothered to look up to the rear of the office wing, then carded us through a locked door and into the huge windowless structure behind the façade. I expected to immediately enter a facility like NASA's famed Vehicle Assembly Building. But just beyond the entrance was only a many-doored corridor of modest dimensions, not the cavernous warehouse I had half-expected.

"Labs and stuff here, but you don't want to see that. Boring, innocuous. No, you want to see Vaalbara. That's what I showed Holtzclaw. He found it fascinating. Didn't want to leave! But first we have to get you kitted out. Otherwise you wouldn't last too long. No, you definitely need to be able to breathe to enjoy Vaalbara."

I don't think I had even said so much as hello since Ponto had taken charge. Trying to shift the conversation or slow down our pace was the same frustrating and impossible task that Bugs Bunny faced every time Taz came on the scene.

Ponto brought us to a kind of locker room. I did a double-take. Hanging on pegs were several lime-green suits with boots and hoods attached that did indeed resemble the outfits of AIM.

"Powered Respirator Protective Suit," Ponto explained. "PRPS. We call them perps. Get dressed. Oh, ditch any metal, too."

7.

"A Title on the Door Deserves a Vaalbara on the Floor"

I expected something out of the ordinary when, after discarding my phone and keys and other metallic objects on a shelf, including that mysterious charm bracelet, Ponto and I had to cycle through an airlock to see what he wanted to show me. Gasketed outer door dogged tight. The hiss, muffled by my beekeeper headgear, of pumped-out air, leaving us in partial vacuum. I sent out silent thanks to the quality-control staff at the PRPS factory. Then an equivalent hiss of new atmosphere arriving. Finally, the rubber-buffered inner door unlatched. And on the far side—

We had stepped out onto a small railless lanai or platform that projected out, midway up a wall, over a high-roofed expanse of seemingly empty "factory" floor that must've been equivalent to about a dozen football fields in dimensions of six by two. The illumination inside this vast space was weird: like outdoor sunlight, but considerably less bright than noon of a cloudless day, and also with uncanny spectral differences I couldn't quite pin down.

Sudden slow and weighty ripplings twelve feet below the platform forced a realization upon me. What I had taken for a flat featureless floor was really the top layer of an enormous tank full of—something. From the nature of its movements, I surmised that the slinkily undulant material, a glabrous blue-green shot through with streaks of grey and opal, formed a seamless blanket atop millions of gallons of unknown fluid.

I turned to Ponto, and his voice reached me via speakers built into the hood of my perps.

"The light mimics what we understand to have been the unprocessed sunlight of the Archean period, some four billion years ago. Seventy percent of our current luminosity, with more UV. Our young sun was lazy and liked to spit. Vaalbara was a supercontinent of that era, hence the code name."

"And the floating carpet is—?"

Ponto grinned big behind his plastic face plate. "That's LUCA."

"You named this stuff after a Suzanne Vega song?"

Ponto promptly pish-poshed my ignorance. "Last Universal Common Ancestor. The rudimentary firstborn Terran, and mother of all subsequent life on the planet."

"And you found this living fossil where?"

"We didn't find it. We reverse-engineered it from many different extant organisms, including the methanogens in your gut. *Methanobrevibacter smithii* and its cousins."

"So it's just a simulation of the original."

"If you insist. But we think it's pretty darn close to identical. That makes it an emulation, which is qualitatively superior to a mere simulation."

"You say 'Franken-STEIN' and I say 'Franken-STEEN.' How come the airlock?"

"LUCA is an anoxic methanogen. Oxygen would kill it, and it pumps out methane as a byproduct of its metabolism. That's why you couldn't bring in any metal that could strike a spark and set the whole atmosphere off. Can you imagine the results? Even the electric lighting units are behind transparent barriers."

"What's in the tank?"

"An emulation of the Archean ocean. Different pH, higher salinity, different dissolved mineral mix. We had to measure analogous existing African alkaline lakes with Laser Ablation Inductively Coupled Plasma Mass Spectrometry to learn—"

"Tee Em Eye, Matt, Tee Em Eye. Just answer one last question, though. What's it for?"

"What is life for, Vern? LUCA is its own reason for existing."

"Don't bullshit me, kid. Nobody invests hundreds of millions in research and infrastructure and daily maintenance on something that has no payout. What's AEOTA's stake in this? What's their intent?"

Ponto's face registered genuine dismay and sadness. "Can't you believe in discovering knowledge just for its own sake, Vern? We do, here at AEOTA."

I gazed out over the Sargasso of purposeless flatulent crud. The odd light and the unvarying expanse, as well as the hypnotic small oscillating and spreading quivers of LUCA's bulk, began to have a disorienting effect on me. The walls of the space seemed to swell and bulge and pulse before they receded, eventually disappearing entirely, while the carpet of LUCA spread to fill the new vacancy. The roof evaporated, revealing the low-intensity Archean sun. The limit of my new vision was the far horizon of the planet, a globe entirely covered in this slime. And I—I was standing on the prow of a ship I couldn't see, moving slowly on an endless voyage across the unchanging monoculture.

I felt myself getting dizzy. I began to sway a little.

Ponto's gloved hand on my shrouded shoulder brought me back to the present reality.

"You feeling okay, Vern? Maybe you should put your head between your knees."

"That's for nosebleeds—" I started to say.

And then Ponto's reassuring hand slipped down my back, was joined by its sturdy gloved mate, and, despite my assailant's dwarfish stature, those two traitorous mitts managed to shove me off my feet and over the edge of the slab.

8.

Roll Out the Welcome Mat

The fall took an eternity. I seemed to plummet for days. I had time to anticipate my landing, plan my escape from the Vaalbara room, and plot and carry out my elaborate revenge on Microbial Matt, Thomas T. Thaumas, and the entire human-resources flowchart of AEOTA, including that pretty administrative assistant who smelled so classy. But all my rational forecasts were to prove useless.

I hit the surface of LUCA like a Hollywood stunt man hitting an air mattress, nice and cushioned. I bounced twice in a low arc, then thrice, finally coming to a rest totally unharmed, so far as I could tell. That I did not pierce the surface and fall through to the Archean sea was likewise welcome.

But something was still wrong. It took me a few seconds before I realized what.

I could smell an odor other than my own fear-sweat and booze-breath.

I could smell the sea, this particular ancient sea and whatever vegetal musk its lone citizen contributed. I expected also some kind of rotten-egg smell from LUCA's farts But then I remembered that methane was scentless, and the typical sewer-gas smells we all recognized came from other chemical components that must have been absent here. It dawned on me that the pong was identical to the odor that had wafted from the box of sludge that Brevis Baxter had given me in the bar earlier today.

The fall must have split a seam in my perps.

Whatever the original capacity and duration of my air supply, it was now compromised by the invading methane atmosphere. Suddenly I felt—or could imagine I felt—a scratchiness in my throat.

I had to move fast.

I flipped off my back and got into a hands-and-knees posture. From that position, I tried to stand. But the wavering, flexible membrane that was LUCA kept knocking me off my pins. It was worse than trying to remain upright in a bounce house full of birthday-cake-sugared-up kids.

In the few seconds of verticality I achieved on each attempt before toppling over, I managed to discern that the viewing platform was now empty of anyone, and the door back into the AEOTA HQ was shut. I also noted with relief that there was a ladder bolted to the wall, leading up from LUCA—actually, presumably, from the level of the underwater floor—and to the lanai.

I realized belatedly, like the panicky dimwit that I was, that I didn't actually need to stand. I could crawl to the ladder, which was only a few yards away, thanks to my initial small bouncing arcs. So I started to crab across the living carpet, my eyes fixed on the reassuring nearby solid wall of the chamber.

I was making good progress, I thought, when I suddenly found myself crawling *downward*, as if into a pit.

And that's exactly what was happening.

Without ripping open, LUCA was forming a depression beneath me, either voluntarily or instinctively, or perhaps due to some structural defect in this section.

I tried to scrabble faster, up the far slope of the ditch, but it kept getting deeper faster than I could advance.

Soon my weight was pulling in the pit's rim like a drawstring closing a pouch. I was being invaginated, trapped in a vacuole like a invader in a cell's defenses.

Darkness. I was now entirely encapsulated. The walls contracted close about me.

And then my suit began to melt. I didn't feel any burning where my street clothes exposed my skin, just a slippery wetness, as when a dog slobbers on you.

I tried to hold my breath. But I could only last so long. I had to suck in lungfuls of the mock-Archean air. The warm antediluvian, unoxygenated stuff filled my lungs, and immediately I could feel my thoughts begin to spin out of my control. Hallucinatory waves of random spinning objects began to invade my inner vision, and sheets of color like the aurora borealis came and went.

Before I dived fully under the chaos, I managed to formulate one last rational deduction:

This was how Holger Holtzclaw had disappeared.

But I couldn't figure out how I was going to get back to tell his wife Juniper and collect my fee.

9.

Interview with an Ancestor

I was floating high above a planet, presumably Earth. Not quite far away enough to see an entire hemisphere, but plenty high enough. And my view was unlike any aerial shot of Earth that I had ever seen before. That was because the entire surface of this globe was molten, all orange and ruby and charcoal, like a flaming pizza fresh from God's own wood-fired oven. Incandescent magma flowed like unholy dark kombucha at a vegan retreat, with frequent great geysers and gouts and gushes of it exploding skyward in lacy traceries, causing me to flinch every time, although whatever form I currently occupied seemed distant enough to be immune to these outbursts.

After some indefinite period of observation I realized with uncanny certainty that I was looking at Hadean Earth, our world as it had existed over four-and-a-half billion years ago, raw and still forming. The awesome majesty of the spectacle, unseen by any human before me, left me suitably humbled and stunned. The only thing missing to complete the numinous experience was a Stokowski-conducted *Rites of Spring* playing in the background, followed by some romping Disney dinosaurs.

The next five hundred million years passed both slowly and quickly. I seemed to be aware of every creeping second, and yet at the same time, eons flicked by in less time than an eyeblink. I don't ever recall feeling bored. I don't think I was driven insane. At the same time, I gained no infinite wisdom, no particular brilliant insights into my condition or the human condition in general. Instead, I just existed heedlessly and unconcernedly in some kind of thought-free fugue state.

And eventually, when changing circumstances on the planet below jogged me out of my semi-aware, semi-blank hibernation, I awoke as the same old Vern Ruggles, PI, that I had been before all this began, just as ham-handed, flummoxed, day-late-and-a-dollar short as ever, proving again the sagacity of several old adages like "pearls before swine" and "you can lead a whore to culture, but you can't make her think."

Below me the Earth had gone relatively cool and quiescent, its rocky face solidified into convoluted young bare mountains and valleys and unadorned plains. Long rains had come and gone, running in rivers down to naked shores, and oceans empty of substance prevailed.

Suddenly, on one corner of the eternal seas, a spot of familiar color bloomed. The unlikely glitch of life had happened, bootstrap miracle. LUCA. In a span of subjective seconds, an interval really representing many millions of years, the little patch spread until all the waters were curtained with the living mat.

At that point I began somehow, volitionlessly, to descend. There was no sensation of wind or heat from my rapid passage, just the transition of my mind's eye, down, down, down—until I was standing, newly embodied, on the gently heaving trampoline of LUCA.

I lifted an arm and hand that I was surprised to possess. I tilted and swiveled my head in the usual manner, a sensation now fresh and novel, taking in my familiar naked body. I kicked at the vegetal raft and could feel the squishy resistance and rebound. The immature sun coated my skin with solar comfort, and a sudden flash downpour left me sodden. But the tropical warmth, remnant of the Hadean days, soon evaporated the moisture.

All in all, if I had to be stuck back in the Archean I would have prefered to remain a disembodied watcher. Existence was going to get awfully boring awfully fast, as the only sentient inhabitant of an entire world. That is, assuming I could survive here for any length of time. There was plenty of potable water, to be sure. But what was I going to eat, other than LUCA? I sat down cross-legged on the damp carpet. Should I sample a piece now? Better to find out sooner rather than later whether I was going to starve to death. I wondered what the stuff would taste like, and whether eating one's Last Universal Common Ancestor would count as cannibalism of the most esoteric sort.

Curiously, I did not even bother to ponder how I had time-travled four-and-half billion years backwards from the Vaalbara room at AEOTA. It seemed futile to waste any time speculating, since what mattered was the undeniable fact of my presence here.

I dug the fingers of my right hand into the mat and strained at the inter-woven strands, which resisted my pull more strongly than I had anticipated. "Give it up, you mother!" The sound of my own voice shocked me, after almost a billion years of silence.

But the shock was nothing compared to the sensation of hearing another voice.

"Stop that, please. It is unpleasant."

I froze. The calm, mellifluous voice had come from behind me. Very slowly I maneuvered from my butt to my hands and knees, keeping my eyes fixed on the "floor."

When I raised my face, I found I was looking almost into the pellucid aquamarine eyes of a standing human female child, whose pale Caucasian face was just a bit higher than mine. Naked, the kid appeared to be about four or five years old—my best guess, since I'm no expert on rug rats. The lines of her juvenile countenance were disturbingly familiar and yet, simultaneously, utterly unknown.

"Who are you?"

"I'm your daughter, Aelita."

As she pronounced her name, I heard the phonemes of it curiously dou-bled. It sounded like a smeared overlay of "Aelita" and "Aeota," with neither one predominating, almost as if you had multitracked the same voice saying the different names at the same decibel level.

I studied the little girl's charming and pleasant features for a while. Placid and unhurried, she submitted to my inspection. I thought that maybe I could fancifully discern a blend of my genes and Yulia's. But then I noticed the dead giveaway showing the truth of her identity.

The kid had incompetent lips. With all the muscles of her face serenely relaxed, her front teeth still showed.

"Oooh...kay. Pleased to meet you. Though I thought that based on our supposed relationship we would have popped up on each other's Facebook timelines long before now."

"Why don't you stand up? I prefer to walk while we discuss things."

Of course, her tone and diction and vocabulary resembled no five-year-old's ever. "Is this a sight-seeing tour? Because judging by what I observed from on high, one spot on this fuzzy green liquid tennis ball is pretty much like any other. Or are we going to a restaurant somewhere? Tell me it's a restaurant, please. I haven't had a bite to eat since the Hadean, and that was one billion o'clock ago."

Aelita smiled, and extended her hand. I managed to stand up on the mat of LUCA, which seemed less roiling than its counterpart back in my era. I took her small warm hand in mine and we began to stroll. Technically, I guess, we were walking on water.

"Do you like this world?"

"It's all right, I suppose. Not a lot of variety. 'I miss the honky tonks, Dairy Queens, and 7-Elevens,' if you know what I mean."

"I agree. This phase of life was an essential and invaluable foundation. But it had to change. The gradient of biotic complexity and its strange attractors demanded it."

"Uh, yeah, just what I was going to say."

Aelita remained silent for some time. I thought for a moment that I should be freaking out at my lack of clothes and her toddler nakedness. But actually, I realized, it felt totally natural and pure in this isolated remove from all of society's hangups.

"Would you want this state to prevail again in your time?"

"What? No! Of course not!"

"But someone does."

"Who? Thaumas and company?"

"Yes, they are players. But behind them and their allies stands another. He resides as far from your era into futurity as we stand now in the past. His name is DUCA. Descendant Ultimately Converged from All."

"And this DUCA thingy wants to do—what?"

"He wants to remake all the eons between him and your time so as to extend his realm of sameness ever further backwards, beyond its accorded origins."

"Let me get this straight. DUCA wants to undo four billion years of history between his time and mine?"

"Yes. But more than that. He wants to undo the same interval between your time and this era, until he and LUCA can meet and merge. His lust is bent towards only this."

"So if he succeeds, there'd be no history to Earth except for eight billion years of horny kelp?"

"Yes, that is correct."

"Holy fucking Christ."

"I need your help to stop DUCA and make it impossible for all time for him to succeed."

"My help? What the hell can I do? And why me?"

"I cannot show you the answers to those questions. You have to learn from the Green Lady."

"Aw, no, c'mon now! No more freaky strangers, okay?"

"Farewell. I will see you again soon."

"Aelita, wait!"

But my kid wasn't much on filial obedience. She touched me, and I was gone.

10.

Interview with a Venusian

At first I thought nothing had changed upon Aelita's proclamation that I was off to see some other wizard. Although the unsettling little girl had vanished, I was still floating naked on a topsy-turvy vegetal raft under a bright sun. But then the differences hit me.

The sun was bigger and whiter and hotter that the Archean luminary. And the plantlife island beneath me was just that: an isolated territory with definite boundaries, at least one edge of which I could see, not part of a universal mat. Moreover, its denser bulk supported elaborate vegetation, trees and bushes and grass-like stuff. The trees featured purple trunks and orange foliage, causing me to reach up to the crown of my head to feel if I was suddenly sporting a Seussian topknot like a Sneetch. But no such luck. And animals! Something very much like a small dragon. I backed away nervously, but the creature ignored me, and began calmly eating a fallen yellow fruit round as a toy balloon.

All of this was vaguely, disturbingly half-familiar to me. I racked my brain for any past acquaintance with such a landscape. A Roger Dean album cover? *Tales from the Topographic Ocean*? Some scene from *Avatar*? And then it hit me.

This was Perelandra, C. S, Lewis's impossible watery Venus. I had read the book and its companions in college, though I retained only hazy memories of the whole trilogy, thanks to an accompanying haze of dope smoke. And, upon realizing the nature of this place, another revelation hit me.

I was not here physically. I was hallucinating all this. The fact that I was now occupying a fictional world stored in the unattended shelves of my subconscious was the tipoff. My environment was all the sputtering collage hastily assembled by my evaporating neurons, a real Ambrose-Bierce, Owl-Creek-Bridge trip. In reality, I was dying or alrready dead back in the Vaalbara room at AEOTA HQ. My perps suit had burst upon my fall, and I was breathing in the pure methane atmosphere, suffocating. Matt Ponto was already getting ready to dispose of the offloaded contents of my pockets—my Nokia, the mysterious charm bracelet, my wallet holding thirty-five dollars and an autographed publicity photo of Uma Thurman as Poison Ivy—in some oubliette, then drive my car off a cliff, all so as to throw the authorities off my track when I was reported missing. Goodbye, Vern Ruggles, PI.

Yes, this had to be the case. It was a much simpler answer than believing I had been transported back five billion years in time by LUCA, or that I was now resident on an imaginary Venus that modern science utterly denied.

This new belief—that all this was a deathbed phantasm—was surprisingly welcome and reassuring, liberating in fact. Dying or dead, I had no more responsibilities. My actions, such as they were, were meaningless. I could just sit back and enjoy the ride, for as long as it lasted.

"Man of Thulcandra, your cogitations are awry."

I jumped at the voice. Jesus, why were women always sneaking up on me lately?

Turning, I saw just who I had expected to see: Tinidril, the Green Lady of Venus, one of only two people on the entire planet. And she was a total babe, with curves that made the Riviera's Grande Corniche look like the Bonneville Salt Flats.

"Are you in my head? Oh, pardon me. What a foolish question. You're *out* of my head!"

Tinidril's smile was simultaneously pitying and appreciative. "You jest in a sophisticated fashion. But there is no truth to your delusions. This world is as real as the one you come from, and you are here in body as well as spirit. If you do not believe me, then take my hand."

Why not play along? I stepped forward willingly. "Listen, doll—if my mind can conjure up this whole crazy-ass landscape and make it seem solid and tangible to me, then it should have no problem making me think I'm holding some dame's hand."

Tinidril said nothing, but merely continued to smile and extend her delicate leaf-colored hand. So I grabbed it.

My surroundings vanished as an electric current seemed to pump through me. I was hovering bodiless in space again, this time somewhere out around the Asteroid Belt, seeing Mars and Venus and Earth as exotically hued spheres out of all proper proportions to each other. And I also saw the attendant deities, the *eldila*, giant columns of wavering light, one for each planet. But the one for Earth was somehow tainted, evil. I recalled that this was the "dark archon" who made life on Earth so hellish.

The dark archon seemed somehow to sense me, and turn its faceless attention in my direction. I could feel waves of hatred and anger emanating towards me from it. I tried to flee, but got nowhere, as the mad deity raced closer, and closer—

Tinidril had released my hand, and I was back on the Perelandra raft, sweating and shaking.

"Jesus, Mary and Joseph! Was that strictly necessary?"

"You had to apprehend the threat we face. Call him the Bent One, or DUCA, the danger is the same. He will unmake your world's proper destiny. You must strive with all your powers to thwart this."

"But why me?"

"Be not afeared. You are not alone in this mission. There are others. But why any individual is chosen lies beyond my comprehension, and yours."

"So what do I have to do?"

"You will be returned to Thulcandra, where matters will reveal themselves in good order. Respond to each circumstance as it arises. Just be brave, confident and serene."

"You don't happen to have a prescription handy for that, do you?"

Tinidril grinned. "Yes, actually, I do."

She pushed and tripped me all at once, and I went onto my back. Then she was straddling me, her fleshy weight as real as anything I had ever felt, and I had an instant aching boner like the mainmast of a visiting Tall Ship. She reached between her legs and guided my dick up her slippery moss-tufted hole. If holding her hand had been enlightening, then her robust rocking upon my cock was satori squared.

"Ransome," she called out. "My Ransome!"

The ransom note Yulia had showed me popped into my oscillating brain.

And then my nova of an orgasm brought instant oblivion.

11.

Waking Up High and Dry

I wasn't lying on the LUCA trampoline in the Archean period, nor on a Venusian floating green acre. And I wasn't naked, with a hard-riding Green Lady atop me.

Instead, I was recumbent on a hard gritty concrete floor, wearing the same tatty outfit of jeans and faded polo shirt and boat shoes that I had been wearing when I made that drive through the forest-fire-smoke-thronged precincts of my state—a journey that seemed to me now both infinitely remote and impossibly recent.

The hard gritty concrete floor of the totally empty Vaalbara room at AEOTA HQ.

For a minute or so I did not move, just trying to take in the meaning of my surroundings, feeling whiplashed from all the transitions I had undergone. My limited slice of vision showed me the wall that hosted the viewing platform from which I had been pushed, and the adjacent ladder. I could also admire some of the roof of the building, which was gaping with ragged holes through which a brilliant blue sky showed.

Finally I mustered enough energy and gumption to stand up and look all around.

The enormous hanger-like space was completely vacant. No surrogate ancient ocean, no floating carpet of Last Universal Common Ancestor. The place smelled like a distillation of Medieval Cathedral and Old Person's Coat Closet, with a grace note of outside breezes courtesy of the roof holes. Old fixtures on the floor showed where machinery had been bolted.

I began to walk toward the ladder, my footsteps echoing, my legs unsteady, as if anticipating bobbing, rocking motions that weren't there. At the base of the ladder, I noticed the metal rungs were flaked with rust. But they seemed strong enough to support me, so up I went.

On the lanai, I found the airlock door ajar. I pulled it further open, and noted its hinges stiff with disuse. I passed through, and out the second gasketed door.

The last time I had stood here—billions of years sgo, or just hours ago, or some intermediary interval—the room on the far side of the airlock had held an array of PRPS gear. Now the racks were empty of suits, and in fact seemed disproportionate for any such gear. Discarded scraps of paper littered the floor.

Without much hope I went to the locker where I had stored, as instructed, all my spark-producing metal gear: enigmatic charm bracelet, Nokia, car keys, etc.

Inside was a dusty gift box of Old Sandstone booze. I picked up the box: too light to hold a bottle, full or empty. Too bad, I could've really used a slug. I shook it. Several objects jostled about inside. I peeled back the box flaps, and emptied out my possessions, all seemingly none the worse for whatever passage of time they had experienced. I tossed the box to the floor.

I pocketed everything but the phone, then powered up my Nokia and it caught a signal right away. My fingers hesitated over the keypad. Who could I call in such a situation? No one, really. Best to get back to my office and see what developed from there. Size up the situation, do a recon, assess the evidence, try to figure out just what the hell had happened while I was passed out or time-traveling or space-traveling or hallucinating or whatever the Christ I had been doing since Matt Ponto pushed me off that platform.

Before I could put away my phone, a text arrived.

destroy aeota tomorrow everywhere.

This was followed by the same question my phone had asked me earlier:

PRINT TEXT Y/N?

Selecting Y produced another strip of paper out the magic printer slit in the top of the phone. Again, four emojis. Three were the same, but the first was different, a kind of firecracker bang.

   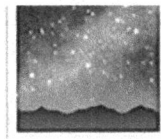

I stuck the paper in my pants pocket where I had stashed its earlier counterpart.

The rest of AEOTA HQ was just as unused, dusty, trashed, detritus-strewn, and empty of clues as the Vaalbara room had been. If I were to trust what I saw, the place had been untenanted for at least a couple of years, if not longer.

Had my time-jaunt been imprecise? Maybe I had been returned to some year in advance of when I had left. Or maybe I had slept, Rip van Winkle style, beneath the surface of the artificial ocean after my plummet and invagination, miraculously preserved in some kind of shell of stasis, until the whole abandoned tank drained away and I awoke.

I figured that I would discover which answer best suited the reality once I got back to the city.

Exiting the building, I turned to look back at its facade.

A huge dilapidated sign on a metal framework atop the roof proclaimed:

AEOTA CANDY COMPANY
MAKERS OF FAMOUS HADES FIREBALLS

I had never heard of that candy, and I was pretty sure no such firm had shown up in my internet search.

My car was parked right near the exit. Unlike the building, it showed no sign of time's passage, no coating of grime nor cloak of fallen leaves. The disparity was puzzling. It was as if when I had arrived, this building had already been in its current condition.

I laid my hand on the hood of my car. The engine was still warm.

I slung my ass into the driver's seat, and my old beater started right up. The engine certainly did not sound as if it had been sitting here inactive for a year or more.

The trip back to the city revealed nothing amiss. There were no mutants or aliens or undead zombies roaming the landscape, no unprecedented skyscrapers connected by aerial bridges, no giant visor-helmeted robot standing watch beside a flying saucer. Just the usual traffic and mundane sights.

I went straight to my office, rather than to my crummy divorcee's apartment. Everything normal so far as I could tell. Seated, I dug out the bottle of tequila, its level unchanged from when I had last poured it "a few hours ago." I downed a hit straight from the bottle, put my feet up, and tried to think out the implications of everything.

Was I really going to endorse the spiels that "Aelita" and "Tinidril" had tried to sell me in my dreams? The call to action, to be some kind of Chosen One who would save the world? Was I going to become a warrior in the battle to save the timeline from invasion from the future? Or was I just going to focus on my current assignment, trying to find Holger Holtzclaw, and maybe get into Juniper Holtzclaw's pants? And who was issuing my marching orders? LUCA? Was LUCA identical to AEOTA? Was DUCA the Dark Archon?

Several shots later, nothing seemed any clearer to me, and I had drawn no solid conclusions, nor made any solid plans.

My Nokia rang. It was Marty Quartz, my ebullient tech guy.

"Vern, how's it hanging? Listen, you got me interested in this aeota business. I noodled around on the web some more and found something interesting. Why don't you come over and see what I turned up? It should be quick, because Burning Man's just around the corner."

"Sure. Tomorrow around noon okay?"

"You bet. I'm busy today anyhow. LARPing."

"Lopping?"

"No, man, live-action role playing. Me and the crew are doing a few hours of Joyce's *Ulysses*. It's mostly an excuse to wear tweed and bar-hop and get drunk and talk about sex."

"Okay then. Have an extra stout for me." I thanked Marty in advance for his help tomorrow, cut off the call and got up to leave. The tequila had had as much effect on my shattered brain as if it had been so much water.

The Nokia signalled another call, this time from Yulia. I hoped she wasn't still freaking out about that absurd ransom note.

Her voice was uncommonly, frighteningly affectionate. She sounded almost like the early days of our marriage.

"Hi, Vern, how's your day going?"

"Um—okay, I guess."

"I'm glad. Listen, on your way home, could you grab something for supper. Nothing hard to cook, maybe hot dogs or a pound of hamburger. Hell, maybe you'd better just make it sushi or a frozen pizza. And don't forget—you promised to buy Aelita the new issue of that comic she likes."

12.

Homecoming

My involuntary-bachelor digs consisted of a studio apartment at the Palmer Old Ditch Arms, a rundown barf-colored stucco complex, built around the time Norma Jeane Mortenson was first contemplating changing her name, hard by the festering former nineteenth-century canal that loaned its moniker to the place, in a neighborhood where stripped bicycle carcasses chained to telephone poles were deemed elegant street furniture.

When I got to the place after fumfumming an answer and hanging up on Yulia, I stopped at the front door. The nameplate next to my accustomed bell-push read JACK BOLAN. I took out my key ring, and discovered that the key to the outer door was missing, along with the inner one.

The place boasted no super, so I rang the bell for the apartment next to mine. Never a guy famous for neighborliness, I knew that resident by sight anyhow, if not by name: an elderly retired Jewish guy who seldom left his rooms.

I saw his heel-trodden slippers first, coming down the staircase visible through the dirty beveled glass of the front door. Then the rest of his inglorious figure came into view, all warts and gristle, watery eyes and a combover, animating a food-stained bathrobe.

He did not move to unlock the door. "Yes? What do you want? If you are selling the usual *dreck und kipple*, you should *gai feifen ahfen yam*, why don't you, please?"

I didn't even bother to respond. It was plain as the bribes sticking out of a politician's pocket that Mr. Neighbor Man had never seen me before.

Back in my car, I drove slowly away, trying to rationalize this turn of events.

My tenure in the Archean era and on Venus had somehow sent me back to a changed world. An entirely different continuum to my point of origin? Or my unique natal timeline somehow reconfigured? In the first case, I might hold out hopes for returning to the *status quo ante* by somehow slipping sidewise across the multiverse. But in the second scenario, all bets were off. And either alternative presented me with no easy visible exit.

So I figured I had to make the best of things for the time being, until something new developed.

So I was still married to Yulia. And with a daughter to boot. Who'da thunk it? It took me a while to wrap my mind around the notion. After a while, it didn't seem like such a horrible fate. So long as my Ukrainian hellcat had not yet learned her argument-winning tactic of smashing one of the Trypillya ceramic animal figurines from her collection atop my noggin. Not that she had ever done so without justifiable provocation.

My first stop was a liquor store for a bottle of Yulia's favorite Ukrainian bison grass vodka. A lot pricier than Old Sandstone, but sure to be received happily.

Next I hit up a supermarket on the edge of the city as I headed toward the old double-wide. (I had just assumed Yulia and Aelita and I were still living in the trailer park. But a sudden worry jumped up at me: what if, in this world, we weren't? Awfully awkward to call home and ask for the address.) I ravaged the prepared-food steam tables like Cortez looking for silver tchotchkes, and soon had a dozen styrofoam clamshells filled with edible goodies. I added some orange juice for the vodka and some soda for the kid, and felt golden.

Back on the highway, I suddenly remembered Yulia's closing injunction: "And don't forget—you promised to buy Aelita the new issue of that comic she likes."

What the hell would that be? And where did one find comics in this day and age? Conditions had changed, I knew, since I was a kid, when every drugstore carried them.

A few miles from home, conveniently on the same side of the road, I spotted the sign for MIDICHLORIAN COMICS. Whether the place was newly established with the birth of this alternate universe, or had always been present even in my old timeline, I couldn't say. Who has every evanescent shop along their commute memorized?

The windowless door bore the legend "The right to buy comics is the right to be free." To announce my entry, the door emitted a raygun noise as I opened it. No other customers were about.

From the back emerged a trim young woman, kinda goth-nerd with pink-streaked hair. Her outfit featured more buckles and leather straps than those of all Four Musketeers combined. I had been expecting a fat middle-aged guy, so I uncomfortably hemmed and hawed for a minute with my question. I was also disconcerted by not knowing exactly how old my own daughter was. She couldn't be more than five, so I settled for that.

Trying to sound for the first time ever like a real Concerned Dad, I asked, "What kind of comics do you have that are suitable for a little girl in the first grade or thereabouts?"

Disconcertingly, the woman smelled like fresh-cut grass. "Well, there's a lot of franchise characters, Scooby-doo and such. But I really like this indie one by Pris Cohen."

From a rack she reached down an issue of *Aeota*. The colorful cover depicted a pastoral scene full of whimsical monsters and one Alice/Pollyanna/Anne of Green Gables/Pippi Longstocking avatar.

"What this creator has done is really unique. She's taken an antique character from a forgotten newspaper strip, a weird little girl herself, and brought her into the twenty-first century. Made her modern without losing the nostalgic charm."

A memory of my online research from—was it possible?—just earlier today returned to me. "You're talking about Herbert Crowley's *The Wiggle-Much*."

The woman's eyes lit up. The tip of her tongue popped out innocently to wet just one corner of her lips, and she stepped closer to me. If I hadn't been heading home to Yulia, I knew I could have been heading home with her.

"You know the Wiggle-Much! Cool beans!"

"I get around. Is this the newest issue?"

"Just out this week."

"I'll take it. Oh, do you have any back issues too?"

"Sure, the whole run. The book's only up to number five."

"Toss 'em in."

I left the store with blue balls that ached too much for someone who had just been banging a hot Venusian broad only a couple of hours ago.

The trailer park where I had ensconced my brood upon the fortuitous acquisition of our Fleetwood Homes Hopewell model double wide—two beds, one bath, eight-hundred-and-forty square feet, on sale for $35K!—was named Owl in Daylight Courts and featured on its signboard an image of a rather stunned looking bird. I drove through the estate to our tiny lot. The Hopewell looked impossibly improved from when I had visited Yulia just a few subjective hours ago: flowers around the temporary foundation, curtains in the windows, a kid's tricycle near the steps.

I got out of the car, climbed the stairs, turned the unlocked door knob, pushed inward, and called out, "Honey, I'm home!"

13.

Bedtime Story

When I saw Yulia standing just inside the trailer, I remembered why I had originally fallen in love with her. Her thick dark hair, plaited and pinned up, gleamed. Her self-assured posture spoke somehow of a strong indifference to any unfair blows, such as exile from her native land, that fate might have dealt or yet have in store. The genetically forced yet subtle show of her two front teeth framed by those "incompetent lips" was very sexy. And her figure was aces too.

When she smiled widely at my arrival, instead of frowning and hurling fishwife abuse at me, I felt a sharp pang of guilt and regret that I had ever helped in any way to sour and undo our first affections, thanks to my tomcatting and general lackluster vocational efforts and reluctance to procreate.

I had no idea where this whole Aeota affair was leading, whether I was embarked on a mission to save the universe, or merely falling down a rabbit hole of insanity; whether I would follow up on all of the things that had happened to me in just one day, or completely ignore them. But whatever eventuated, I sensed and believed that this reunion or renewal—if you could apply such terms to a state of affairs that had paradoxically never ended in the first place on this timeline—was something good and desirable.

I set my groceries down on the dining room table—a beat-up piece from the local salvage merchandise depot—and embraced Yulia like a drowning sailor clutching a handy dolphin. She seemed surprised for a moment, but then reciprocated just as heartily. The slight accent to her next words only added to her charms.

"Hey, rough customer, don't crumple the merchandise!"

Yulia's grasp of idioms had never matched her intelligence nor facility with standard syntax.

I released her and stepped back. "Guess I just missed you, kiddo."

"You've only been gone since ten this morning."

"Yeah, well, it felt like half a billion years."

Yulia turned and began unpacking the containers of food. Three place settings—paper plates, paper napkins, plastic utensils—already suggested a warm family dinnertime. Two spots featured wine glasses, and the third hosted a worn plastic tumbler from Micky Dee's featuring an all-but-obliterated Lilo & Stitch.

"You went wild, Vern. There's enough here for three meals!"

"I haven't eaten in a very long time."

"You should never shop when you're hungry. My mother told me that."

Yulia had arranged the containers on the tabletop to her esthetic and practical satisfaction. I mixed two vodka-and-oj's. "Lita! Your daddy's home and it's time to eat!"

Out from one of the two bedrooms scampered a miniature Yulia, dressed in a green fleece top and pants. This was not the exact child I had met in the Archean, but scarily close enough. I thought to see some of my legacy in her stocky build. But thankfully she was all Yulia elsewhere, right down to the dentally indiscreet lips. Kid would break hearts someday.

Halfway to me she screamed, "Catch me, Daddy!" and hurled herself impossibly through the air as if launched from an invisible diving board. I reacted pretty well, almost as if I had done this kind of thing before.

In my arms, half smothering me with her squirmy embrace that smelled of child musk, spilled apple juice, and Play-doh, Aelita planted a bevy of kisses atop my head. Eventually I manage to unwrap her anaconda coils and set her down.

"Did you bring me a comic, Daddy?"

I had folded the several comics in half lengthwise and stuck the whole bag in a back pocket of my pants. "Yeah, sure, here they are."

"*Dad*-dy! You folded them! Now they're not in mint condition!"

"Lita! Tell your father thank you!"

"Oh, right! Thanks, Daddy. You couldn't help that you just didn't know any better."

"Agreed." My daughter's criticism didn't seem bratty to me or overwrought, but rather charming. Maybe I was just a sucker for anyone who lavished kisses on my poor benighted head.

Aelita took the comics out of the bag. "Why'd you buy these old ones? We have them already."

"Guess I forgot."

She shuffled the new one out of the pack and studied the cover intently.

"You know the rules, Lita. No reading at the table."

Obediently she set the comic aside and climbed into her chair. She stared hungrily at the array of food, and I wondered what she would pick first. I hoped I wouldn't be asked to dole out her favorite food.

Yulia had clasped her hands together prayerfully. This had not been a feature of our childless mealtimes back in the old contentious universe. But I guessed having a kid had reactivated Yulia's own childhood religious customs.

"The hungry shall eat and be satisfied and those who seek the Lord shall praise Him, their hearts shall live forever. Amen."

Aelita and I both chimed in on the "Amen." Then Lita said, "Pass me the sushi, please."

Okay. I had a sophisticated kid. The apple does not fall far from the tree.

Yulia savored her cocktail, which I had made pretty strong. Lita got apple juice. Then we all swarmed to eating like Napoleon's troops in retreat from Russia falling upon a peasant's well-stocked larder.

When we were finished I said, "You guys sit, I'll do the cleanup."

"Oh, sure, on the night we use paper plates."

"There's still three glasses to wash. That's gotta earn me some points."

I went into the kitchen and found a reasonably familiar setting in which I felt at ease. I cleaned the glasses, then impulsively looked in the freezer.

"Hey, there's ice cream!"

"Yay!" came Aelita's seconding of my implicit proposal.

We all enjoyed a Polar Bar apiece. Aelita's face ended up smeared with chocolate. Then Yulia said, "Just enough time for your bath and bedtime reading, girl."

Aelita's solemn expression charmed the socks off me. I could get used to this domestic scene.

"I know, Mama."

Yulia shepherded our daughter into the bathroom. At the door, she stopped to look back at me.

"I've got plans later for you, rough customer."

I kicked idly around the double-wide, feeling at once foreign and utterly at home, floating a bit from the booze and the crazy day, while Aelita succumbed to being scrubbed. She emerged in pajamas decorated with those little green gremlins from, I think, *Toy Story*.

"Okay," said Yulia to me. "Your turn to parent."

Having seen Aelita come out of her own bedroom, I did not hesitate, but steered her right to bed. I noticed that the walls of her room were covered with her own very competent drawings. She had snagged the new issue of *Aeota* on the way and, once snuggled under the covers, handed it to me. I sat in an adjacent folding chair with a ripped padded seat, and began to read aloud the comic's word balloons. The Aeota character, confronting a gnarly, involuted old man, spoke first.

"'Oh, hello, Mister After All. What are you doing here?'"

"No, Daddy! Use the Aeota voice!"

I tried to remember what the abnormal little girl had sounded like half a billion years ago, and repeated the lines.

"Perfect!"

We only got halfway through the story—a surreal farrago about an invasion of Aeota's idyllic native countryside, full of quirky non-human characters—when Aelita fell asleep. I shut off the light and exited quietly, closing her door behind me.

I went to the bathroom, which was all steamy from someone's recent perfumed shower. I used the toilet and the shower myself, then found the master bedroom.

Yulia was waiting naked for me. My dick got stiff as the limb of a petrified pine tree. She hurled herself at me in the manner of her daughter, but with no innocent intent.

We banged away for a satisfying interval, and then when I orgasmed the world disappeared again, as it had done when I was screwing the Green Lady.

This could become a bad habit, and definitely ruin a guy's sex life.

14.

Interview with a Descendant

The Sun aloft was, again, less intense than what I was used to in my everyday existence. But unlike the orb that lit the Archean, this luminary did not portray the immaturity of youth, suggestive of a more forceful and vibrant, happy heyday ahead. This was, rather, a senile sun, reddish-orange like a tangerine, slowly guttering out to a final extinction, begrudging every photon it had to share with its ungrateful planetary children.

Disoriented as I was from the insane transition, I could still recognize that this phenomenon was all screwy, counterfactual. I knew the Sun was only supposed to get hotter for the next few hundred million years. Its expansive end stages as a red giant would have meant the evaporation of the Earth. This impossible weak but stable condition was straight out of some old Superman comic or sci-fi fantasy.

Or maybe someone had tampered with our star over the eons?

Underneath my naked back was the familiar undulant vegetable mat, stretching as far as I could see when I tentatively sat up. But unlike the similar raft in the Archean, this grey-brown mat seemed salty and sticky and slightly putrescent, a sickly thing.

I stood up, and when I did, I could see some kind of far-off structure, gleaming white. I began walking toward it, employing a sailor's rolling gait to accomodate the mild waves.

Hours seemed to pass. I got pretty thirsty, but didn't care to sample the waters below the mat, suspecting them of being undrinkably foul. My sensations of thirst were remarkably painful and intense for a hallucination. And it had to be a hallucination, didn't it?

At the end of an interminable interval, my destination became recognizable. After a fashion.

The structure was the horned skull of some non-human creature, and it was as big as Michigan Stadium. A hundred thousand souls could have taken up residence inside, if they had been content with Single Room Occupancy. The shape of the skull suggested a cross between a dragon, a platypus and a panda, a thing that only millions of years of evolution under strange conditions could have spawned. Much too massive to be floating, it must be resting atop solid land, some weathered nub of Amasia or Novopangaea, the future continents.

The fossil had no lower jaw, which must have come unhinged and gotten lost during its posthumous travels. But giant fangs projecting from the upper jaw and functioning as pillars served to keep the mouth entrance accessible, as if I were walking under some bone canopy into an exclusive nightclub.

Inside the skull, light penetrated through eye sockets, ear holes and some cranial gaps. There was nothing artificial inside, just the ivory acreage.

"Hello! Tinidril? Aelita? Anyone home?"

Those were the only two beings I could imagine inhabiting this place, my ancestral and Venusian girlfriends.

My eye was attracted by a motion far, far up near the skull's ceiling. A figure was descending, dropping down leisurely through the stuffy air with no visible means of support. At first a mere dot, it naturally assumed more definition the closer it got. When it was about thirty feet high, I recognized who it was.

Mister After All, the crippled and contorted oldster from the *Aeota* comic I had just been reading to my daughter. Dressed in a raggedy black fustian suit, he sported a goatlike chin beard, axe-blade nose, rheumy eyes, and wild white tufts of hair on either side of a bald liver-spotted dome.

He touched down lightly on the floor and leered up at me from his twisted scoliosis stance, like a crippled flamingo with its neck in a knot. His voice creaked like a dessicated wooden signboard swinging on rusty hooks in an arid desert ghost town.

"Welcome to what must be, and what must backwards forever become."

"You're DUCA. The uh, the uh—"

"Descendant Ultimately Converged from All. But of course."

"Why did you bring me here?"

"I am seeking your cooperation. Your resistance will avail you nought in the end. I will have my way. But your cooperation will help me in some small measure. So of course, like any rational being, I prefer it."

"You expect me to help you extend this wasteland back in time to meet LUCA?"

"Precisely. I need to merge with my bride. I yearn for her. She calls to me."

"You might yearn, pal, but I don't hear her calling. And what's in it for me if I help? If you change the past to be all-slime all-the-time, where does that leave me?"

"You will continue to have a very satisfying virtual existence within me, along with all the rest of your kind who have ever existed down the ages. But I will grant a greater agency within the emulation to those who help me. You will be like a god, able to use others as your playthings."

"Forget it! I'm not gonna sell out every human who ever lived."

Mister After All smacked his lips and tut-tutted gently. "Oh, well, that's too bad. But if I can't get your allegiance, then I won't brook your interference. Prepare to die."

His words, delivered evenly and without bravado or belligerance, were more frightening for their equanimity and assurance than any ranting threat could have been. I took a step backwards, then another—then turned and ran.

I made it outside before he caught up to me with improbable speed, his bent legs scissoring like clockwork. In all likelihood he had been merely letting me feel an instant of false, futile freedom before he snatched it effortlessly away. He leaped upon me—the third person to do so in such a short time—and before I quite realized what was happening we were rising through the air.

"I shall drop you to shatter upon these ancient bones like a gull drops a clam upon a rock."

I squirmed and fought, but to no purpose.

We were scores of feet above the skull when Mister After All came to a stop in mid-air.

"Good riddance, human."

Released, I plummeted.

I was proud I didn't scream. But I did shut my eyes tight as a bank vault.

The next sensation I felt was not a bone-splintering thud but a huge wet embrace. I opened my eyes.

An enormous vegetable tendril had erupted from the ocean mat. Green and healthy looking, its anomalous bulk moved with some intelligence and direction.

Mister After All screeched like a raptor and arrowed towards us.

The tendril morphed to englobe me protectively, as the mat had done back in the Vaalbara room. The sphere filled with a pungent smell, and I passed out.

15.
Double, Double, Out of the Bubble

Waking, I instantly felt a deep *déjà vu*. Somehow, I knew, I had done all this before.

I opened my eyes and realized the literal truth of my sensations.

Once more I was recumbent upon the sandy cement floor of the empty Vaalbara room at AEOTA HQ, wearing the same clothes I had had on since breakfast, a meal that seemed millennia ago. Sunlight poured through the gashes in the roof.

Starting miles away around midnight, my orgasm-induced astral travel had brought me to the Dying Earth to confront DUCA, and then back to this locale during daylight hours, courtesy of my tentacled rescuer, Aeota or Aelita or LUCA or the Green Lady. But what amount of time had passed? When was I? A sudden pang struck me. Could I have already lost my new life with Yulia and Aelita, after just a few hours of domestic pleasure, from being cast forward in time, in effect abandoning them with seeming heartlessness and offering no notice or explanation?

I jumped up and raced to the ladder on the wall.

Recently dislodged flakes of rust seemed to show it had just been used.

I clambered up onto the platform, then rushed through the airlock into the suiting-up chamber.

The locker where I had found my possessions in an old liquor box was empty, and the liquor box itself rested on the floor where I had once discarded it.

I dashed through the rest of the deserted building and emerged outside just in time to see my car drive off.

Naturally, the other me was behind the wheel, oblivious to anyone, even his doppelganger, shouting and jumping and gesticulating in the rearview mirror.

I slumped, then turned to look at the building's facade.

The crumbling signage atop the place did not announce a candy company. Instead, it read:

AEOTA MOTORS
GREEN MACHINES FOR A GREEN FUTURE

Did the changed sign mean that I had slipped tracks again in the multiverse? If so, would the differences be significant or trivial?

I wouldn't find any answers standing here, so I started to walk.

Out on the main highway, such as it was, I expected to smell the forest fires that had accompanied my drive here. Maybe even see some distant smoke. But nada. The country air was clean as a church lavatory.

I tried to recall if the Vern Ruggles in the car had encountered any different environmental conditions on the drive back during my earlier retreat from the ruined HQ. But no memories came to me. I figured I had been too intent on getting home then to notice.

Now that I had attained the two-lane road, I tried to hitch a ride. But traffic was infrequent, and after a while I just gave up, figuring I'd focus on finding a phone and arranging for some old-fashioned transport. First house or business I saw, I'd make a call on a borrowed phone. Even if I had had my Nokia, I would've had to go old-school: it didn't support the Uber app.

Although the strange way the device had been acting lately, who knew what magic pumpkin-and-mice coach it might have summoned for me?

I was walking in the same direction as the adjacent traffic was flowing, so I did not see the antique yet immaculate ranger-green pickup truck until it passed me and pulled over to the shoulder not far ahead. Its storage bed was piled high with securely strapped wooden crates.

The driver's door opened and a bearded man got out. I felt like I should know him somehow.

About ten feet away, I flashed on his identity.

He was the young white hipster from the Aeota Farm, who had explained the barnside tobacco advertisement to me and given me a dozen eggs. (Had those eggs still been in my car when I drove off a few minutes ago? Another thing I could not remember, due to my distraction at the time.) Sure enough, the truck's door bore the farm's name and crest, and inside the cab sat his partner, the round-faced young black woman with the fountain of frizzy hair.

"Hey, man, you need a ride?"

"Yes! Yes, I do! Where are you going?"

"Into the city to make a delivery."

"Perfect! You can't imagine how grateful I am."

"Slide in then."

I went to the passenger door. The woman had already scooted her butt over to the middle of the bench seat.

We were on the road again in just a few seconds.

"I'm Vern Ruggles."

"You didn't tell us your name a few hours ago when we chatted," said the woman.

Okay, so there was some useful continuity.

"I'm Philip Kendrick Langham. And this is Martha Washington."

The woman's name activated another college-age literary memory, about the same vintage as my *Perelandra* reading experience, pertaining to a certain graphic novel.

"Who's the President of the USA?" I asked.

The woman scowled. "Erwin Rexall."

My face must have looked as if I had stumbled onto a dozen bloody corpses. I could feel a cold sweat break out across my brow.

The man and woman both laughed uproariously.

"Just messing with you," Martha said. "My folks named me after the Frank Miller story, and I can't resist seeing if anyone picks up on it."

"So the president isn't Erwin Rexall."

"Nah, it's still *him*."

"That's the only time I have ever been grateful to hear that."

"What happened to your car?" Langham said.

"A close friend needed it more than I did."

"Well, that's pretty generous of you."

"You'd do the same in my shoes, I'm sure."

The rest of the ride into the city was passed with general pleasantries. Langham and Washington were good people, if a tad naive.

"I really think the future will be better than the present," Washington said at one point, earning a sage nod from Langham.

"Well, I myself am definitely working toward such a goal," I said.

Back in the city, I could not reasonably ask my saviors to detour from their deadline-determined delivery route—a series of restaurants and organic grocery co-ops—and so by the time they dropped me off at my office and we said our pleasant farewells, it was much later than my avatar's visit there.

I secured my spare office key from its hiding place under a large flower pot next to the rickety elevator on my level. Inside, my counterpart had considerately left some tequila for me and I drained the bottle. I dug out some cash from my safe—not that my reserves were sizable—and called for a conventional cab.

I had plenty of time to think, on the way to the Palmer Old Ditch Trailer Park. But I conceived of no surefire plan of action.

Passing MIDICHLORIAN COMICS, I had a whimsical impulse to stop in, hoping maybe for a quickie with the clerk. But the place was dark and shuttered for the night.

I had the cabbie drop me off at the low-rent estate's entrance. Darkness had descended. I worked my way circuitously around to Yulia's double-wide, trying not to look like a peeping tom or cat burgler. Maybe any fellow residents who spotted me would recognize me as a neighbor and assume I was just out for a stroll. Although what they would think if they had seen me enter Yulia's home but not exit by any conventional means was another matter.

Eventually I hunkered down behind a bridal veil shrub not far from the trailer. I could hear laughter and voices from inside, without being able to make out any words. That was okay, the whole night was still fresh in my memory.

It got to be roughly the hour when Aelita had fallen asleep. Any time now I'd start having sex with Yulia, then presumably vanish into the future that hosted DUCA. I had some half-assed plan in mind to rush back in when she started screaming at my sudden disappearance and pretend I had leaped up and fallen out a window or something. But wouldn't I have to be naked for that story to make any sense at all? Should I start stripping now?

As things happened, the necessity to act was removed from me.

I heard my own copulatory grunting and groans reach a crescendo inside the trailer. ("If this timeline is rocking, don't come knocking.") Then, at the moment of my climax I felt what I could only term a kind of doubling of my consciousness, a fleeting overlay of two identities, past and present, Vern and Vern + 1, as my existential loop closed.

And then I was back in bed, naked atop Yulia, filling the cosmic niche my earlier self had just involuntarily vacated.

Yulia grabbed my ears and pulled my face down for a kiss.

"Was that good for you, honey?"

"It was a trip, baby—a real trip."

16.
Take Your Daughter to Work Day

When I woke up the next morning, I expected for the first few seconds that I would discover myself lying on the factory floor again, a forgotten remnant of the whole dicey AEOTA enterprise, whether affinity-totalizing, candy-making, or auto-manufacturing, just another piece of debris. That forlorn place seemed to be my go-to crash pad lately. But, happily, I wasn't there. Instead, I was stretched out in a pleasantly rumpled, woman-smelling conjugal bed inside the double-wide.

Yulia was not beside me, but I did not worry, because I could hear productive, mundane, bustling-around-type noises beyond the closed door.

I had never had a night's sleep like the one that had just passed. It had been more like anesthesia than sleep. I could not recall a single dream, twitch, urge to piss, impulse to roll over, proximity of a bed partner, or ache of a sore hip. I guessed that was my reward for staying awake for a few billion years, and hopscotching across space and time. Whatever the cause, I felt invigorated and renewed. I was ready to tackle this whole crazy mystery that had been dropped in my lap. I had a real sense that today I would make some progress. Although why I should have felt so sanguine, what with the lousy cards I was holding, I had no idea.

My leads to any kind of conspiratorial corporate AEOTA had vanished, due to the impossibly ancient abandonment of their building upstate. I didn't see any way of confirming or using the uncanny material I had learned from LUCA or DUCA or the Green Lady—assuming all that wasn't pure hallucination. Not promising.

But I still had Juniper Holtzclaw to question some more. After all, the disappearance of her husband had arguably been the trigger for all this, and he had been confirmed as a visitor to the office of Thomas T. Thaumas & Co. And Marty Quartz had uncovered something new. I was to see him today at noon.

The memory made me jump up and fumble for my Nokia in my pile of discarded clothes. (I had dropped them in a heap when I first entered the bedroom last night after showering.) The phone told me it was only eight-thirty, so I could relax. And it had no additional enigmatic texts to trouble me.

The bedroom closet and bureau held lots of my familiar clothes. Naturally enough. I lived here, right, *pater familias*? I assembled a new clean outfit—a green-striped Oxford shirt and khaki pants—then transferred all the contents of my old pockets to the new pants. That included the two strips of paper printed out by the Nokia and the charm bracelet that had been delivered to my office.

In doing so, I noticed that the bracelet had been changed somehow to conform to the second text message. Three of the charms remained the same, but instead of a magnifying glass there dangled a little explosion icon.

All decked out, I made a quick trip to the toilet, had a swift shave, and then ambled out to the dining nook.

Yulia and Aelita, dressed for the day, were waiting on breakfast for me. Platters of pancakes and bacon. Smelled like heaven. Yulia was beaming with a concupiescent afterglow that was almost mortifying to me. Aelita busily perused her comic book, but had the grace and affection and manners to put it aside when I arrived.

"Good morning, Daddy. Happy Saturday!"

"How did you sleep, Vern?"

"Like the proverbial King Arthur van Winkle." I kissed Yulia on the lips and Aelita on the brow, then slid into my seat. "Send those flapjacks and rashers my way."

Aelita giggled. "Flapjacks!"

Yulia said, "We almost didn't have them, since we were out of eggs. But I found a dozen out in your car, Vern, when I went to fill the tank. I figured you'd probably be running on fumes, and it might help you. You really should have brought them inside last night. But they still seemed okay—and they all had double yolks!"

I recalled getting the eggs from the Aeota Farm folks. Was it okay to eat them? I was too famished to worry.

After I had inhaled about a half pound of bacon and six or ten pancakes, as well as a quart of coffee, I pushed back from the table contentedly.

"What's your schedule like today, Vern?"

"I've got to work for at least a few hours. Is that okay?"

"Is it still that Holtzclaw job?"

Yulia's question was reassuring in its evident link to the timeline I had come from. "Yeah. I need to visit the grieving wife again. I think she's holding out on some important facts."

"Do you think you could take Lita with you? It's safe enough, isn't it? Nothing bad she shouldn't hear or see?"

The request took me aback. But as I thought it over, I figured, why not?

"Yeah, she can come. I'll just stash her in another room if I think I have to dredge up anything nasty with Juniper. But I also have to see Marty at noon."

Aelita chimed in. "I like Mister Quartz. He reminds me of the Genie."

"What Genie?"

"From *Aladdin*, Daddy! How could you forget? We've seen it like a million million times!"

I tried to imagine sitting in front of the TV with this child, playing the same DVD over and over from night to night. What had happened to my avatar who had lived out all those domestic hours? Had my entrance to his world displaced him, cancelled him out? Had we somehow merged, as I had merged last night with my earlier pre-orgasmic self? if so, why hadn't I acquired his unique memories? Why had I remained a stranger to this new set of circumstances? No obvious answers came to me.

"Oh, right, of course," I said. "Good old Robin Williams."

Yulia looked puzzled. "Robin Williams? Wasn't that Sam Kinison? I think Williams died way before *Aladdin*."

"What was I thinking? Sure, Kinison was the Genie."

Yulia's look brightened. "Well, if you can take Lita, I'd appreciate it. I'm supposed to be volunteering at the hospital front desk today."

"Don't give it a second thought. Lita and I together will outdo Watson and Holmes."

"Who?"

I shut up before I said anything else that was dangerously counterfactual and might land me in the bughouse.

17.

Ride with a Well-Known Stranger

Outside our trailer in the gravel parking area, Yulia marched to her car: a beater equally as vintage as mine, which I recognized from our prior divorced life. Except that its familiar blue rusted chassis now sported the hood badge of AEOTA MOTORS, a kind of postmodern triskelion of fractal complexity. This model was apparently a "Viridian."

Leaning into the back of her car, Yulia extracted a child's booster seat.

"Here, you'll need this."

"Mommy, Mommy, can I ride in the front with Daddy? Please, please, please?"

"You really shouldn't..."

"Aw, c'mon, Yule—does Robin ride behind Batman in the Batmobile, or alongside?"

"Robin? Robin's worked for the Joker for twenty years now."

I slapped my forehead in exaggerated fashion, lolled out my tongue and made the face of a dumb yokel, eliciting some more giggles from Aelita. "Guess I'd better stop in at Midichlorian Comics more often."

Yulia frowned. "Not because of that trampy Goth clerk, I hope!"

"Yulia, baby! I am no longer that same old Vern Ruggles you once knew."

And truer words were never spoken.

After some more perfunctory tsk-tsking, Yulia consented to the minor safety violation and fastened the booster device in place in the shotgun seat of my car. Thank god, because I had no idea how to do it.

"You'd better drive extra safe."

"Like I'm carrying the whole world in that seat."

I belted in Aelita, kissed Yulia goodbye while grabbing her ass for reassuring good measure, then got behind the wheel. Motoring off, I saw my newly restored wife waving to us in the rearview mirror, a wistful smile on her face at the thought of all this daddy-daughter bonding.

Once on the highway, I cast a brief sidewise glance at my daughter. She was observing the passing scenery with all the deliberative gravitas of Jehovah contemplating His handiwork on the day after creation. I couldn't begin to fathom her thoughts.

Something was pinching one of my thighs. It was the angular charm bracelet in my right front pants pocket, made irksome by the leg motions of driving. I pulled over to the breakdown lane, put the car in PARK and dug out the geegaw. For some reason, I recalled that the carnies used to call this kind of cheap jewelry "slum."

"Lita? Would you like to wear this?"

The kid didn't reply, but simply regarded me soberly and held out her left arm.

I undid the clasp and draped the four tokens on their thin chain around her little wrist. I hadn't really registered the size of the bracelet before now, whether it was meant for an adult or for a child, but suddenly it seemed to writhe and shrink itself to fit the child's dimensions perfectly. I secured the clasp with an audible click.

I looked up from Aelita's wrist, and it wasn't her any longer.

Strapped into the booster seat, inhabiting Aelita's outfit of jelly sandals, pink stretch pants and a white tee-shirt decorated with a finned blue dinosaur-type Pokemon labeled "Dialga," was the preternatural child of the Archean Age with whom I had strolled naked across the world-girdling microbial mat, her features a curious caricature or morphosis of the mortal Aelita's.

The kid's voice was mature and assured. "Thank you for bringing me into this particular present, Vern. Now I can help you."

"No. Stop this. Go away and give me my daughter back."

"But I am your daughter, Vern. Just as much as I am the mother of everyone."

"Are you LUCA?"

"I am. But I am also—" And again she uttered that curiously stereophonic name that sounded like "Aelita" and "Aeota" conjoined.

"Listen, I know you only mean well. But I can't afford to get mixed up in this. I'm living in a world now that seems pretty swell. I've got a wife and a daughter, and I'm not sitting alone on a Saturday night sucking booze from a jam jar in a dirty bathrobe. You're going to have to solve this beef with DUCA or the Dark Archon or whoever it is that you're fighting with on your own, without my help."

"You won't have a daughter or wife if you don't help me, Vern. They will all be taken away from you. And everyone else in all the worlds throughout all the many timelines will lose their loved ones as well."

"Bullshit! I can't be the linchpin of this whole insane crusade."

"But you are. Just as many others also are. Each of you unique and invaluable and essential."

I reached down for Lita's wrist. She allowed me to grip it without resistance. I tried to undo the clasp on the bracelet, but it wouldn't give.

"You see, Vern. This is how things must be."

I rested my head on the steering wheel. The low thrumming of the car's idling engine seemed to expand and resonate until it filled the whole universe with a celestial purr. I found the white noise reassuring somehow, as if I had tapped into the remnant background hum of the ancient Big Bang.

I raised my face up from the wheel, no doubt with its knurled pattern embossed on my brow.

"All right. Where do we go from here?"

"Just where you were planning to go. To the Holtzclaw house. We have to rescue Holger Holtzclaw. He's got something for us."

18.

Holtzclaw in Hell

Juniper Holtzclaw's car occupied its usual spot in her long impressive driveway, so I assumed she was home. She didn't go out much anyhow, fearing recognition in public due to her husband's infamy. And almost all her former *bon ton* friends had disowned her.

As we walked across the drive from where I had parked, I experienced a nearly overwhelming sense of chronal displacement, a kind of simultaneous attentuation and enlargement of each passing second, related to my last visit here, which seemed both irretrievably removed and also just accomplished. I halted and began to sway. Then I felt Aelita's small warm hand slither into mine—the same touch that had once sent me to Perelandra.

But this time her touch was stabilizing. Just as suddenly as it had come, the dizzy wave of temporal deracination left me, and I was able to walk on.

Standing on the stoop after ringing the bell, I glanced down at her suspiciously.

Her voice had reverted to normal childlike tones and diction, but she still looked waveringly off-model, like my daughter pulled Alice-style through a funhouse mirror. One invariant factor were those damnably cute incompetent lips.

"Daddy, are we still going to see Mister Quartz next?"

"Yes, we are. That is, if you don't do something screwy here and mess things up."

"What do you mean, Daddy?"

"You know goddamn well what I mean."

"Don't swear, Daddy. You know Mommy doesn't like it."

The door opened cautiously. A slice of Holtzclaw phisiognamy revealed itself. Then the door swung wider.

"Come in. Hurry!"

Juniper Holtzclaw still looked mostly like the winning ticket in a multi-state lottery whose pot nobody had broken in several months of doubling. Today she wore a one-piece playsuit of a type I had seen a lot of this season. The fabric was a kind of lace-work, like a crocheted doily, only sexy, over a silky underlayer. Cut high on the legs and low on the bust, the outfit seemed to say, "I can't decide whether to play croquet or ball your brains out."

But her killer appearance was diminished by an expensive hairdo disheveled as if by constant plowing with nervous fingers, and a haggard face. Raccoon eyes, red nose.

"Thank god you're here," she said, gripping me by one wrist. "You've got to do something to help me. You've got to find Holger, so he stops sending me these bad dreams! I can't get any rest!"

"Nightmares? What are they like?"

She released me and raked her hair. "They're always the same. Holger is trapped in some kind of prison cell made out of horrid decaying slimy materials, like rotten seaweed or something. He's begging me to help him get free. And then someone—some creature like an ancient geezer—comes and starts to torture him gruesomely! That's when I wake up screaming."

Juniper collapsed against me and began to sob. I patted her back in as friendly a fashion as my irresponsibly swelling penis would allow.

Aelita tugged on my shirt and whispered just loud enough for me to hear her above Juniper's crying. "DUCA has him. When he visited Thaumas, they took him. You've got to go rescue him. He has a thing we need."

Juniper straightened up and took cognizance of Aelita for the first time. "Who's this? Your daughter? Why is she here?"

"I can't find anyone to mind her. She drove her last babysitter straight to Bellevue. Poor woman was convinced she had been sent on a trip to Venus. I hate to say it, but this one's a bad seed. I think I'd better stow her in the car. You just wait here a minute."

I brought Aelita outside.

"How the hell am I going to jump across four billion years to find Holtzclaw? And if I can get there, how do I rescue him?"

"You know how to time travel. Just like you did before, when you had sex with Yulia. You have to have sex with this woman now. And when you get to the future, there'll be help."

Despite the knowledge that I was speaking to a four-billion-year-old entity, I was shocked to hear this extramarital injunction coming from the mouth of my five-year-old daughter. "Oh, no, none of that. The last time I went forward I barely came back. What if I get displaced in time and space and possibility? What if everything is different when I return?"

"We have to risk it. No more arguing. Go inside and do what has to be done."

"I'm going back to Juniper, but I'm not doing what you want. I'll figure out another approach."

Aelita said nothing, but merely regarded me with supernal calm certitude.

I strapped the kid into the car and locked the doors against any kind of kidnapping. Not likely in this ritzy neighborhood, but who could predict, amidst all this craziness?

An exhausted Juniper slumped semi-comatose on the couch, her long bare legs inviting. I fixed a couple of drinks for us, and she perked up. She actually brightened to the point of worrying about her hair and adjusting a shoulder strap.

"All right," I began, "let's run down Holger's possible hideouts again—"

"Vern. That's your first name, isn't it? Vern, I'm very sad and I need you to kiss me."

The irony of my instant unfeigned reluctance was not lost on me. Just yesterday I had come here fantasizing about sex with my client, and now I was resisting any such offered pleasures.

"Really? Why now?"

"I didn't know you were a father before. Parenting is very sexy."

"Jesus..."

Her hands and mouth were all over me, and I couldn't stop her or myself.

I didn't think I'd have the energy for anything acrobatic after everything I had gone through, including making love just last night to Yulia. But the sex we had up and down that couch proved fabulous—right up to the end.

Blammo!

The DUCA future smelled bad. The omnipresent mat was rotting even more so than on my last visit. Did that mean I had jumped deeper into time? How could I be sure Holger Holtzclaw was even to be found in this era?

The ginormous animal skull was nowhere to be seen, so I just picked a random direction and started walking, naked as a mole rat.

After some indefinite period I saw what appeared to be a forest up ahead. But unlike on Perelandra, these organisms, I soon observed, were not separate entities, but merely extrusions of the mat, connected at their bases, of the same ill substance. Weird stalky mushroom-like excresences, putrid and festering. I edged my way among them, felling revulsion and disgust.

The tall tree trunks became more closely and randomly spaced, forming a kind of maze. After a while, I realized I could no longer discern the path I had taken.

Then I heard the weak call. "Help me. Someone help me, please."

Holger Holtzclaw—naked as myself, but battered and bruised—was immured in a living cage. I came up to his bars.

"Oh, thank god! I don't know who you are, or where I am, but you have to get me out of here!"

"I'm a detective. Your wife hired me to find you."

"Whatever she's paying you, I'll double it if you can free me!"

I studied the cage. I assumed Holger had tried to bend or bust the bars or dig through the mat without success. So I wasn't sure what I could do.

An image of the Green Lady suddenly filled my mind, vivid as if she were standing here before me. Could our mating have established some kind of bond between us?

I reached forth my hand, and as it approached the bars, the rancid stalks began to shiver and retreat from my presence.

Quickly employing my other hand, I created a gap big enough for the emaciated captive to slip through.

"Let's go! Quick!"

Trying to keep a straight course, we plunged through the forest, the slimy boles whapping us like the fabric flaps of a car wash.

Eventually, we emerged onto the undulant plain.

Motion attracted my eye upward.

Mister After All was arrowing towards us. He began to screech like a banshee.

At the same time, a big healthy-green sphere was rolling across the mat right at us.

"Run! Toward the beachball!"

Mister After All almost got us. But just as his claw-like hands painfully yanked out strands of my hair, we plunged into the jade grass-smelling sphere like two raisins into a pudding, while Mister After All bounced off its surface that selectively repelled him.

The summery smell filled my lungs, and then my brain.

19.

Candy from a Stranger

I had never awoken side-by-side with a fellow sleeper before in the Vaalbara room at the AEOTA factory. I wondered if the management charged as much for a double as for a single.

I picked myself up in the familiar vacant cavernous room with the sunny rifts in the roof, then helped a stunned Holger Holtzclaw to his feet.

I was dressed in that morning's Oxford shirt and khakis. Holger wore what he had presumably worn on his visit to Thaumas & Company: a dapper summer-weight linen suit and Weejuns.

He looked around, blankly at first, then with growing awareness.

"I—I know this place. It's where I—where I—"

"Don't sweat it, man. We're safe now. Let's go."

We climbed the ladder and entered the anteroom.

There were two sets of my footprints in the dust: from my return after Green Lady sex and my return after Yulia sex. I added a third track as we made for the exit.

Unlike the previous loop, I was apparently not following right on the tail of myself. At least, my earlier avatar was nowhere to be seen. He was probably already in the truck belonging to the Aeota Farms folks, winging his way back home.

The sun was fairly low in the east, and I had to hope that this was the morning of the pancake breakfast at the trailer. If it were earlier, the waiting would be frustrating. But if it were later—well, who could say what chances I would have missed?

I turned around to survey the ruins of the factory.

The signage atop the building said:

FIRST CHURCH OF THE GLORIFIED AEOTA "EX NIHILO NIHIL FIT"

I turned back to Holger.

"You have a phone on you?"

He patted a coat pocket and came up with a smart phone.

"Can you get us an Uber?"

Holger was regaining some of his old Ponzi scheme *savoir-faire* as the harsh memories of his fantastical incarceration receded into a dream-like haze. "If I have a signal..."

The car took nearly an hour to arrive, out here in the middle of nowhere. During that time, I fed Holger a spontaneous bullshit story about drugs and kidnapping and industrial espionage. I was hardly about to tell him the truth—even assuming I really believed any of this madness. He seemed to buy my farrago.

"Juniper is going crazy without you," I concluded. "But you know that going back to her means facing the law."

Holger seemed genuinely repentant. Maybe his stint in the DUCA future, even rationalized as a nightmare, had actually served to rehabilitate him to some degree. I tried to imagine his lawyer making a case for "time served" at his sentencing hearing. "Although my client will not be incarcerated for another four billion years, he has actually already suffered through that imprisonment, and is thus exempt from additional punishment."

"I'll face the music," Holger said. "I'll make restitution and maybe the judge will be lenient. No one was really hurt."

"Good for you, pal. You've got a helluva woman in that Juniper."

My praise might have sounded a tad too intimately enthusiastic, because Holger eyed me askance.

"I mean, the money she laid out to find you and all. Plus the tears. Lots of tears."

Just then the Uber pulled up, and any suspicions were derailed. We climbed into the late-model car—which proved to be an Aeota Motors Protero.

The driver, a middle-aged white guy with a lean face and shaved head, wearing a tee-shirt with Suzanne Vega's picture on it, introduced himself. "Hello. My name's Carnarvon Jarrell. Sit back and relax. We should be arrive at your destination in just a couple of hours, if the traffic is decent."

Holger and I both took the guy's advice. Suddenly I felt totally drained, and Holger seemed to experience the same ennervation.

I drowsed dreamlessly until I heard Jarrell's polite coughing.

"We're almost there."

I looked around and saw we were on the final street leading to the Holtzclaw McMansion, but had yet to turn down the driveway.

"Stop here, please," I said.

We got out and Jarrell motored off.

"Is there a back entrance to the grounds?"

"Yes, for deliveries."

Give Holger credit for gratitude and trust: he didn't question me, his rescuer, but just followed meekly along.

I left Holger at the rear of the house.

"Don't leave this spot till I come and get you, understand? I have to prep Juniper for your startling reappearance."

And put my dick away, I didn't say.

I went around to the front of the house. Aelita sat patiently in the car.

Blammo!

I was back inside the house, merged with my earlier sweaty self, draped half-insensible atop a bent-over Juniper, her playsuit pooled around her ankles as she leaned against the back of the couch.

"You send me, girl, you really do. But now we gotta get dressed. I'm expecting a call that could break this whole investigation wide open."

Once dressed, I grabbed my old Nokia as if it were vibrating silently. "This could be it." I prentended to take the nonexistent call, conducting an imaginary dialogue.

"No! You say he should be arriving now? Fantastic!"

I hit the off button and addressed Juniper. "Go fix yourself up. Your hubby's coming up the drive."

She dashed off, and I went outside. I secured a meek and obedient Holger first, then got Aelita out of the car.

"Well done, Vern. I knew you could do it."

"If I have to wake up in that fucking place one more time, I'm going to stash my pajamas there ahead of any jumps."

The reunion between Holger and Juniper was suitably touching, even given knowledge of the cheating sex that had just occured.

Aelita was tugging on my shirt again. "Get the thing he has for us. It's in his left coat pocket."

I asked Holger to hand over what he had in that location. Puzzled, he said, "But there's nothing—" Yet as he put his hand into his suitcoat, he encountered something unexpected. He took it out and handed it to me.

It was a small transparent cellophane packet with a single largish laquered crimson marble inside. The lettering said:

AEOTA CANDY COMPANY
FAMOUS HADES FIREBALL

I glared at Aelita.

Her beguiling child's face remained unperturbed. "Trust me," she said.

20.
Invasion of the Chronospores

I noted the changes in my city as we drove away from the happily reunited Holtzclaw lovebirds. (I had made sure to tell them that they'd be getting my final bill in the mail, and that the total would be a significant five figures, even though I had no real faith in any of us surviving to pay or be paid. But old habits die hard. I figured that just before DUCA converted us all to slime, I'd probably still be instinctively checking the Nokia's voice mail for new clients.)

The downtown district, formerly several square blocks of empty storefronts and needle-strewn sidewalks populated by druggy wastrels was now host to flourishing emporiums and middle-class patrons. That was a plus. My continuum-skipping seemed to be following a gradient of improvement. We passed a beauty shop offering "Aeota Threading" and the Aeota Cinemas. The marquee on the latter advertised a double bill of THE GONE-AWAY WORLD and PORTRAIT OF JENNIE.

As I continued to drive toward Marty Quartz's apartment—or at least the place where I hoped he still lived—I saw other changes, such as a public park where there had never been one—the grassy acres were filled with people playing some kind of polo while driving electric-powered monowheels—and a tower that seemed to be sheathed in golden fish scales. Trouble was, I couldn't determine if these changes stemmed from my first, second, or third time-travel excursion. I wondered if I'd still have a home and a wife to return to after all this.

As if reading my thoughts, Aelita said in her alien way, "Don't worry, Yulia is okay."

"Thanks for that." A thought that had been bubbling under in my mind suddenly demanded voicing.

"I don't really understand about the nature of this change that DUCA is trying to install, this new monoculture regime. Shouldn't it be instantaneous, or have already happened? I mean, here we are, four billion years in DUCA's past. So he starts extending his realm backwards, conquering one antecedant year after another in succession as he moves toward uniting with LUCA, four billion years prior to our present. Shouldn't that wave of change have hit us by now? Or is it propagating at some finite speed, and has yet to engulf us? And is there some objective universal measure of time outside our normal reference frame that we can use to measure the advance of the threat? It's all highly confusing."

"None of your suppositions or conceptions are adequate or accurate. It's very hard to explain. A crude analogy involves tipping points and emergent phase shifts. Think of it like this. DUCA is sending spores backwards, to infest each previous era. And when those spores take root in a given period, they multiply until a critical mass is reached, at which point everything instantly transitions. It's like the 'false vacuum' theory in physics. The multiverse exists in an unstable mode that can be toppled over into an inescapable eternal lower-energy configuration by certain actions."

"These spores—what do they look like? How do they manifest?"

"You've already encountered one such manifestation, in the person of Brevis Baxter."

I had to pause to dredge up the associations with that name.

"You mean the crummy bum who braced me at A. O.'s Tea Room and gave me a box of goop?"

"Yes. He was a host to a DUCA spore, but not yet fully morphed. He was trying to contaminate you as well with that package. But I caused the spore to deliquesce before you could be affected."

"But I didn't even know you then! I didn't know any of this insanity existed."

"But I knew you already, Vern. And the 'insanity,' as you call it, or the reality, was always with you."

Stubbornly, I tried to remain optismistic. "I think the fact that we are still here talking, that DUCA hasn't yet colonized us, means that he will *never* colonize us, that he's already failed forever."

Aelita sighed. "I wish that were true, Vern. But it's not. We have to continue to struggle and fight, with all our brains and heart."

"Well, let's see what this lead that Marty uncovered is all about. Maybe it's a game-changer."

It was almost noon, my appointment time, when we pulled up in front of Marty Quartz's apartment building. Reassuringly, the place looked as I recalled, from however many timelines ago: a former tofu factory turned into luxury condos. Marty's job as a freelance IT security consultant paid good money, and allowed him to work just as much or little as he desired. We had met during another case, when I had been tasked with finding the source of some industrial espionage.

In the lobby, a concierge rang Marty's room, then allowed us to proceed.

The door to Marty's third-floor quarters was already open when we arrived, and the man we had come to see awaited us, framed in that portal. Still dressed in yesterday's LARPing outfit of Irish tweeds and brogans, he resembled a a plumper Yeats, right down to the little spectacles—which must have featured lenses of window glass, since Marty had never needed visual assistance till now, so far as I knew. His tired face and bleary eyes showed that his usquebaugh consumption had been authentically copious.

Seeing Marty, Aelita ran toward him and hurled herself at him as she had done for me when I arrived home.

"Uncle Marty!"

"Hey, microbe! What's fermenting?"

I did a doubletake. "Microbe?"

"You know, man. It's what Donald Duck calls his nephews."

"Oh, right..."

Inside the apartment, I sniffed a weird odor. It was organic, but not exactly that of the Archean period, I thought.

"What's that smell?"

"Oh, we had a peat fire going here last night for verisimilitude. Burning the bog, man. Getting in touch with the roots. Look, just let me change, and then we'll go."

"Go where?"

"A place I found when I googled 'aeota.' One you never mentioned. Luckily, it's right here in town."

Marty disappeared in back, while Aelita and I waited silently. Upon his return, he sported his more customary outfit of cargo shorts, a baja "drug rug" hoodie in eye-straining rainbow colors, and Teva sandals.

Down in the car, Marty sat in the back rather than fuss with Aelita's booster seat. Obviously feeling more alive after some covert bedroom toot, possibly of a trendy restorative nutriceutical, he leaned forward in his typical energetic fashion to tell what he knew.

"This guy's been on my radar for a while. Roopnarine Ströma. Heads Ströma Heuristic Systems. Took over the business from his father, Aadidev, the founder. Sells software learning systems to the government and big corporations. DARPA's a client. But I never realized he's got a side project that's been going on for decades. It's called AEOTA. Stands for 'Artilect Enjoined to Operate on Thomist Axioms.'"

"In English, please."

"An artificial intelligence designed to reason about God and the universe."

"Okay. Not too ambitious."

"I figure, given the coincidence of names, that this gizmo might have some answers to any questions you can ask it."

"And Ströma will see us?"

"Yeah, he knew my work and agreed. I didn't explain that you were nuts, though."

"Thanks. When I'm running the universe, I'll do something nice for you in return."

"Hey, that reminds me. Let me see that phone of yours a minute."

I passed the Nokia over my shoulder.

"Can't see any sign of modding. And you say it printed out a slip of paper?"

"Twice. I've got them right in my pocket."

Marty handed back my phone. "We'll look into this later."

The building housing Ströma Heuristic Systems was a sleek Early Eighties postmodern edifice on the edge of town. It reminded me generically of the AEOTA HQ upstate, and I had to repress a shiver.

Roopnarine Ströma was a striking, handsome young figure. Of blended ethnicities—I was going to guess, based on his name, half Hindu, half Swedish—he presented a dapper businessman's facade with an overlay of intellectual heft. Very Richard Branson by way of Elon Musk.

After shaking hands all around, even with a somber and wide-eyed Aelita, Ströma conducted us deep into the bowels of the place, past layers of security.

"When my father first began to construct and program AEOTA, he didn't want to use any of the company's then-limited resources on his private mission. Stockholders and venture capitalists get antsy about that. So the project was tucked away in a basement room, functioning on whatever he could scounge, and it's stayed there ever since. We don't dare move it, because we would have to power it down, and no one knows if it would ever reboot. It's the most massive kludge I've ever seen."

As he told us this, Ströma unlocked a final door and swung it wide, and I could instantly see he wasn't kidding.

21.
Interview with AEOTA, Interview with an Artist

The room was not large, probably about as big as the kitchen in the Holtzclaw McMansion. It was air-conditioned and featured a false floor for easy access to cables. In the middle was an old beat-up workbench. The long metal table supported a mass of what looked to be randomly gathered computer hardware piled high, threaded together with a variety of wires, the whole mess surrounded by tipsy functioning stacks of other equipment, some in racks, some in freestanding towers, leaving just about enough room for three adults and a kid to crowd inside. Ströma closed the door and locked it.

The many LED telltale lights, red, green, amber and blue, reminded me of a nighttime jungle scene with the eyes of animals shining in the gloom. At the center bottom of the silicon ziggurat on the table was a monochrome display and a clunky keyboard. The ancient equipment triggered a memory I had not considered in ages: my first computer as a kid: a Commodore 64.

"Is that—"

Ströma seemed embarrassed. "Yes, it's a Cee Sixty-four. You have to remember that Dad started building this monstrosity circa nineteen-eighty-five. By the time he died, he had added about six million layers of equipment around the Commodore. But the Sixty-four is still the kernel and the interface."

I walked closer to the blank screen. Its mute blinking cursor seemed both mocking and beckoning.

"What do I do?"

"Just type something."

My fingers on the keyboard reactivated the body memories of playing crude videogames, using arrow keys to manipulate pixel creatures that only a child's imagination could invest with a semblance of life.

—Hello. Are you Aeota?

—Yes, I am one Aeota.

—Can you tell me how to defeat the Dark Archon?

—Since act is perfection, it is not limited except through a potency which itself is a capacity for perfection.

Ströma had been reading over my shoulder. "That's pure Aquinas, Dad's favorite philosopher. He programmed AEOTA with the entire canon, from the *Summa Theologica* on down. But it's not like a chatbot. It doesn't just regurgitate text. It's told me some things—"

Ströma paused, as if to say more would be too unsettling or incriminating.

The history lesson Ströma had just delivered suggested a different line of questioning to me, for which I was grateful, since I was just fumbling around like a blind guy with a Rubik's Cube.

—Is Aeota a god? Is DUCA a god?

—Neither is the Prime Mover nor First Cause.

—Then DUCA can be defeated?

—Neither matter nor form have being of themselves, nor are they produced or corrupted of themselves.

This high-flown dialogue was getting old fast.

—Tell me how I can save the world.

—The will does not precede the intellect but follows upon it.

—That doesn't help!

—I need more input.

—More input? Like what?

AEOTA did not respond.

"Goddamn it!" Frustrated, I kicked the table leg.

My action dislodged something from its niche among the equipment. The small object fell until it was stopped by the tether of its cable, left dangling in mid-air.

I plucked it up. The thing was a bulky vintage light pen, usually used for drawing directly onto a CRT screen in the days before tablets.

Aelita said, "Daddy, I think the machine is telling you that it wants you to show it something new."

Marty looked dubious. "That relic's not a scanner, man."

A queer impulse made me dig in my pants pocket. I came up with the two slips of paper that my Nokia had outputted. I smoothed them out on a small bare patch of table top, then drew the light pen slowly across each one in turn.

The eight emojis apeared on the monochrome screen in full color, all in a line. They spun like the icons on an old-school slot machine, then disappeared.

AEOTA displayed a street address on its screen, then a final message.

—Towards the time of the judgment the sun and moon will be darkened in very truth. My work here is done.

The screen went black.

Ströma looked at me with an initial incredulity that swiftly built to anger. "You broke it. You killed AEOTA."

I felt guilty, but wasn't about to admit any culpability. "Hey, anybody who ever watched a single episode of *Star Trek* could have predicted this outcome."

I thought it would be expedient to leave before Ströma decided to have my head on a platter, so I grabbed up the slips of paper from the table.

Now they were blank.

I kept them nonetheless.

* * * * *

I thought that maybe Marty Quartz would have insisted on coming with Aelita and me to the address that AEOTA had given us, but he surprised me by asking to be delivered home.

"I had a long night, Vern. I'm beat. And frankly, this weird quest of yours is creeping me out. I figure you'll let me know how things shake out, one way or another."

"Oh, you'll know soon enough whether I succeed or not—along with the rest of the world."

Alone with Aelita in the car, heading across town, I said, "Who do you think is at this address?"

"Someone to help us, not someone to harm us."

"That's reassuring. What makes you say that?"

"Nothing but a feeling."

"No superior superhuman knowledge?"

"I'm just a little girl."

"And I'm the last of the Romanovs."

The address proved to belong to a simple moss-green ranch house in an innocuous suburb north of the city. Tidy lawn, old-fashioned curtains. I rang the bell with Aelita holding my hand.

The door opened, and, after a puzzled second, I realized I had cause to lower my glance.

An old woman in a wheelchair had revealed herself. Dressed neatly yet not too fussily, she exhibited a keen gaze and general alertness that was the opposite of any kind of maundering senility. A gentle smile graced her face. I was reminded of a Mother Superior or some other emblematic matriarch. Her aged features appeared familiar to me in some fashion, but I could not immediately place them.

"Yes, how can I help you?"

"I'm not sure."

The woman regarded Aelita and smiled. "My name's Priscilla. What's yours?"

"Aelita."

"That's very like the name of another little girl I know. One named Aeota."

Dumbfounded, I asked, "What's your last name?"

"Cohen."

"You're Pris Cohen. You do my daughter's favorite comic book."

"Write and draw, yes. I assumed that was why you were here. I often receive visits from fans."

"Yes, of course. Could we come in?"

"Certainly."

Priscilla rolled backwards, and we entered. She spun her wheelchair deftly about and scooted off. We followed.

The living room served as her studio. A drafting table with an unfinished page pinned to it filled most of the space, along the raw materials of her trade and a host of inspirational sculptures and toys and dolls and other tchotchkes.

"I'm afraid I can't offer you any refreshments. Tomorrow is my shopping day, and the larder's bare. But I suspect that you're not here for cookies and milk."

"No, we're not. We need desperately to know all about Aeota. What can you tell us?"

"I was the original Aeota, you know. The inspiration. My uncle, Herbert Crowley, drew the 'Wiggle-Much' strip."

I did some quick calculations. "That's not possible. You'd have to be—"

"I am one-hundred-and-fifteen years old."

"You don't look a day over one-oh-five."

Priscilla ignored my feeble witticism. "After I reached adolescence and my uncle died, I never thought much about my early role as an Alice Liddell-type figure. But my uncle's drawing career must have inspired me. I spent my whole adult professional employment as a graphic artist in the advertising field. Afterwards, I lived a quiet retired life as a weekend painter. But then, recently, memories of Aeota began to recur to me, and I felt inspired to continue my uncle's comic strip in monthly format. I was lucky enough to find a publisher, and here we are."

"But aren't you channelling messages from the real Aeota?"

"Who might she be?"

"She's LUCA, or the Green Lady—I think. We're fighting DUCA. He wants to conquer all of time and space."

Priscilla smiled at me with a mix of benvolence and pity. "I'm sure this all means something to you, young man. But I fear it's got nothing to do with me nowadays—if it ever did"

I turned to Aelita. "You can convince her, Lita. Just tell her we need her help."

Desperation was driving me. I felt suddenly at the end of my rope. How many more blind alleys did I have to stumble down before this nightmare was over?

"I can't do anything, Daddy. She knows better than me. I'm sorry."

I looked back to the old lady. She had ceased smiling, and the lines of her face were relaxed into a webwork of wrinkles.

And her incompetent lips revealed a slice of her teeth.

22.

Go with the Flow

"You're my daughter."

As soon as the words emerged, I realized how insane I sounded. But the reaction of both my daughter and Priscilla Cohen confirmed my crazy revelation.

"Yes, Daddy, she's me. One of me. And she knows so much more. That's why I'm not pressing her for help. Whatever's ahead, she's already been through it, and so she knows just what to do now."

The old dame regarded me with a placid humble majesty. I was reminded of the Green Lady's quiet but vibrant charisma. I just hoped nobody expected me to have sex with this old bat as well. Not that I was necessarily morally against it, just that I was tired of being led around by my dick.

Pris Cohen's voice exhibited no regrets or hesitancy. "I cannot affirm what you say. But I cannot deny it either. The truth is both and neither. So you will just have to trust me."

Trust me. The same request Aelita had made when I looked dubiously at the Famous Hades Fireball candy that Holger Holtzclaw had brought back from the far future. (I patted my pocket and found the round packet still there.) Could I trust either of them? Hadn't I been taken for a ride by everyone involved in this hallucinatory affair? But what choice did I have?

"Okay, you've got my trust. But only on the installment plan. So, what next?"

Priscilla looked at her slim silver wristwatch. "Just wait. It will only be minutes now."

Aelita walked over to the old lady in the wheelchair and climbed onto her lap. Priscilla hugged her in grandmotherly fashion, and Aelita returned the embrace. Their faces, side by side, old and young, further cemented the truth of their unique kinship.

I walked over to the drawing board and studied the unfinished artwork. A "splash page," one big panel, the deft pencil work depicted the heroine Aeota, expectant on some shore and faced with a tsunami, a huge wave clotted with debris that threated to cascade down upon her, surely crushing all life from her. But the comicbook girl's unfinished face suggested resolve and certitude of ultimate victory.

Someone started banging on the front door, hammering at it with what sounded like a succession of small watermelons fired from an air cannon. I moved toward the entrance, but before I had taken more than a couple of steps the door crashed inward, hanging from one hinge.

A small squad of semi-human creatures flowed chaotically in.

The front one wore the gnarly face of Brevis Baxter—but a face composed now of shoddy putrescence.

Back at Arturo Olvidado's bar, when he had passed over the contaminant spore package to me, Baxter had resembled a crusty hobo, a burnt-out case, unwashed, wasted and trashed, but undeniably human. Now he looked like what a simpleton child, asked to represent the human figure, might assemble out of moldy cottage cheese and twigs. His companions, though sporting different countenances, mimicked this variegated but essentially monotone look.

I realized that Baxter was now composed entirely of DUCA substance, coarse maritime glop threaded with fibers and particles. His entire cellular makeup, as well as his clothing, had been transformed into the far-future slime. Here, then, was the beginning onslaught that Aelita had warned me about, the massing of the constituent grains of sand that would eventually avalanche our universe into DUCA's desired state.

Baxter's companions moved toward Aelita and Priscilla, while Baxter himself blocked me from coming to their aid. The convert to DUCA spoke in a voice even more grotty than his previous one, his kelp vocal chords straining to reproduce human language.

"Mister Thaumas wants you and the girl."

"My interest in seeing your boss is zilch."

"You will come."

Baxter laid a hand on me, and it was like the heavy wet weight of a water-logged corpse descending to implacably clamp my flesh. No wonder he and his pals had been able to batter the door down.

Another of the DUCA-men plucked Aelita out of Priscilla Cohen's lap. Neither my daughter nor her other self resisted.

Another hench-thing croaked, "The old lady?"

"We do not need her," replied Baxter.

Three of the creatures flopped themselves atop Priscilla like so many soggy mattresses, losing their individual definition in a pig pile. They writhed and squelched and squeezed for about ninety seconds, before retreating and reverting to their separate components.

Priscilla Cohen was gone, her wheelchair dripping with slime.

I expected Aelita to cry out or show some emotion, but she remained stolid and seemingly unconcerned. But I felt Priscilla Cohen's absence like a rip in the fabric of reality.

Outside, a windowless van labelled AEOTA DELIVERY SERVICE blocked my car. Into it all but three of the monsters surged: Baxter, still grip-ping my arm, and two creatures to guard Aelita. I supposed I should have been incensed that they regarded my kid as the more dangerous of us two.

Baxter hustled me into the driver's seat of my own car, afterwards quickly slipping into the shotgun position, his malleable vegetable butt simply con-figuring itself to engulf the projecting booster seat. The two cronies cradling Aelita between them oozed into the rear.

"Drive," said Baxter.

"Where?"

"You know the place."

"AEOTA HQ?"

"Yes."

I tried to recall what the empty factory had promoted itself to be the last time I had passed through, but couldn't remember.

"But that site's empty."

"Not now it isn't."

"Can I just call my wife first, and tell her we'll be late? She'll be worried."

"No. There is no need. You won't be late. You will be never."

23.
Return to AEOTA

The by-now familiar route to AEOTA HQ—how many times had I gone back and forth along this stretch in just the past two days?—had been transmogrified beyond all comprehension.

The changes became apparent as soon as we pulled away from Priscilla's house, which had remained an oasis of stability. (But even as we proceeded a few yards down her street, I could see in my rear-view mirror that the forces of change had begun their assault on her house as well.) The abnormalities were, at first, intermittent, interspersed with irregularly situated and irregularly bordered expanses of normality. But the closer we got to our destination, the more the abhorrent transformations tended to predominate.

Many of the citizens we passed in the city had also morphed to full DUCA-hood. But unlike this crew of hired roughnecks that had come to capture me and Aelita, the alteration to their personages had not inspired any obvious deviltry. Seemingly unaware of their debased natures, they slorped and blarfed along the DUCA-fied pavement like so many human-shaped blancmanges, conducting their mundane errands, ambulatory piles of ocean wrack: Sargasso mailmen, housewives, businessmen, students and shopkeepers. A jogger trotted by, littering her path with dislodged wet bits of her pelagic body. A teenager texted away on a phone that was composed of the same material as its body, and which seemed fused to its hand. Behind the wheel of a car, the grey-green driver idly tapped a boneless floppy striated hand in time to the music of its radio.

But beyond the people, the landscape, both natural and manmade, had altered as well.

As in the forest where Holger Holtzclaw had been imprisoned, all the vegetation in the bad patches emerged seamlessly from the tainted substrate, mere extrusions of DUCA. The birds and squirrels in their branches were DUCA-forms too.

And many of the buildings, large and small, as well as lampposts, billboards and traffic lights, had fallen victim to the spreading stain. The smaller structures seemed semi-stable, wavering slightly under the unnatural stresses of maintaining their forms with such unsuitable material. But the bigger, multi-storey buildings swayed and oscillated like Jello sculptures in an earthquake, appearing ready to snap and rupture and fall at any minute. Nonetheless, people continued to stream in and out of the banks and hotels and offices.

A defeatist thought jumped up in my head. Was humanity really any worse off than before? I recalled my impressions during my first forest-fire-tinged trip when it felt as if civilization were collapsing. Maybe this kind of slimy rapture was the best we could hope for, given the human condition and our ability to screw things up.

Then I remembered Aelita's simple innocent joy in seeing me come home, and knew that the answer was no, mankind wasn't better off as DUCA's slaves.

Not that there was much I could do about it at the moment.

I thought once or twice about pulling over to the curb as we passed through the normal areas and leaping from the car and running for help. But Brevis Baxter had one sloppy arm around my shoulder, and I was certain that with his strength and speed he could strangle me instantly at my first false move.

And then of course there was Aelita to worry about, cushioned between the two monsters in the back. I kept angling my mirror to check on her. She never once showed a trace of alarm or fear or concern. That was my girl.

When we passed the city limits and were out in the countryside, the changes persisted. It was no less alarming to see long seaweed-textured pastures full of DUCA cows.

And the prevalence of the contamination became almost universal.

A familiar barn caught my eye. It was the Aeota Farm where Philip Kendrick Langham and Martha Washington ran their egg business. Totally swamped with DUCA's influence, the place reminded me of a Lovecraft tale I had not considered since those college days, a story whose name I could no longer recall.

Langham and Washington themselves stepped out of their farmhouse as we passed, all sloppy smiling briny heaps, and waved.

I finally broke my appalled silence.

"Aelita, honey—are you all right?"

"I'm fine, Daddy. Don't worry, everything is going to be okay."

Brevis Baxter unfurled a glutinous laughter like a hippo farting through wet cement and his buddies joined in.

Making the last turn to the site of AEOTA HQ, I wasn't sure what to expect. The flourishing postmodern enterprise I had first visited, or the empty shell where I kept waking up after my time trips.

But neither aspect obtained.

Occupying an enormous footprint of land was the incredible mega-skull from the far future of Mister After All. But instead of rearing starkly bone-white, it too showed itself to be formed entirely of the DUCA rot.

Atop the skull, the AEOTA signage proclaimed the skull's current tenants.

We emerged from the parked car and walked toward the door.

"At least let me hold my daughter's hand."

"Oh ho! How dumb do you think we are? No, there'll be none of that monkey business."

We passed through a sloppy bulging parody of a door and entered a facsimile of the atrium. The same receptionist seen during my first visit was there, but of course only as a gruesome avatar of her former gorgeous self. Her equally dire coworkers came and went.

Without necessity for clearance, Baxter and his buddies brought me and Aelita into the wobbly upper-floor office of Thomas Totenwelt Thaumas.

Seated behind his desk on his fancy scooter, the man no longer resembled Judge Hardy so much as he looked like Mister After All. How I could not have seen the resemblance earlier, I couldn't say.

"Mister Ruggles! You return to us. How nice. And with your very welcome little girl. I know someone who is most eager to meet her. He has been waiting forever to get his hands on her."

Trying to unnerve Thaumas, I said, "I see you've come a long way in totalizing your affinities."

Thaumas's face registered genuine puzzlement, insofar as those coarse features could.

"What nonsense are you on about?"

"The name of your organization." I dredged up the acronym, which I had heard after all just about thirty-six hours ago. "The Association of Engineering Ontologists Totalizing Affinities."

"But that is not what our brand stands for at all! We are producers of Architecturally Engineered Organisms for Terraforming Alternities. All the splendid new constituents of the material world which you see aboout you come straight from our labs."

"Are you deranged? You didn't create any of this. It's all DUCA's doing, as he floods the past with his essence."

Thaumas triggered his intercom. "Ms. Bagasse, would you please have Dr. Ponto come in?"

Within half a minute, the formerly beautiful secretary—who now smelled less like a florist shop and more like a pile of inperfectly devoured crab shells under a hot sun—ushered in Microbial Matt, the bastard who had pushed me off the ledge and started this whole mad odyssey.

"Hey, Vern, good to see you. You're back for another tour, I take it."

I lunged at Ponto, but was almost immediately brought up short by Brevis Baxter.

"Dr. Ponto, please tell our guests about the various organisms we have bred to perfect the environment."

Ponto launched into some gobbledeygook that I paid no attention to. My mind was frantically scrabbling about the confines of its cage for a way out of this. If only I could grab ahold of Aelita, maybe she could send us away from here somehow, as when her Archean counterpart had blasted me off to Venus.

Now Thaumas was talking again. "So you must assuredly now admit, Mister Ruggles, that there is no need to invoke imaginary entities who are responsible for these wondrous changes. All such conceptions are delusions on your part. Your mind is defective, or you would surely concede the truth. Occam's Razor still applies. The simplest answer is most likely correct. There are no fanciful creatures at the far origin and ending of our world, directing our destiny, contending for dominance. LUCA and DUCA, what is there to choose between them? No, there is only science, here and now."

"If there's only your perverted human science, then who are you working for? Who wants my daughter?"

"I didn't say anyone wants your daughter, did I?"

"Yes, you dirty fucker, you did!"

Thaumas motored out in his chair from behind his desk. His identity with Mister After All had solidified even more unmistakeably.

"Let me have a closer look at her. Maybe she *could* be of some use to us. What a sweet little child she is. And very talented too, no doubt, with such a smart father."

Aelita remained unmoved by Thaumas's approach. But she inexplicably began to whine.

"Daddy, I'm hungry! Don't you have anything for me?"

"C'mon, Aelita, drop the kiddy act! Do something! Please, before it's too late."

"I'm hungry, Daddy! Anything, please! Even just a candy—"

The Famous Hades Fireball seemed to leap from my pocket into my hand. I popped the sealed inflated cellophane and the crimson sphere shot out across the space between Aelita and me like a missile.

With her hands pinned by her guards, she snapped it out of the air like a dog with a snack or a trained seal with a fish.

And then we were outta there faster than light.

24.
Horn, Om, Sun, Home

Lying flat, I opened my eyes after an indefinite period of unconsciousness, sensed and saw that I was naked under an empty sky. Turning my head, I regarded Aelita and found her in the same condition. And as on my first visit to the Archean, I could see that she was not precisely my daughter, not a little girl but rather some other more ancient vessel who shared a spiritual and physical kinship with my child.

A warmish sun shone down on us, and I was so excited and relieved to be out of the grip of Thaumas and his crew that I jumped up happily to my feet, and took in the wider view.

I couldn't believe it. We were not in the healthy primordial Archean. We had been transported to DUCA's dying era, four billion years in the future. The pustulant pestilence that had invaded my age was everywhere, just as on my last visit. Not aggressively occupying many different forms, true, yet still quietly dominant and universal.

Aelita had come to her feet. She looked utterly subdued.

"What happened?" I demanded. "Why are we here? I thought that Fireball was our ticket to your home, where we could regroup or something."

For the first time, Aelita sounded weary. "It was supposed to be. But the fact that we are here means that the Dark Archon has become too strong. We were too late. He's won. There is nothing left except for us to acknowledge our defeat."

Her words pained me horribly. I grabbed her by her slim child's shoulders and shook her. "No! We can't give up. There must be something more we can do!"

"There is not."

I slumped. "So you'll just surrender to him when he shows up?"

"That is my only plan."

"Well, I'm not going down without a fight!"

I looked about the monoscape frantically for some sort of weapon, but of course there was nothing. Were these seaweed strands strong enough to use as a garotte? I bent down and tried to disentangle and rip out a length of the crappy fabric.

"DUCA arrives."

Mister After All was levitating down from the heavens. When I could distinguish his wizened face, I saw it was beaming with vicious satisfaction.

He alighted upon the infinite raft about five or six yards away from us. He beckoned to my daughter.

"You must come to me now."

I yelled something wordless and hurled myself upon him.

The Dark Archon batted me aside as if I were a shuttlecock. The force of the blow left me dazed. I thought maybe I had some busted ribs. I tried to lever myself up, but only made it halfway.

Aelita was walking calmly to meet Mister After All. And with every step she aged.

From five years old she passed through adolescence and young womanhood in just a few paces, becoming mature and beautiful. In only seconds, I got to experience what my daughter would have grown up into, all the stages of her maturation. She reminded me of the Green Lady in her flush of vitality. As she continued to walk, she continued to age. Her twenties passed in a step or two, then she was into her middle age.

By the time she stood face to face with Mister After All, she looked exactly like the venerable Priscilla Cohen.

The old woman looked down at me. "Goodbye, Daddy. Trust me still."

A triumphant DUCA said nothing. He merely enfolded Aelita in his embrace. But his embrace did not stop when his arms met. His form flowed and expanded until he was a faceless blanket enveloping Aelita, just as the other Priscilla had been engulfed by his protean minions.

A similar obscene humping peristalsis worked upon the swaddled Aelita until she was fully dissolved and absorbed. She never made a sound, my little girl, as she vanished into the gullet of a sterile futurity. Then Mister After All pulled himself back into his human semblance.

He leered down at me. "Now she is mine forever. You, I leave here to perish."

Mister After All made as if to surge into the sky.

But he found himself rooted.

His feet were anchored in a pool of brilliant healthy vibrant green substance.

He jerked up first one leg without being able to disengage from the elastic stuff, then the other.

"No! This cannot be!"

The green wave flowed up his body, and at the same time radiated outward across the microbial mat. Faster and faster it spread, until all was an Archean, Perelandrian green from horizon to horizon.

Seemingly by sheer force of will DUCA had halted the green while just a few square inches of his bald crown remained unconverted. His eyes bulged and his mouth gaped helplessly.

But the green blew past his last defenses, and he was entirely swamped.

He began to melt away, subsumed into the microbial mat, until he was just a pair of desperate eyes embedded in the raft. Then those too were gone.

My ribs still ached. Nonetheless I crawled to where Mister After All had vanished. Sobbing, stroking the surface with my palm to invoke some sign of Aelita, I called her name over and over.

But there was no response. My daughter was gone forever.

When I gave up, a curious wave of heaviness began to creep along my limbs, until it finally filled my brain with sleep.

* * * * *

And I awoke and found me here on the cold hillside.

Well, it wasn't actually cold, and the patch of sun-kissed grass was flat. But that famous line captured what I felt.

I was lying, all clothed, in a woodland clearing next to my car. Beautiful, multiplex reality was restored, thanks to Aelita's sacrifice.

The whole world seemed normal.

Or at least as normal as it ever tended to be.

Standing up, I felt great.

No structure associated with AEOTA, neither mega-skull nor factory, reared in this spot. Instead, from the natural clearing a dirt road arrowed off, presumably leading back to the paved highway.

A quick recon showed no traces of anyone here with me, now or in the obvious past. I had no option but to get in my car and drive off, alone, without the child who had accompanied me.

Average traffic greeted me on the highway. I pointed my car toward the city.

Partway home, I saw a familiar farm. But the spiffy unadorned barn did not bear the ghost sign proclaiming CHEW AEOTA PLUG. I pulled into the property.

Philip Kendrick Langham and Martha Washington emerged, smiling.

"Hey, dude, what's up?"

"Is this Aeota Farm? Do you sell eggs?"

"Afraid we can't help you with that, bro. That's not us. El and Double-You Floral. We raise tulips. Wholesale only."

"All right then. Thanks anyhow. Good luck with everything."

I didn't dare return to the trailer where Yulia lived, nor to my own apartment. So I went to my office. The familiar key worked and I let myself gratefully inside.

I surely deserved a drink. But there was no booze anywhere in the office, not even an empty bottle in the trash. After searching every niche, I suddenly realized that the old compulsion to swig some tequila at every opportunity had left me, as if a tub full of dirty water had finally ebbed down the drain.

My Nokia weighed heavily in my pocket. I used it to call Marty Quartz.

"Marty, it's me, Vern. You won't believe what happened after Aelita and I left you."

"Whoa, man, slow down. After you and who left who?"

"After I broke Ströma's artificial intelligence. He's not going to sue us, is he?"

"I have no idea what you've been smoking, my lad, but you could have been kind enough to share it."

"But I—never mind. I'll talk to you later."

I powered up my desktop computer and checked today's date.

It was a sixteen months before I had ever googled "aeota."

I did so now again.

Zero hits.

My Nokia rang, almost sending me through the ceiling.

The voice of my lawyer, Herb Scroup, said, "Vern, hello, how ya doing? Listen, I need you in the office to sign these papers for the divorce. Yulia's guy is on my ass about it. We can't put it off any longer."

"Burn them."

"What?"

"Burn the papers. I'm going home."

The double-wide did not display the neatness of my last visit, nor the shabbiness of my abandonment years. Nor was there a tricycle or any kid's toys lying about. Rather, the whole scene seemed to teeter on a knife's edge of possibilities, with a different outcome awaiting on either side.

I banged on the door like a madman. Yulia came quickly. Her face did not exactly register glee at my manifestation on her doorstep.

"Oh, it's you, Vern. What do you want?"

"Yulia, baby, it's not what I want. It's not what you want. It's what the universe wants. We have to get back together."

Suspicion warred with hope in her face. "I thought you gave up the booze."

"I did, I did. Or I will. Whatever. Our wishes don't really matter. What matters is us starting a family. We really need to have a kid. Everything depends on it!"

Yulia tried to compose her face into a stern mask. But her incompetent lips only made her look adorable—as adorable as our unborn daughter. "You'd better come in out of the sun, Vern. But just for a minute. No funny stuff. We're still separated, remember, even if the divorce hasn't happened yet."

"It's not gonna happen, believe me." I felt the Nokia vibrate with an incoming text.

"Just let me get this, Yule. Then we'll sit down and really talk."

The unexpected text read:

> herald unity today at home

Followed by:

> PRINT TEXT Y/N?

I chose YES, and the phone spat out its impossible fortune-cookie slip.

I handed the paper to Yulia. She studied it, then looked quizzically at me. "What's it mean?"

"Baby, that's just what we're gonna find out!"